DETECTIVE BEANS
&
THE CASE OF THE MISSING HAT

BY LI CHEN

Andrews McMeel
PUBLISHING®

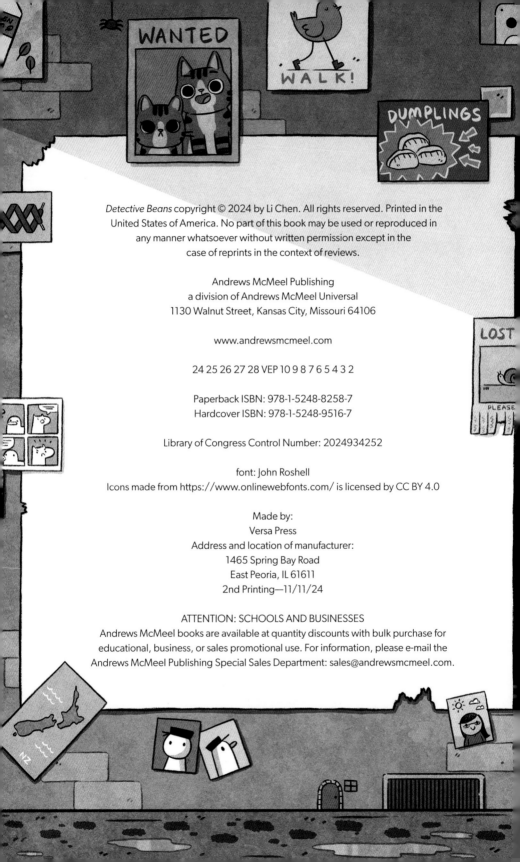

Andrews McMeel Publishing
a division of Andrews McMeel Universal
1130 Walnut Street, Kansas City, Missouri 64106

www.andrewsmcmeel.com

24 25 26 27 28 VEP 10 9 8 7 6 5 4 3 2

Paperback ISBN: 978-1-5248-8258-7
Hardcover ISBN: 978-1-5248-9516-7

Library of Congress Control Number: 2024934252

font: John Roshell
Icons made from https://www.onlinewebfonts.com/ is licensed by CC BY 4.0

Made by:
Versa Press
Address and location of manufacturer:
1465 Spring Bay Road
East Peoria, IL 61611
2nd Printing—11/11/24

ATTENTION: SCHOOLS AND BUSINESSES
Andrews McMeel books are available at quantity discounts with bulk purchase for educational, business, or sales promotional use. For information, please e-mail the Andrews McMeel Publishing Special Sales Department: sales@andrewsmcmeel.com.

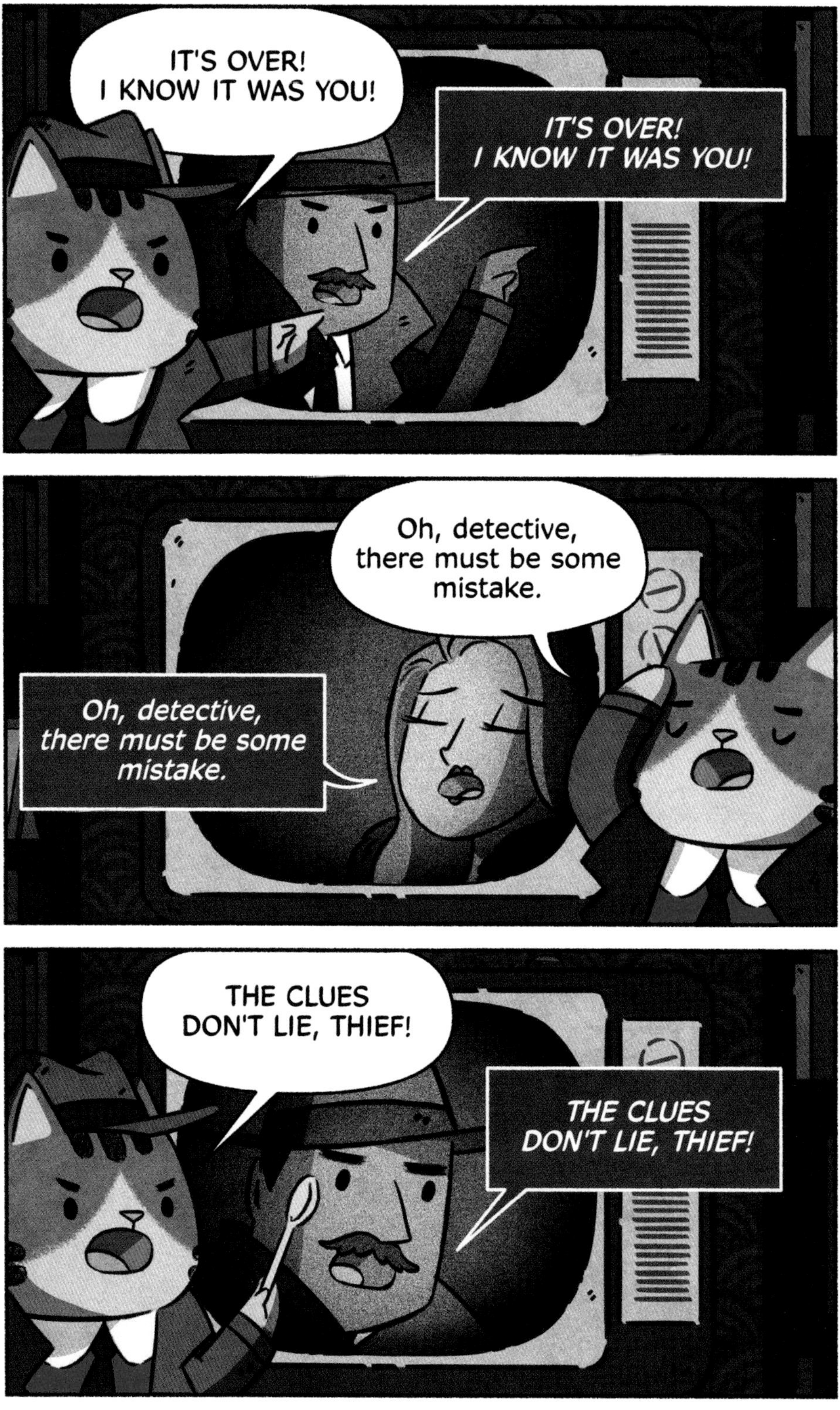
IT'S OVER! I KNOW IT WAS YOU!
IT'S OVER! I KNOW IT WAS YOU!
Oh, detective, there must be some mistake.
Oh, detective, there must be some mistake.
THE CLUES DON'T LIE, THIEF!
THE CLUES DON'T LIE, THIEF!

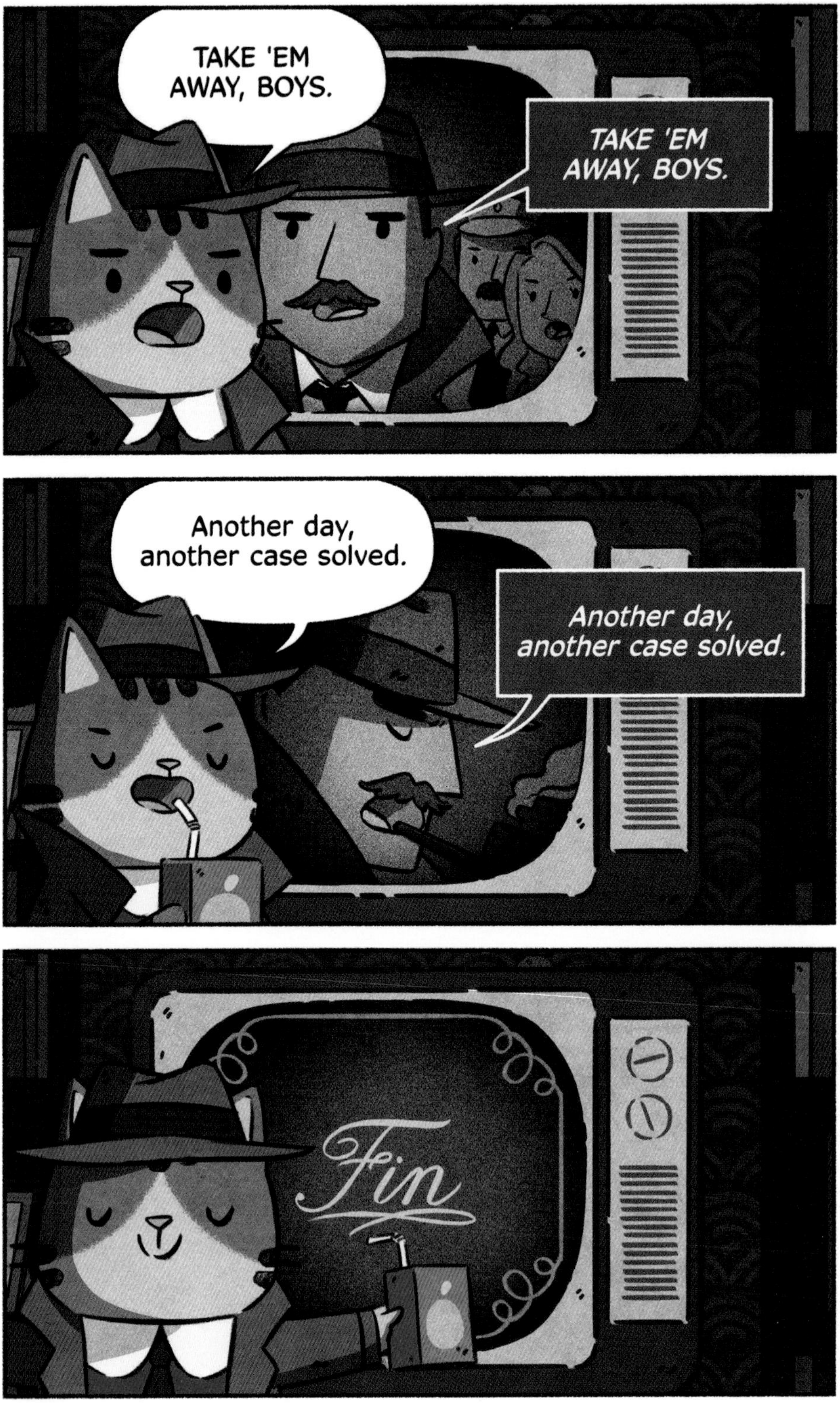
TAKE 'EM AWAY, BOYS.
TAKE 'EM AWAY, BOYS.
Another day, another case solved.
Another day, another case solved.
Fin

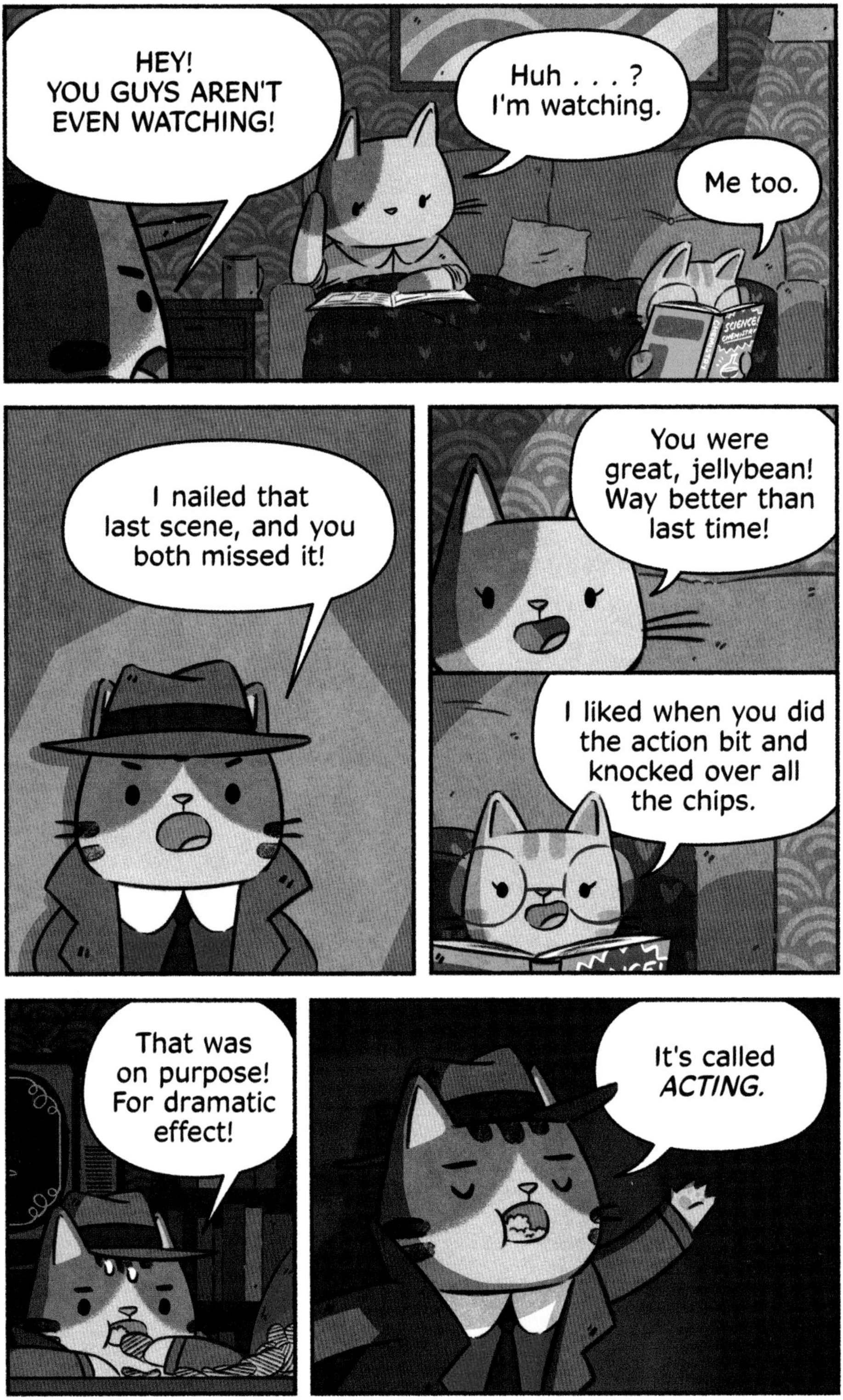

HEY! YOU GUYS AREN'T EVEN WATCHING!
Huh . . . ? I'm watching.
Me too.
I nailed that last scene, and you both missed it!
You were great, jellybean! Way better than last time!
I liked when you did the action bit and knocked over all the chips.
That was on purpose! For dramatic effect!
It's called *ACTING.*

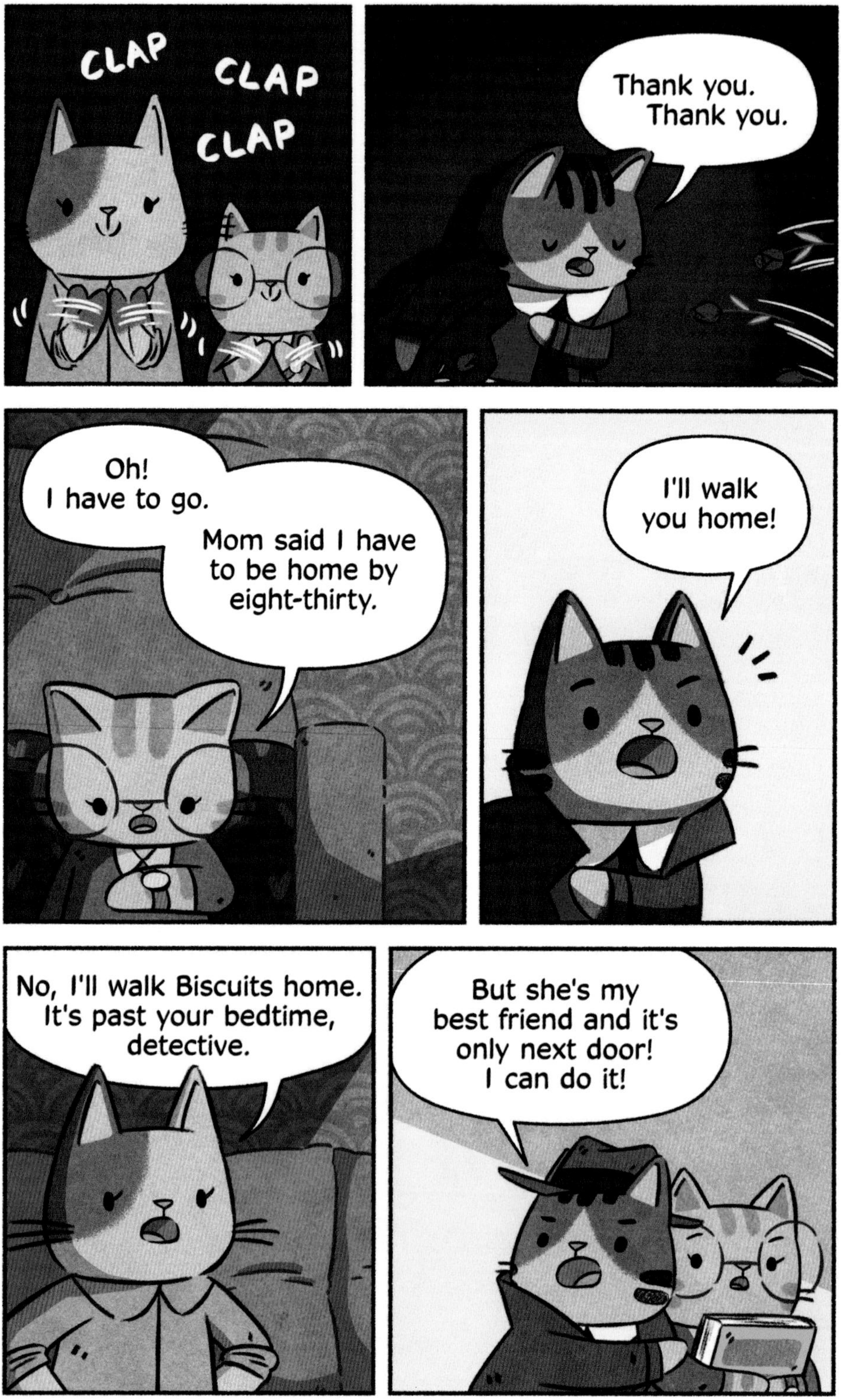
CLAP
CLAP
CLAP
Thank you. Thank you.
Oh! I have to go.
Mom said I have to be home by eight-thirty.
I'll walk you home!
No, I'll walk Biscuits home. It's past your bedtime, detective.
But she's my best friend and it's only next door! I can do it!

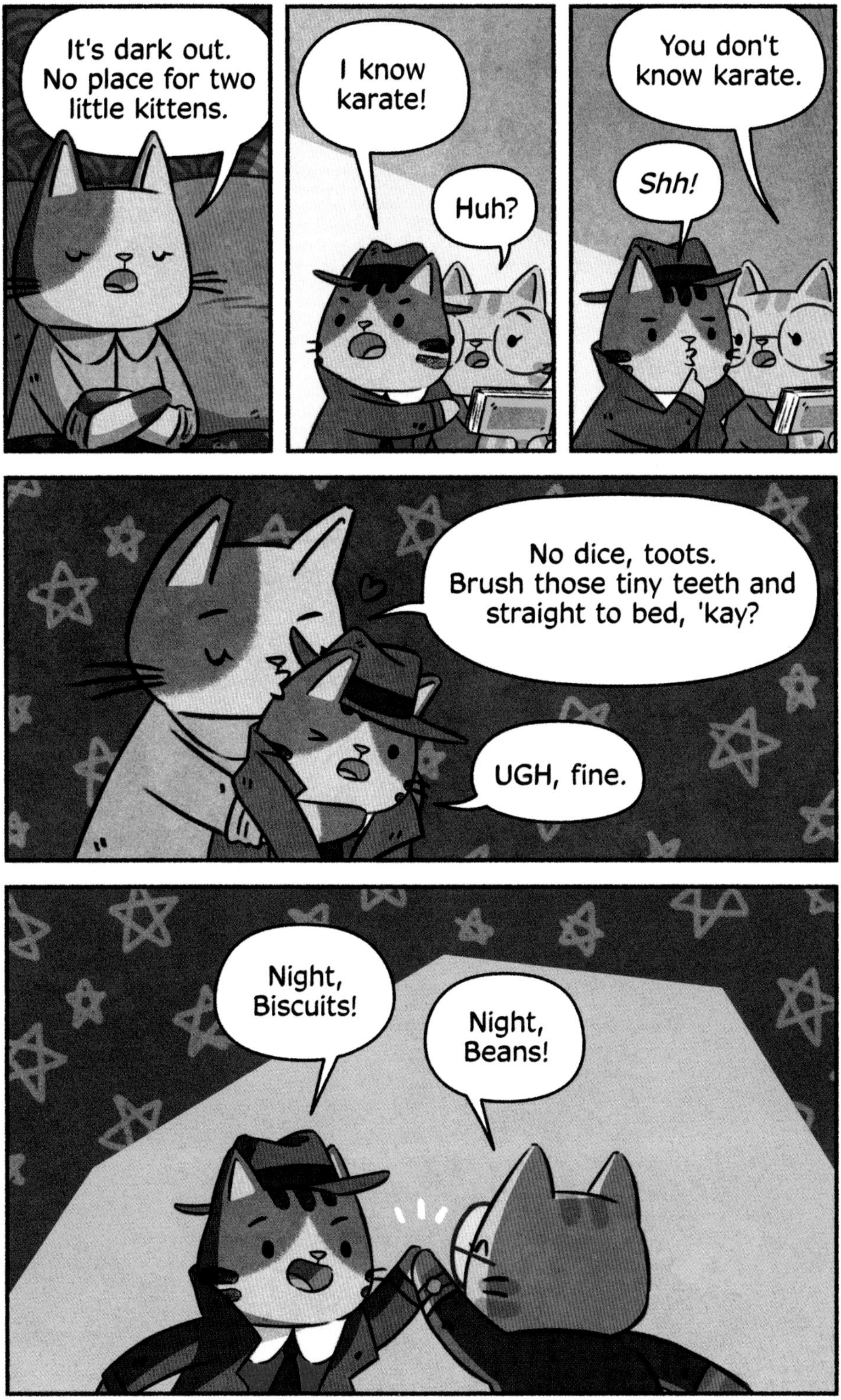
It's dark out. No place for two little kittens.
I know karate!
Huh?
You don't know karate.
Shh!
No dice, toots. Brush those tiny teeth and straight to bed, 'kay?
UGH, fine.
Night, Biscuits!
Night, Beans!

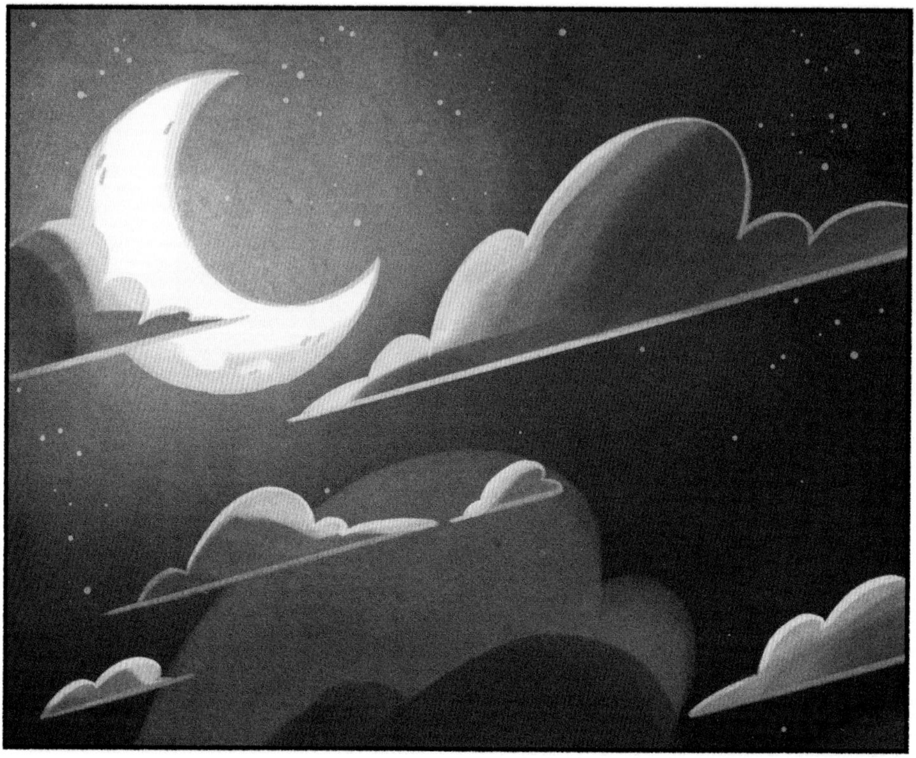

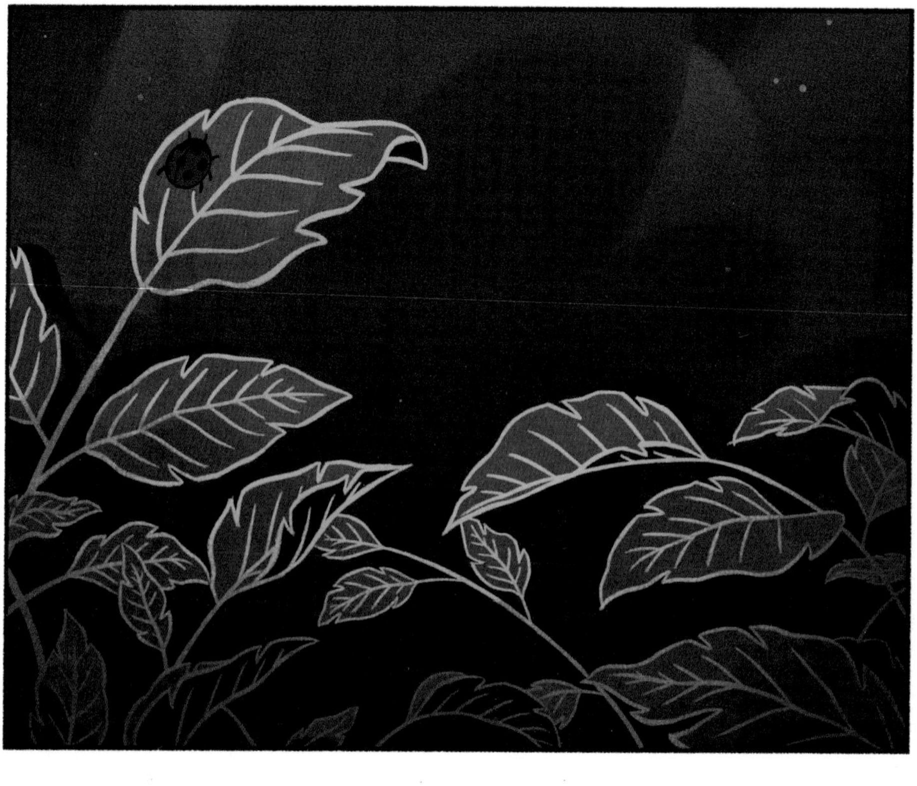

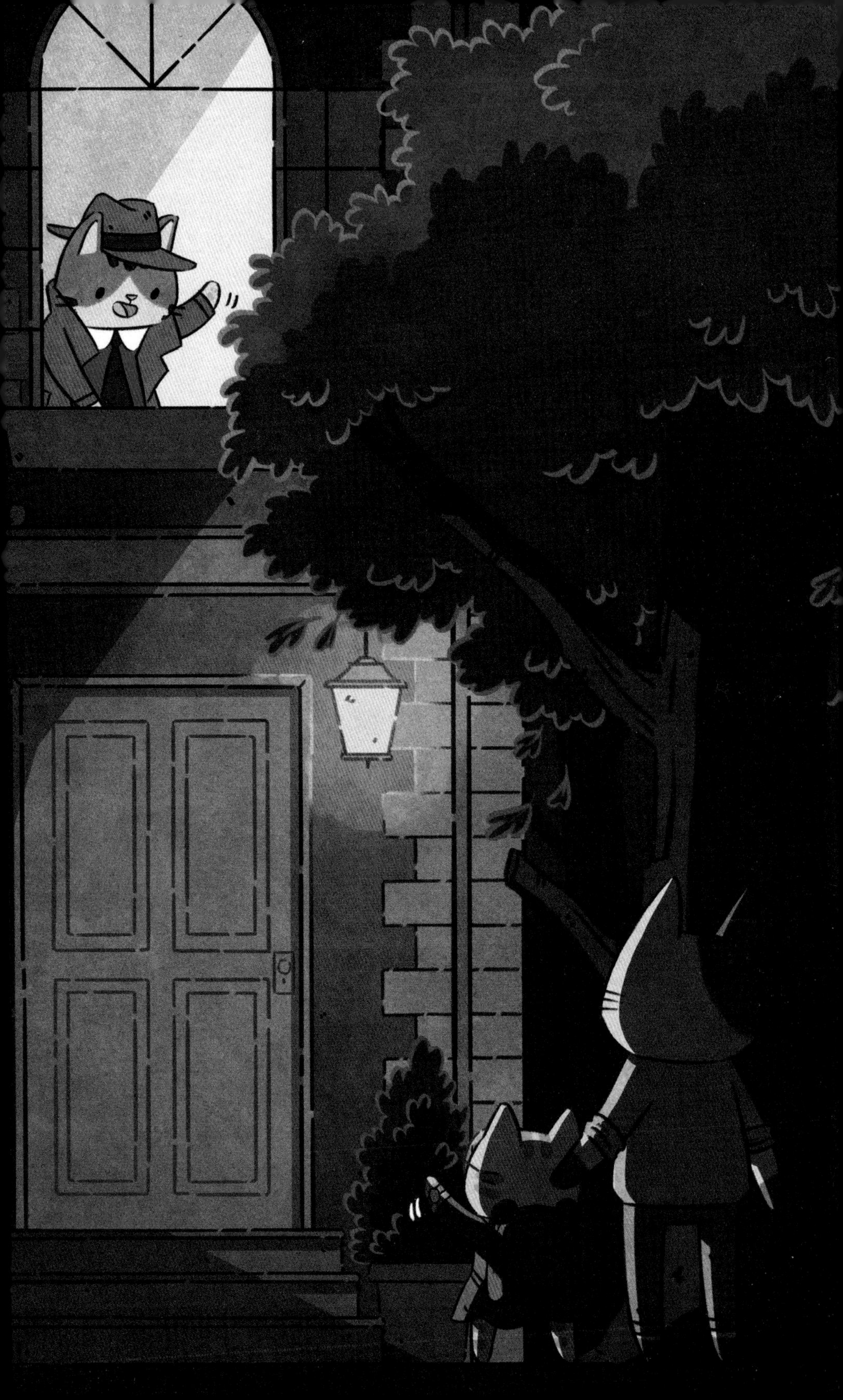

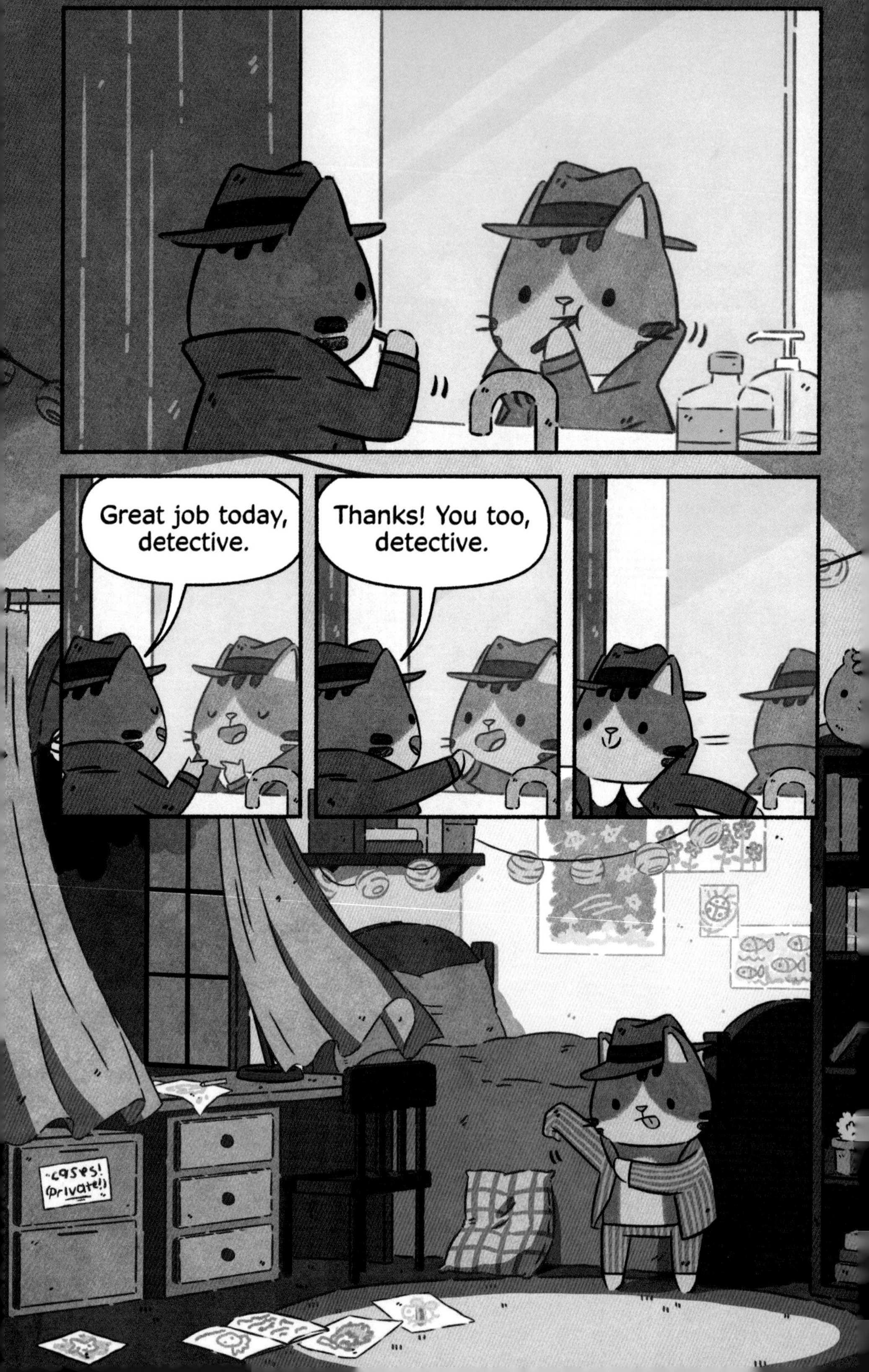
Great job today, detective.
Thanks! You too, detective.
cases! (private!)

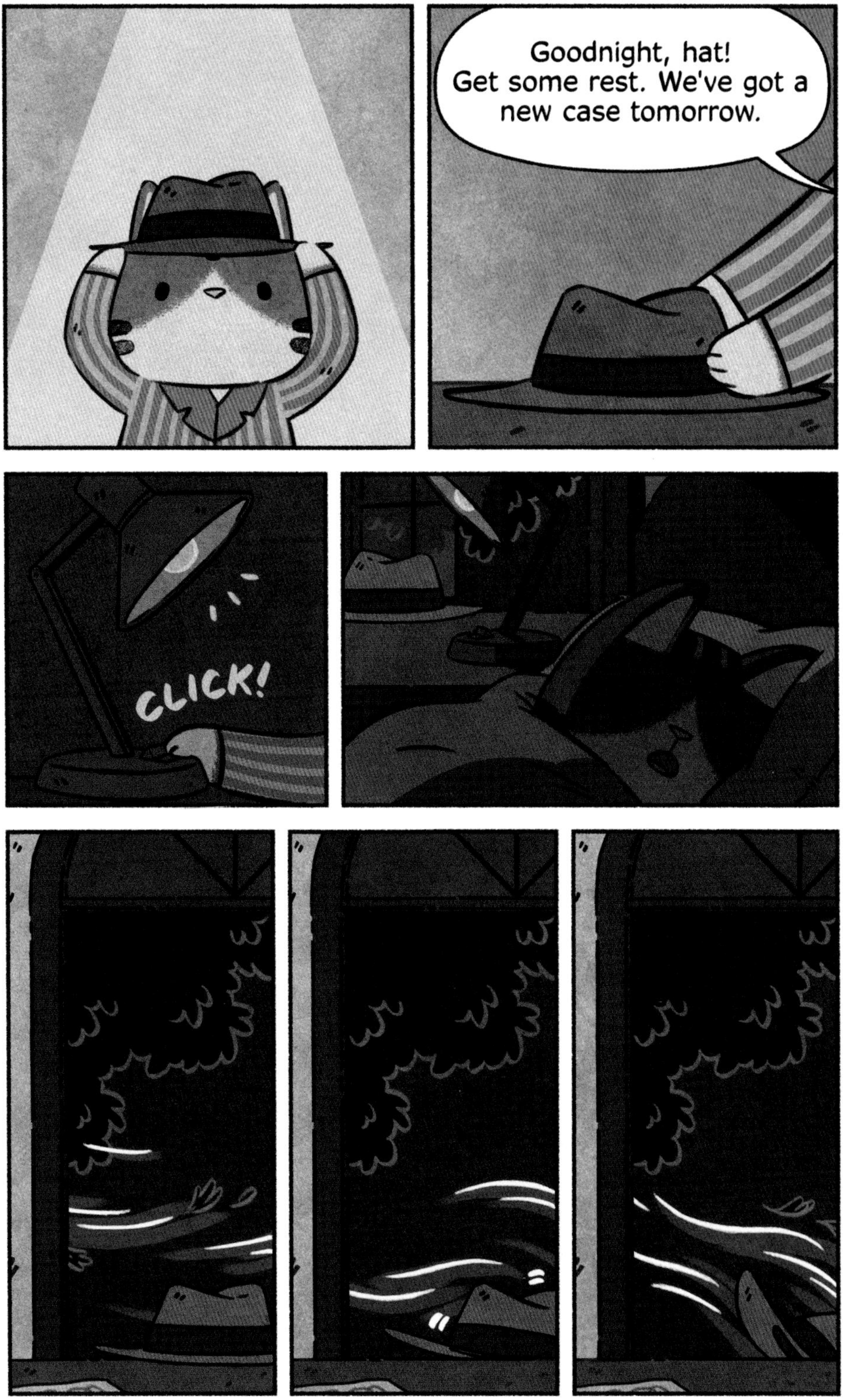
Goodnight, hat!
Get some rest. We've got a new case tomorrow.
CLICK!

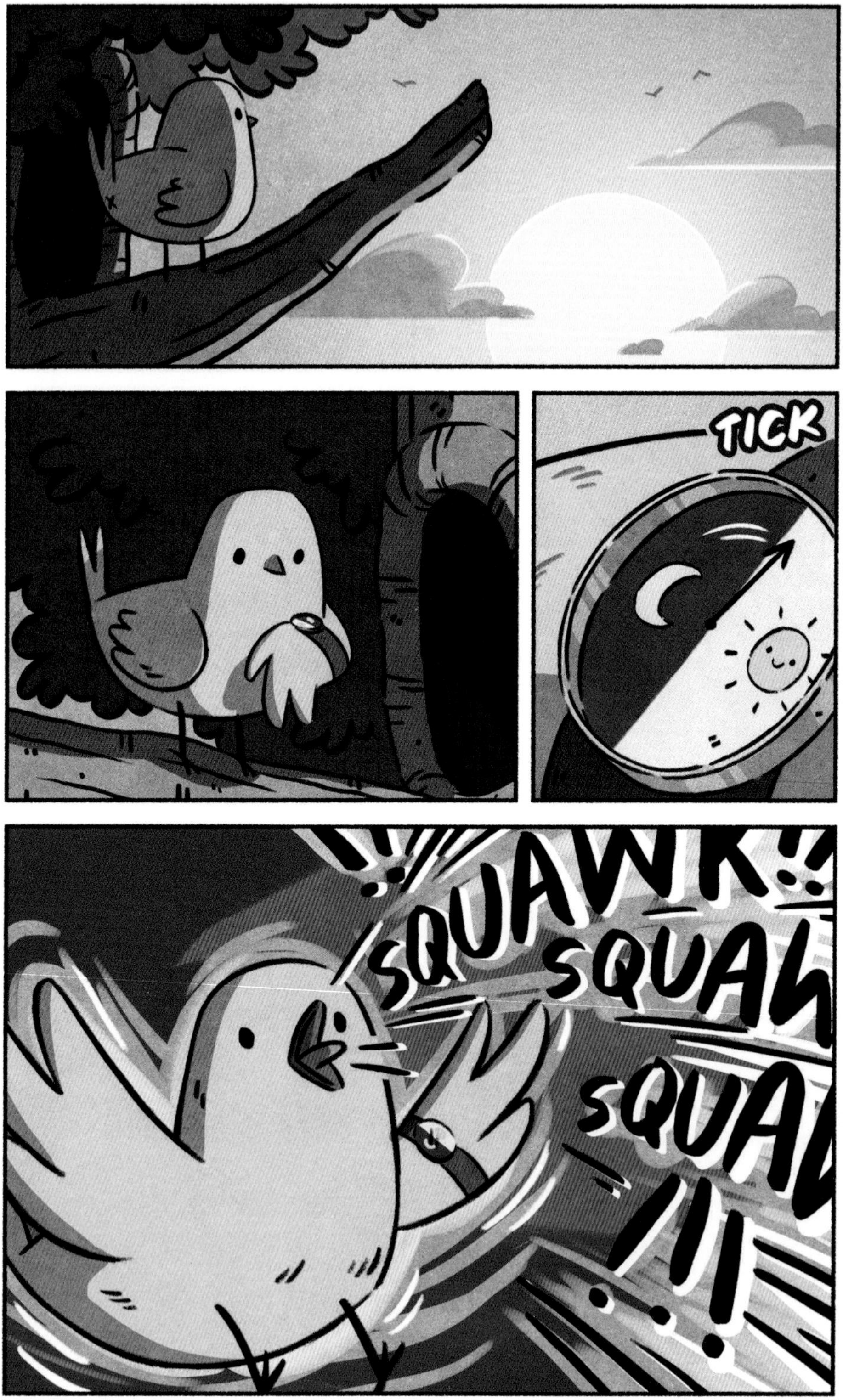
TICK
SQUAWK!!
SQUAW
SQUAW
!!!

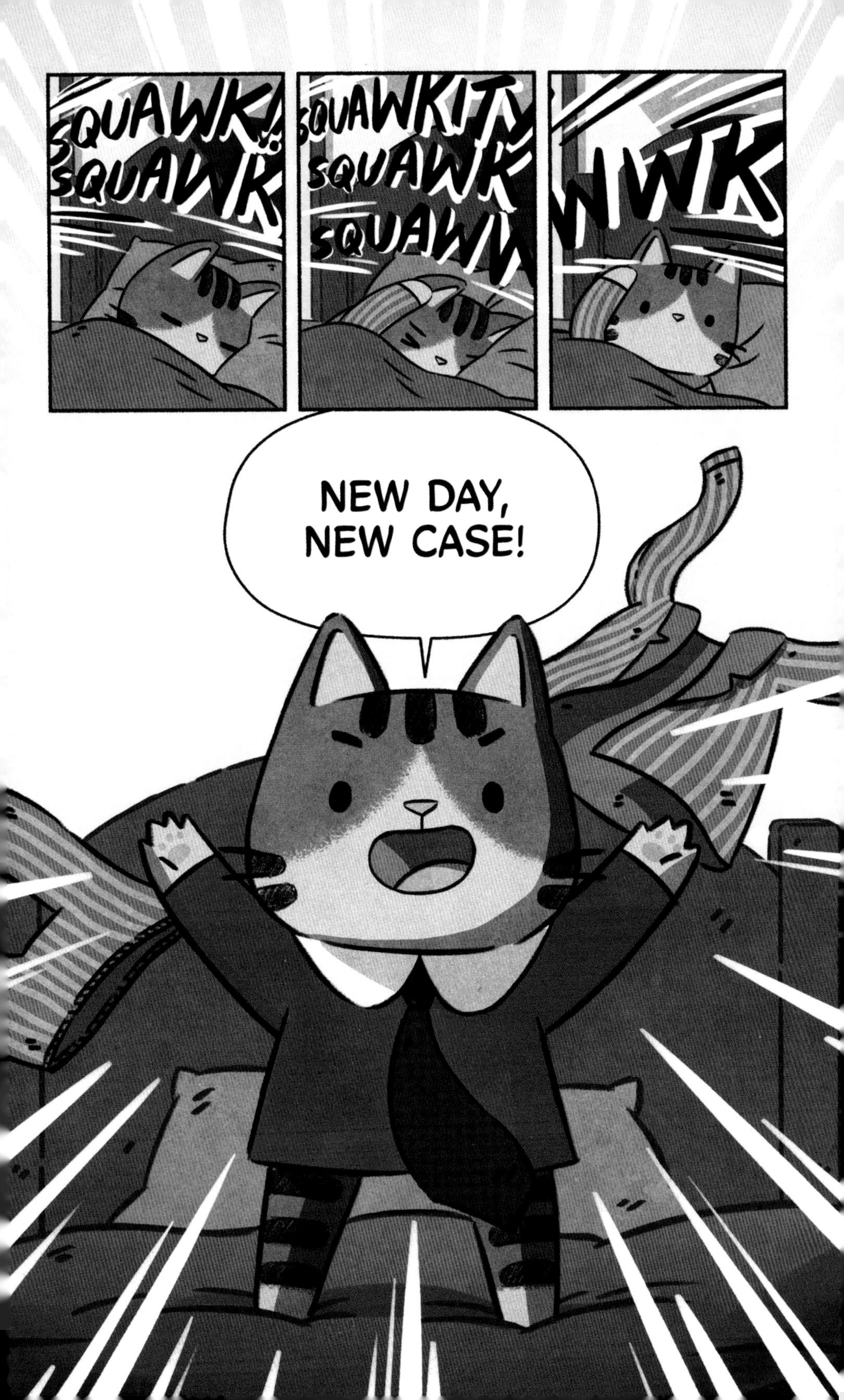
SQUAWK!
SQUAWK
SQUAWKITY
SQUAWK
SQUAWW
WWWK
NEW DAY, NEW CASE!

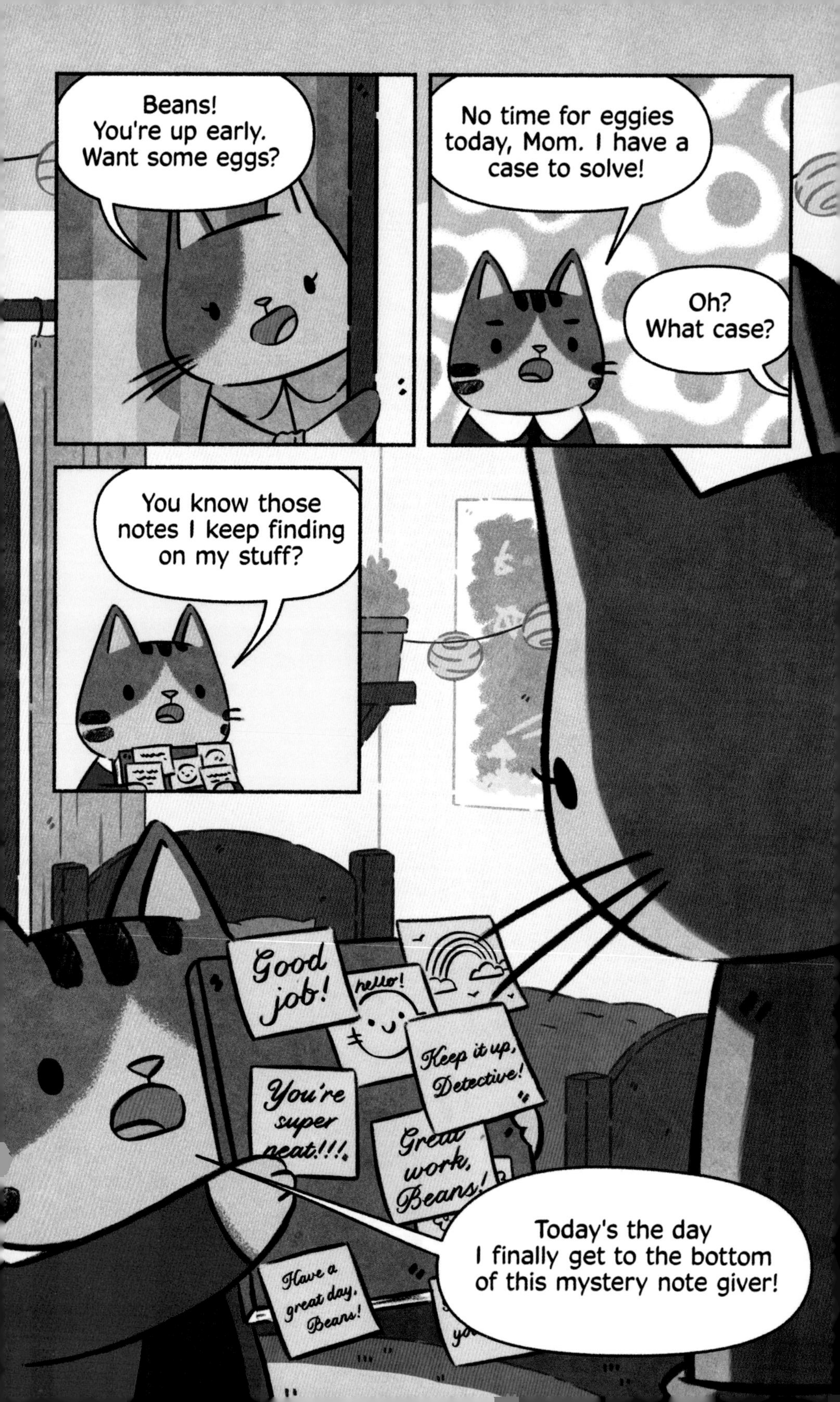
Beans! You're up early. Want some eggs?
No time for eggies today, Mom. I have a case to solve!
Oh? What case?
You know those notes I keep finding on my stuff?
Good job!
hello!
Keep it up, Detective!
You're super neat!!!
Great work, Beans!
Have a great day, Beans!
Today's the day I finally get to the bottom of this mystery note giver!

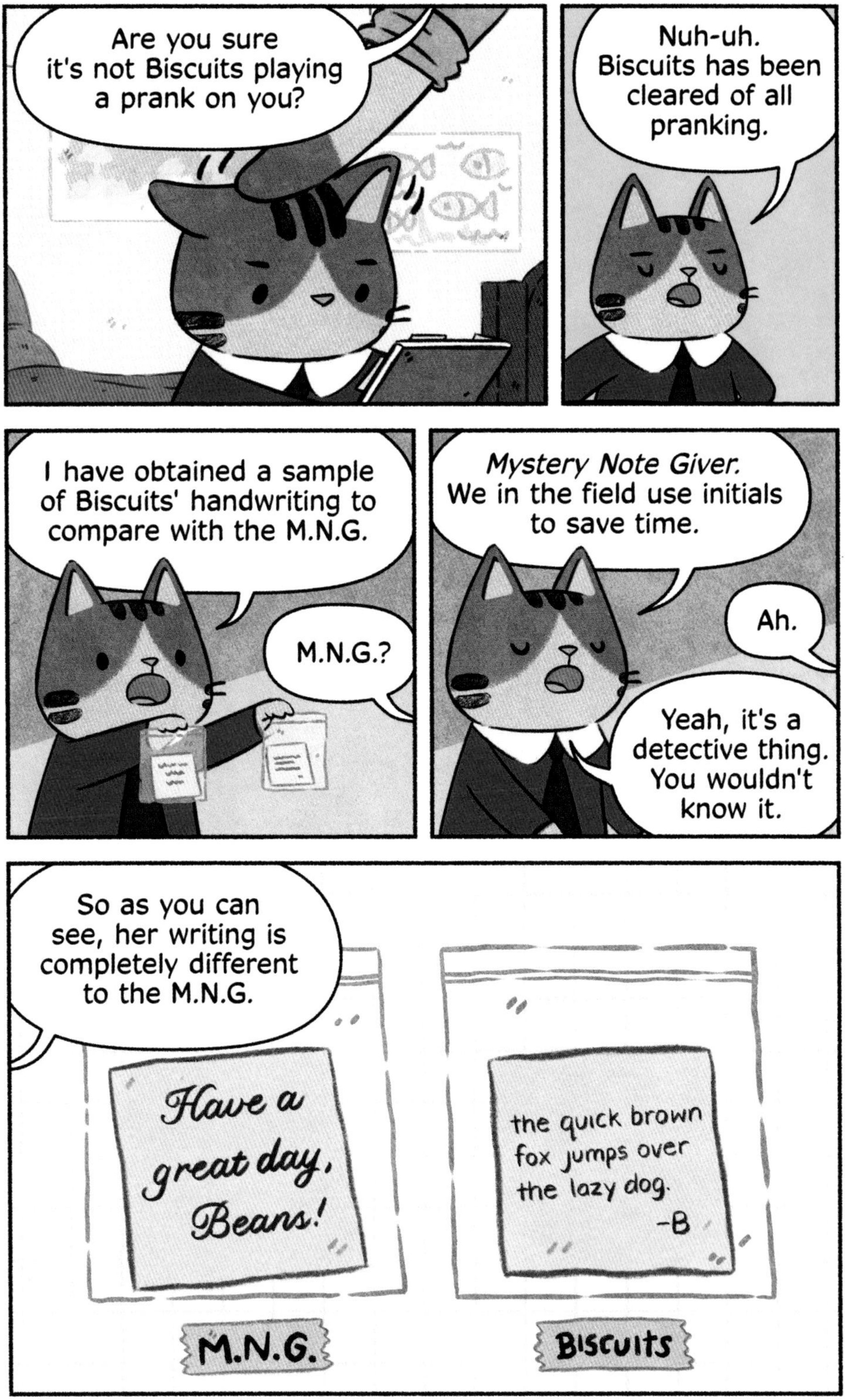
Are you sure it's not Biscuits playing a prank on you?
Nuh-uh. Biscuits has been cleared of all pranking.
I have obtained a sample of Biscuits' handwriting to compare with the M.N.G.
M.N.G.?
Mystery Note Giver. We in the field use initials to save time.
Ah.
Yeah, it's a detective thing. You wouldn't know it.
So as you can see, her writing is completely different to the M.N.G.
Have a great day, Beans!
the quick brown fox jumps over the lazy dog. -B
M.N.G.
BISCUITS

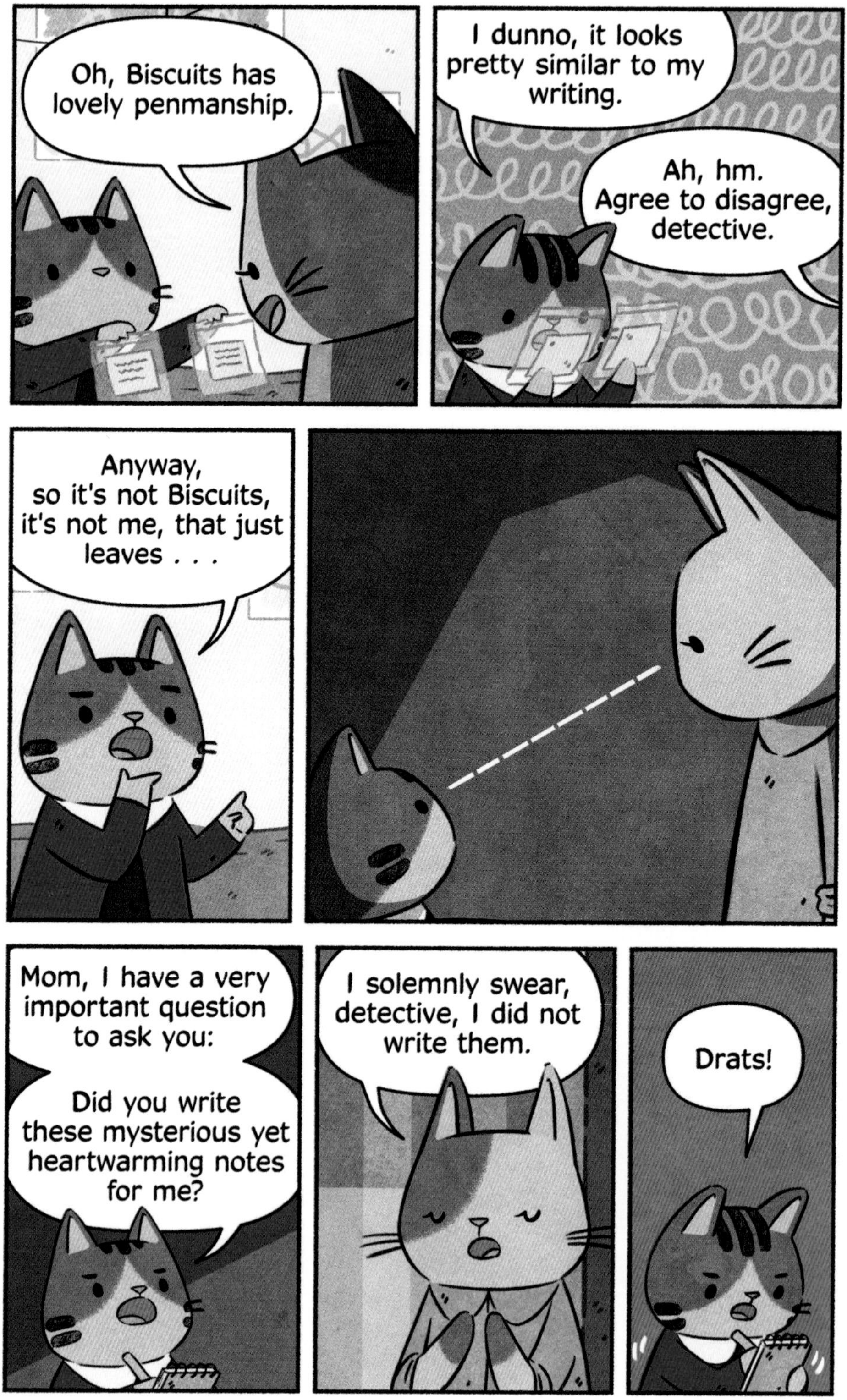
Oh, Biscuits has lovely penmanship.
I dunno, it looks pretty similar to my writing.
Ah, hm. Agree to disagree, detective.
Anyway, so it's not Biscuits, it's not me, that just leaves . . .
Mom, I have a very important question to ask you:
Did you write these mysterious yet heartwarming notes for me?
I solemnly swear, detective, I did not write them.
Drats!

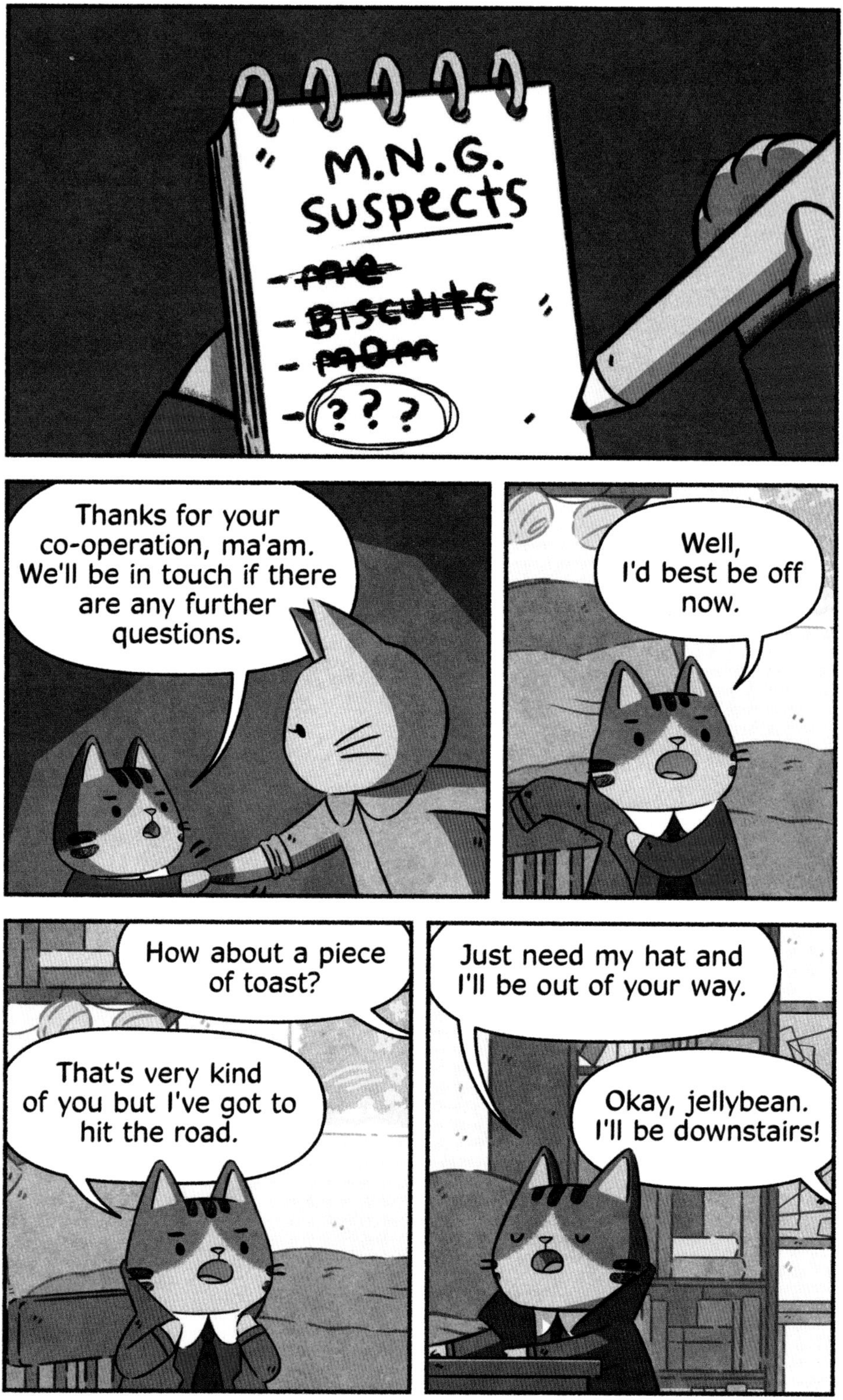
M.N.G. Suspects
???
Thanks for your co-operation, ma'am. We'll be in touch if there are any further questions.
Well, I'd best be off now.
How about a piece of toast?
That's very kind of you but I've got to hit the road.
Just need my hat and I'll be out of your way.
Okay, jellybean. I'll be downstairs!

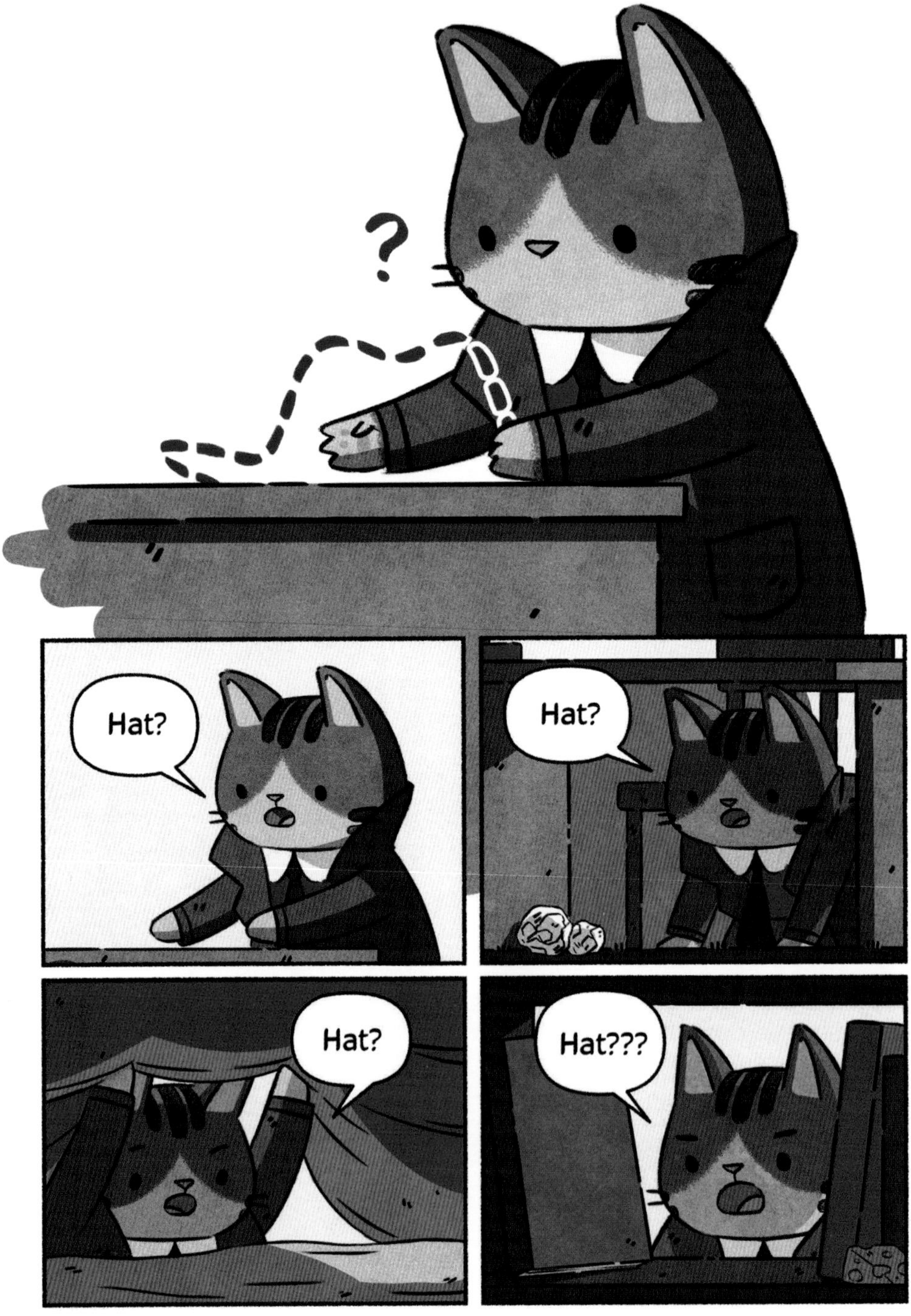
?
Hat?
Hat?
Hat?
Hat???

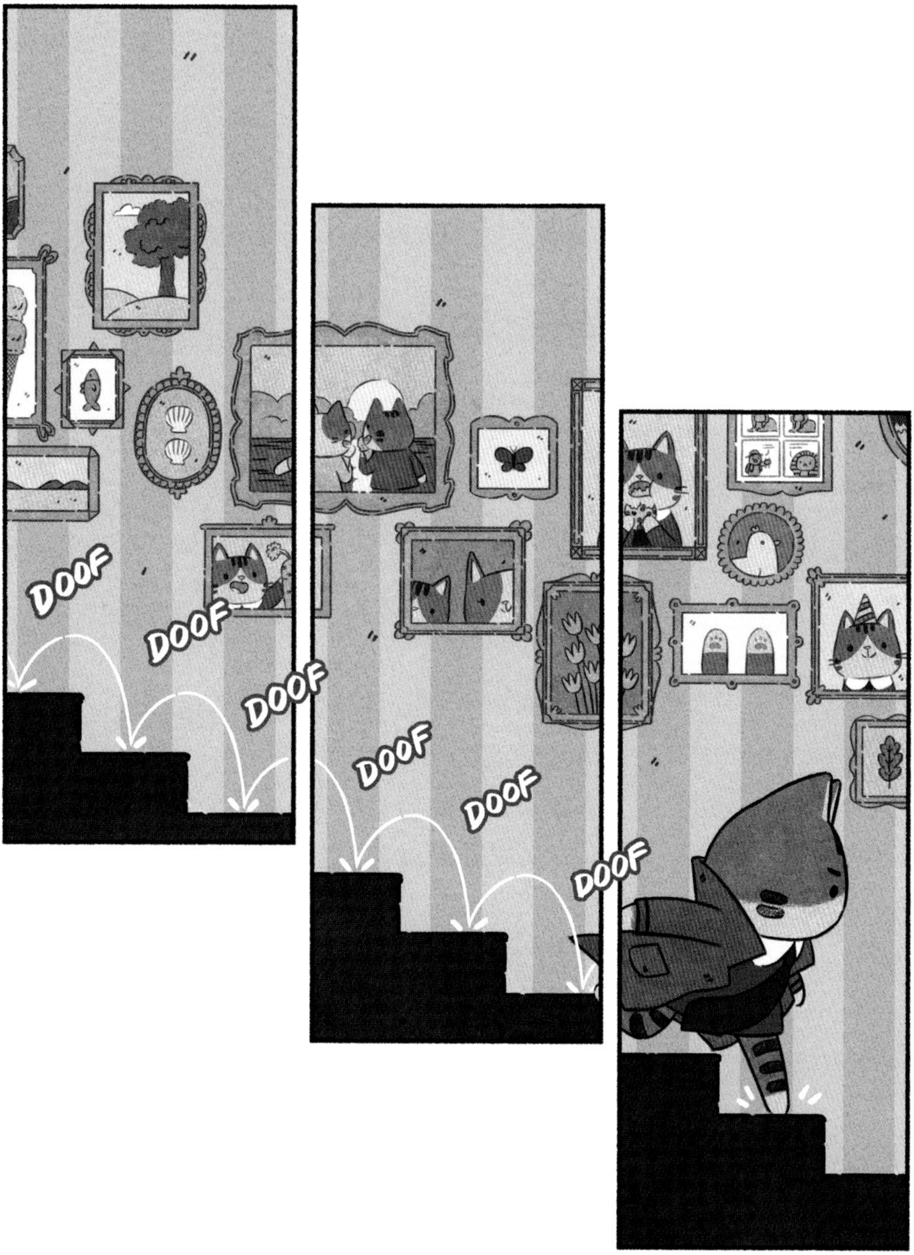
DOOF
DOOF
DOOF
DOOF
DOOF
DOOF

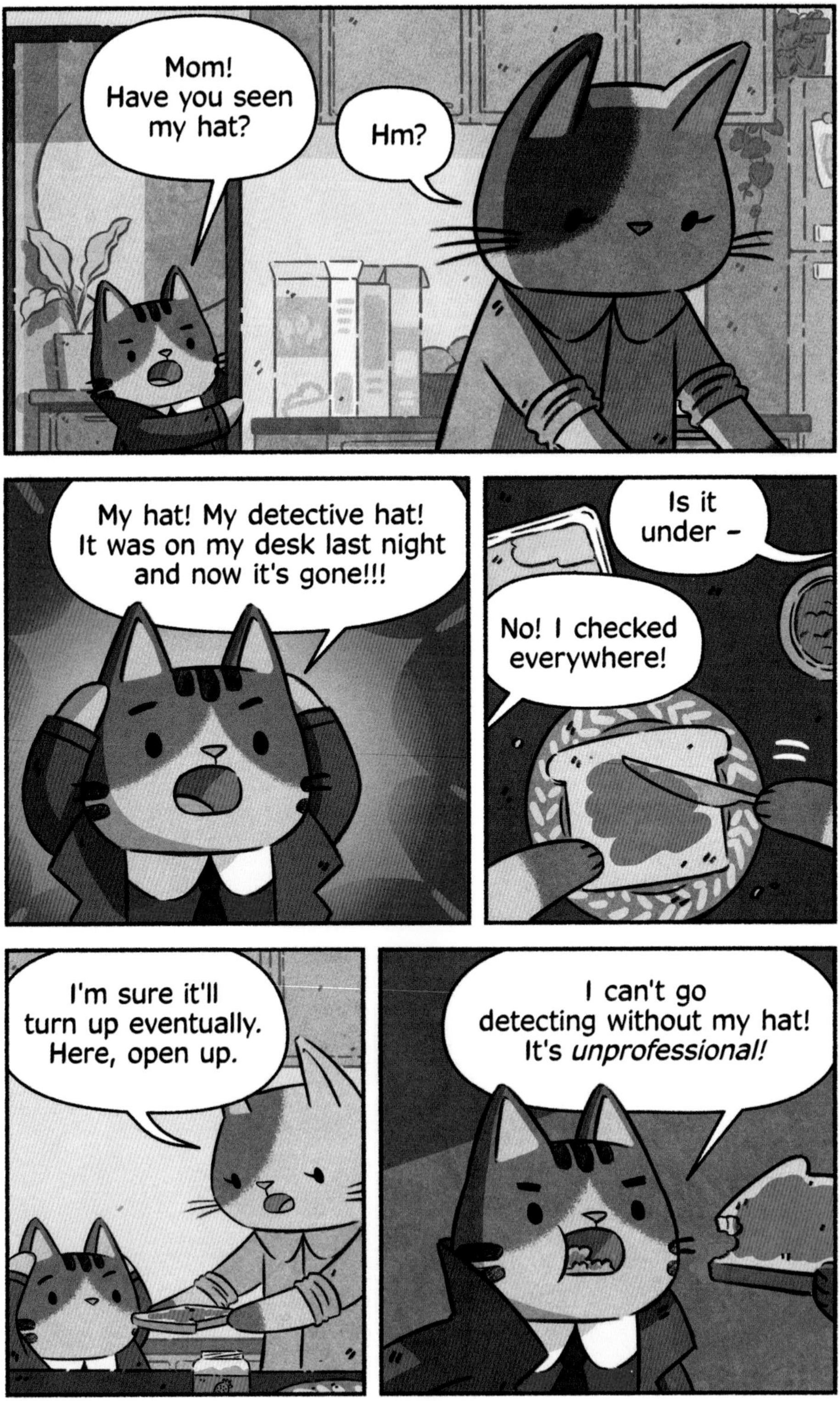
Mom!
Have you seen
my hat?
Hm?
My hat! My detective hat!
It was on my desk last night
and now it's gone!!!
Is it
under -
No! I checked
everywhere!
I'm sure it'll
turn up eventually.
Here, open up.
I can't go
detecting without my hat!
It's *unprofessional!*

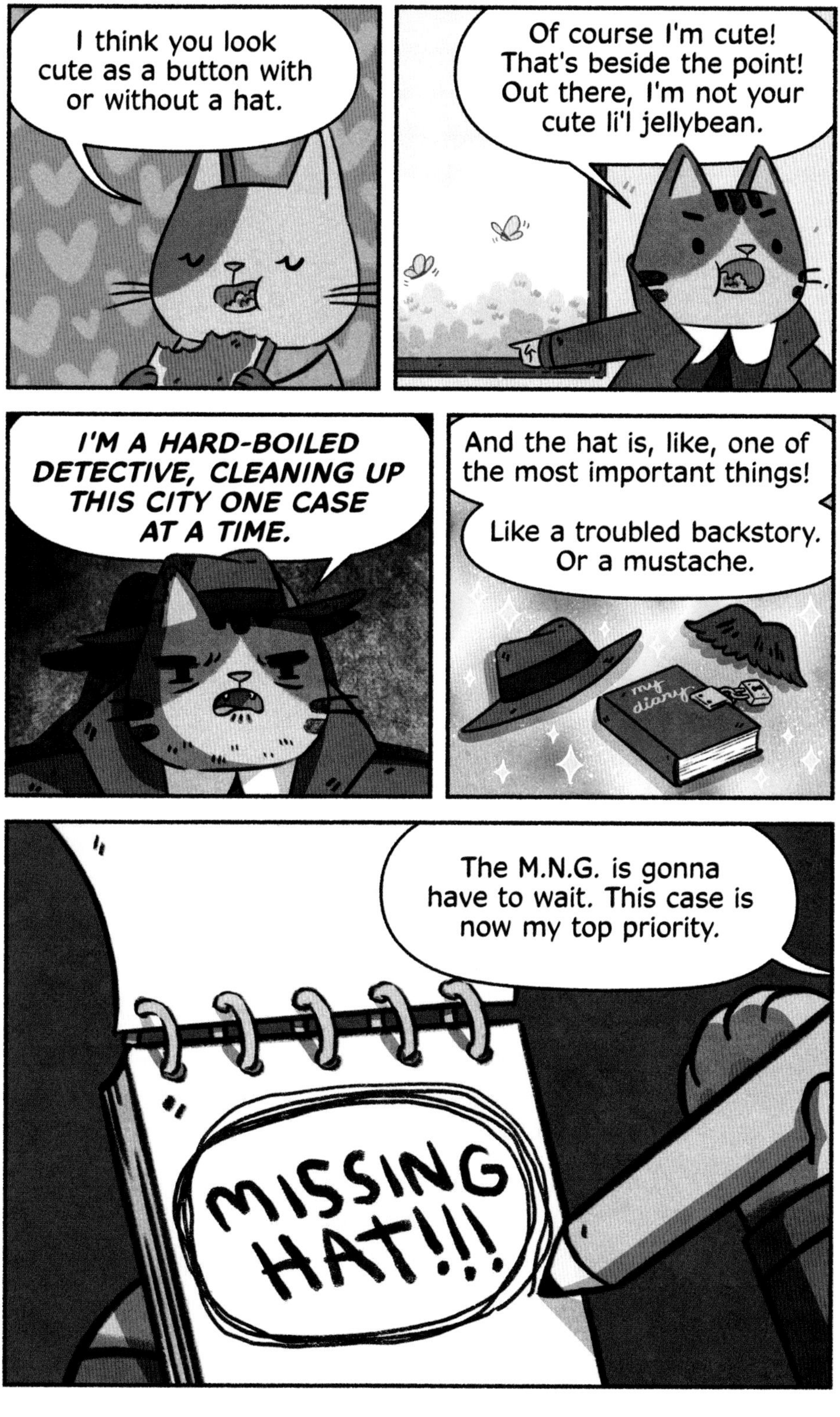

I think you look cute as a button with or without a hat.
Of course I'm cute! That's beside the point! Out there, I'm not your cute li'l jellybean.
I'M A HARD-BOILED DETECTIVE, CLEANING UP THIS CITY ONE CASE AT A TIME.
And the hat is, like, one of the most important things!
Like a troubled backstory. Or a mustache.
my diary
The M.N.G. is gonna have to wait. This case is now my top priority.
MISSING HAT!!!

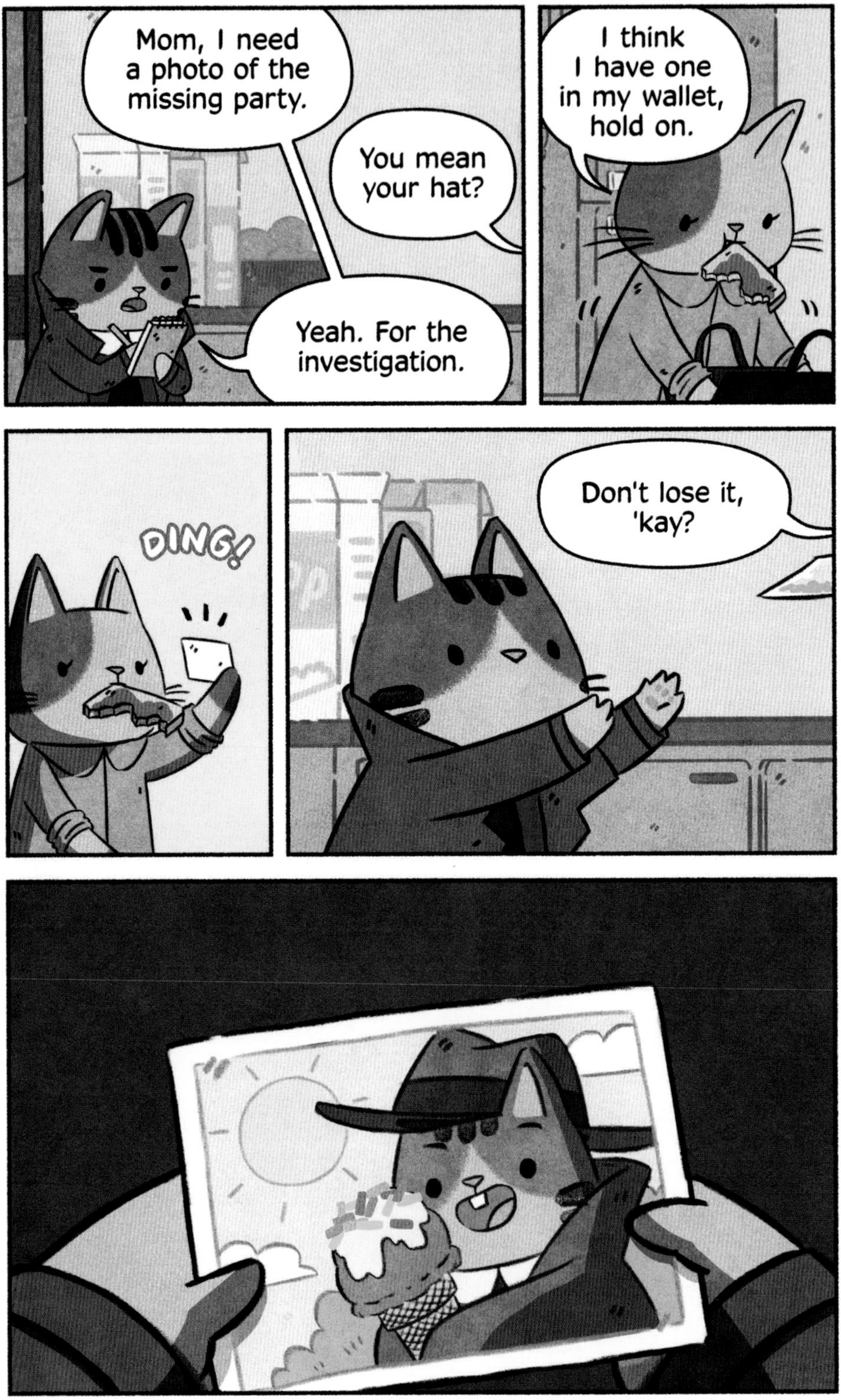
Mom, I need a photo of the missing party.
You mean your hat?
Yeah. For the investigation.
I think I have one in my wallet, hold on.
DING!
Don't lose it, 'kay?

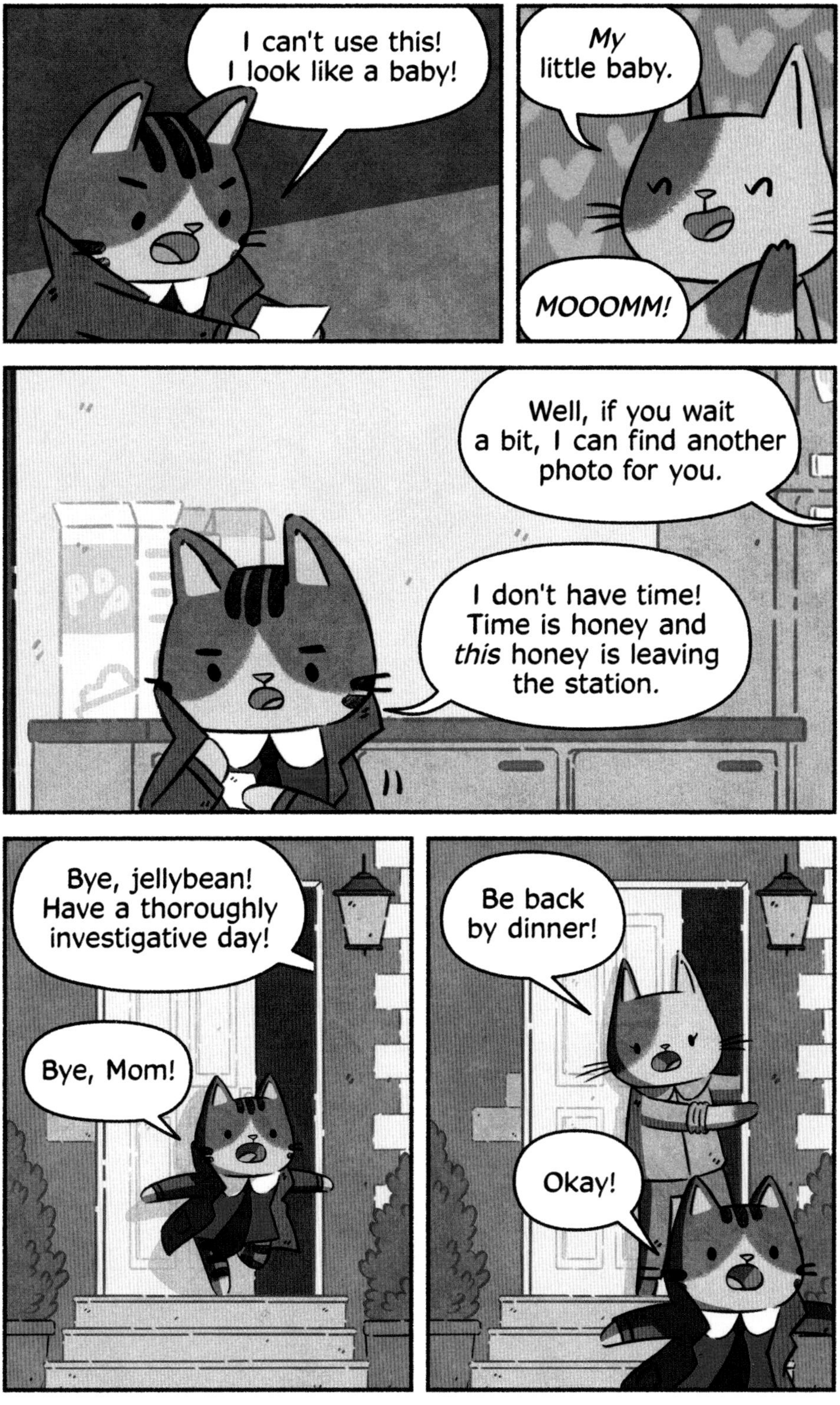
I can't use this!
I look like a baby!
My
little baby.
MOOOMM!
Well, if you wait
a bit, I can find another
photo for you.
I don't have time!
Time is honey and
this honey is leaving
the station.
Bye, jellybean!
Have a thoroughly
investigative day!
Bye, Mom!
Be back
by dinner!
Okay!

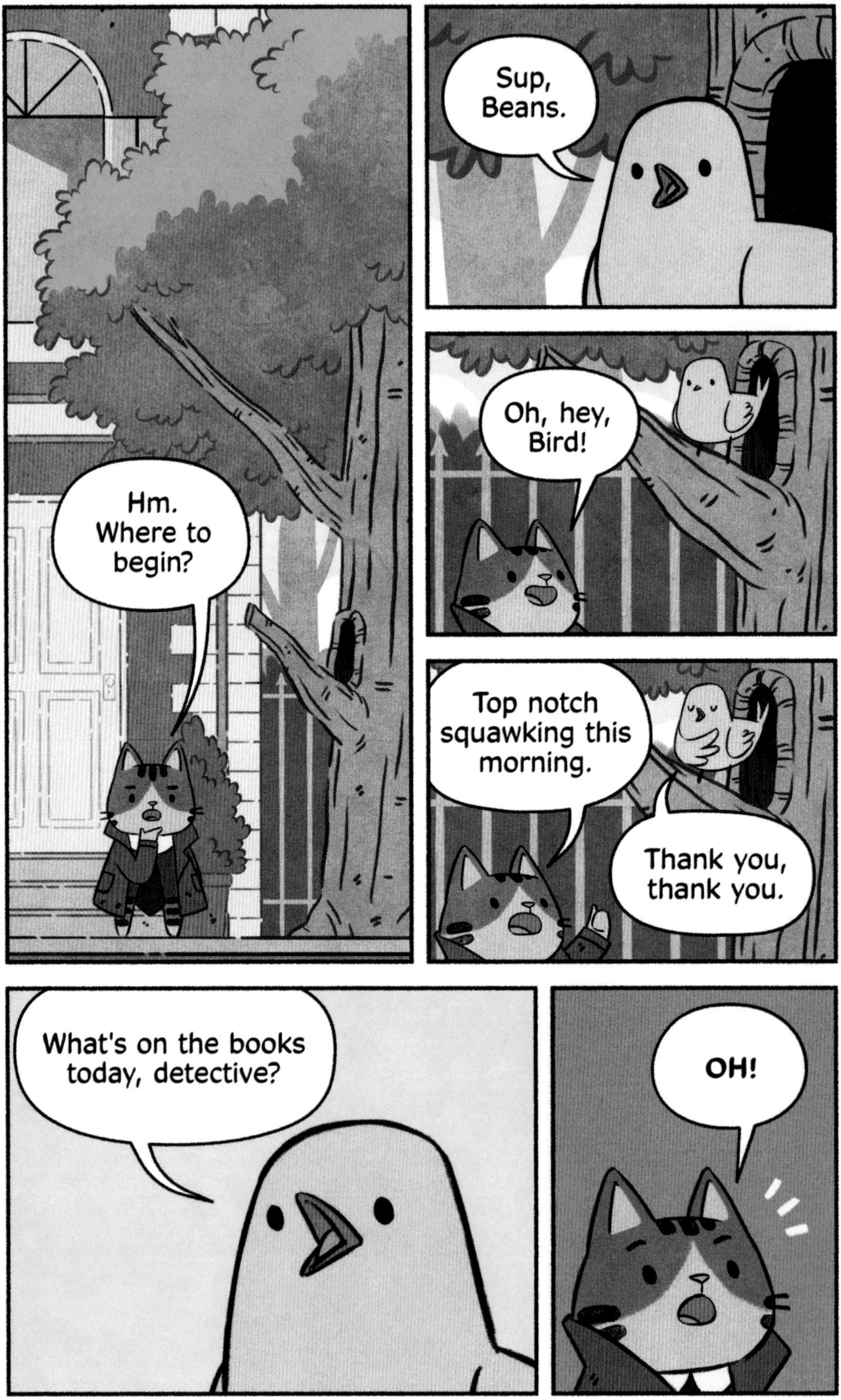
Hm. Where to begin?
Sup, Beans.
Oh, hey, Bird!
Top notch squawking this morning.
Thank you, thank you.
What's on the books today, detective?
OH!

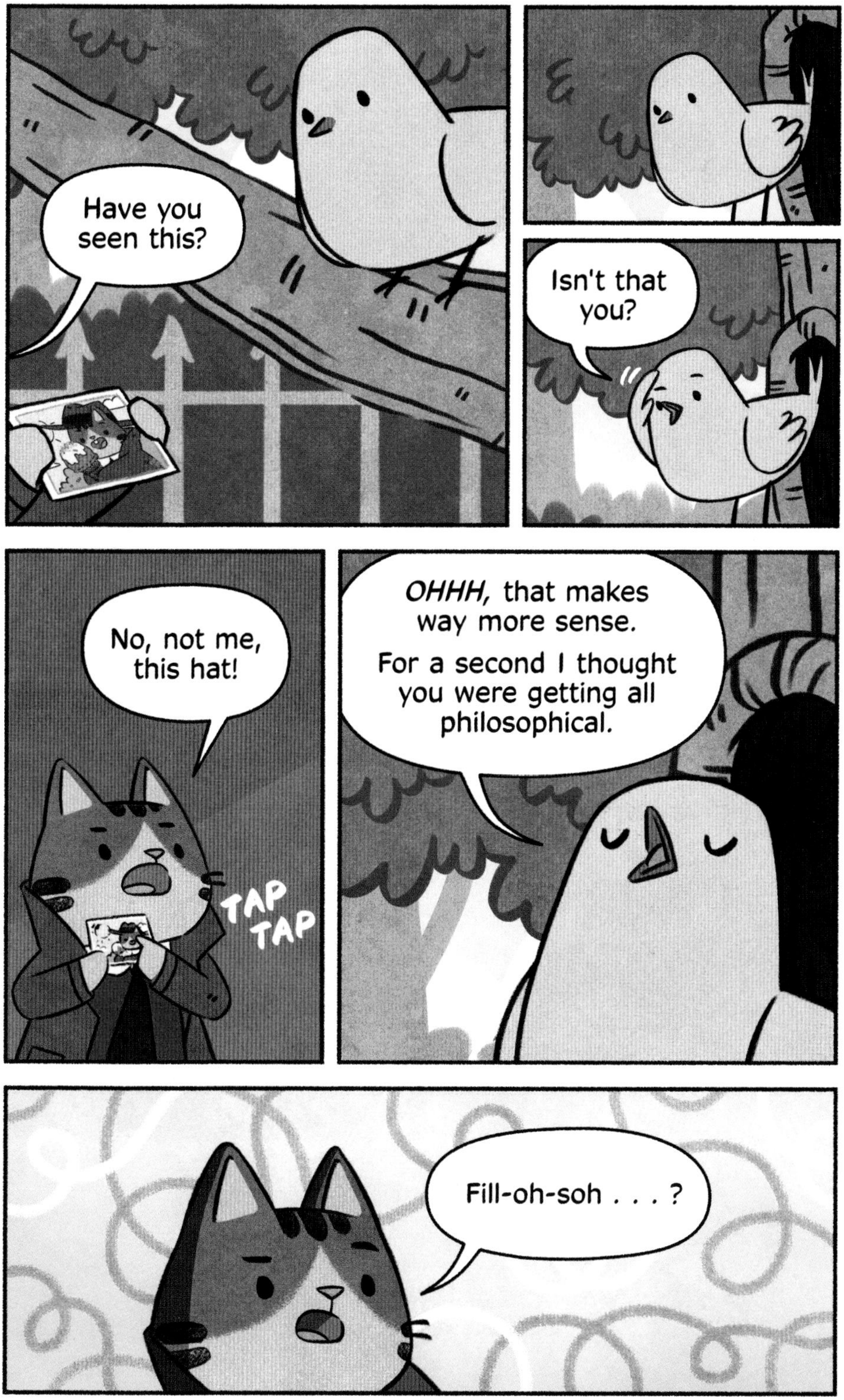
Have you seen this?
Isn't that you?
No, not me, this hat!
TAP TAP
OHHH, that makes way more sense.
For a second I thought you were getting all philosophical.
Fill-oh-soh . . . ?

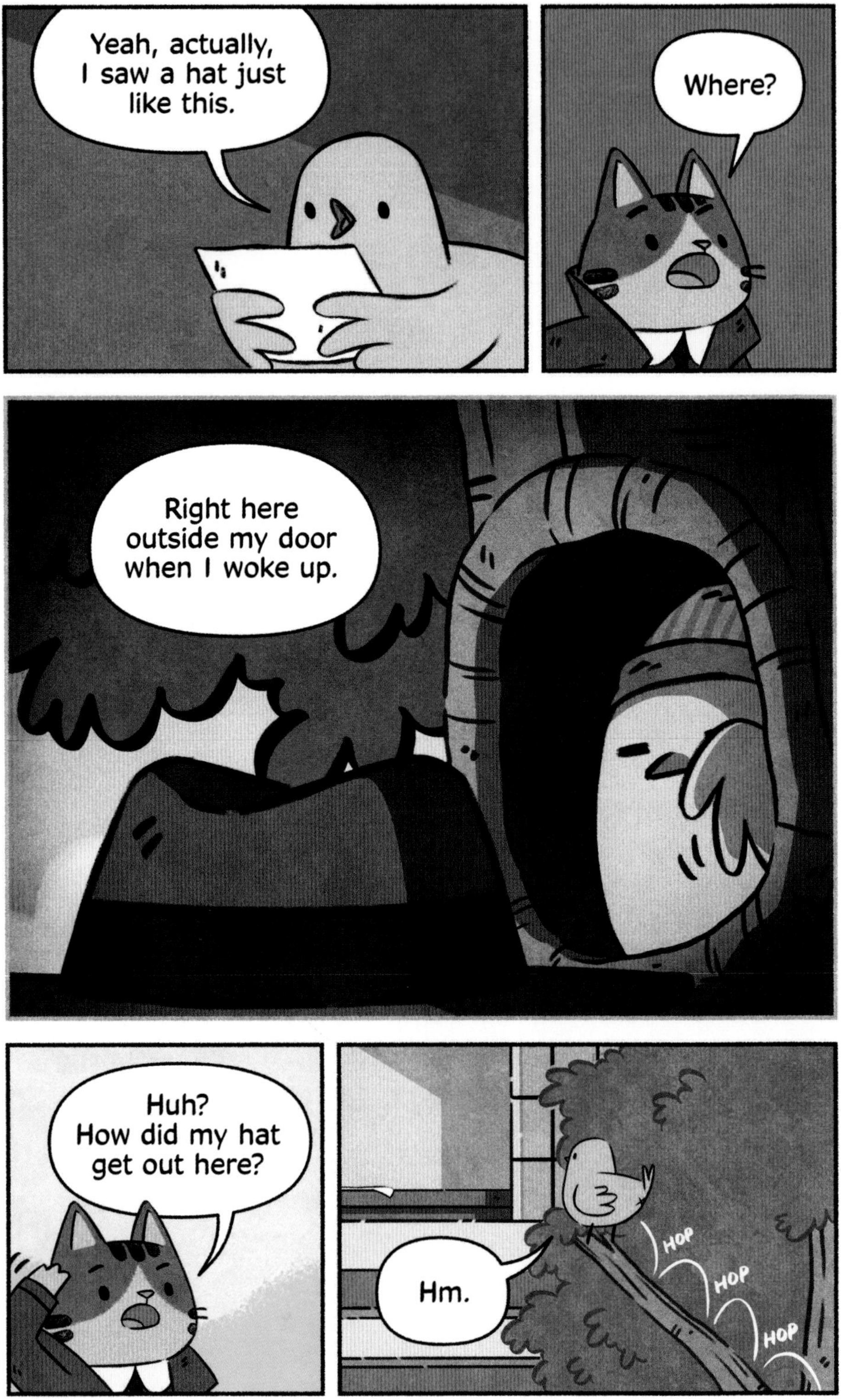
Yeah, actually, I saw a hat just like this.
Where?
Right here outside my door when I woke up.
Huh? How did my hat get out here?
Hm.
HOP
HOP
HOP

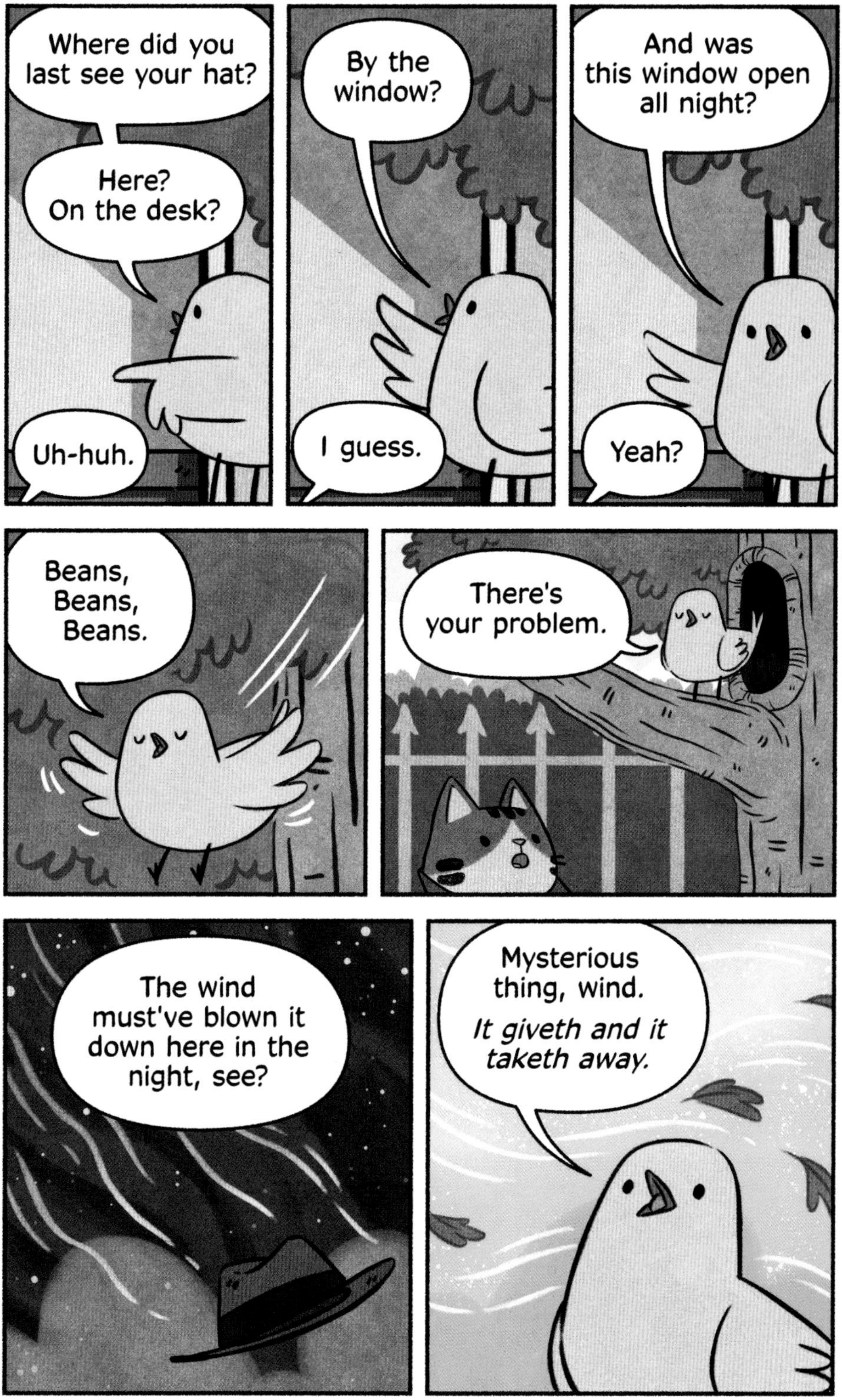
Where did you last see your hat?
Here? On the desk?
Uh-huh.
By the window?
I guess.
And was this window open all night?
Yeah?
Beans, Beans, Beans.
There's your problem.
The wind must've blown it down here in the night, see?
Mysterious thing, wind.
It giveth and it taketh away.

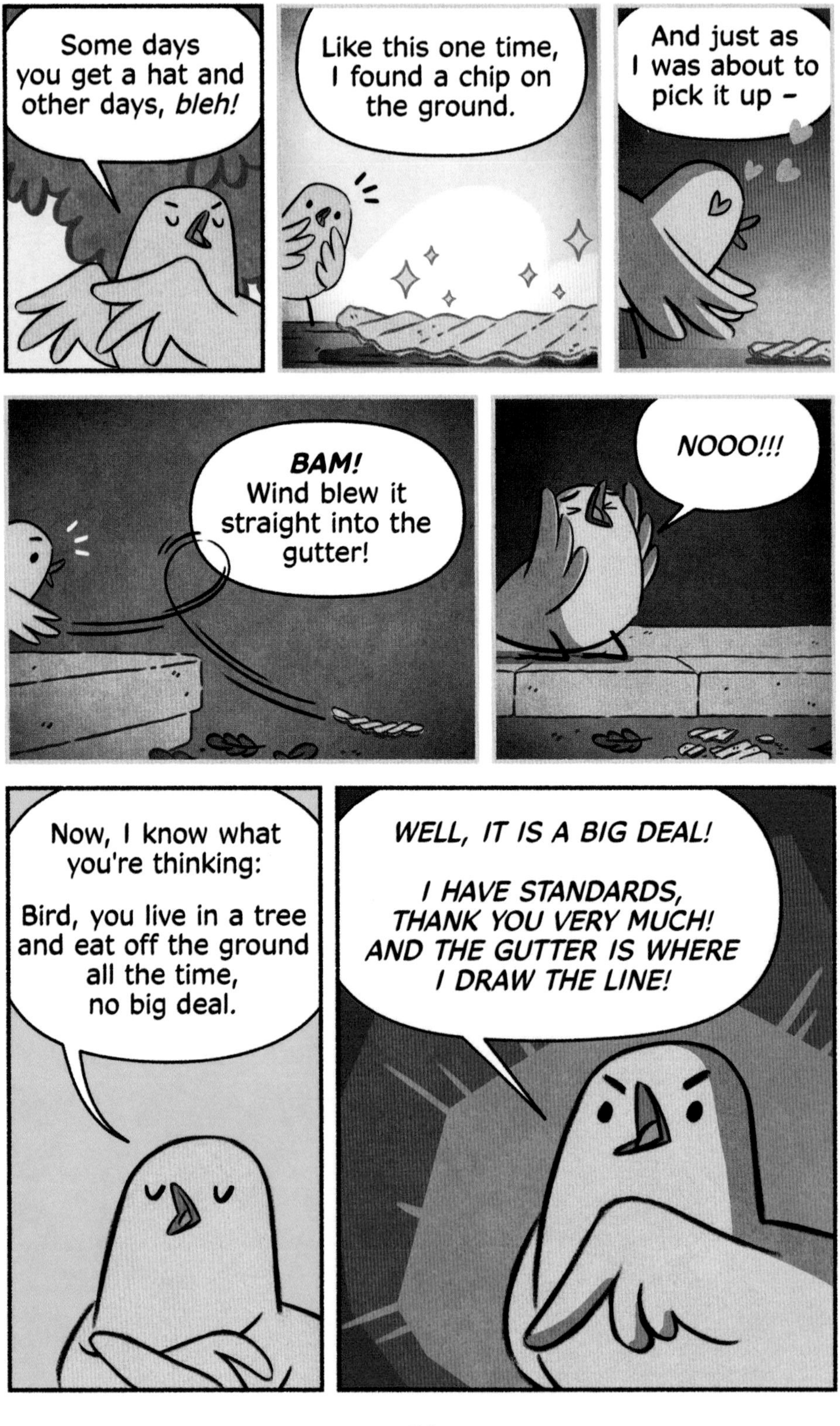
Some days you get a hat and other days, *bleh!*
Like this one time, I found a chip on the ground.
And just as I was about to pick it up –
BAM! Wind blew it straight into the gutter!
NOOO!!!
Now, I know what you're thinking:
Bird, you live in a tree and eat off the ground all the time, no big deal.
WELL, IT IS A BIG DEAL!
I HAVE STANDARDS, THANK YOU VERY MUCH! AND THE GUTTER IS WHERE I DRAW THE LINE!

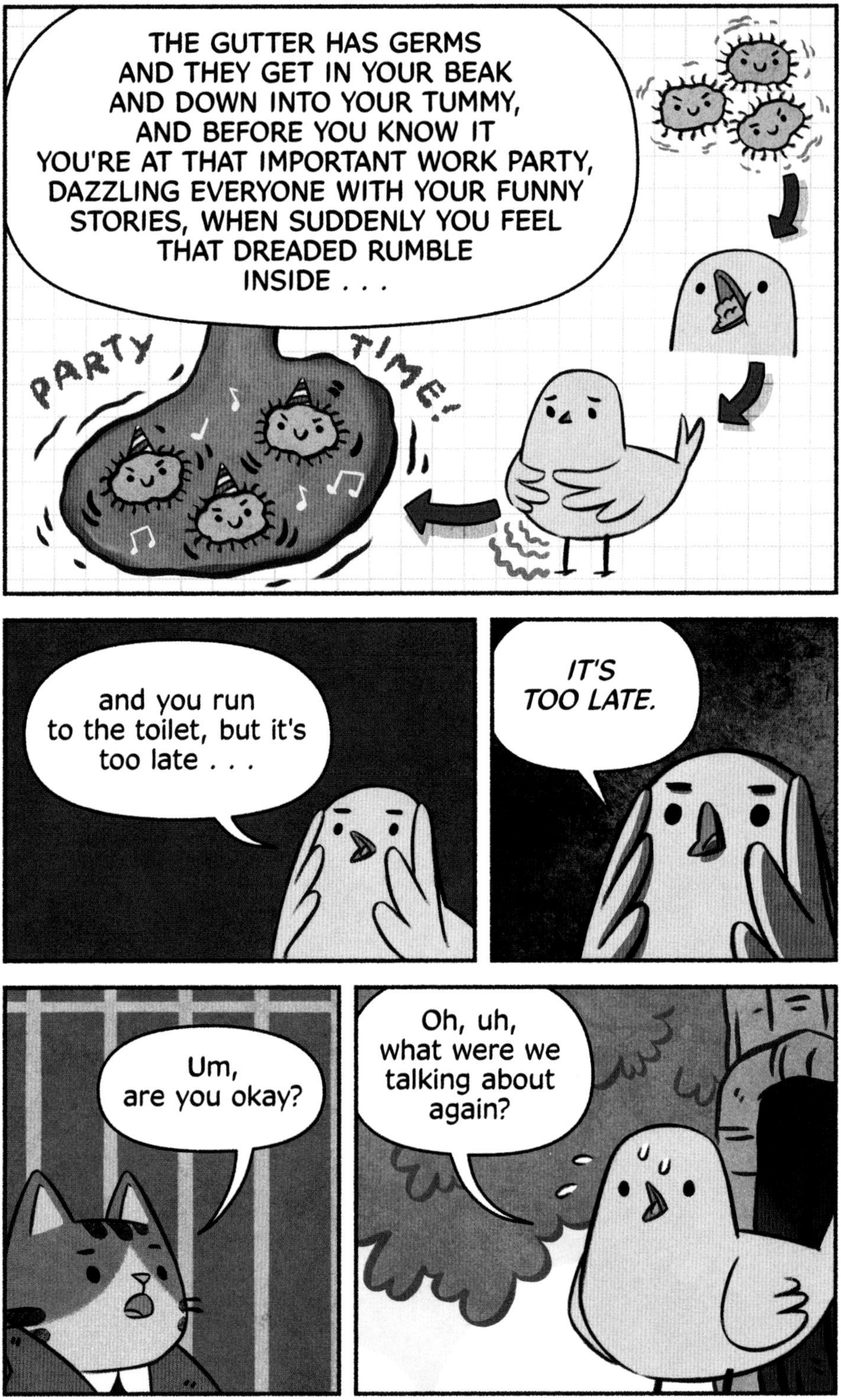
THE GUTTER HAS GERMS AND THEY GET IN YOUR BEAK AND DOWN INTO YOUR TUMMY, AND BEFORE YOU KNOW IT YOU'RE AT THAT IMPORTANT WORK PARTY, DAZZLING EVERYONE WITH YOUR FUNNY STORIES, WHEN SUDDENLY YOU FEEL THAT DREADED RUMBLE INSIDE . . .
PARTY TIME!
and you run to the toilet, but it's too late . . .
IT'S TOO LATE.
Um, are you okay?
Oh, uh, what were we talking about again?

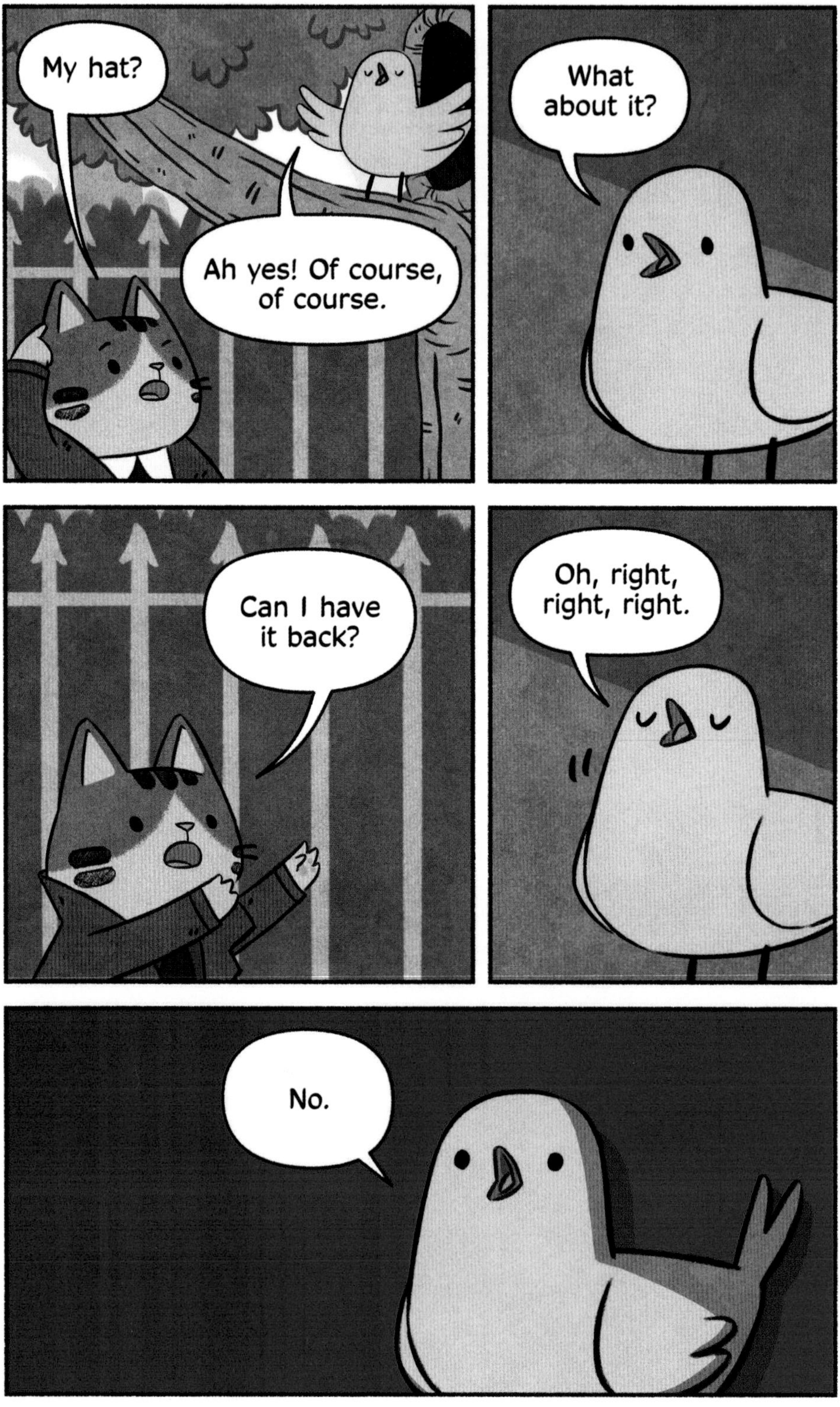
My hat?
Ah yes! Of course, of course.
What about it?
Can I have it back?
Oh, right, right, right.
No.

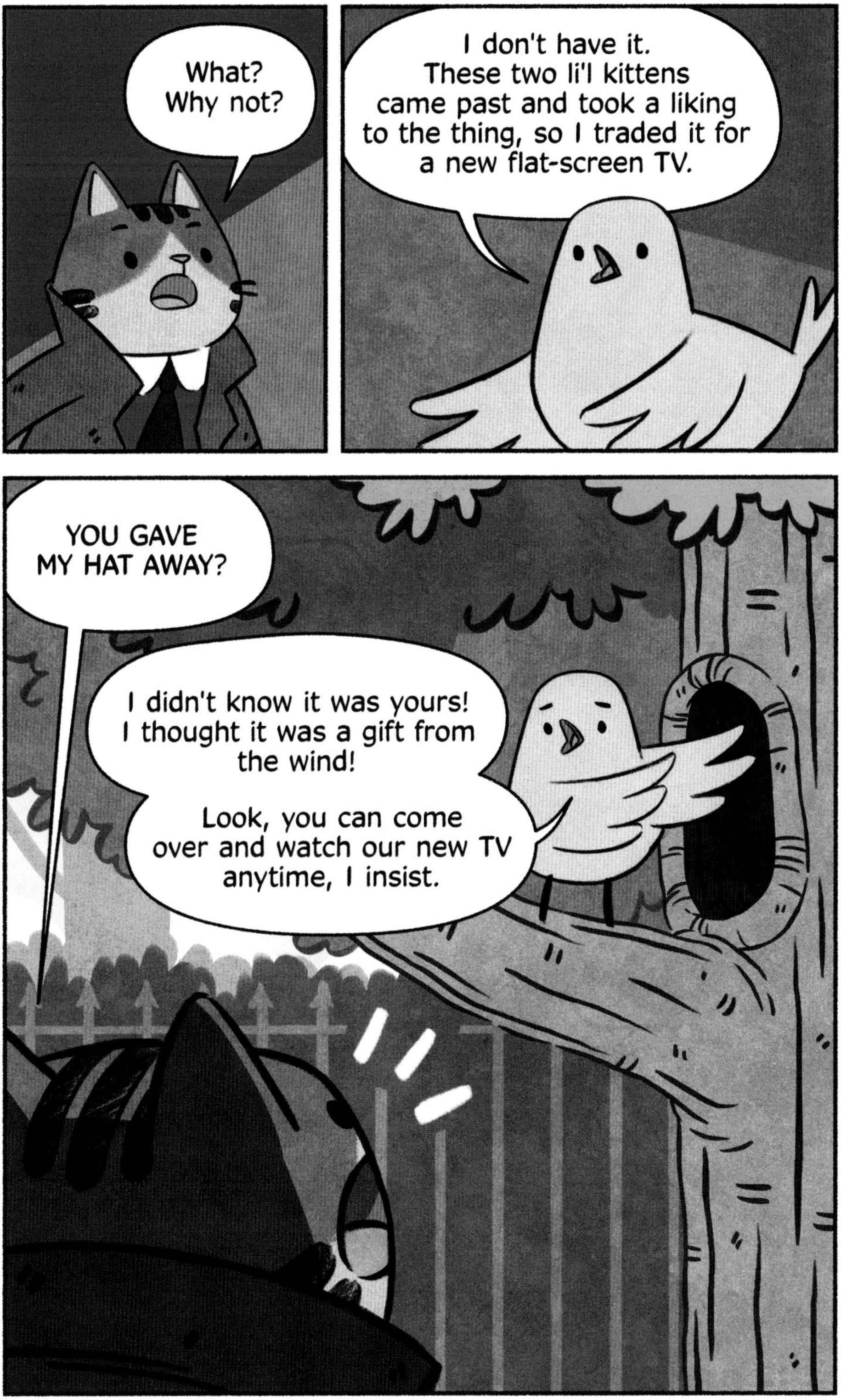
What? Why not?
I don't have it. These two li'l kittens came past and took a liking to the thing, so I traded it for a new flat-screen TV.
YOU GAVE MY HAT AWAY?
I didn't know it was yours! I thought it was a gift from the wind!
Look, you can come over and watch our new TV anytime, I insist.

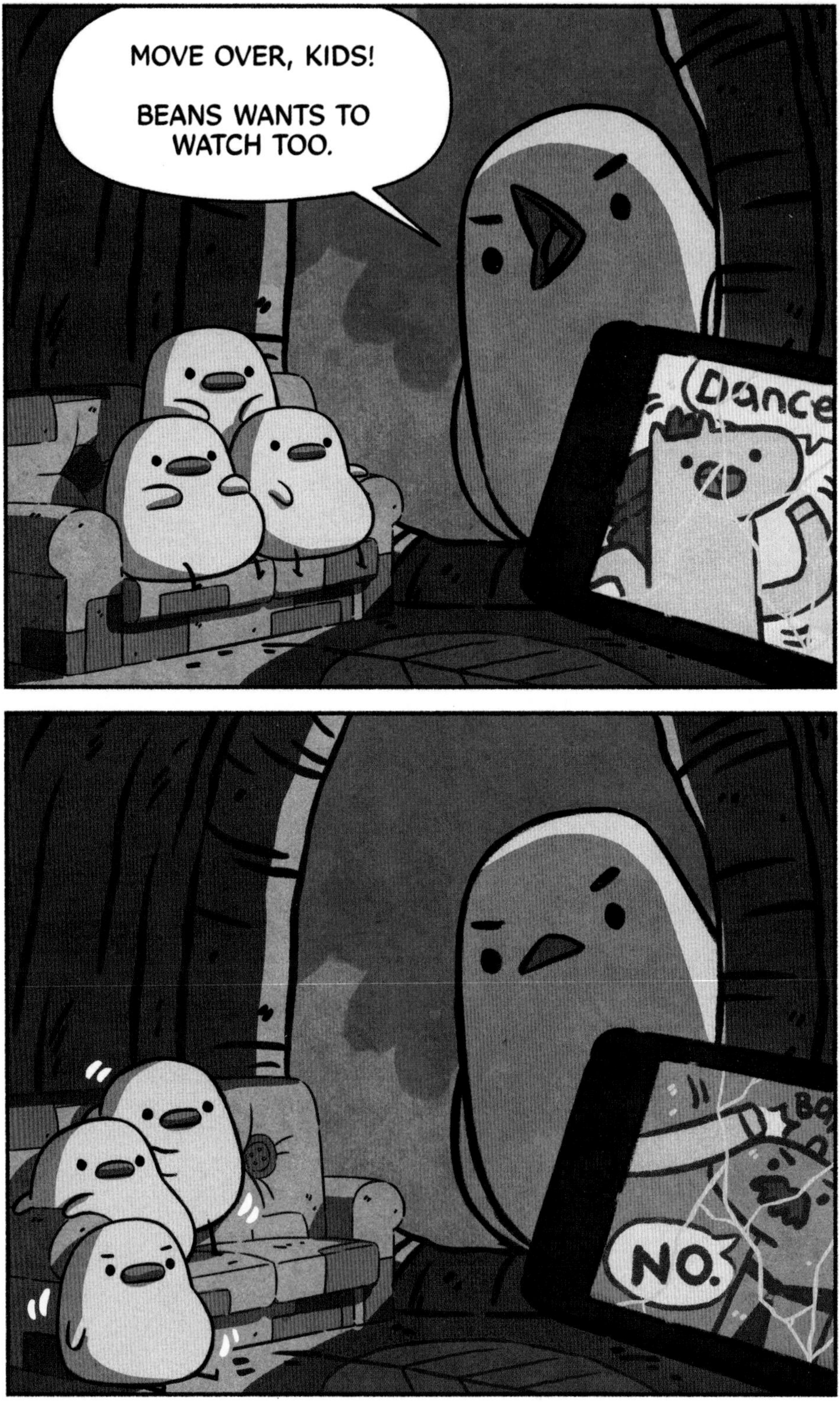
MOVE OVER, KIDS!
BEANS WANTS TO WATCH TOO.
Dance
NO.

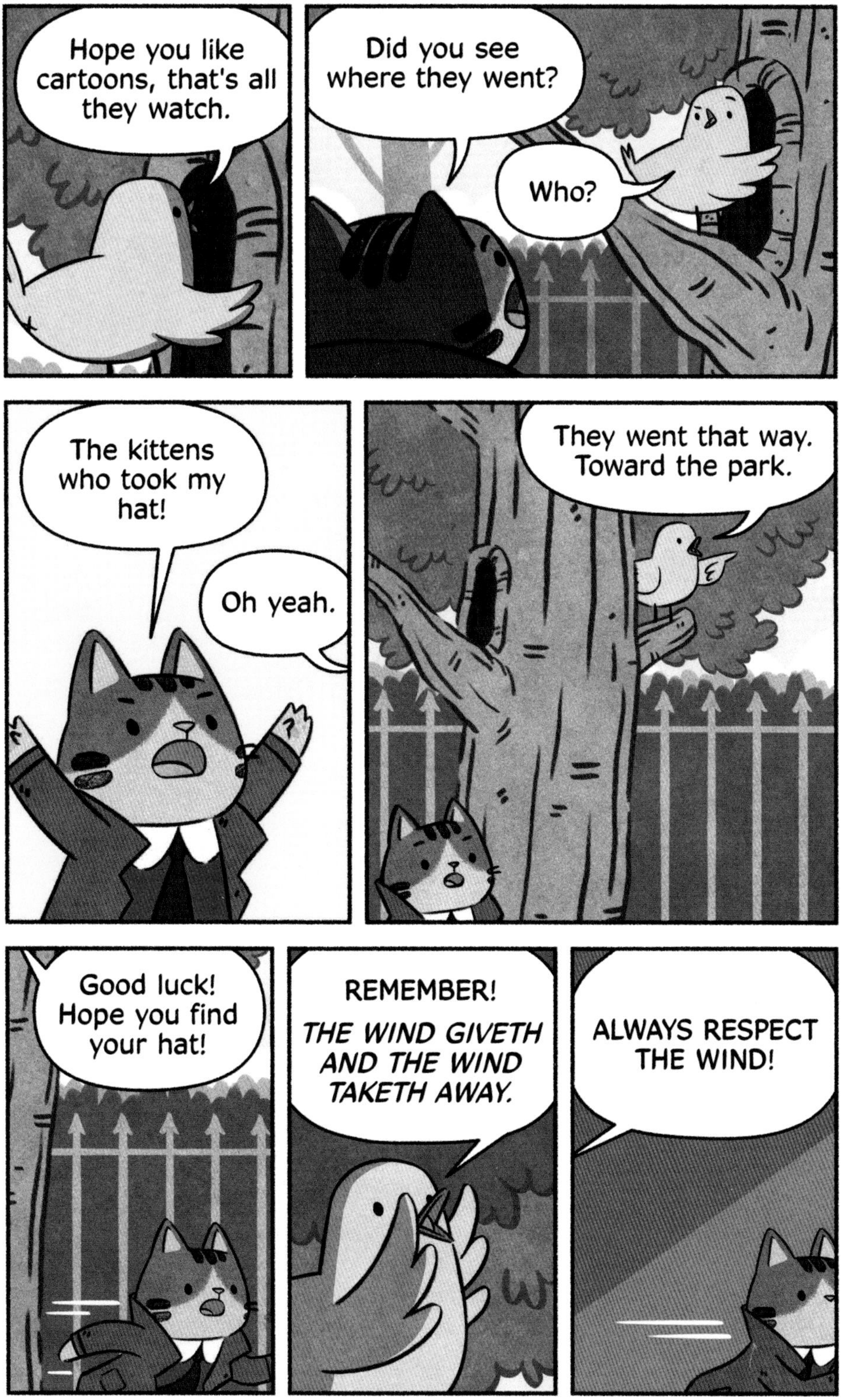
Hope you like cartoons, that's all they watch.
Did you see where they went?
Who?
The kittens who took my hat!
Oh yeah.
They went that way. Toward the park.
Good luck! Hope you find your hat!
REMEMBER!
THE WIND GIVETH AND THE WIND TAKETH AWAY.
ALWAYS RESPECT THE WIND!

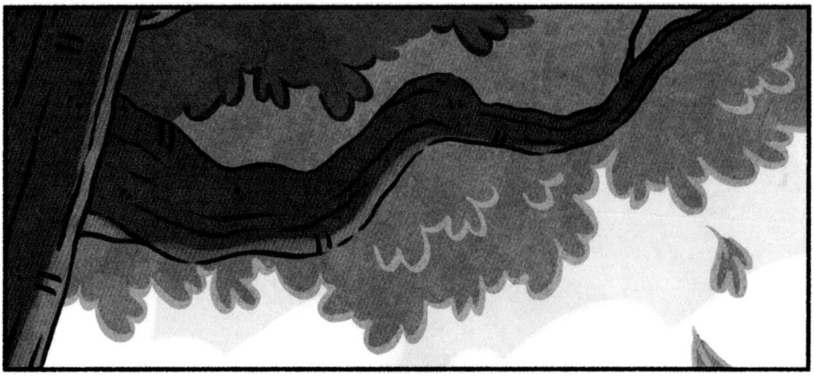

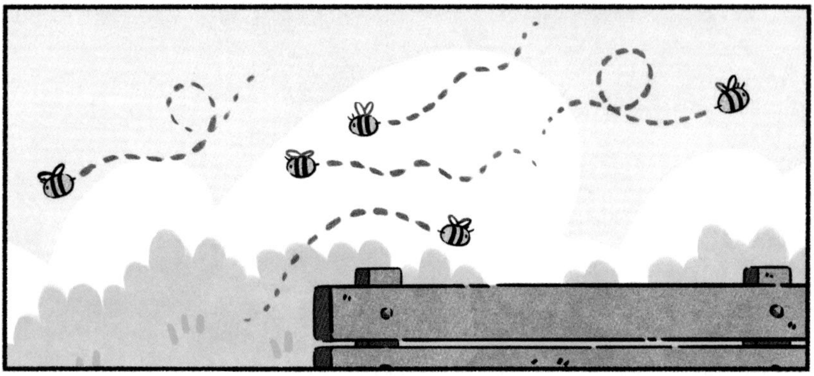

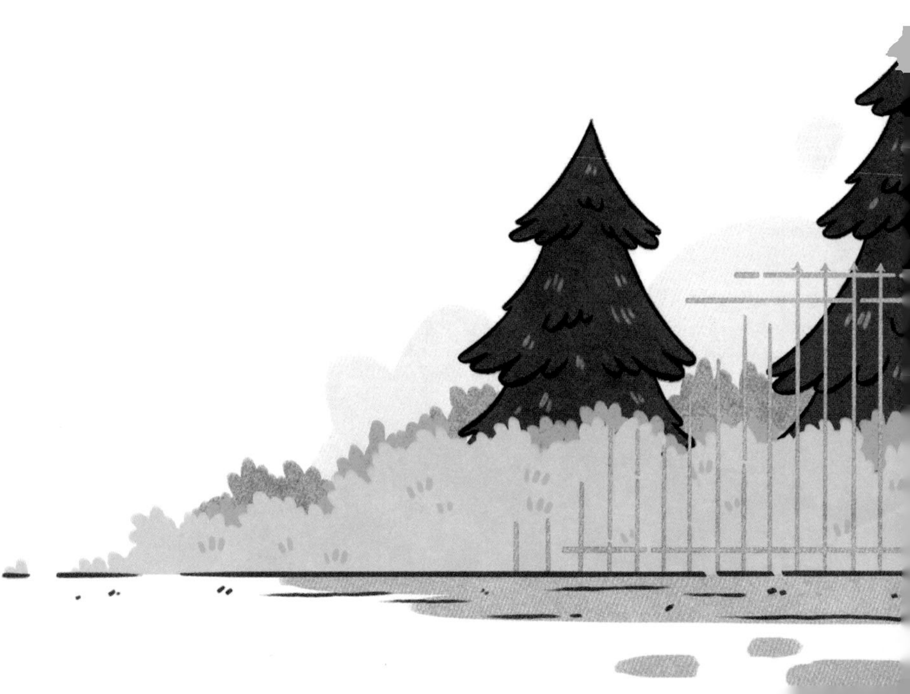

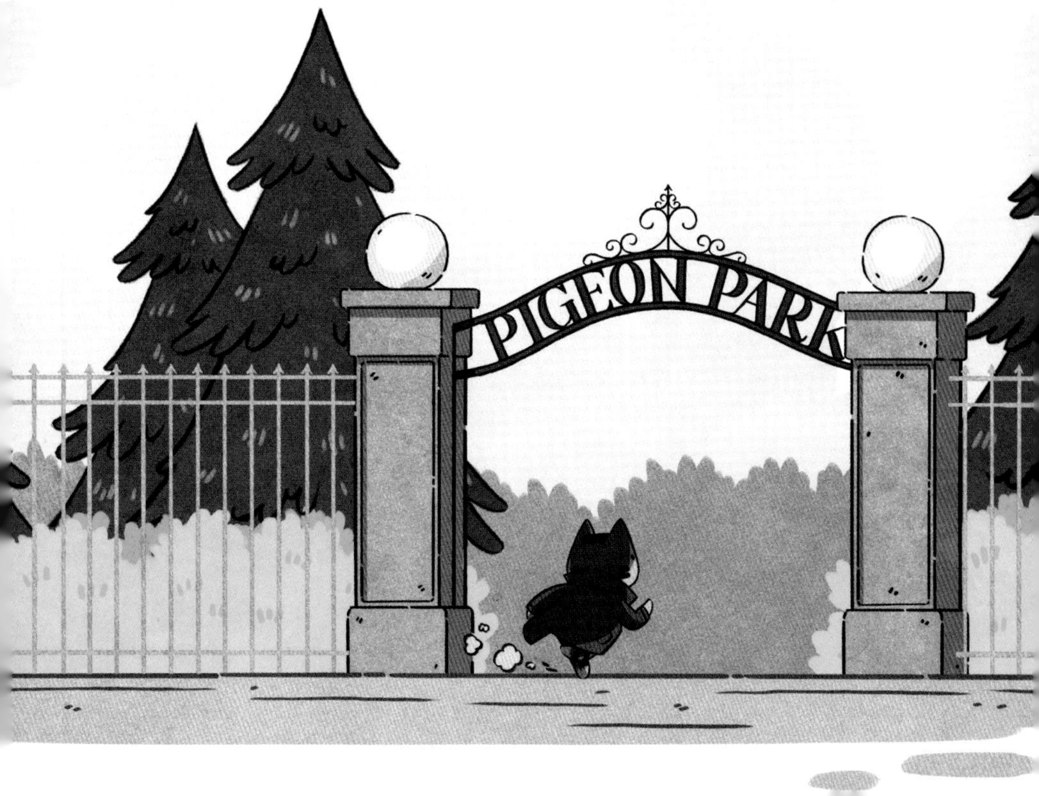
PIGEON PARK

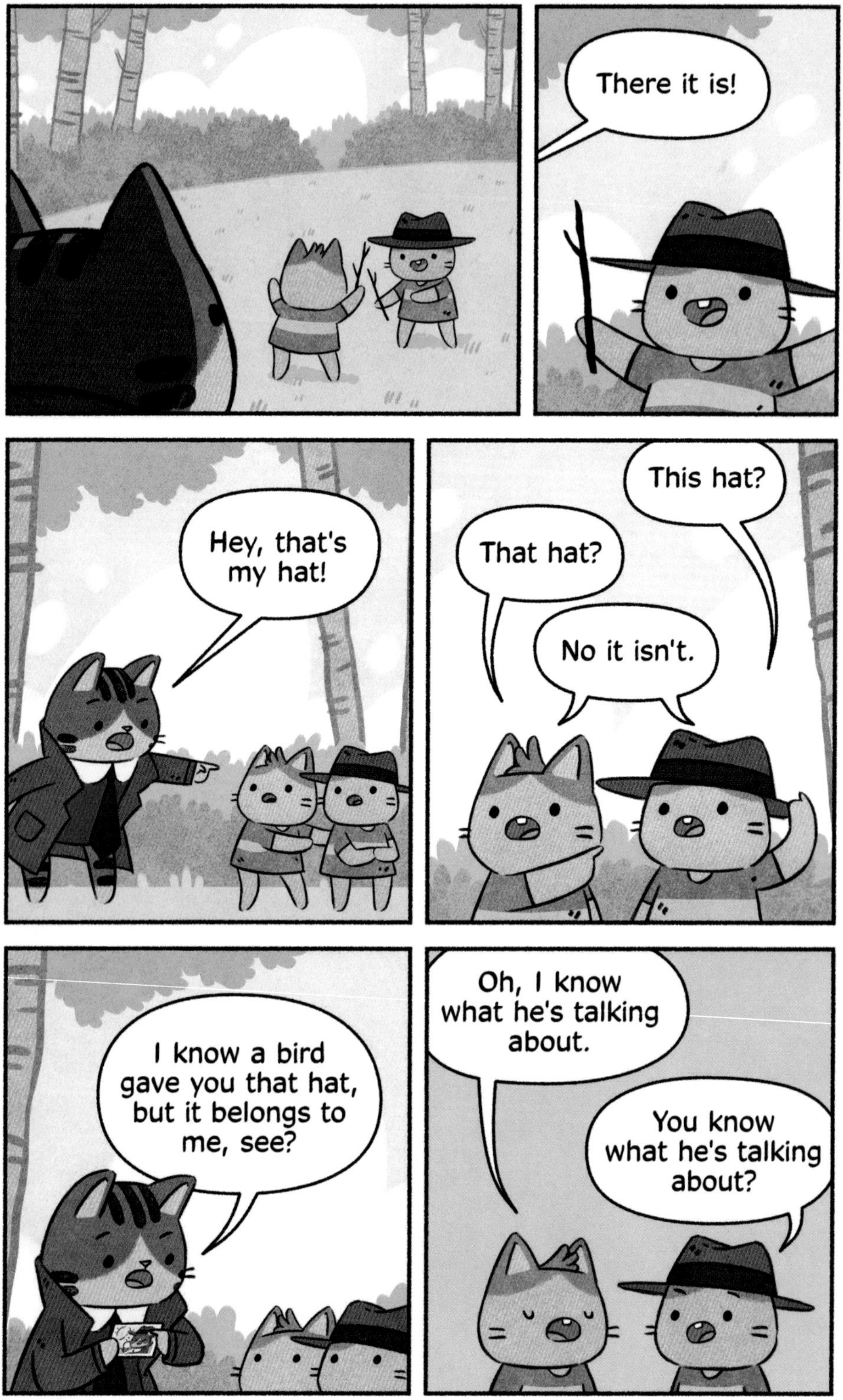
There it is!
Hey, that's my hat!
That hat?
This hat?
No it isn't.
I know a bird gave you that hat, but it belongs to me, see?
Oh, I know what he's talking about.
You know what he's talking about?

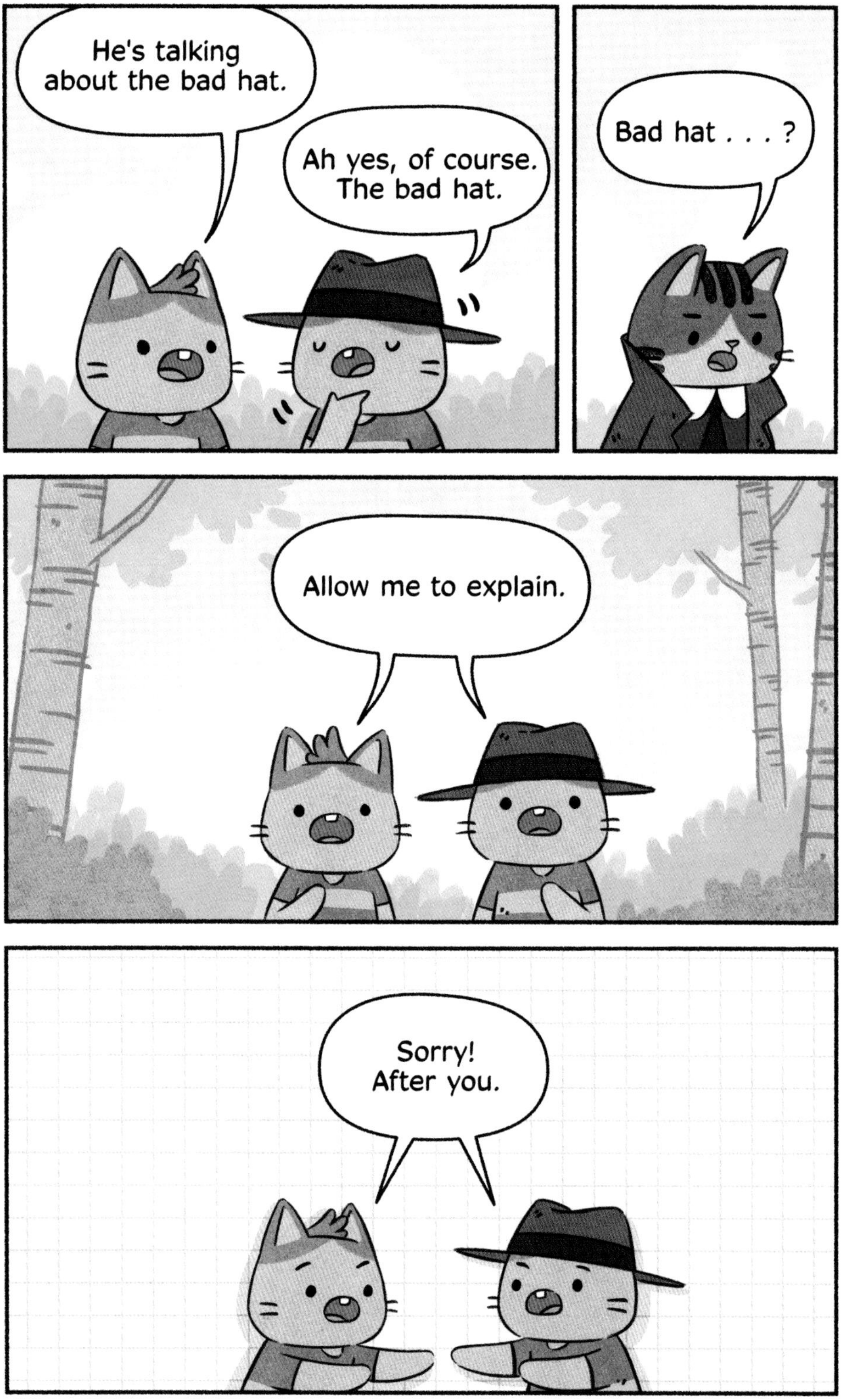
He's talking about the bad hat.
Ah yes, of course. The bad hat.
Bad hat . . . ?
Allow me to explain.
Sorry! After you.

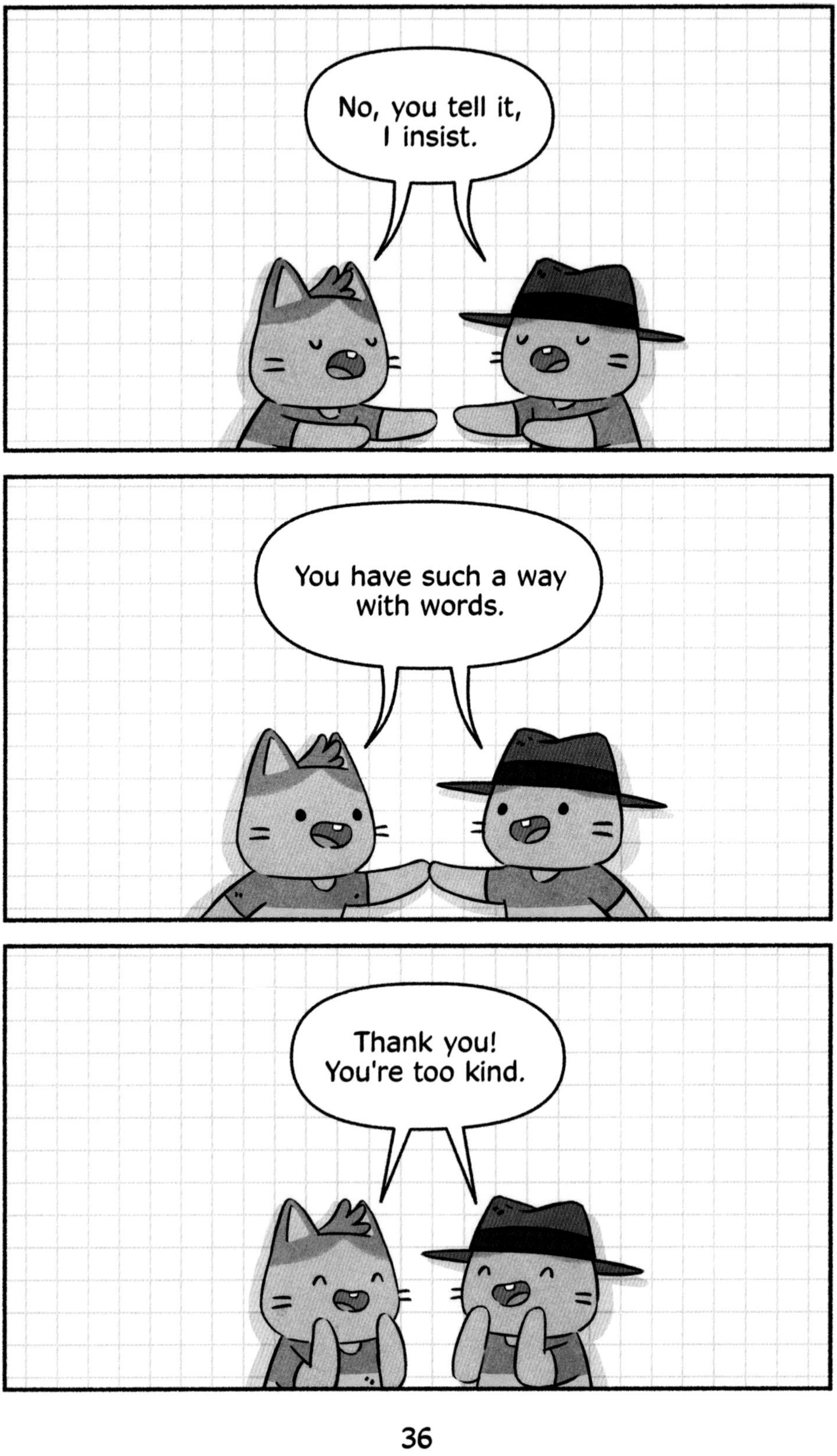
No, you tell it, I insist.
You have such a way with words.
Thank you! You're too kind.

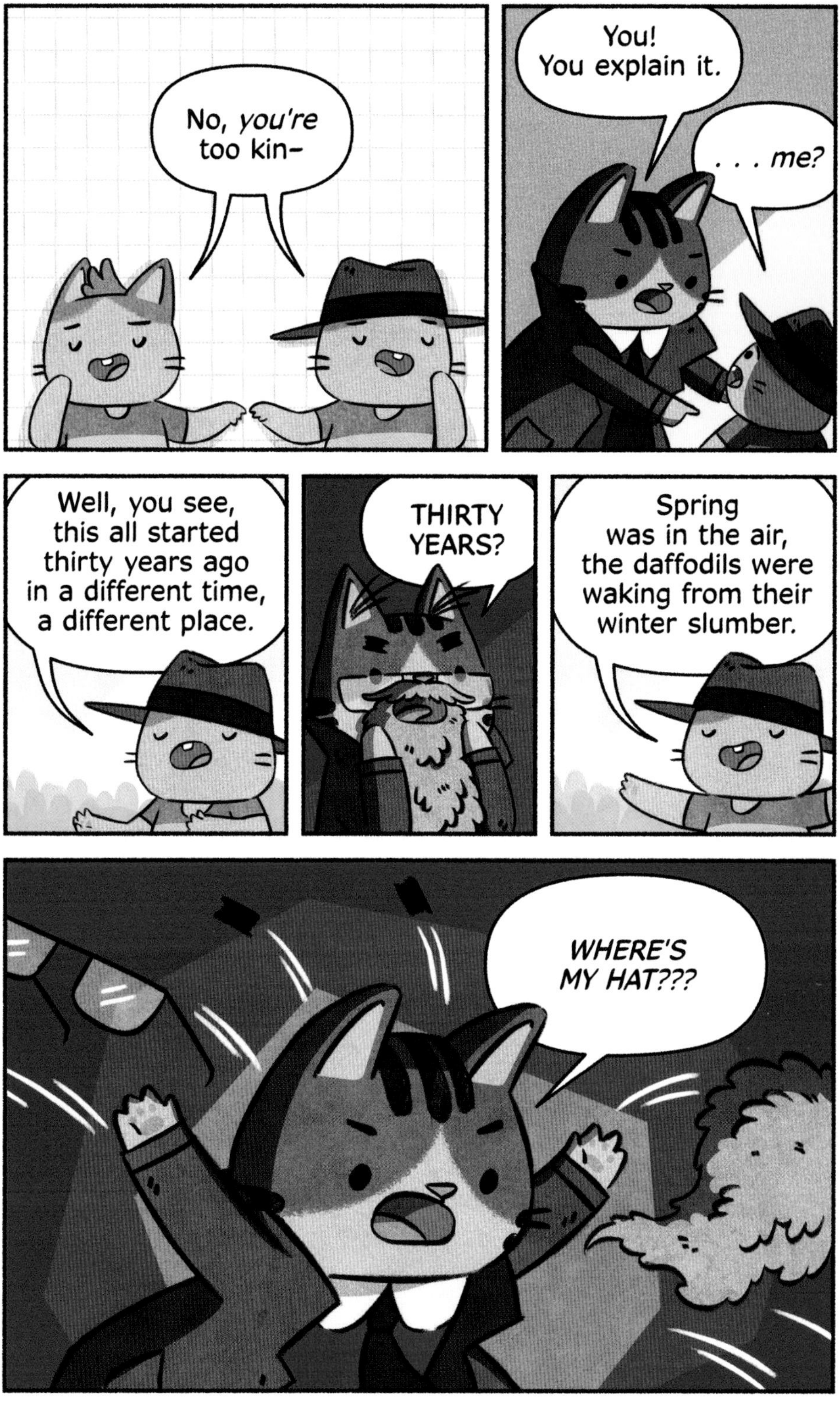
No, *you're* too kin-
You! You explain it.
. . . *me?*
Well, you see, this all started thirty years ago in a different time, a different place.
THIRTY YEARS?
Spring was in the air, the daffodils were waking from their winter slumber.
WHERE'S MY HAT???

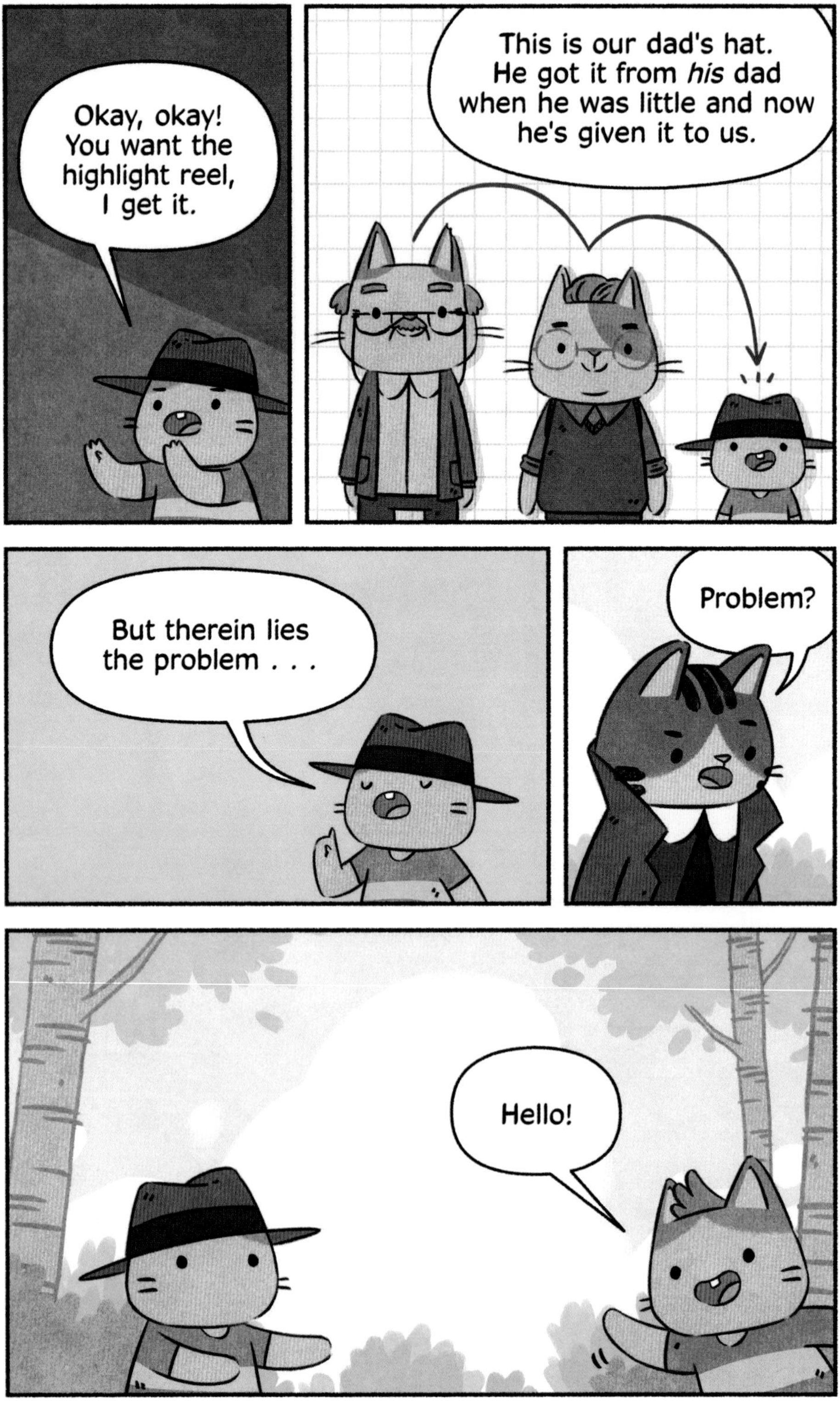
Okay, okay! You want the highlight reel, I get it.
This is our dad's hat. He got it from *his* dad when he was little and now he's given it to us.
But therein lies the problem . . .
Problem?
Hello!

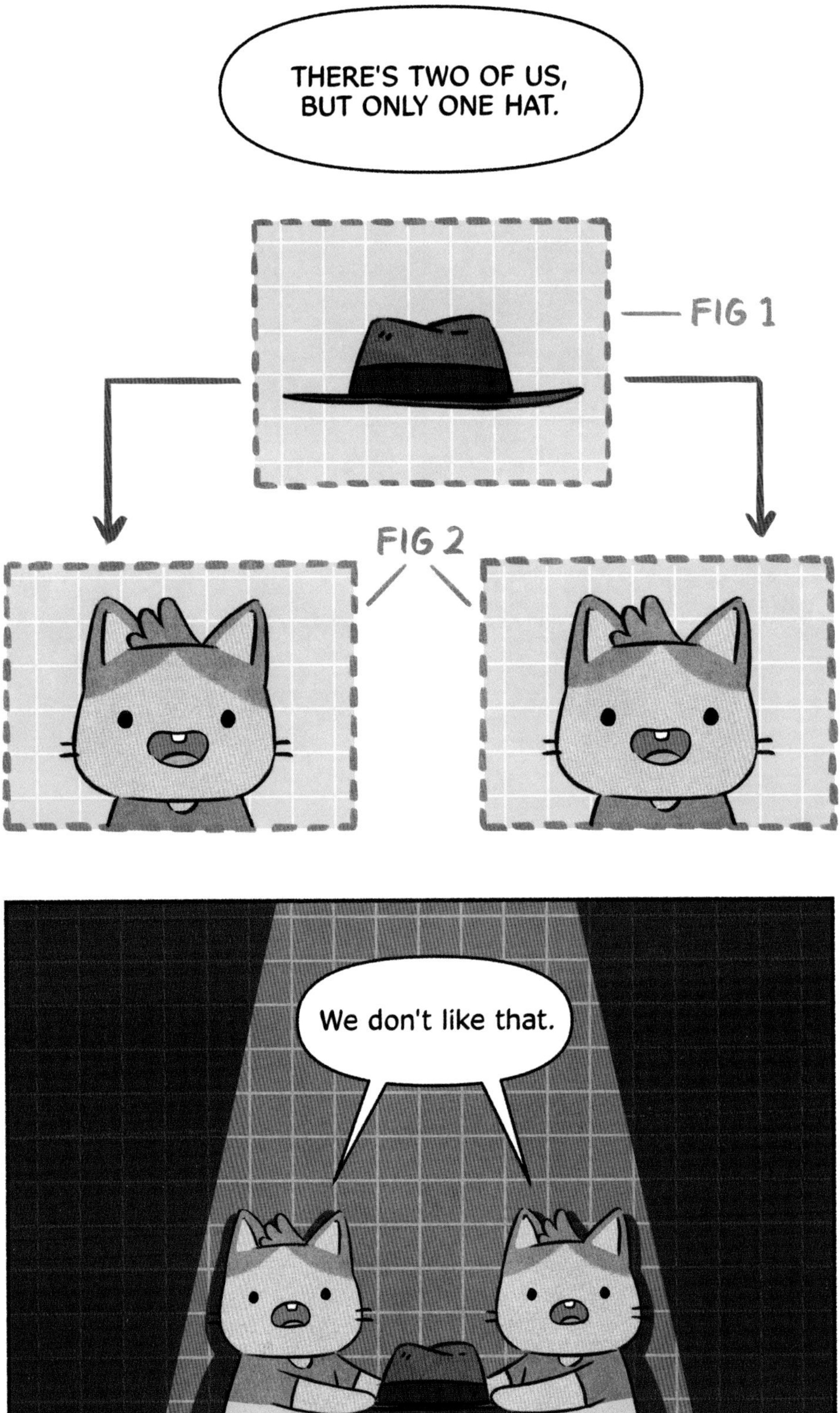
THERE'S TWO OF US, BUT ONLY ONE HAT.
FIG 1
FIG 2
We don't like that.

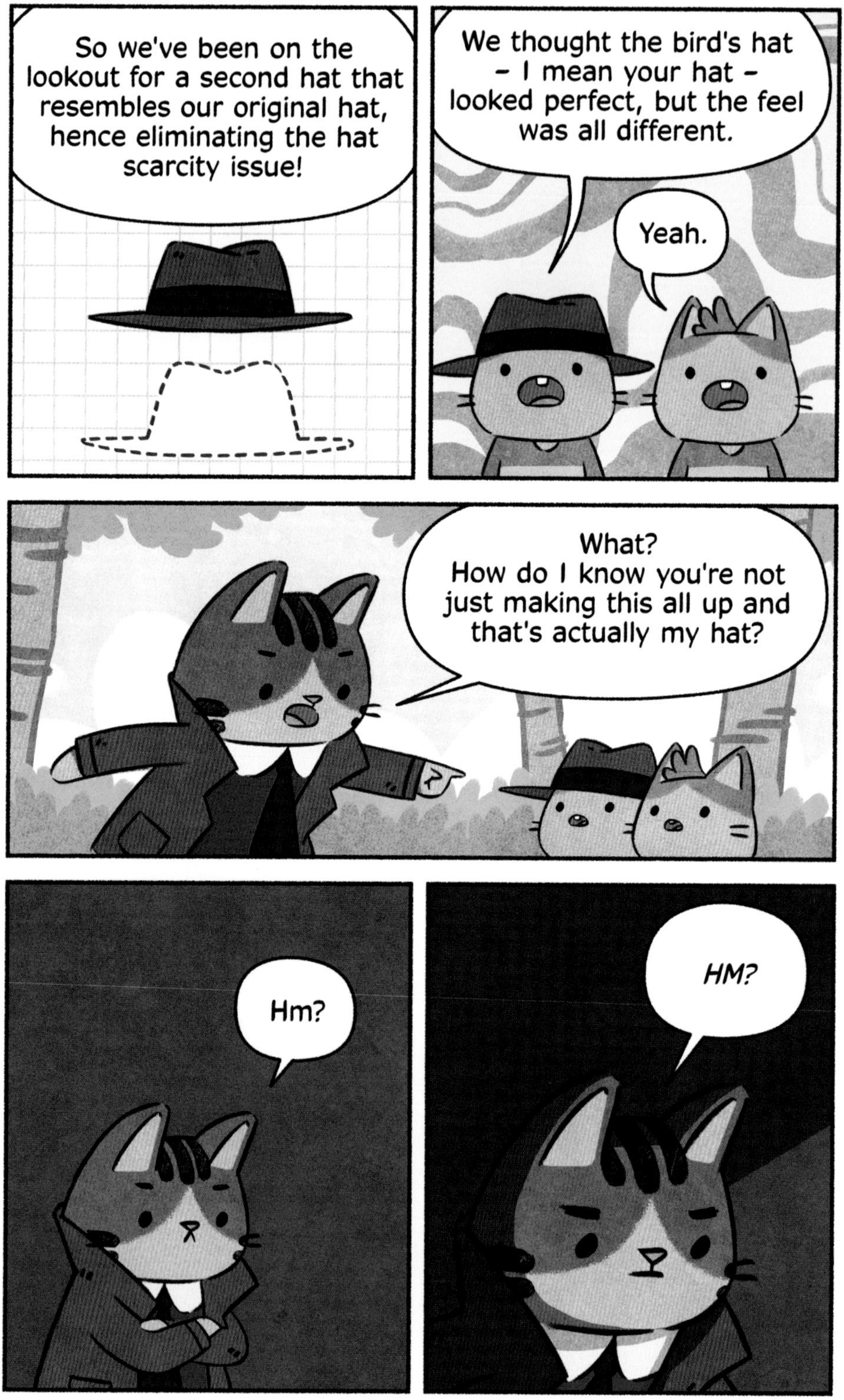
So we've been on the lookout for a second hat that resembles our original hat, hence eliminating the hat scarcity issue!
We thought the bird's hat - I mean your hat - looked perfect, but the feel was all different.
Yeah.
What? How do I know you're not just making this all up and that's actually my hat?
Hm?
HM?

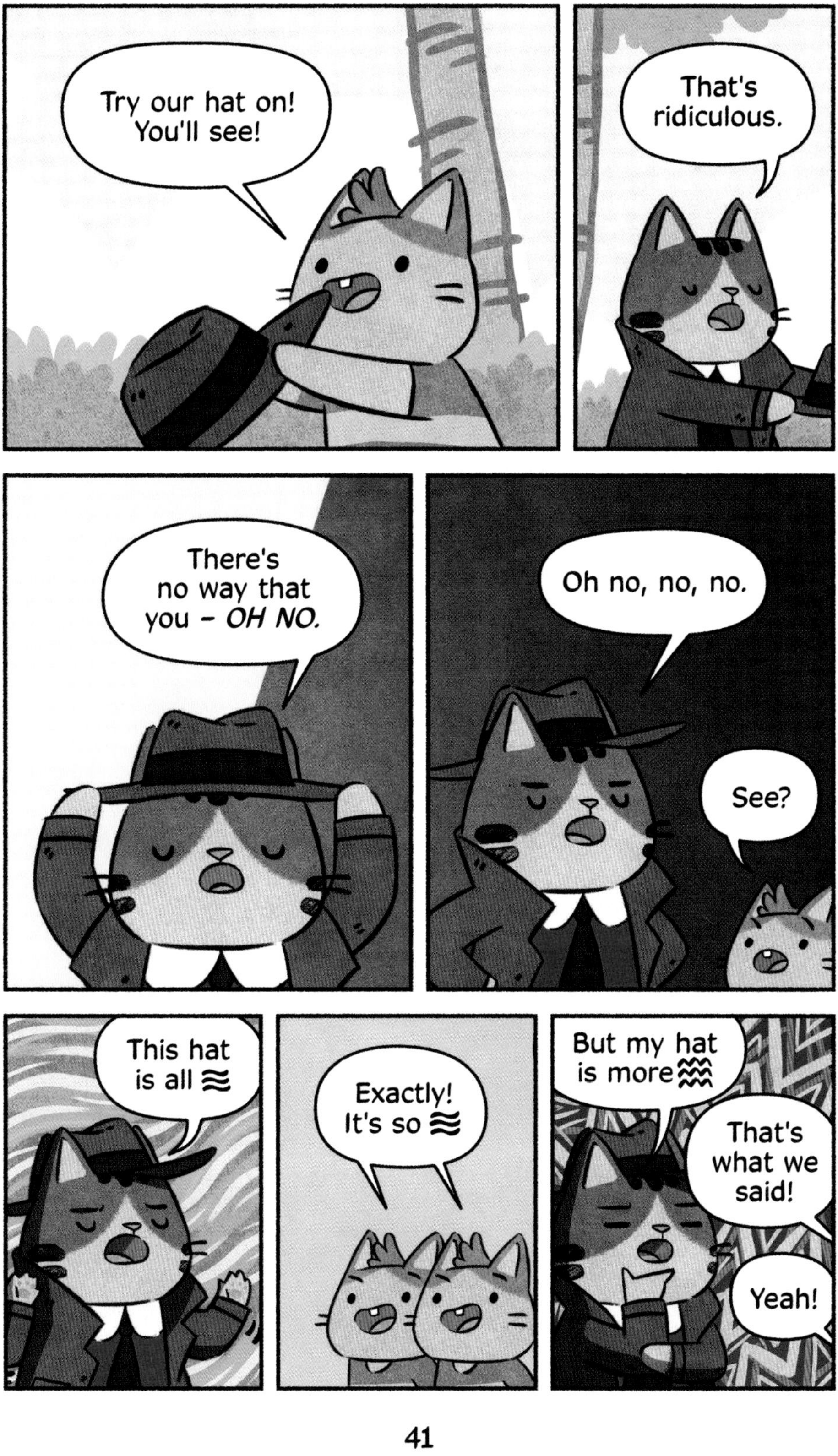
Try our hat on! You'll see!
That's ridiculous.
There's no way that you – *OH NO.*
Oh no, no, no.
See?
This hat is all ≋
Exactly! It's so ≋
But my hat is more
That's what we said!
Yeah!

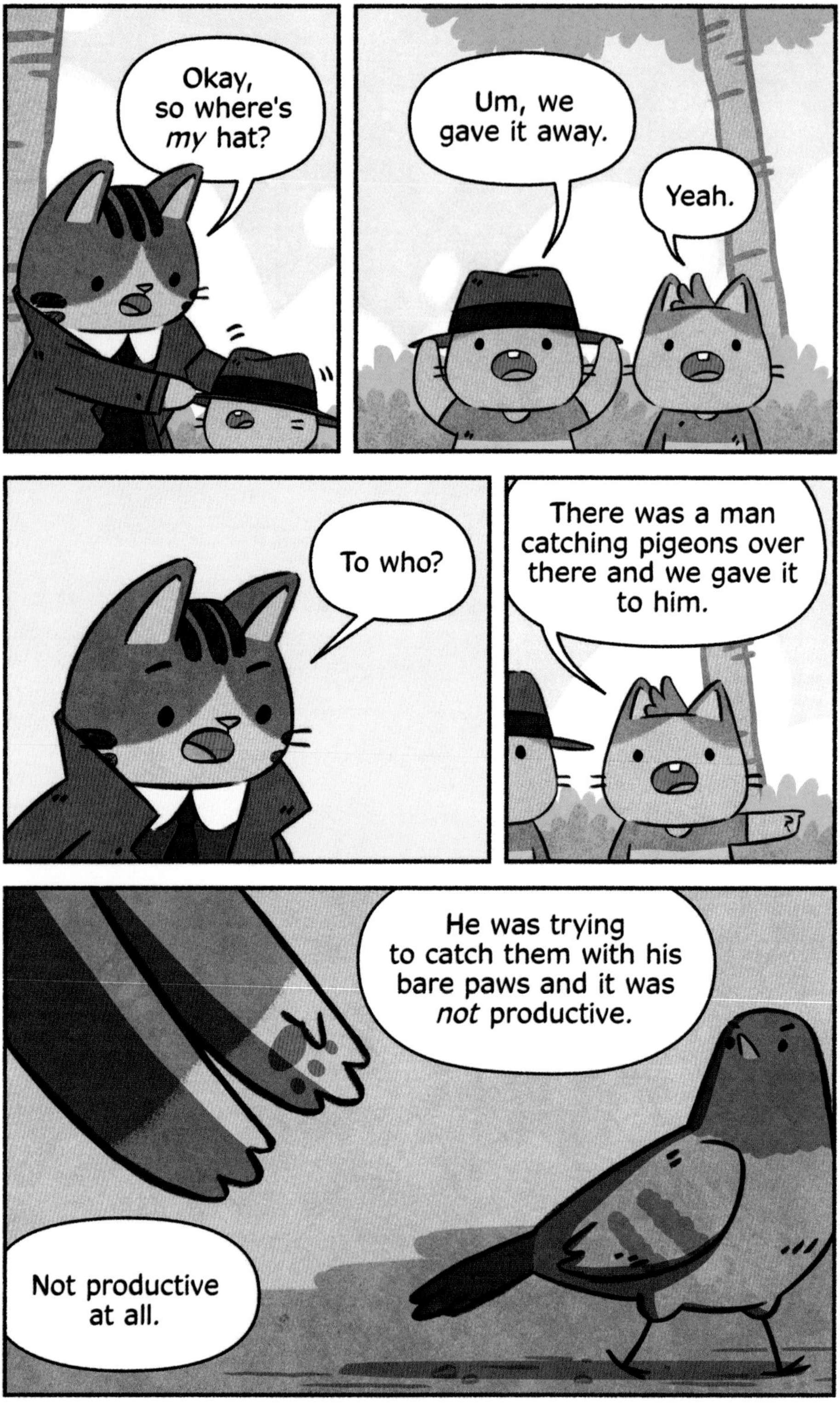
Okay, so where's *my* hat?
Um, we gave it away.
Yeah.
To who?
There was a man catching pigeons over there and we gave it to him.
He was trying to catch them with his bare paws and it was *not* productive.
Not productive at all.

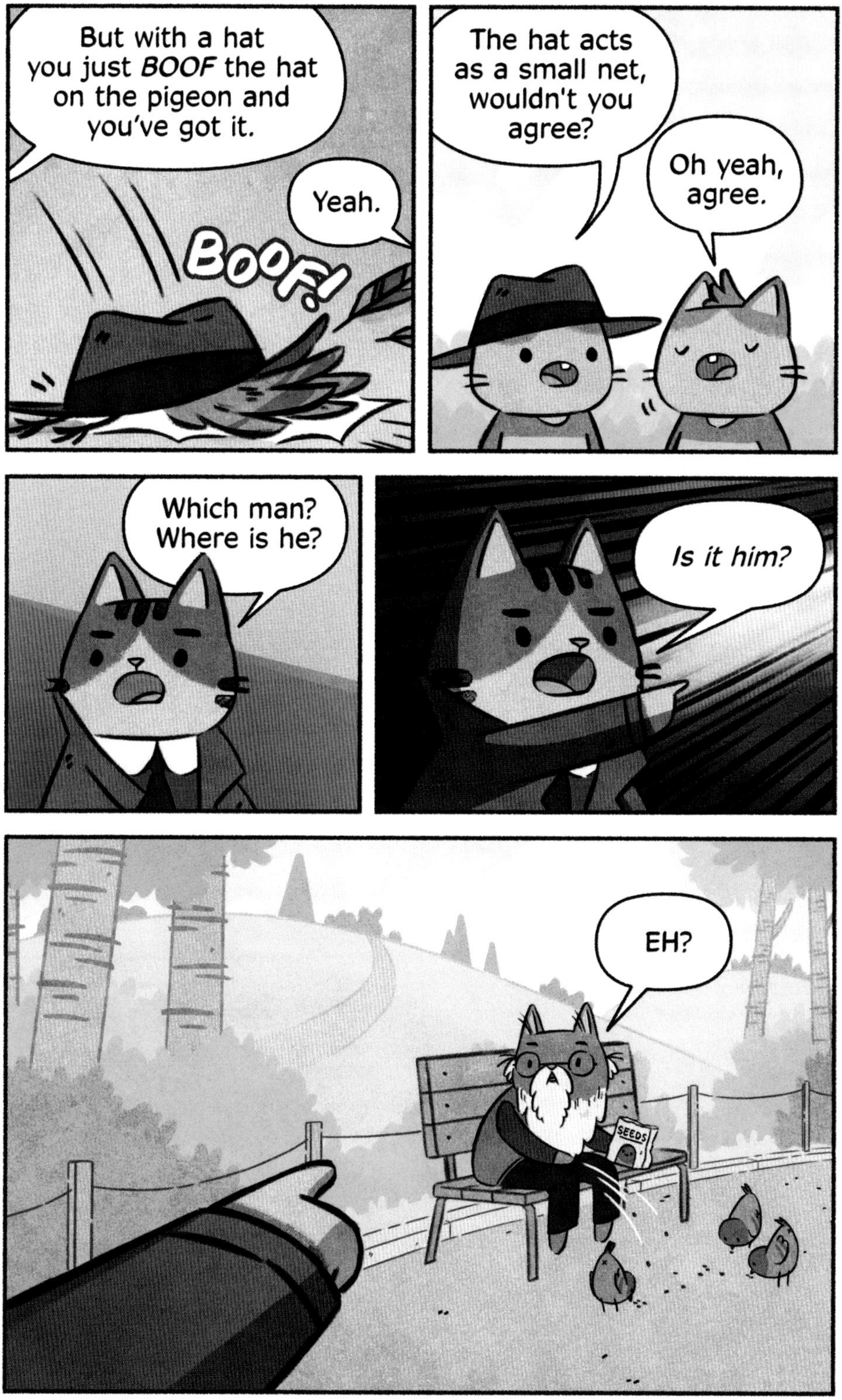

But with a hat you just *BOOF* the hat on the pigeon and you've got it.
Yeah.
BOOF!
The hat acts as a small net, wouldn't you agree?
Oh yeah, agree.
Which man? Where is he?
Is it him?
EH?
SEEDS

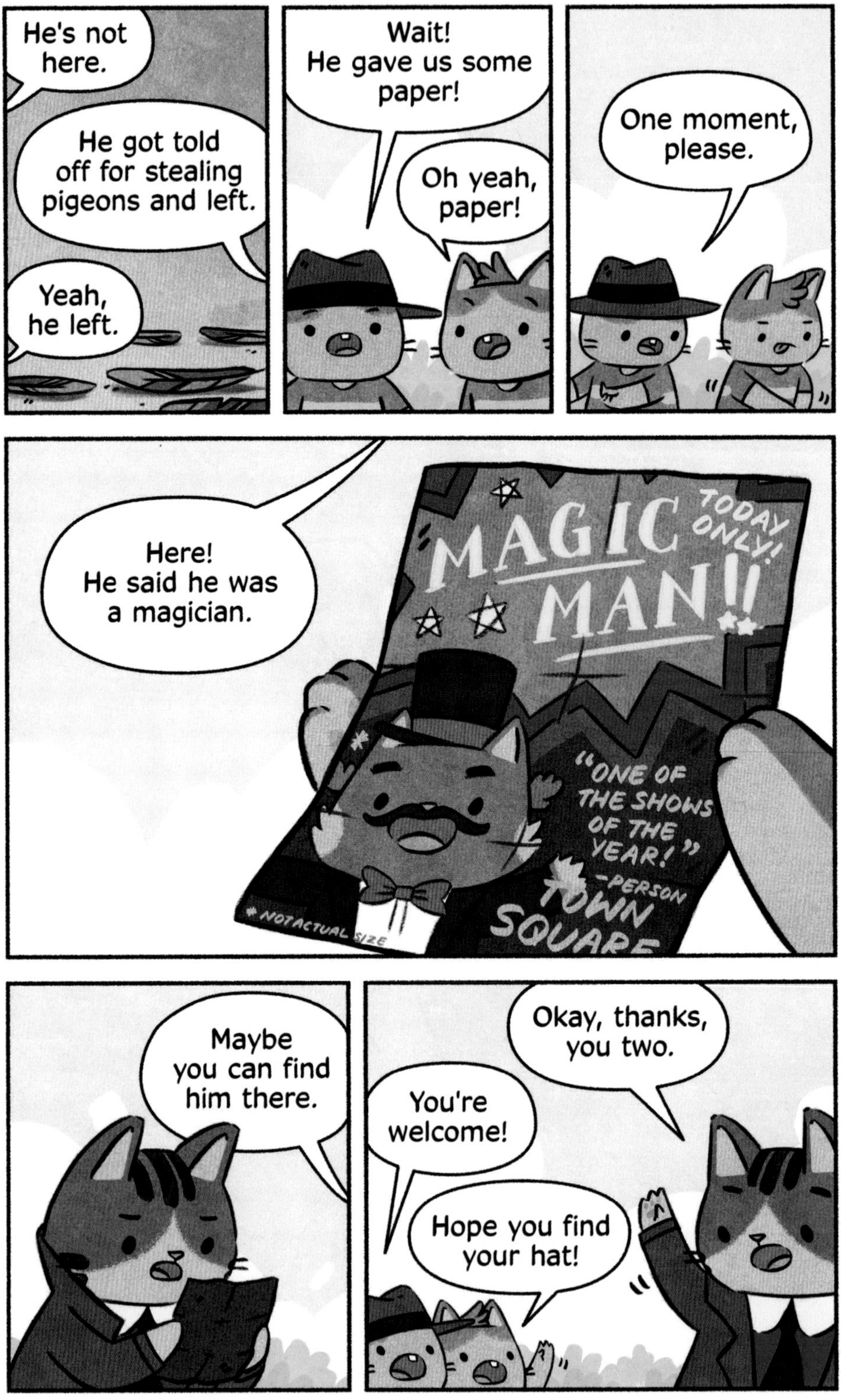
He's not here.
He got told off for stealing pigeons and left.
Yeah, he left.
Wait! He gave us some paper!
Oh yeah, paper!
One moment, please.
Here! He said he was a magician.
MAGIC MAN!!
TODAY ONLY!
"ONE OF THE SHOWS OF THE YEAR!" -PERSON
TOWN SQUARE
*NOT ACTUAL SIZE
Maybe you can find him there.
Okay, thanks, you two.
You're welcome!
Hope you find your hat!

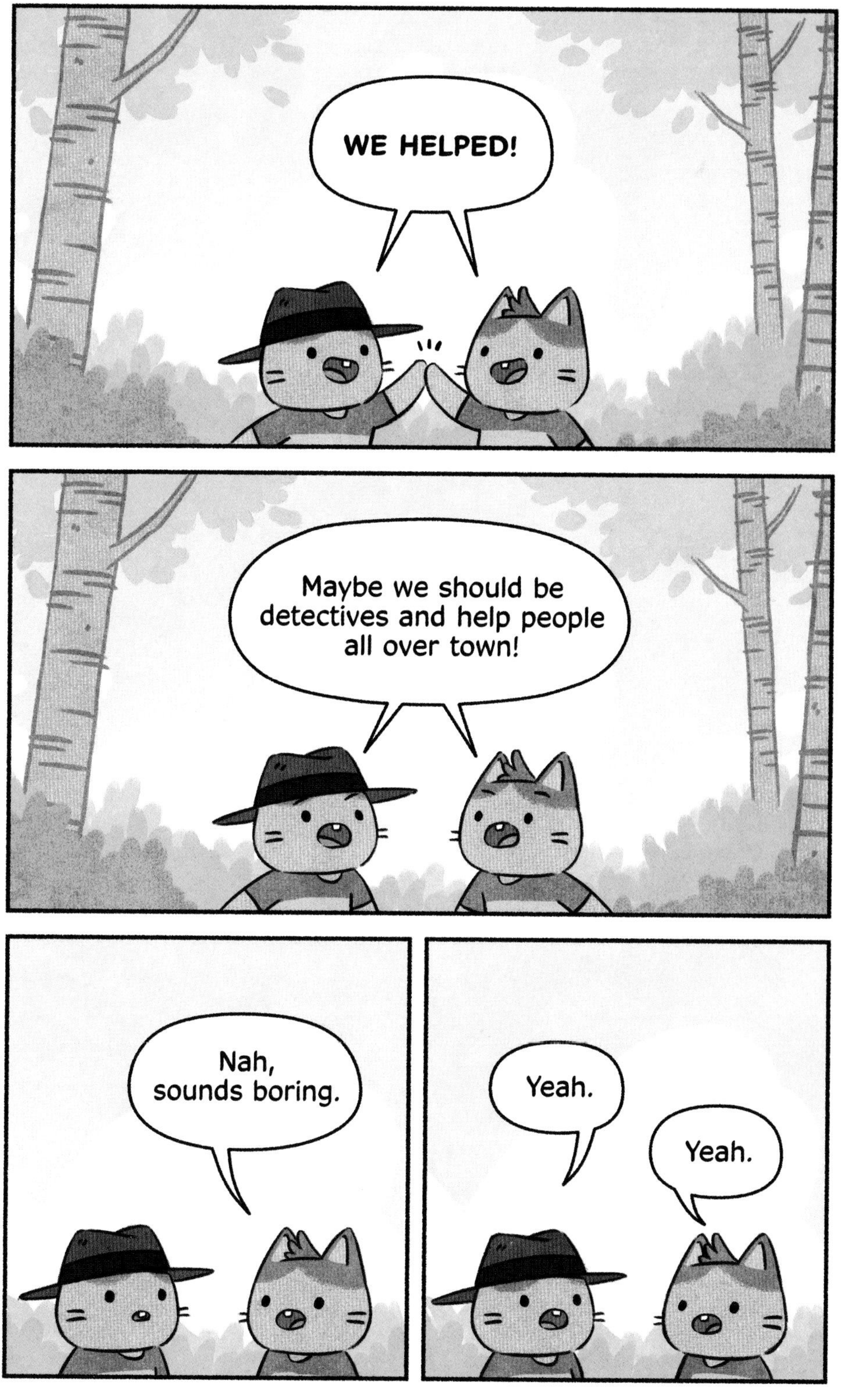
WE HELPED!
Maybe we should be detectives and help people all over town!
Nah, sounds boring.
Yeah.
Yeah.

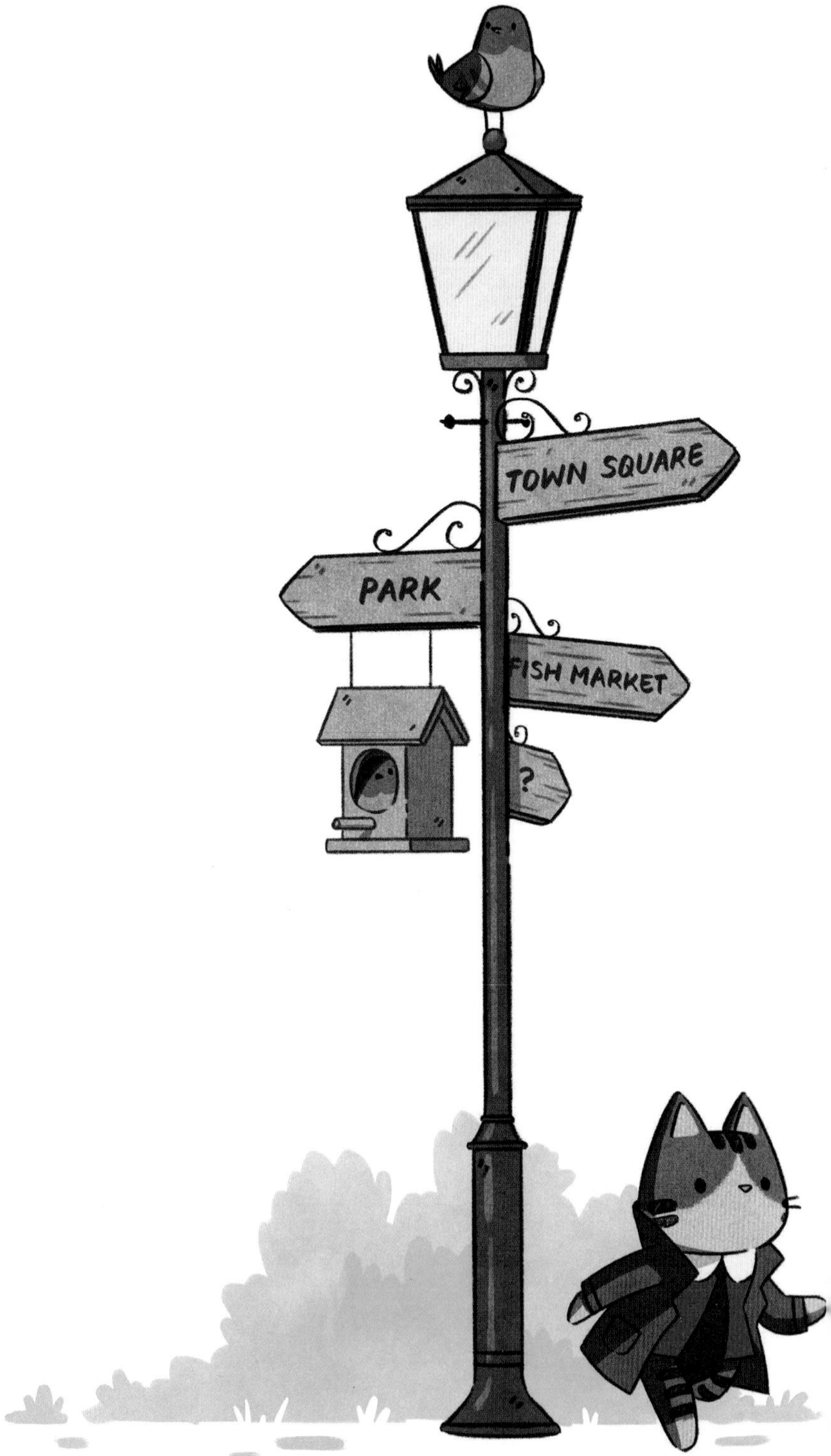
TOWN SQUARE
PARK
FISH MARKET
?

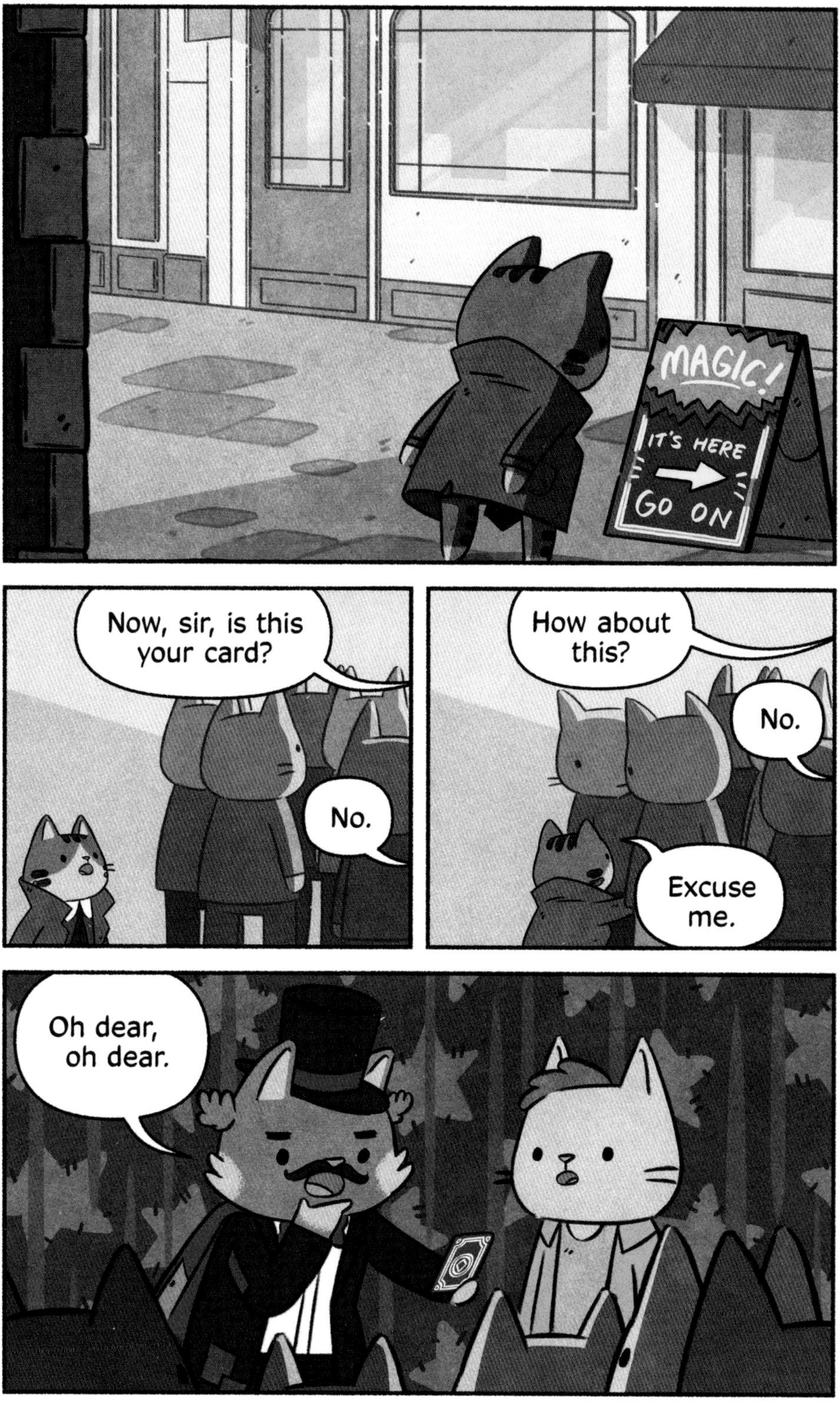
MAGIC!
IT'S HERE
GO ON
Now, sir, is this your card?
No.
How about this?
No.
Excuse me.
Oh dear, oh dear.

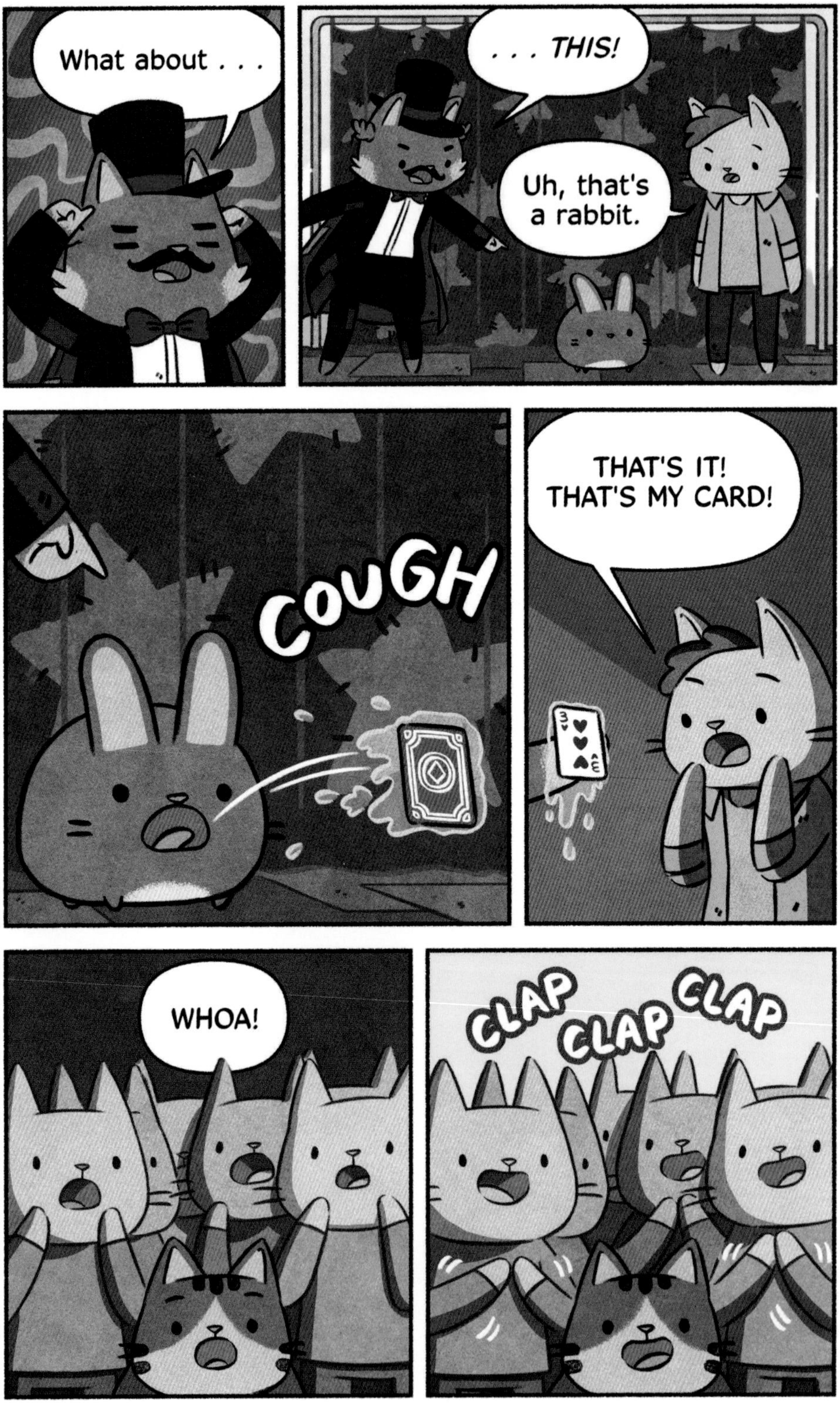
What about . . .
. . . THIS!
Uh, that's a rabbit.
COUGH
THAT'S IT! THAT'S MY CARD!
WHOA!
CLAP
CLAP
CLAP

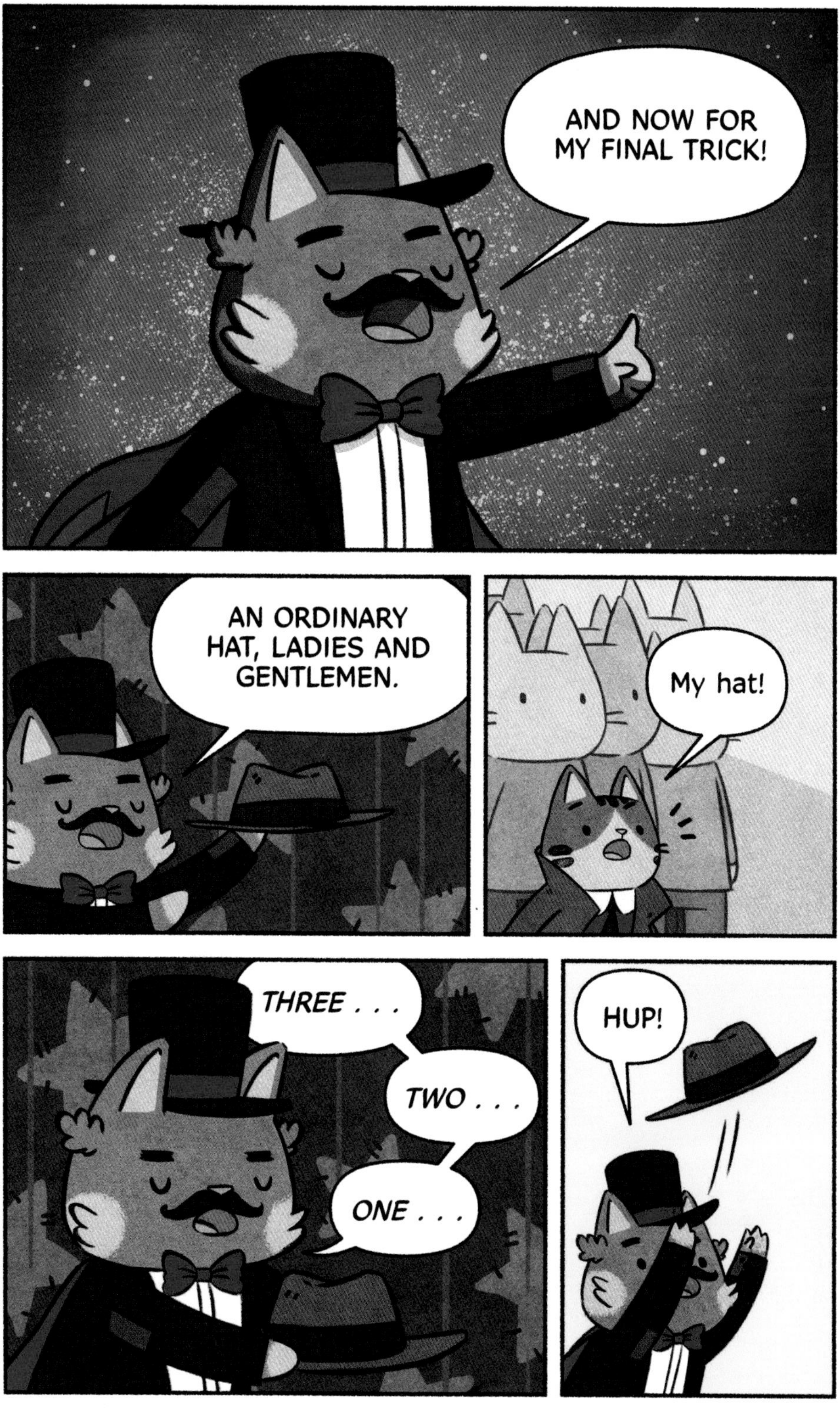
AND NOW FOR MY FINAL TRICK!
AN ORDINARY HAT, LADIES AND GENTLEMEN.
My hat!
THREE . . .
TWO . . .
ONE . . .
HUP!

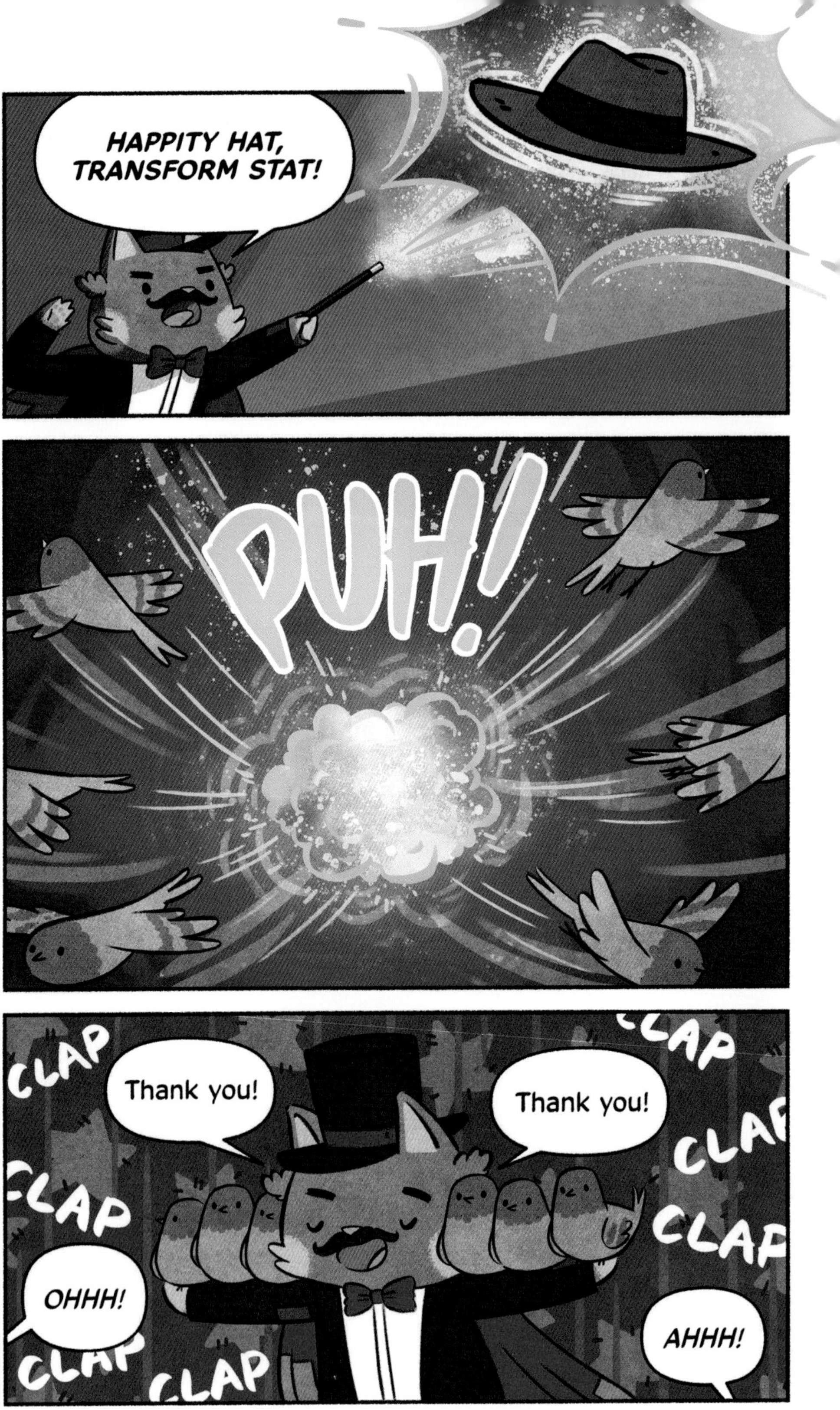
HAPPITY HAT,
TRANSFORM STAT!
PUH!
CLAP
Thank you!
Thank you!
CLAP
CLAP
CLAP
OHHH!
AHHH!
CLAP
CLAP

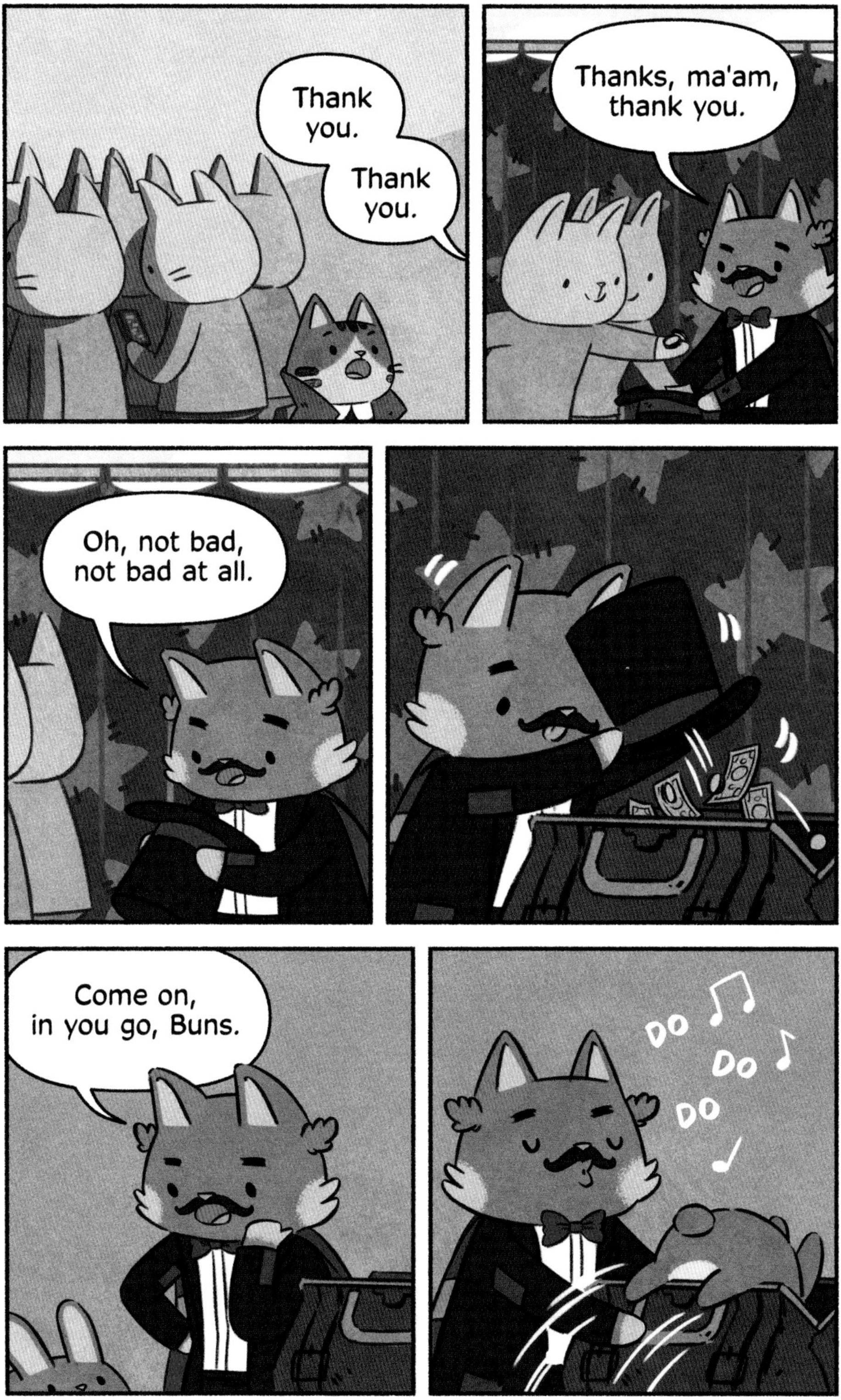
Thank you.
Thank you.
Thanks, ma'am, thank you.
Oh, not bad, not bad at all.
Come on, in you go, Buns.
DO DO DO

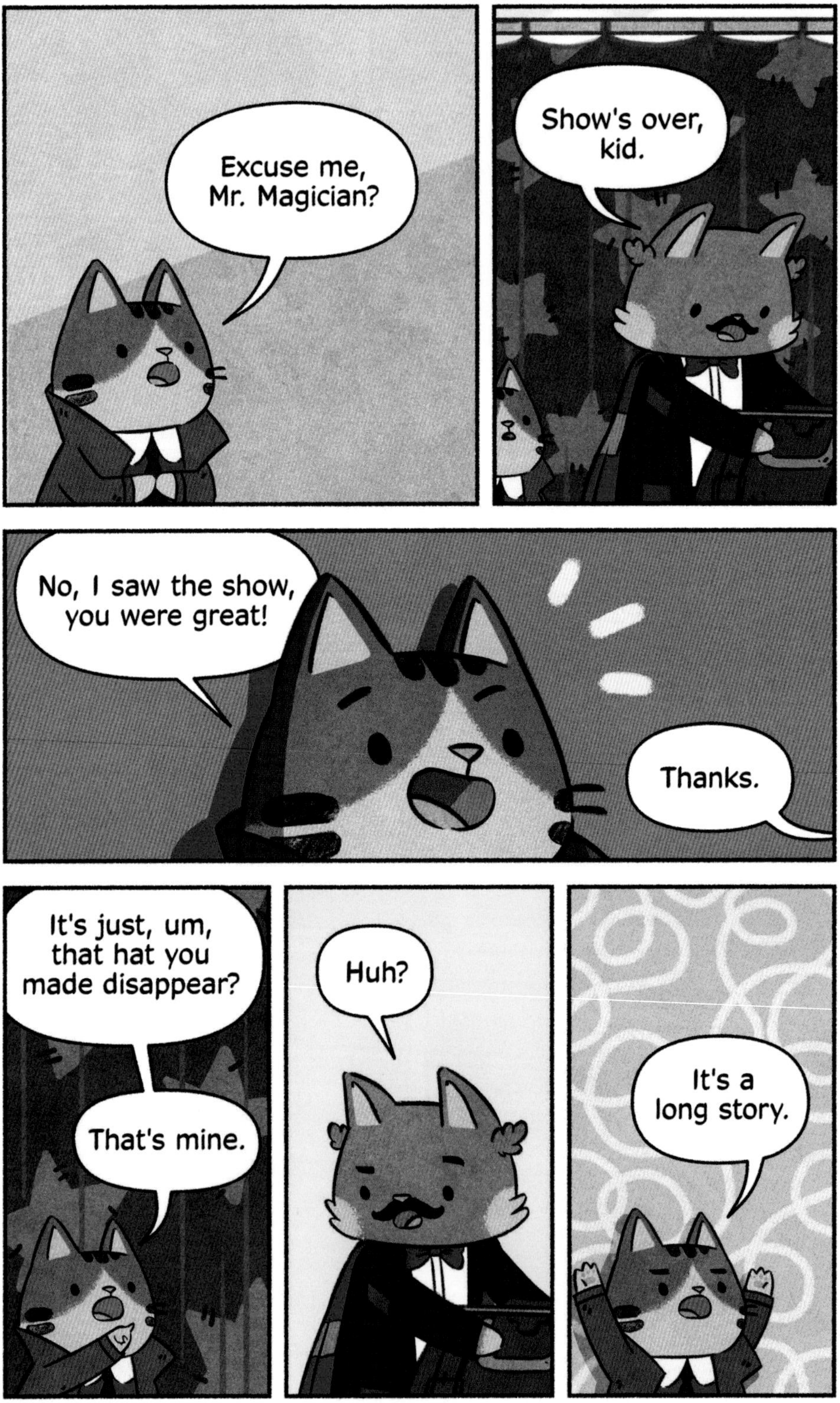
Excuse me, Mr. Magician?
Show's over, kid.
No, I saw the show, you were great!
Thanks.
It's just, um, that hat you made disappear?
That's mine.
Huh?
It's a long story.

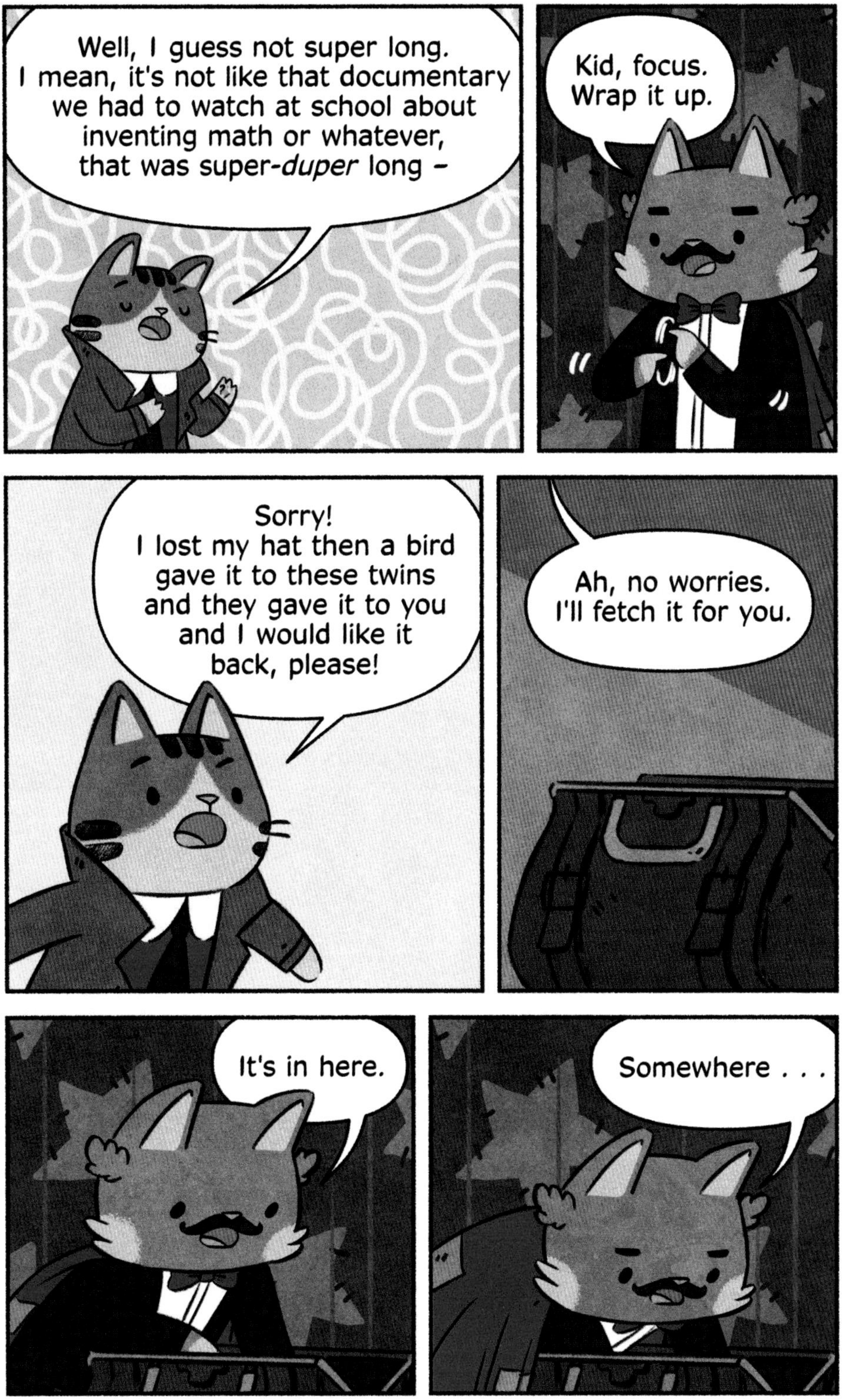
Well, I guess not super long. I mean, it's not like that documentary we had to watch at school about inventing math or whatever, that was super-*duper* long –
Kid, focus. Wrap it up.
Sorry! I lost my hat then a bird gave it to these twins and they gave it to you and I would like it back, please!
Ah, no worries. I'll fetch it for you.
It's in here.
Somewhere . . .

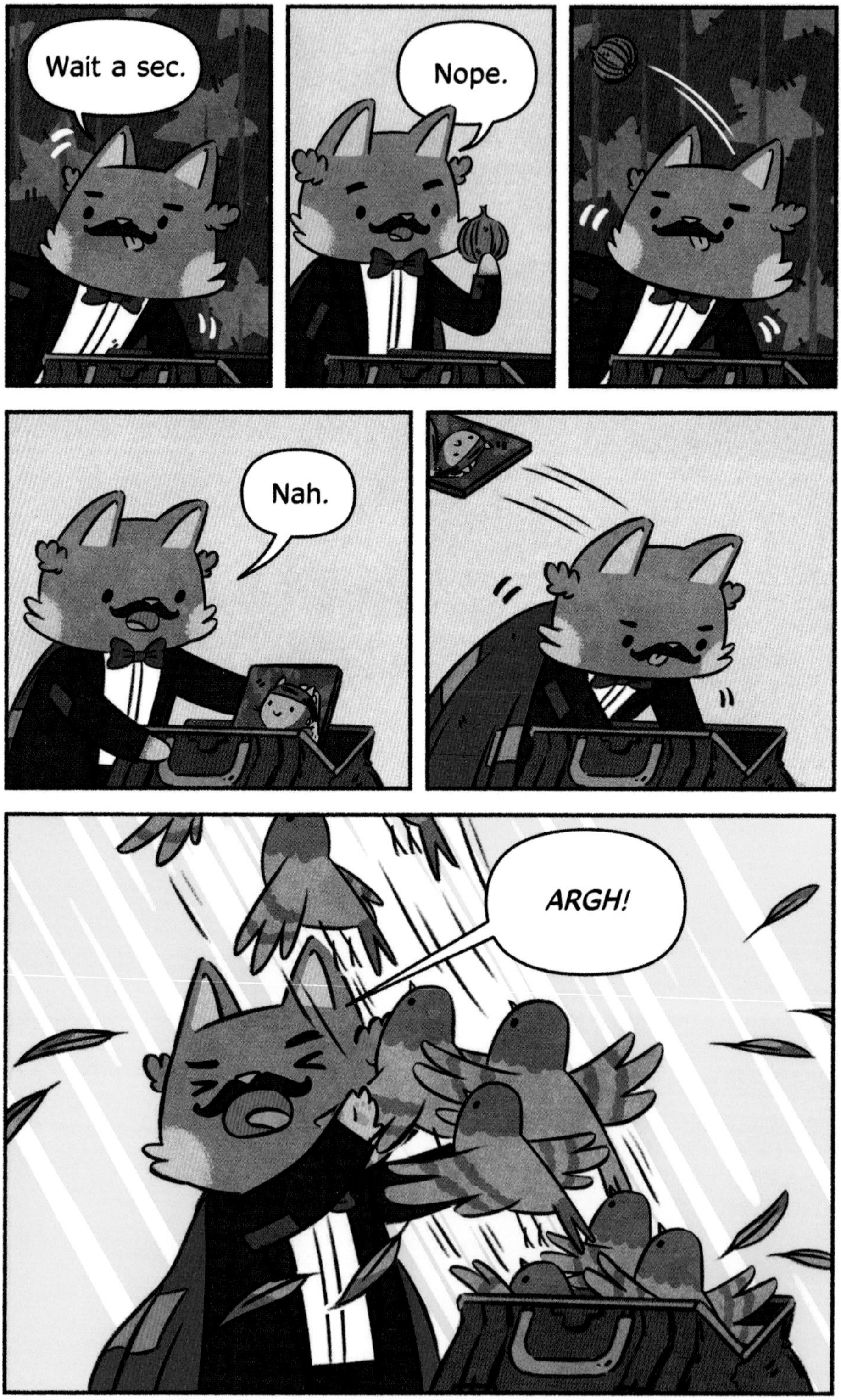
Wait a sec.
Nope.
Nah.
ARGH!

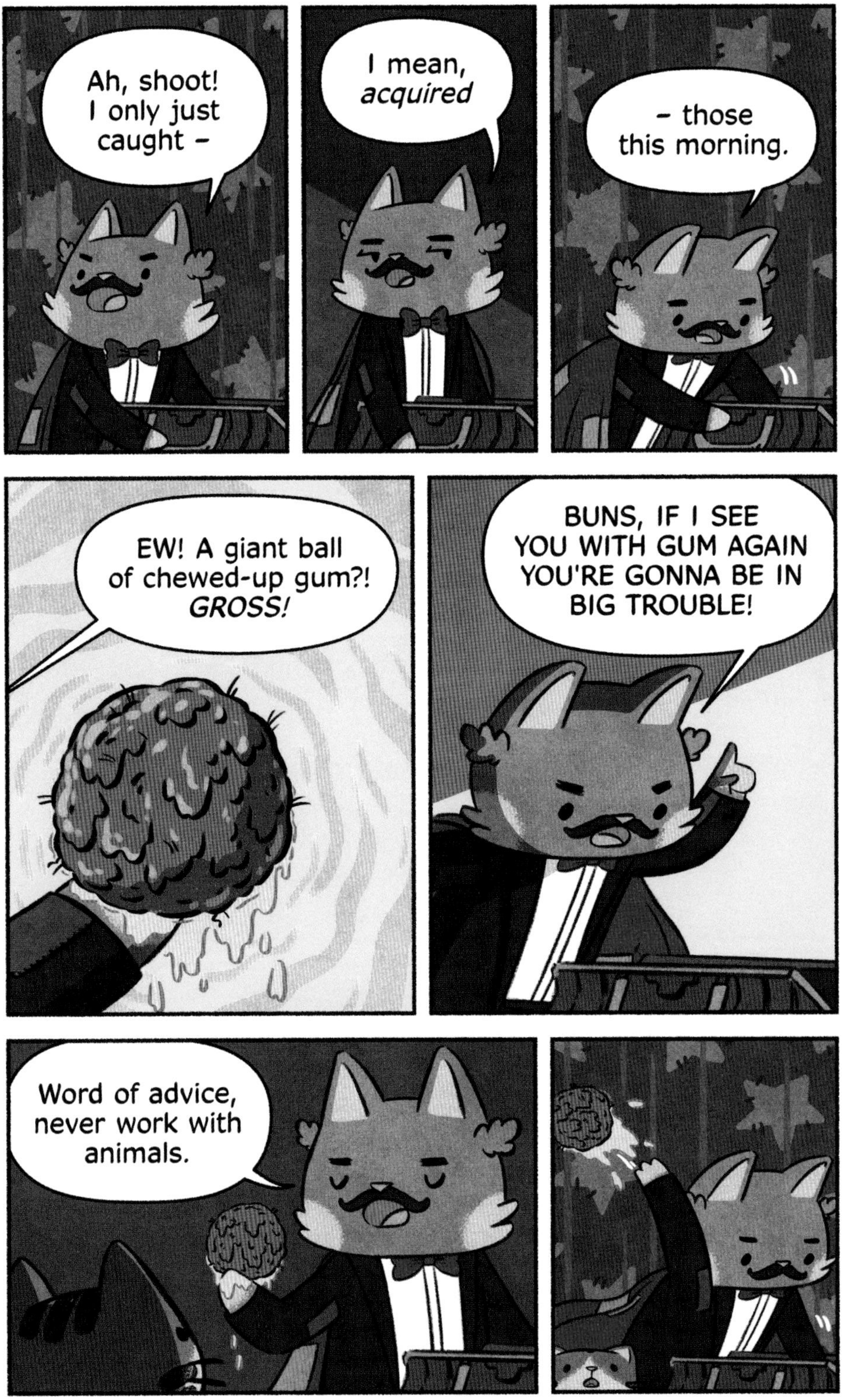
Ah, shoot! I only just caught -
I mean, *acquired*
- those this morning.
EW! A giant ball of chewed-up gum?! *GROSS!*
BUNS, IF I SEE YOU WITH GUM AGAIN YOU'RE GONNA BE IN BIG TROUBLE!
Word of advice, never work with animals.

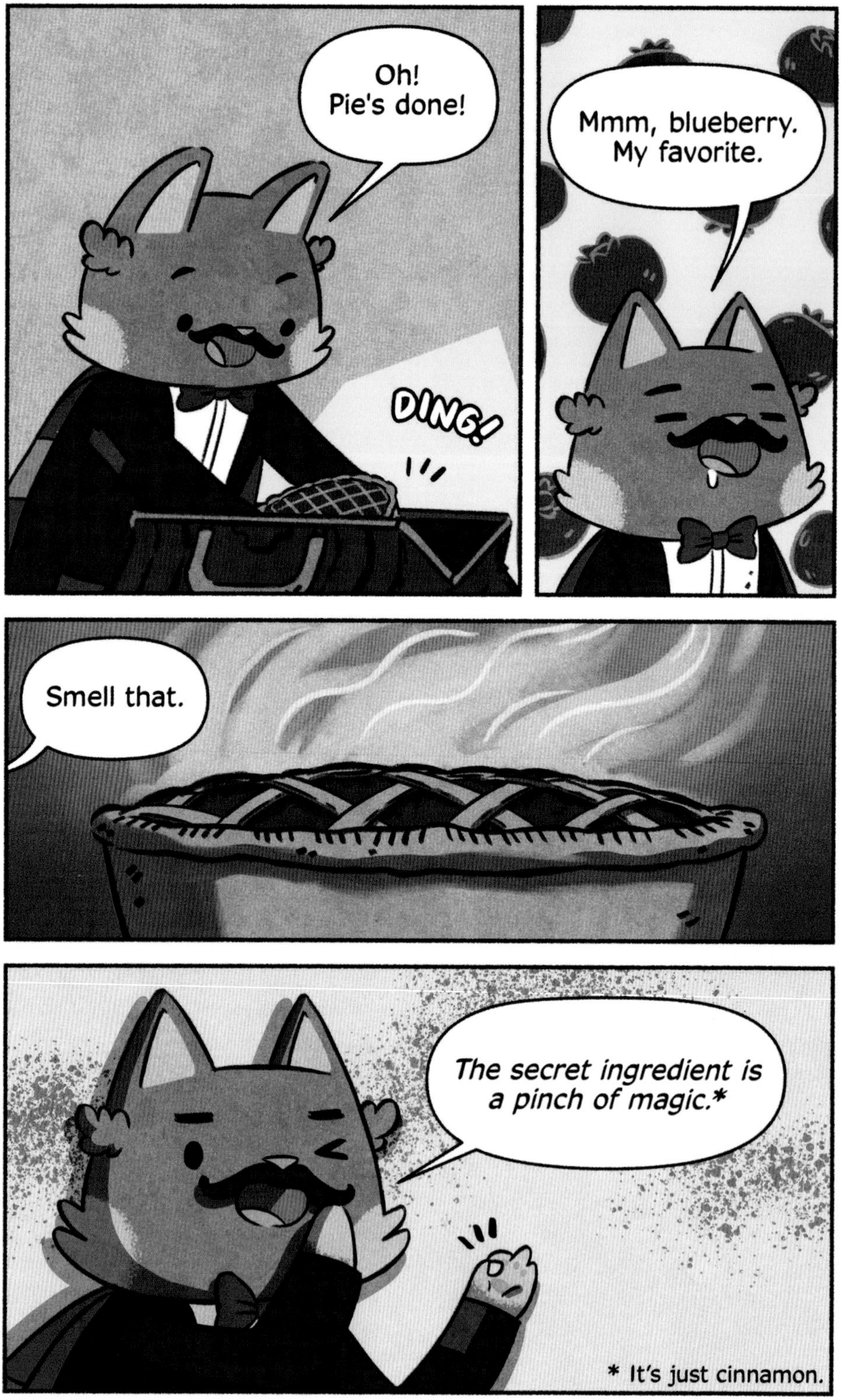
Oh!
Pie's done!
DING!
Mmm, blueberry.
My favorite.
Smell that.
*The secret ingredient is a pinch of magic.**
* It's just cinnamon.

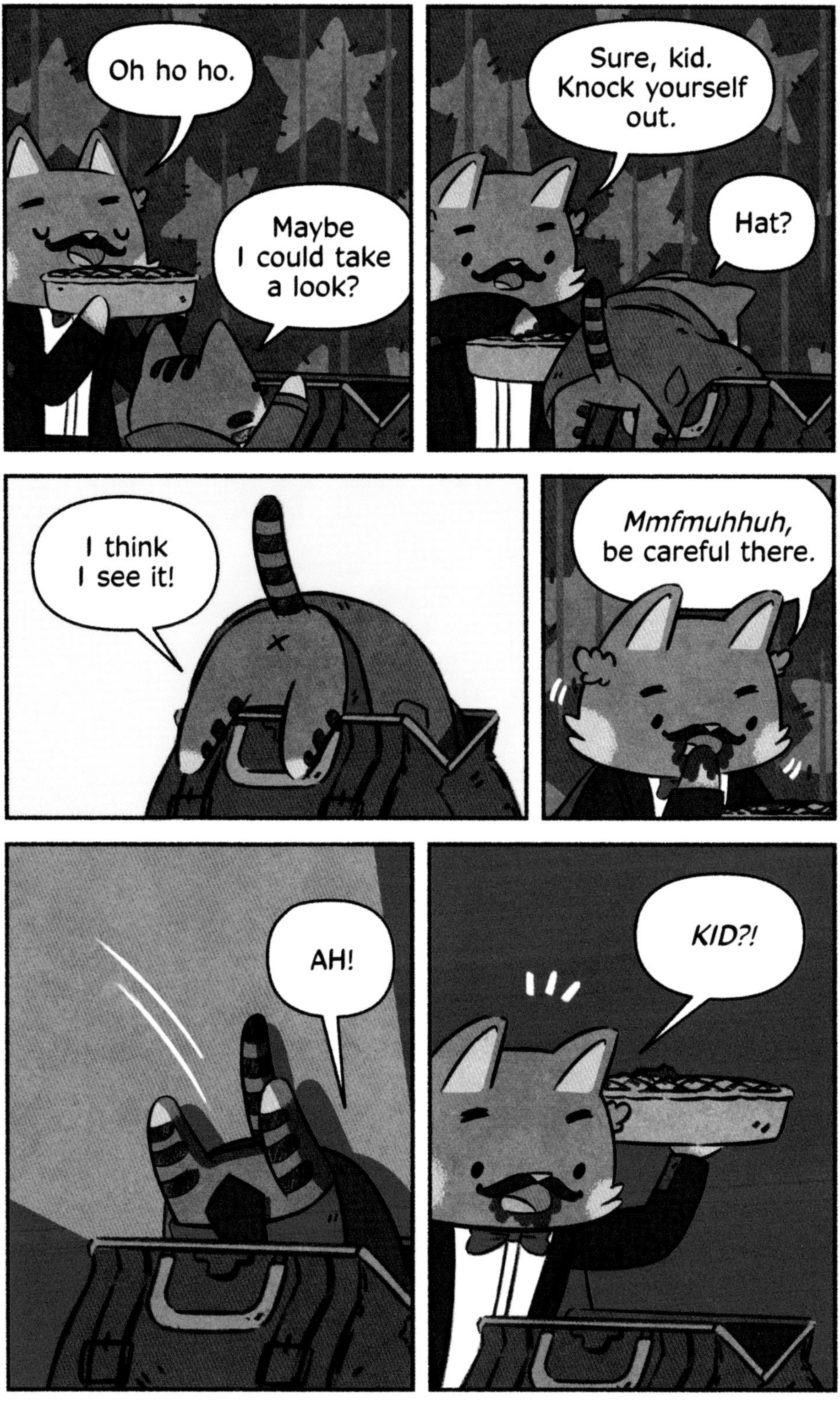
Oh ho ho.
Maybe I could take a look?
Sure, kid. Knock yourself out.
Hat?
I think I see it!
Mmfmuhhuh, be careful there.
AH!
KID?!

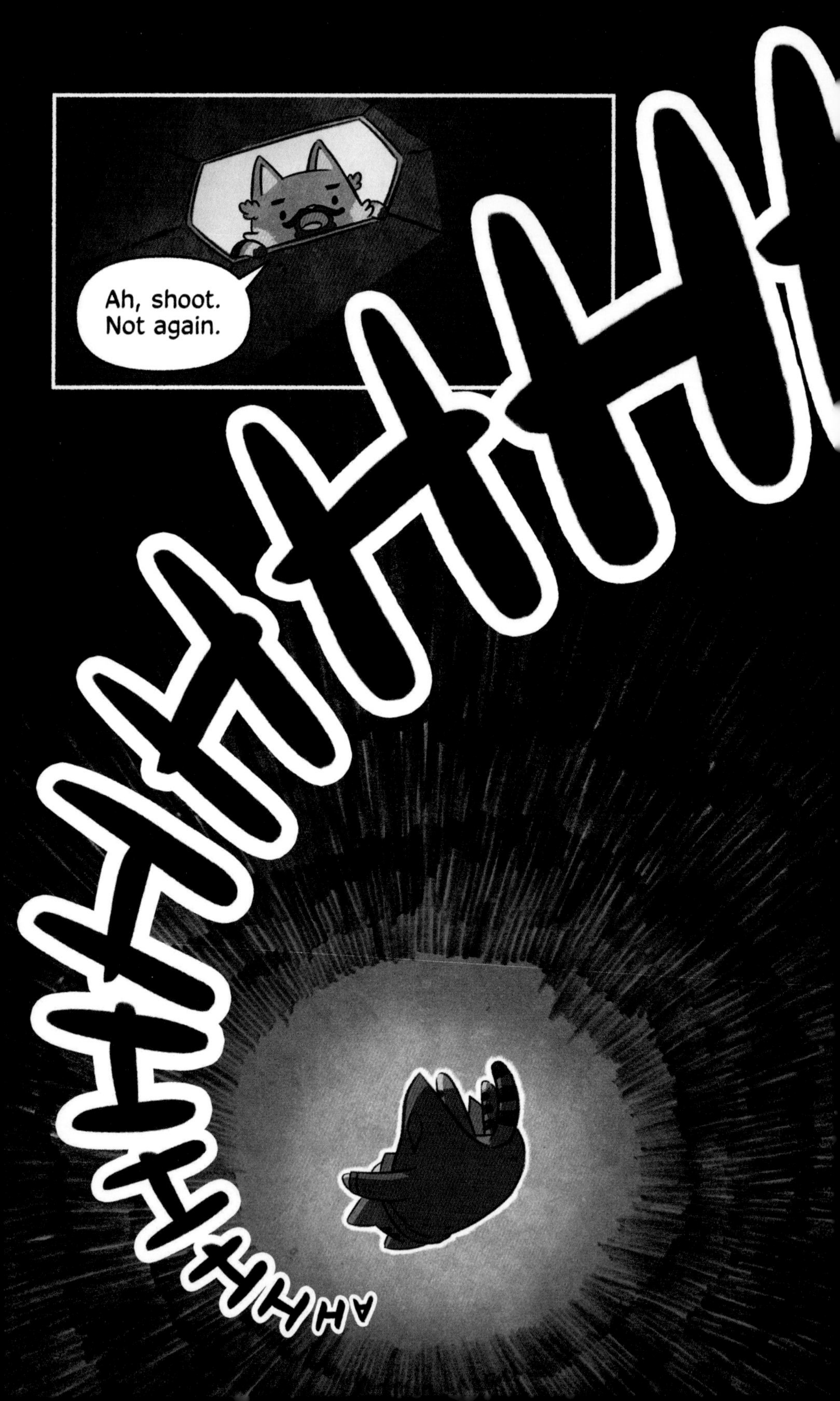
Ah, shoot. Not again.
AHHHHHHHHHHHHHHHH

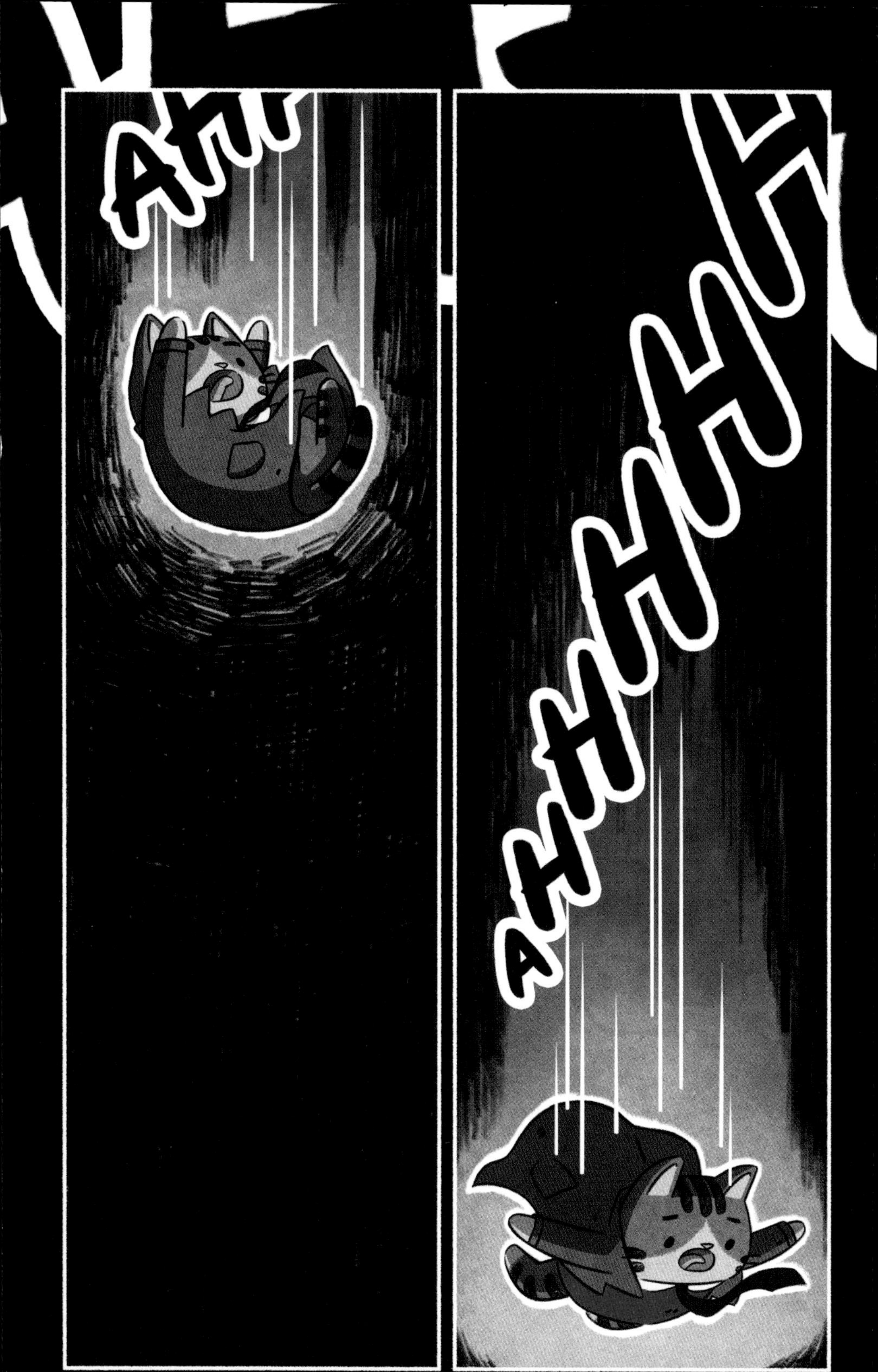
Ahh
AHHHHH

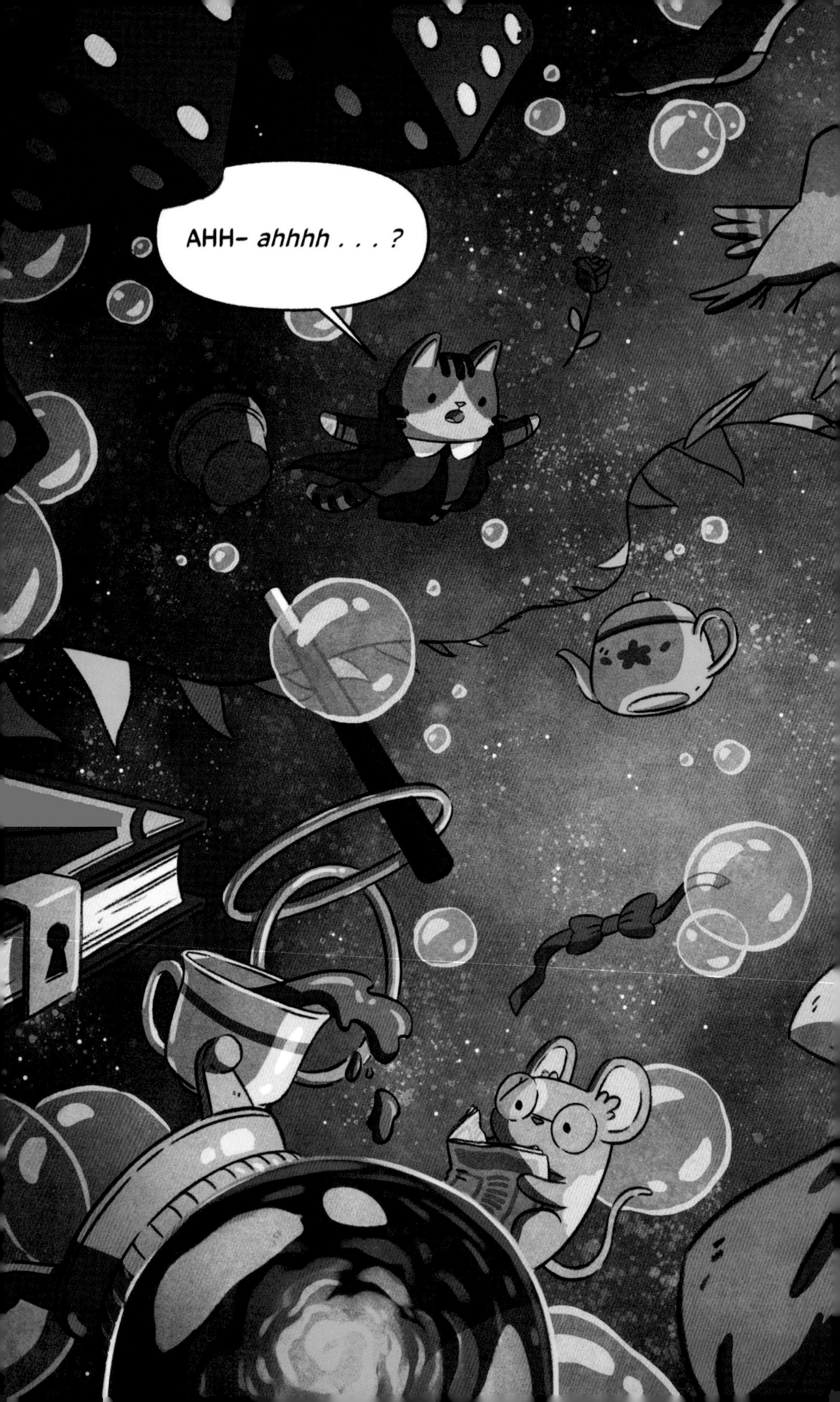
AHH- *ahhhh . . . ?*

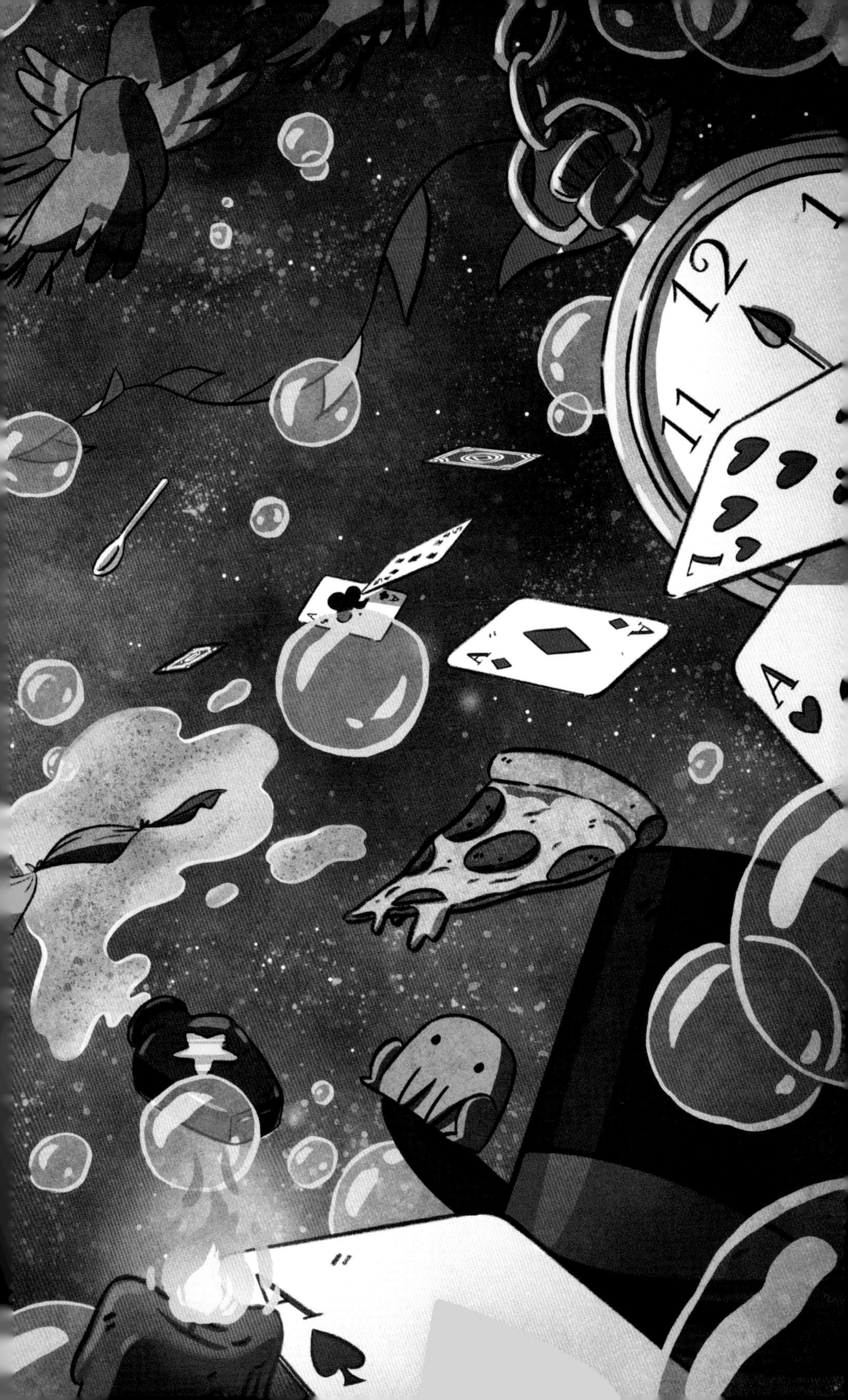

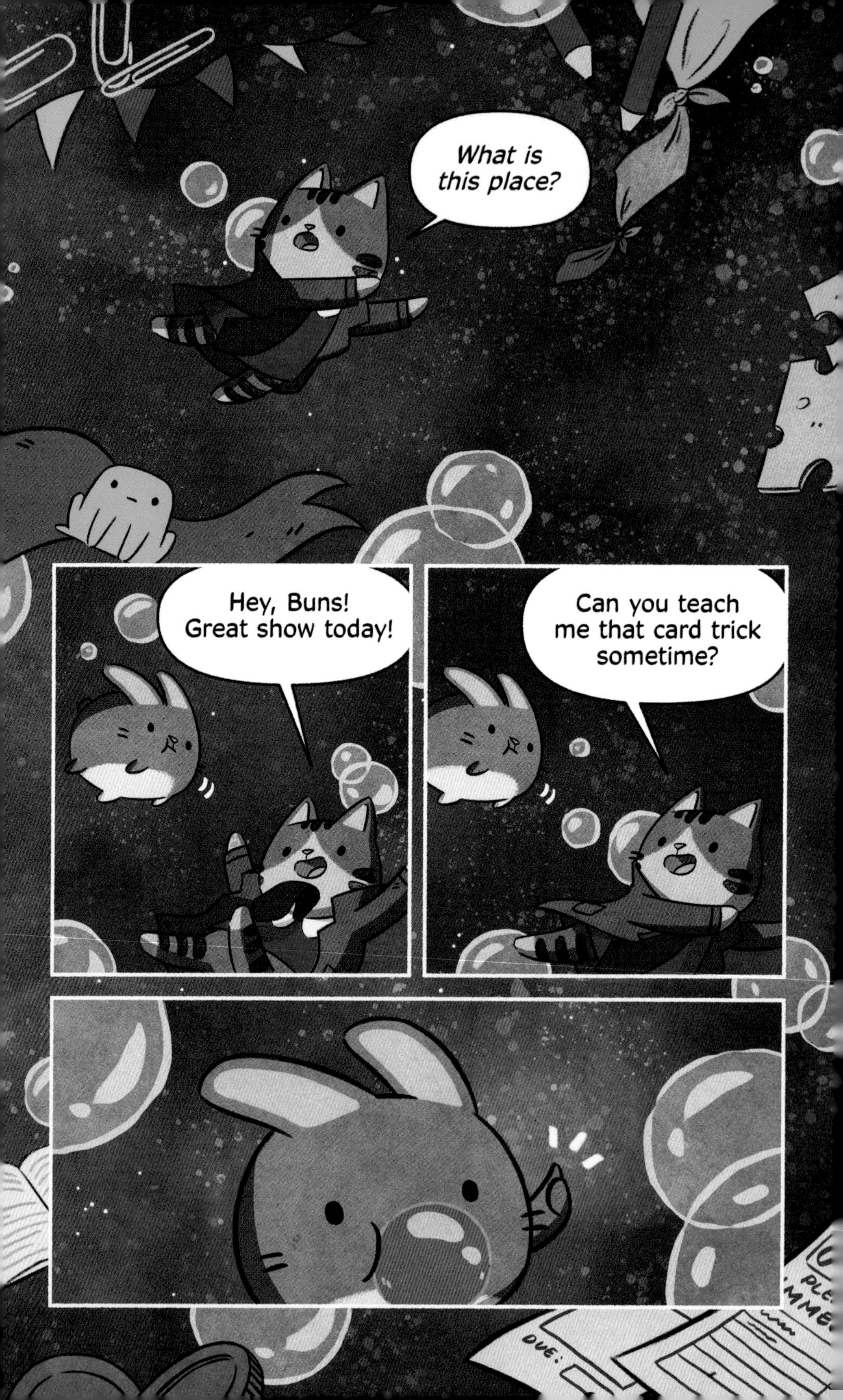
What is this place?
Hey, Buns! Great show today!
Can you teach me that card trick sometime?

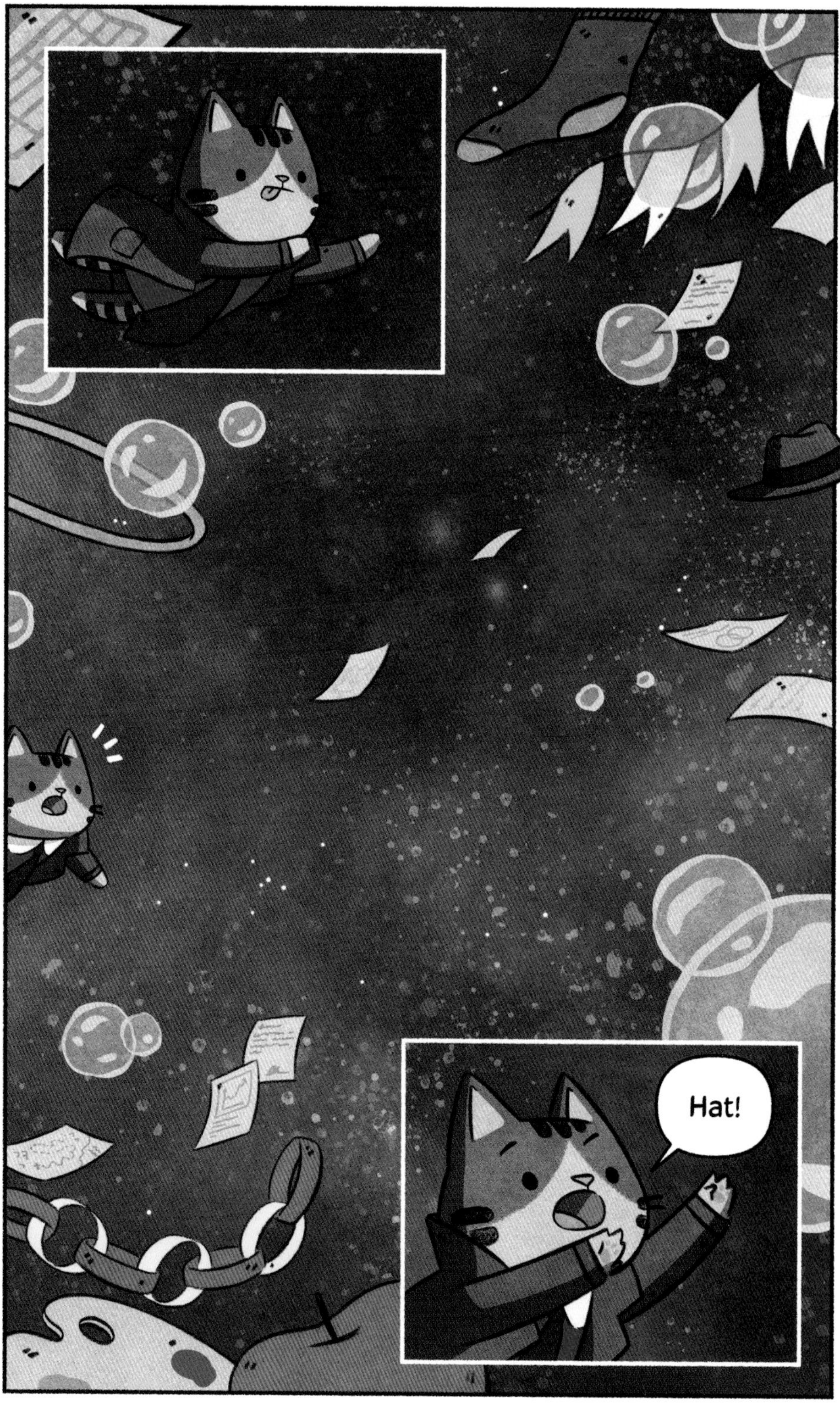
Hat!

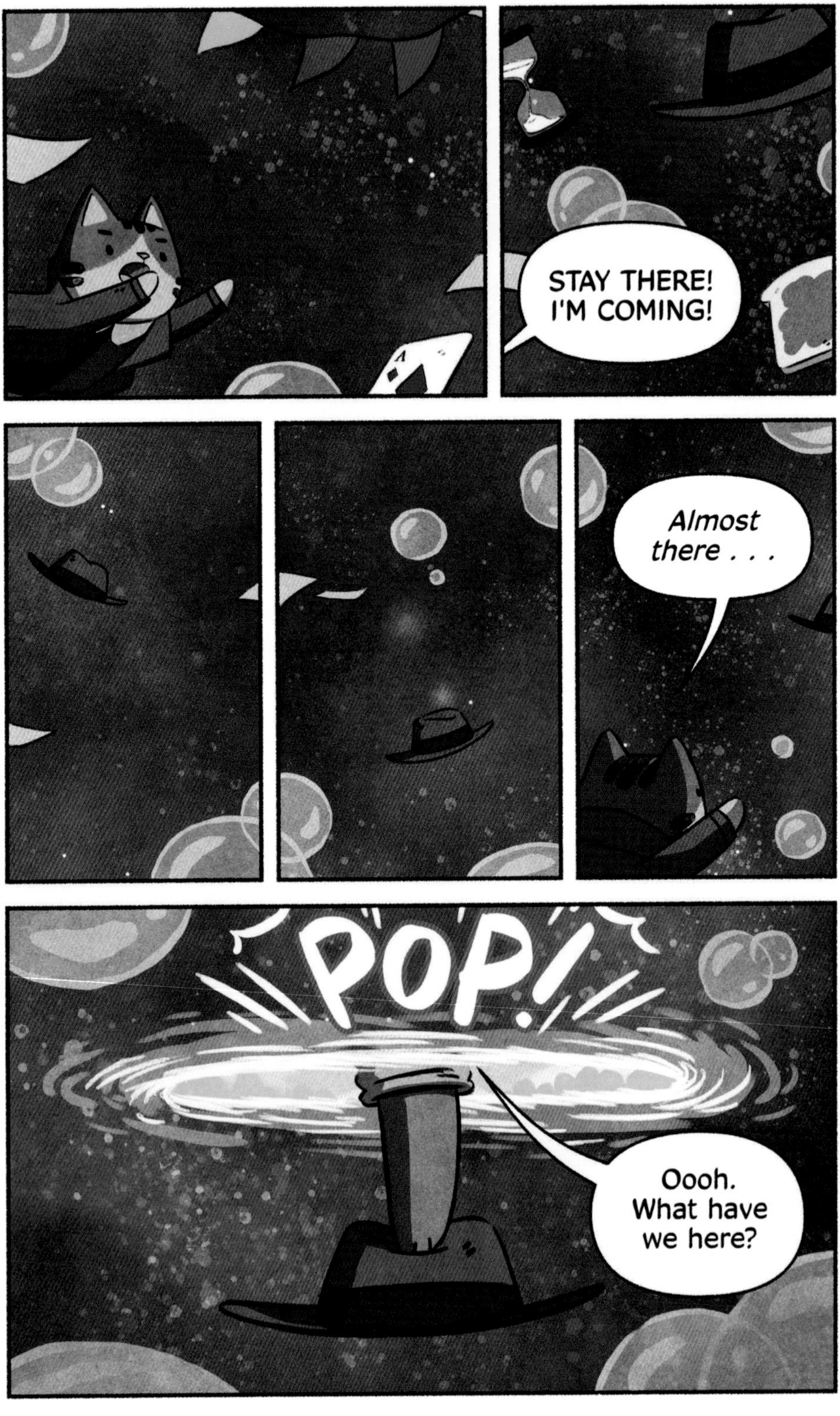
STAY THERE!
I'M COMING!
Almost there . . .
POP!
Oooh. What have we here?

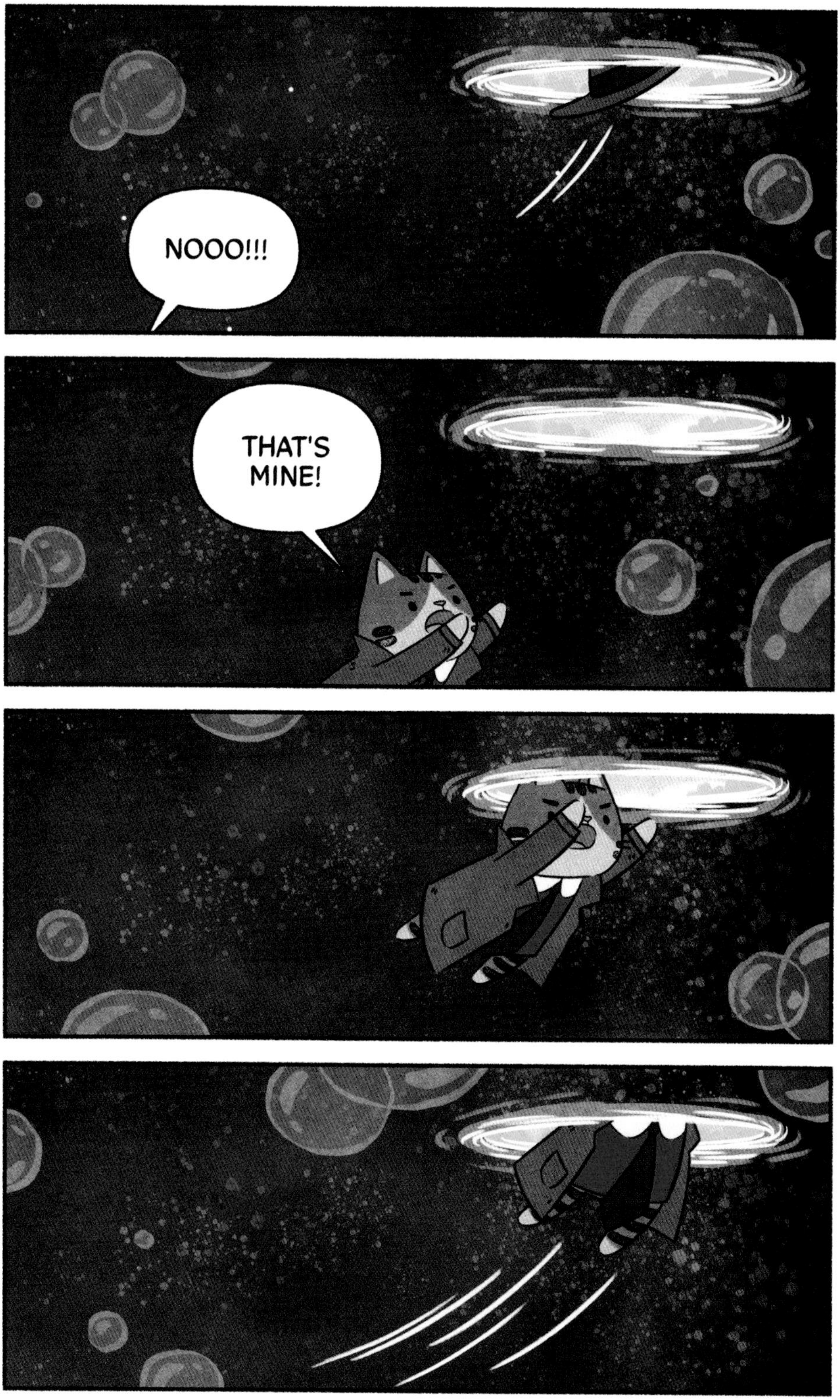
NOOO!!!
THAT'S MINE!

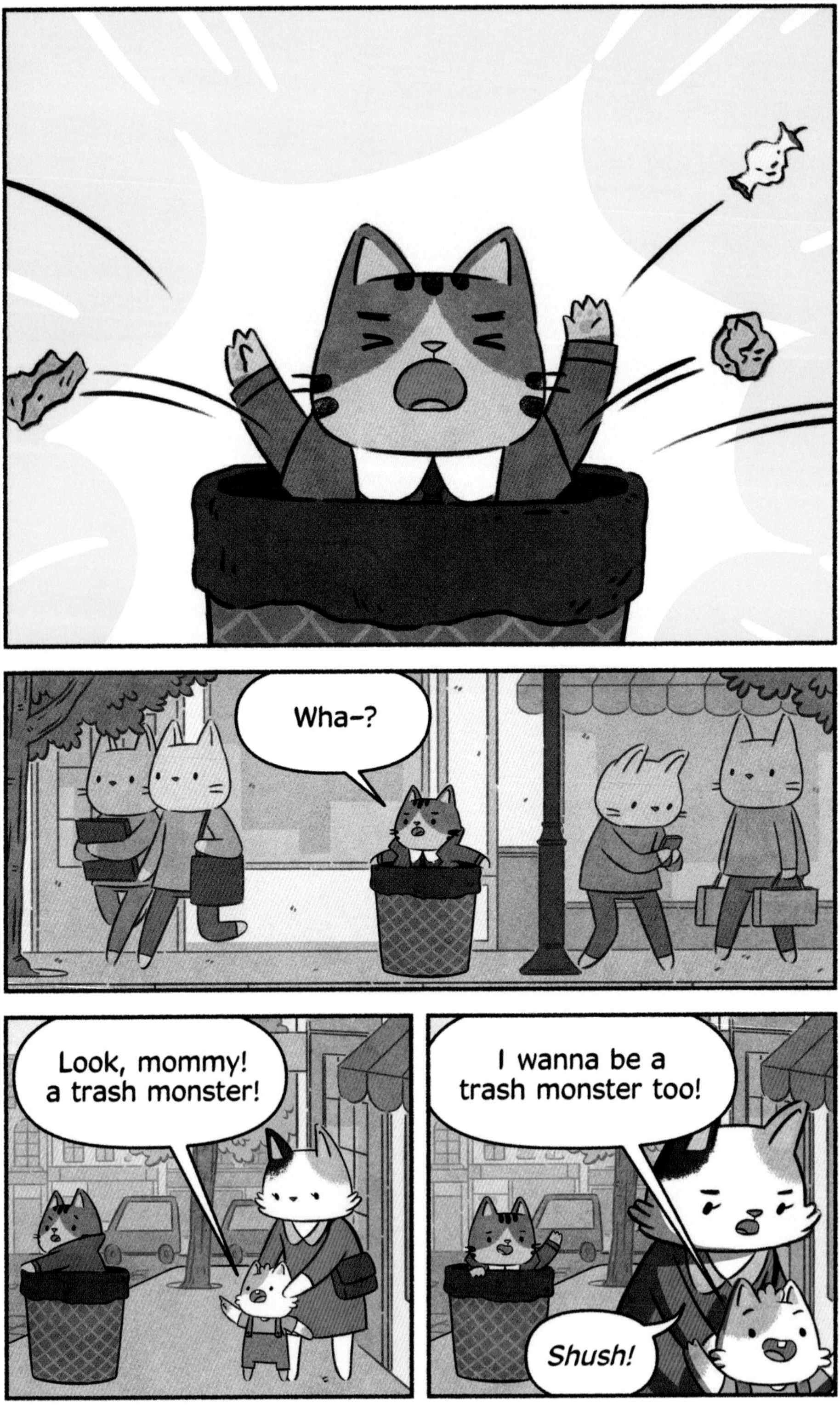
Wha-?
Look, mommy! a trash monster!
I wanna be a trash monster too!
Shush!

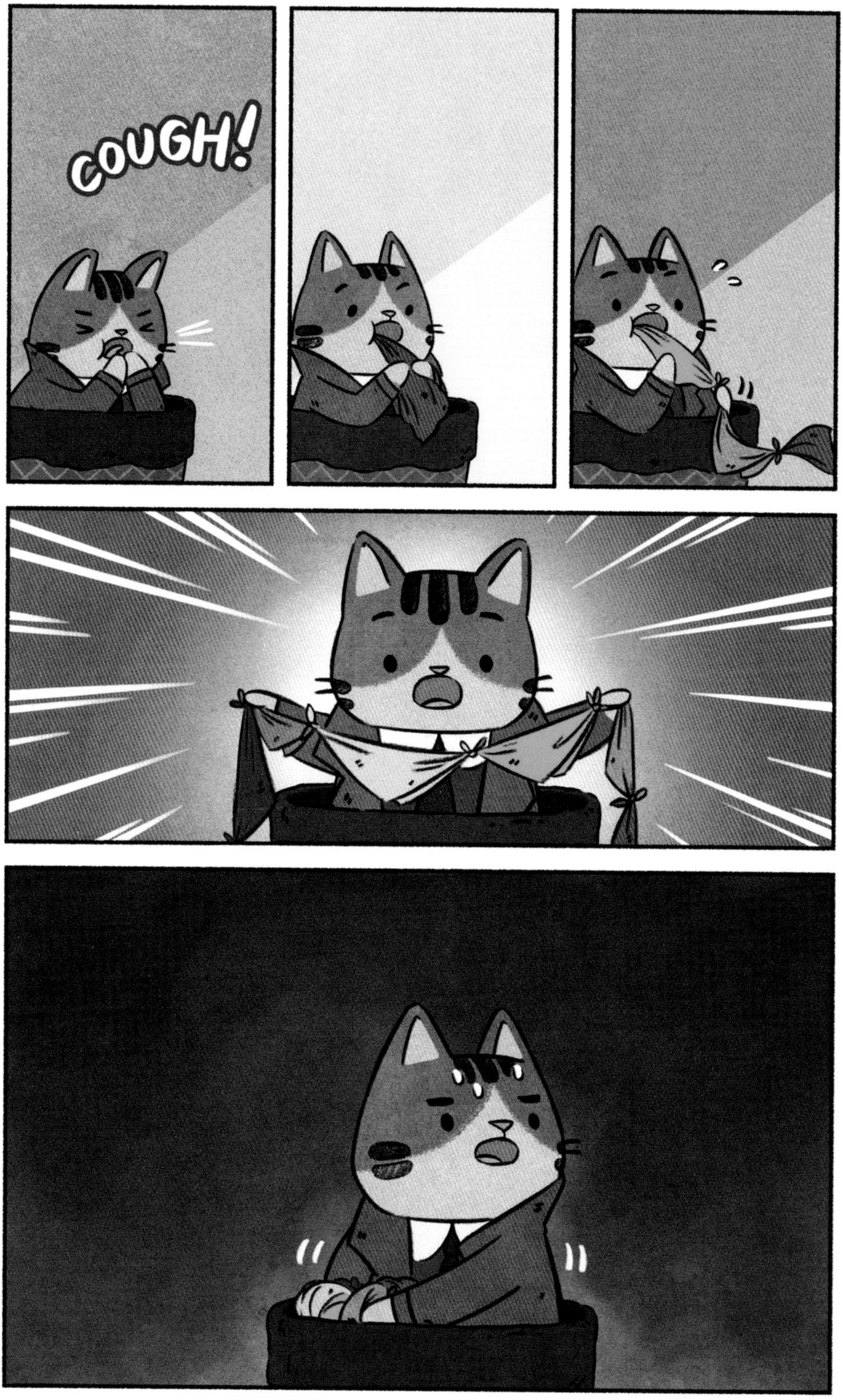
COUGH!

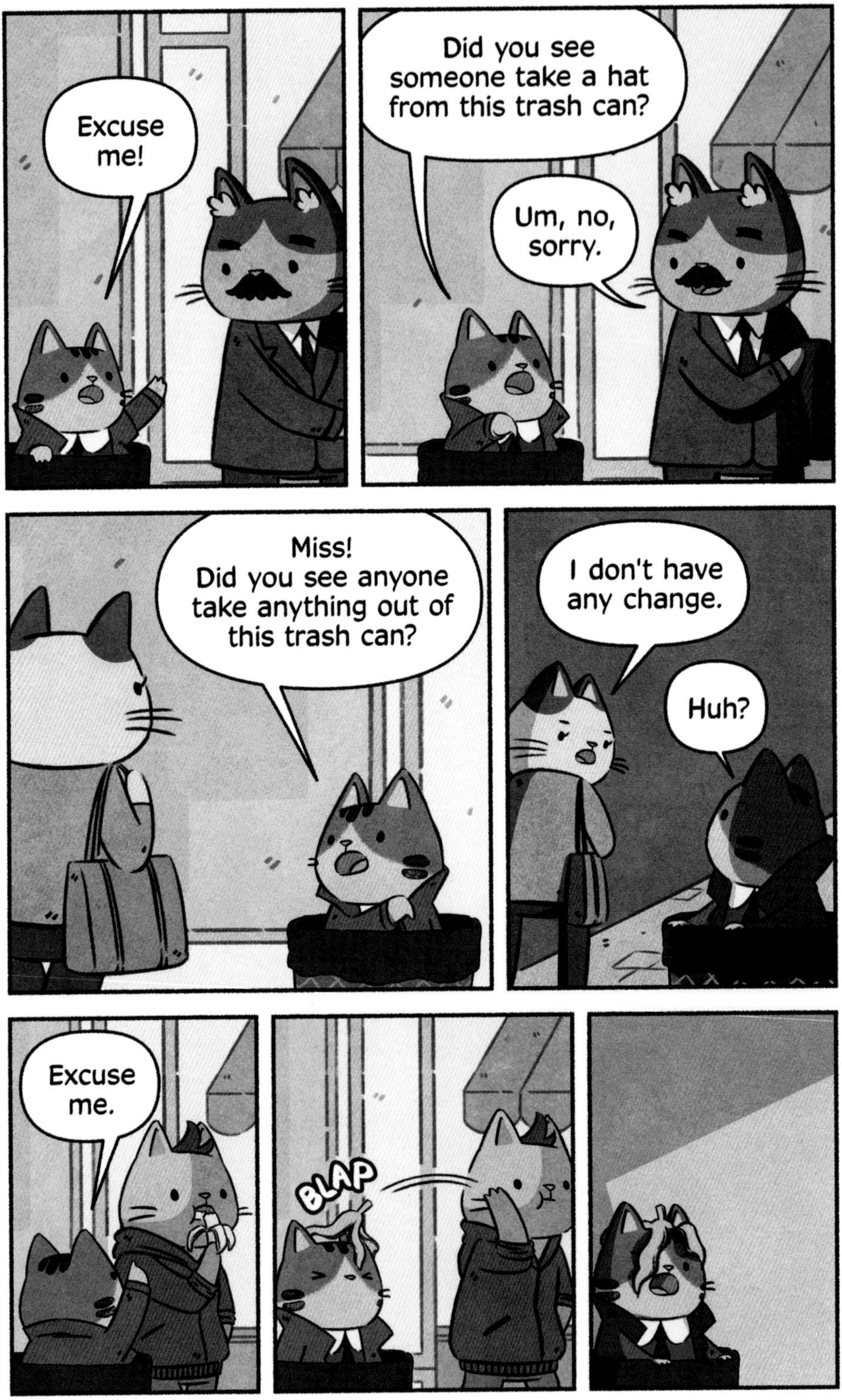
Excuse me!
Did you see someone take a hat from this trash can?
Um, no, sorry.
Miss! Did you see anyone take anything out of this trash can?
I don't have any change.
Huh?
Excuse me.
BLAP

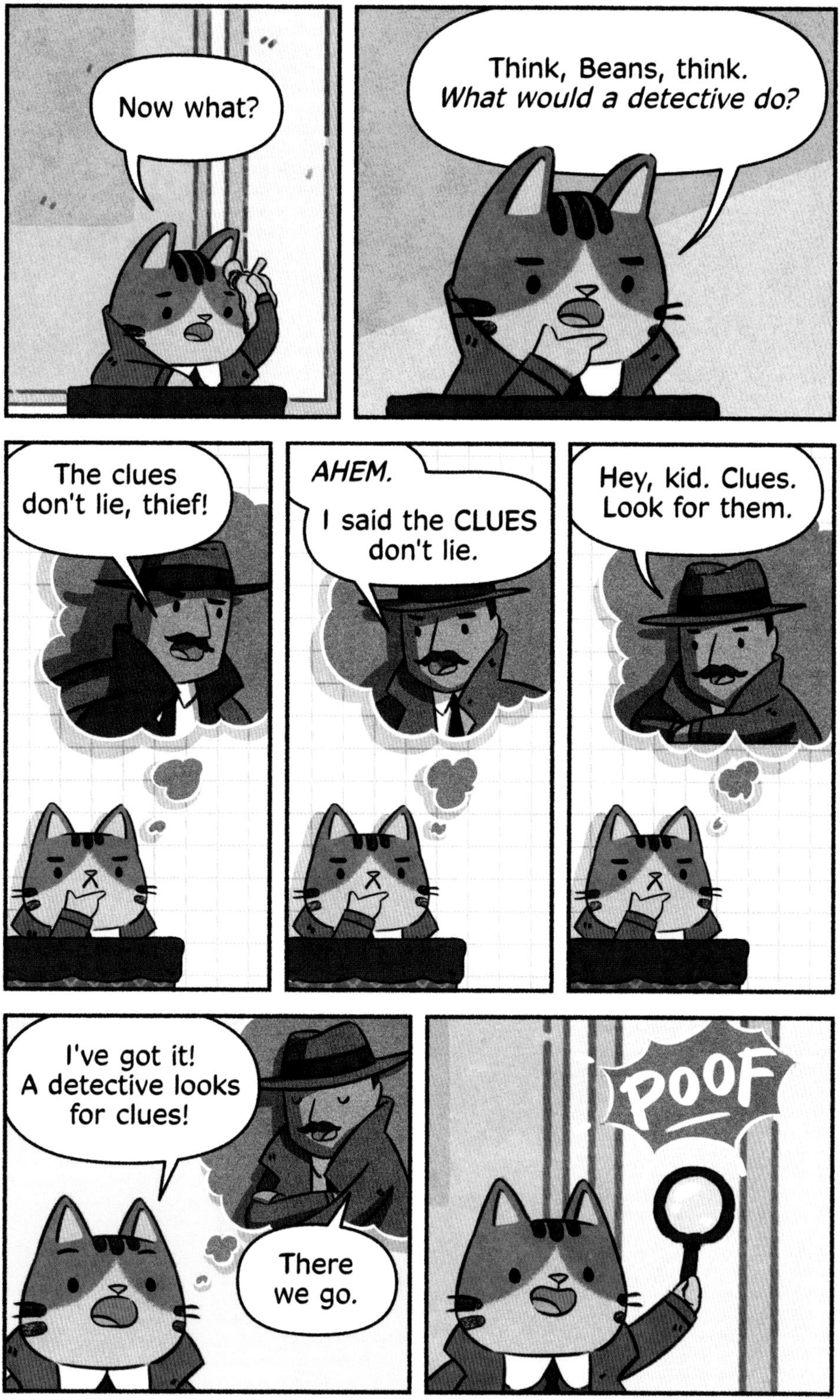
Now what?
Think, Beans, think.
What would a detective do?
The clues don't lie, thief!
AHEM.
I said the CLUES don't lie.
Hey, kid. Clues. Look for them.
I've got it! A detective looks for clues!
There we go.
POOF

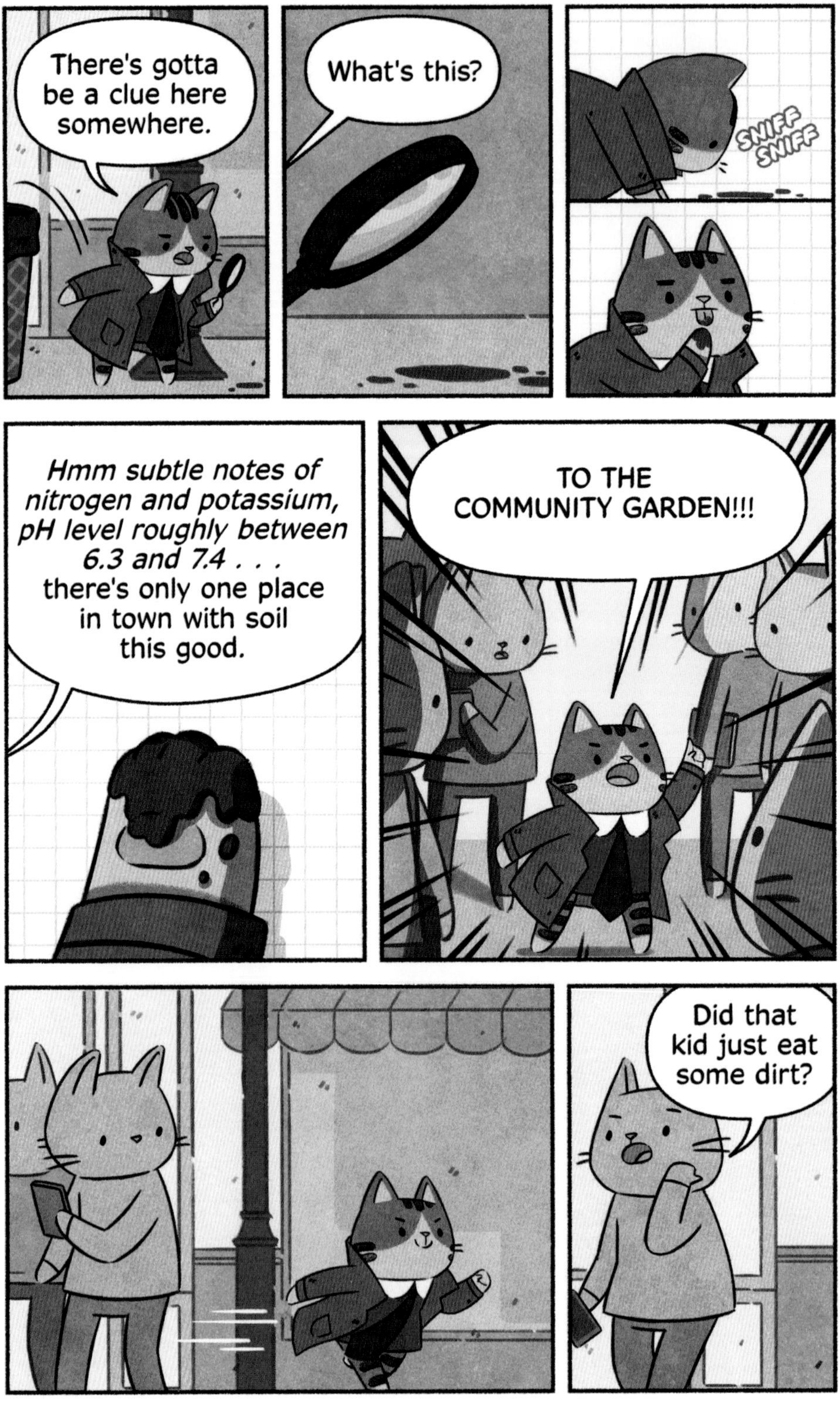
There's gotta be a clue here somewhere.
What's this?
SNIFF SNIFF
Hmm subtle notes of nitrogen and potassium, pH level roughly between 6.3 and 7.4 . . . there's only one place in town with soil this good.
TO THE COMMUNITY GARDEN!!!
Did that kid just eat some dirt?

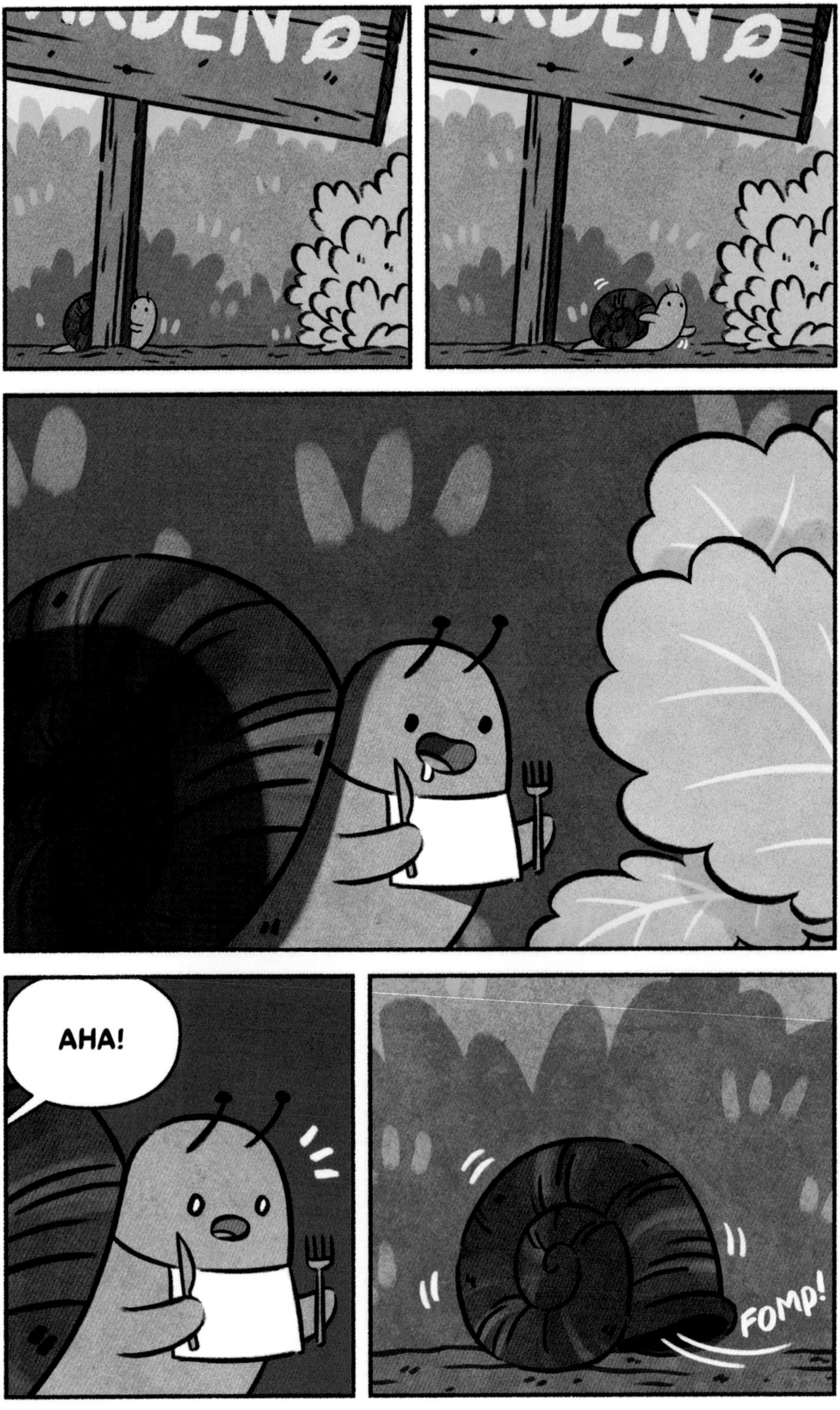
RDEN
AHA!
FOMP!

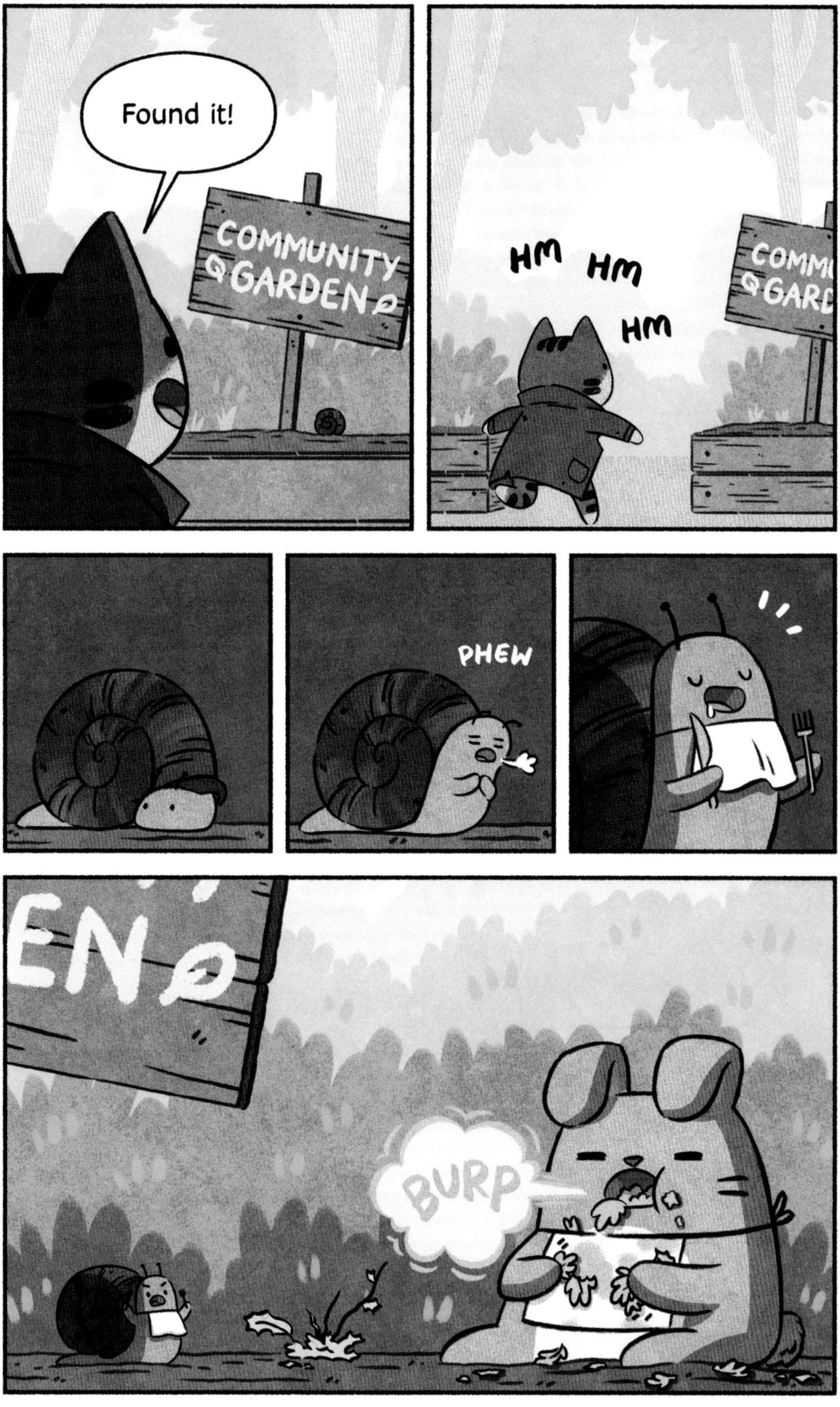
Found it!
COMMUNITY GARDEN
HM HM HM
COMM GARD
PHEW
BURP

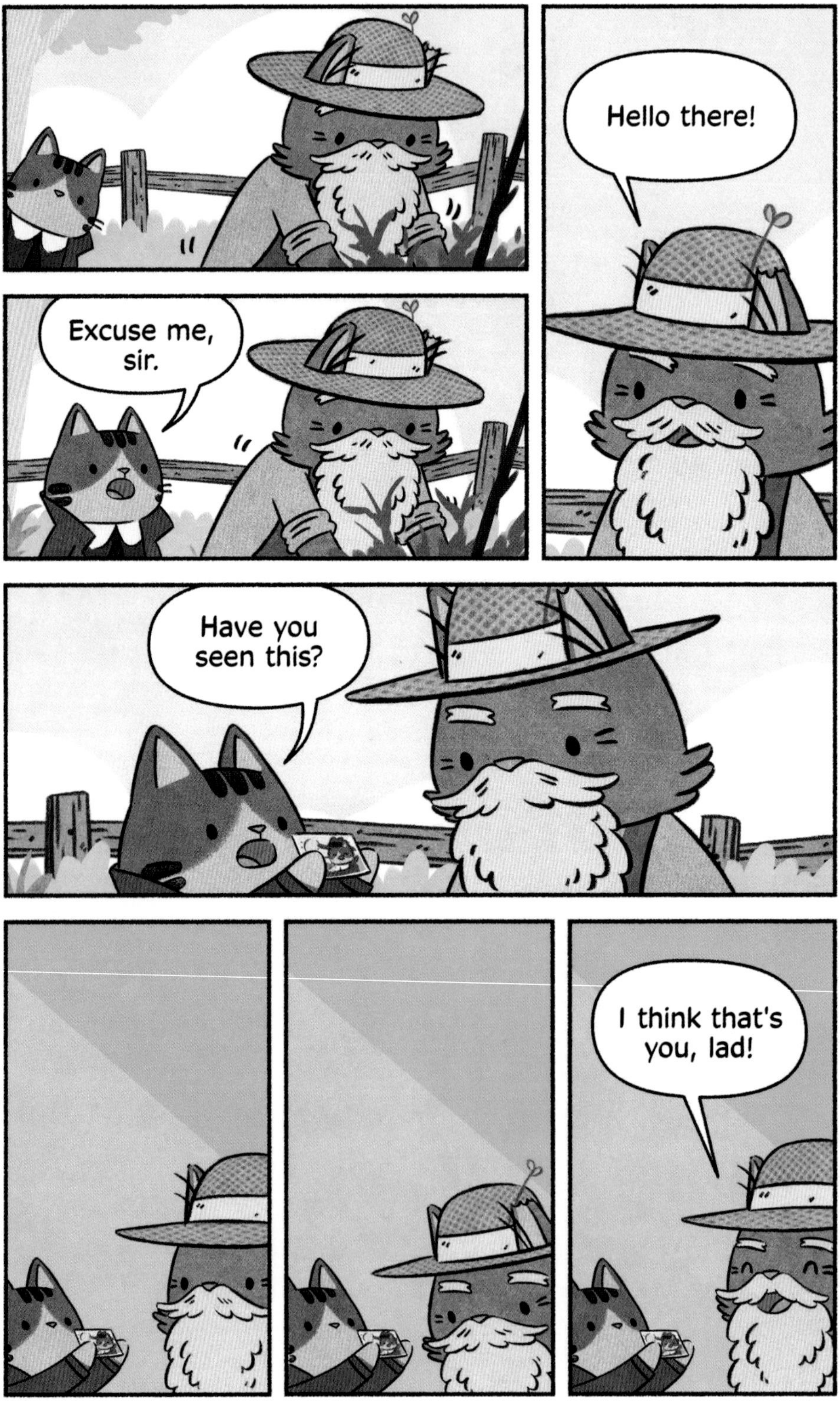
Excuse me, sir.
Hello there!
Have you seen this?
I think that's you, lad!

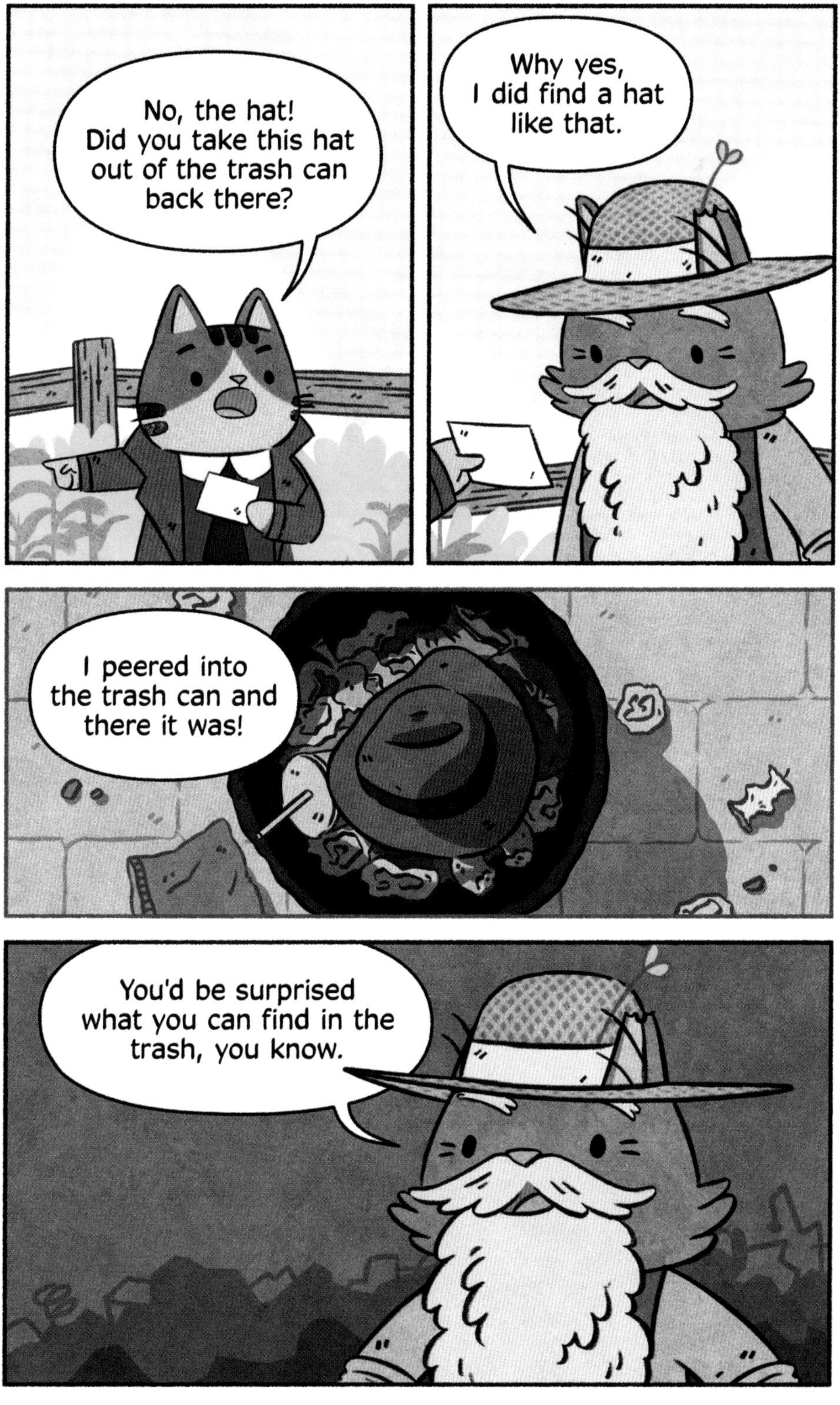
No, the hat!
Did you take this hat out of the trash can back there?
Why yes, I did find a hat like that.
I peered into the trash can and there it was!
You'd be surprised what you can find in the trash, you know.

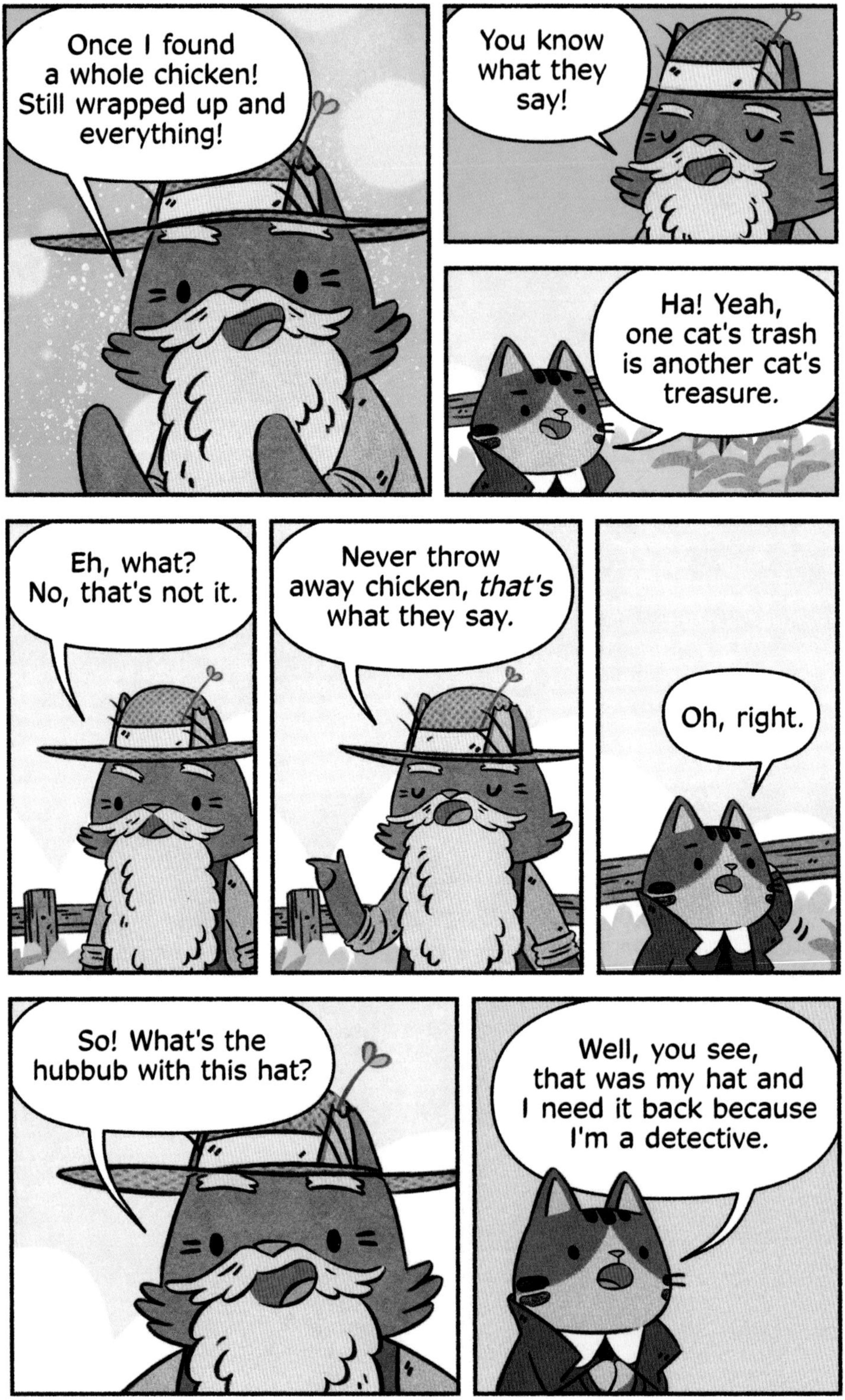
Once I found a whole chicken! Still wrapped up and everything!
You know what they say!
Ha! Yeah, one cat's trash is another cat's treasure.
Eh, what? No, that's not it.
Never throw away chicken, *that's* what they say.
Oh, right.
So! What's the hubbub with this hat?
Well, you see, that was my hat and I need it back because I'm a detective.

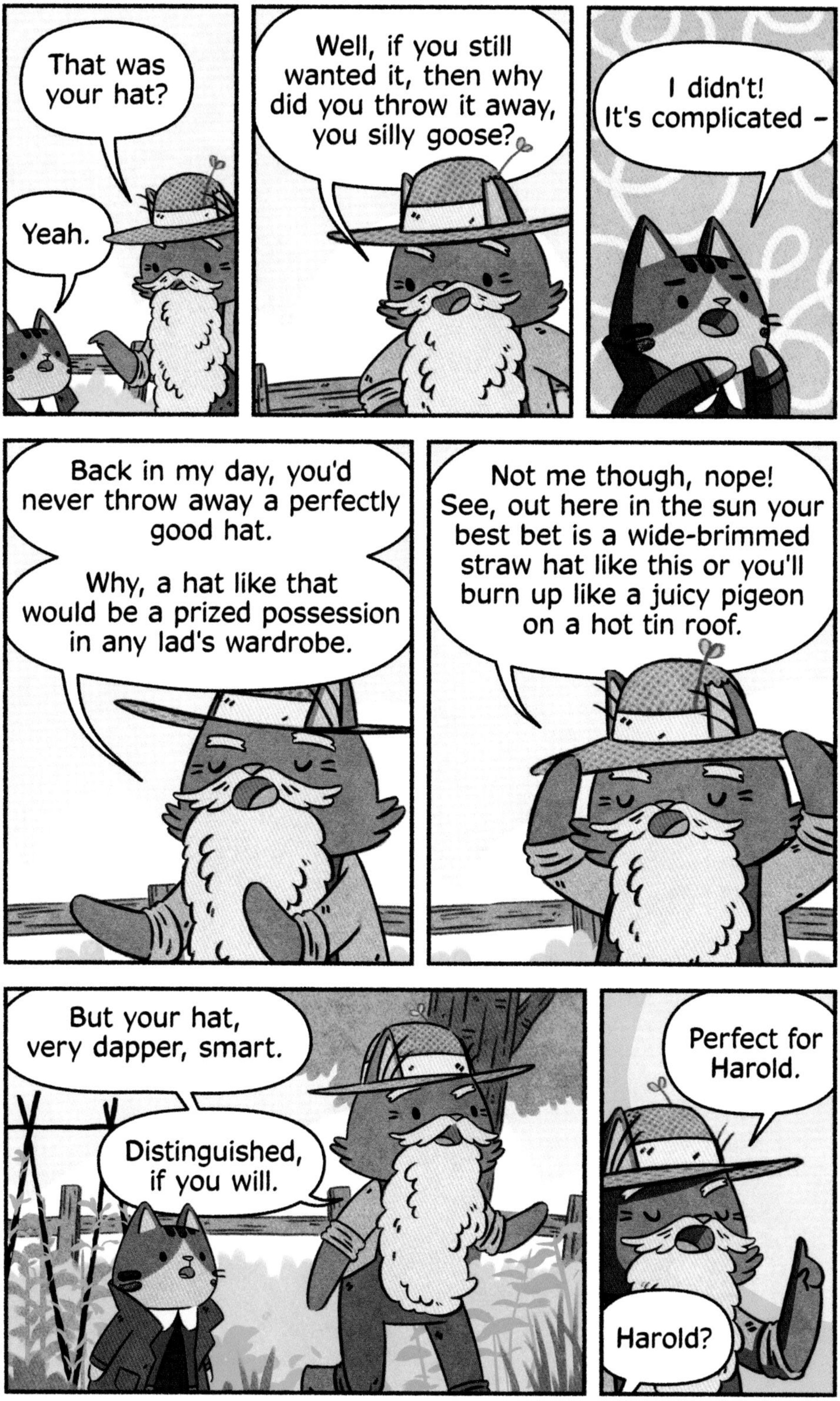
That was your hat?
Yeah.
Well, if you still wanted it, then why did you throw it away, you silly goose?
I didn't! It's complicated –
Back in my day, you'd never throw away a perfectly good hat.
Why, a hat like that would be a prized possession in any lad's wardrobe.
Not me though, nope! See, out here in the sun your best bet is a wide-brimmed straw hat like this or you'll burn up like a juicy pigeon on a hot tin roof.
But your hat, very dapper, smart.
Distinguished, if you will.
Perfect for Harold.
Harold?

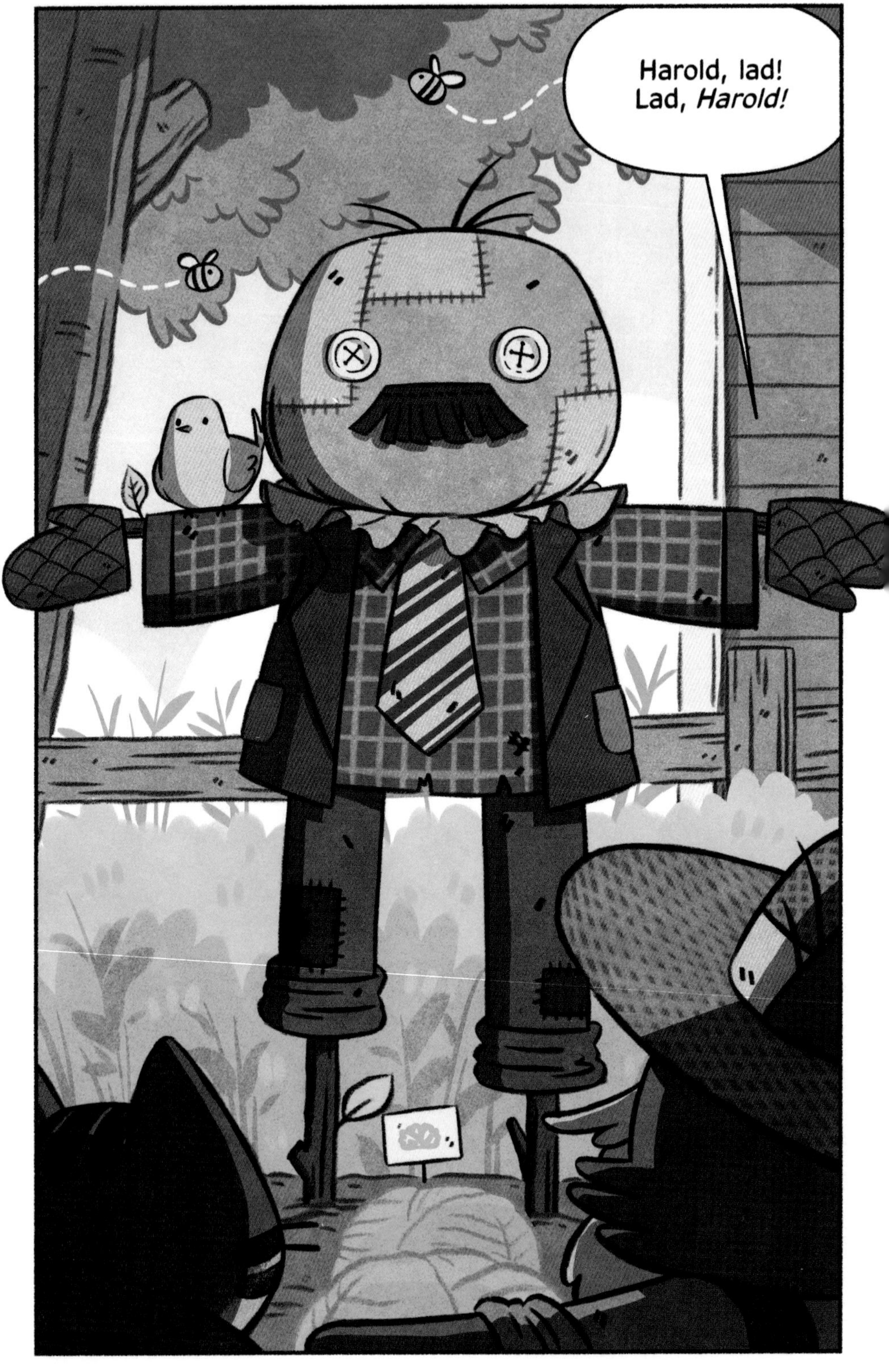
Harold, lad!
Lad, *Harold!*

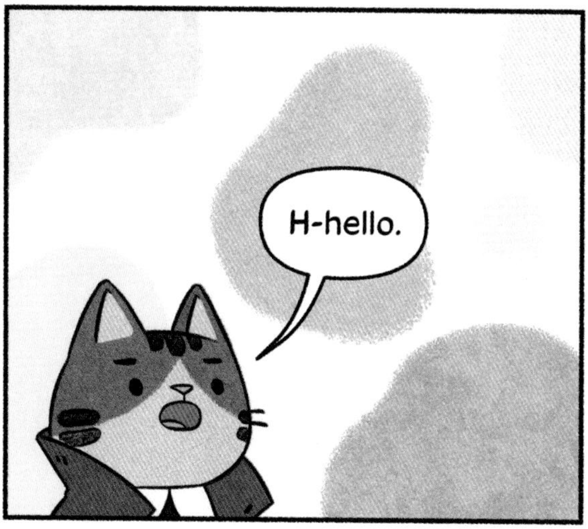
H-hello.

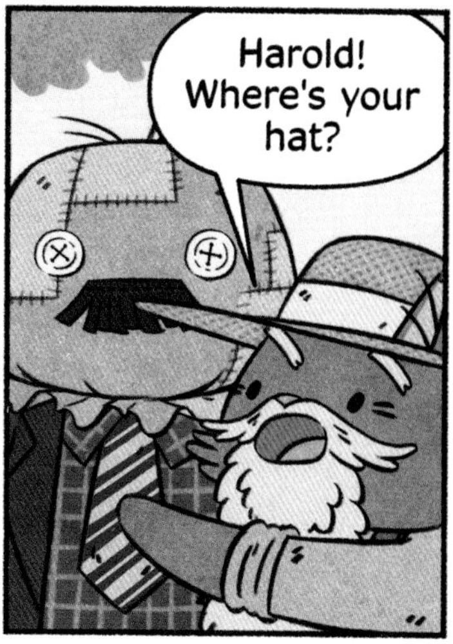
Harold! Where's your hat?

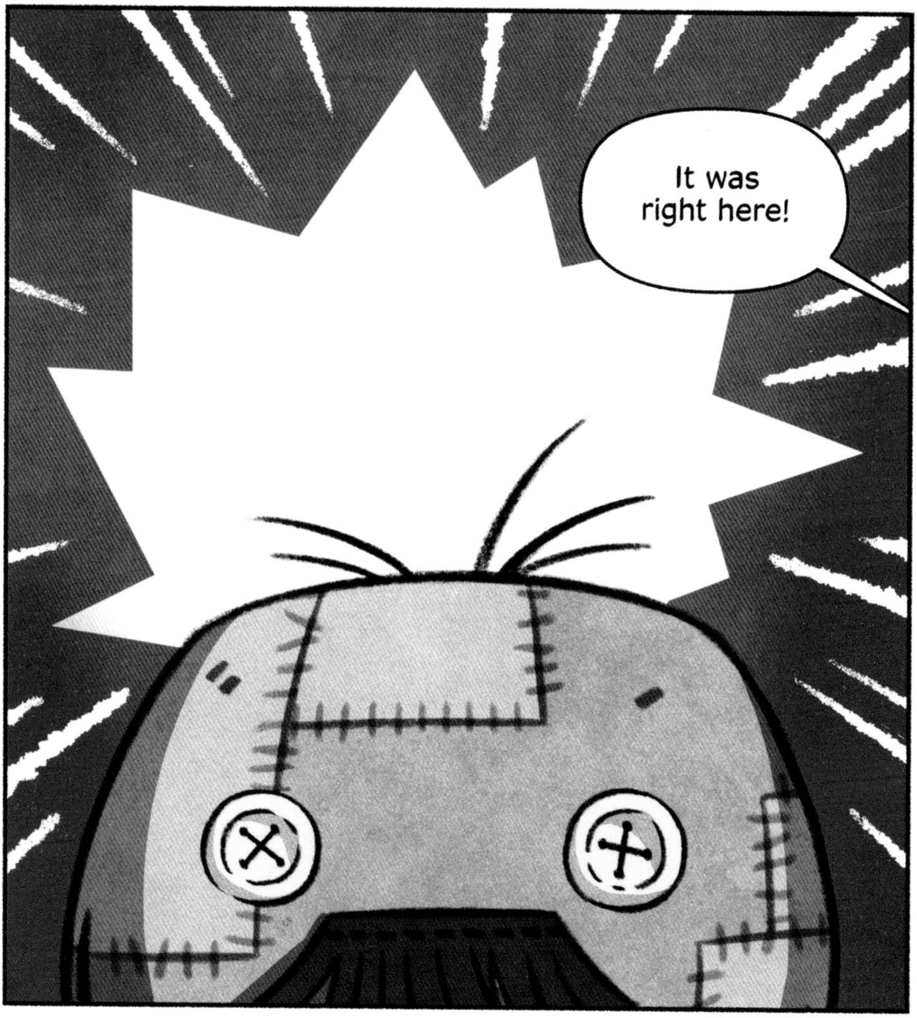
It was right here!

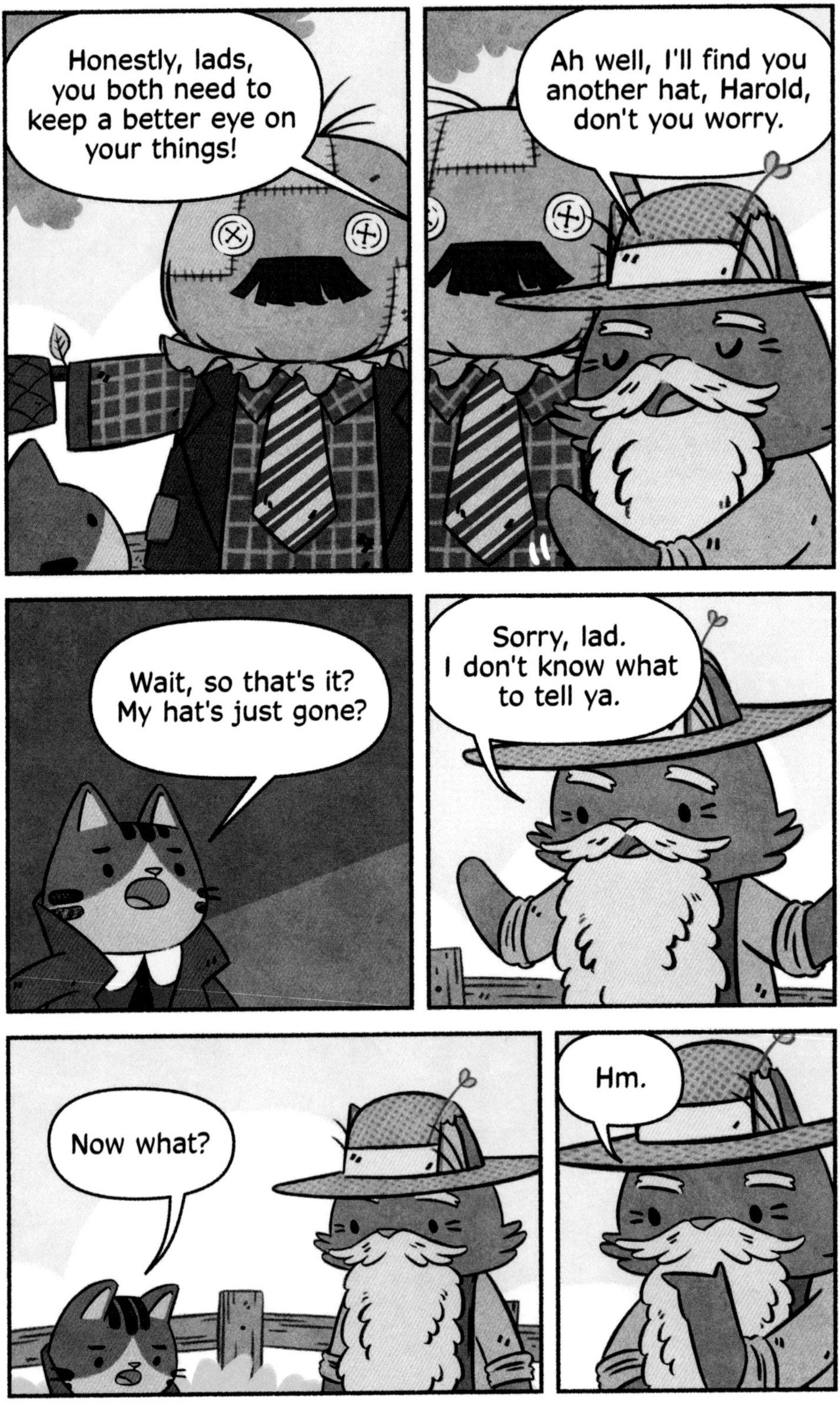
Honestly, lads, you both need to keep a better eye on your things!
Ah well, I'll find you another hat, Harold, don't you worry.
Wait, so that's it? My hat's just gone?
Sorry, lad. I don't know what to tell ya.
Now what?
Hm.

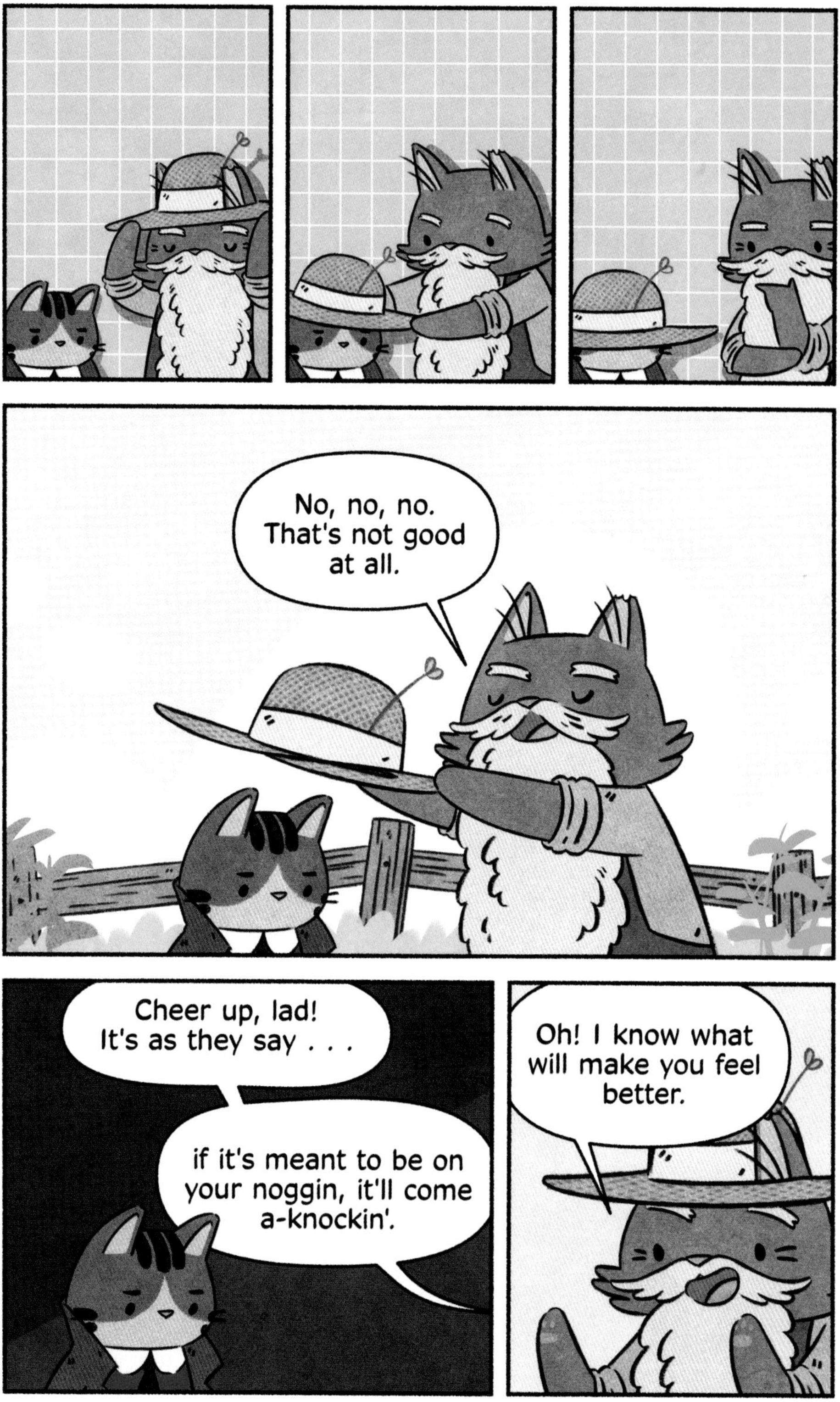
No, no, no. That's not good at all.
Cheer up, lad! It's as they say . . .
if it's meant to be on your noggin, it'll come a-knockin'.
Oh! I know what will make you feel better.

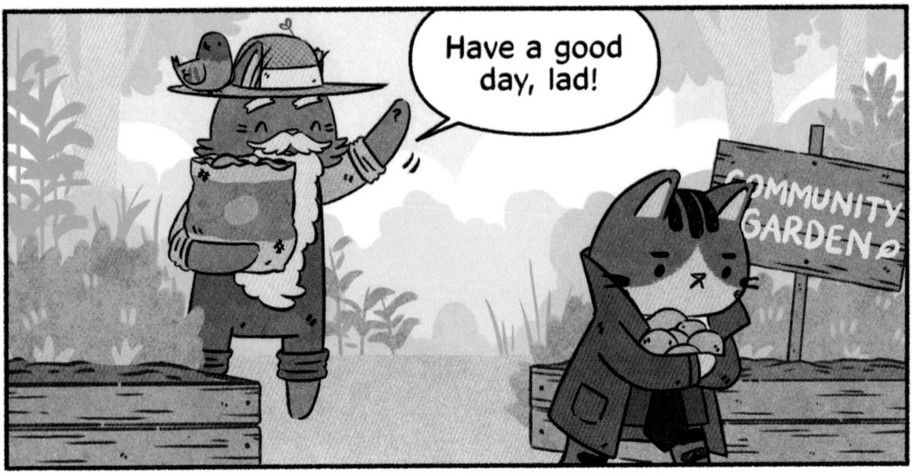
Have a good day, lad!
COMMUNITY GARDEN

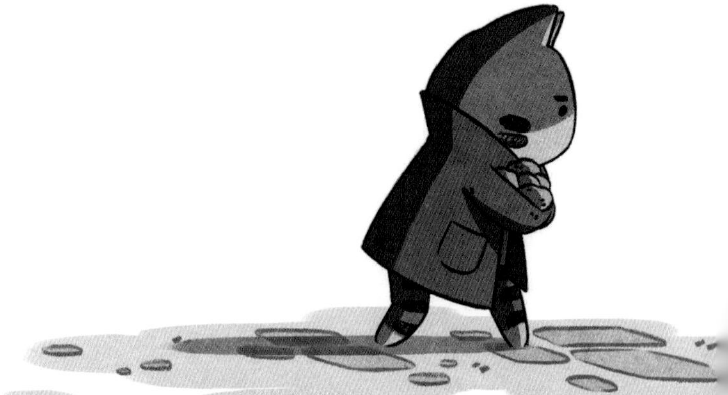

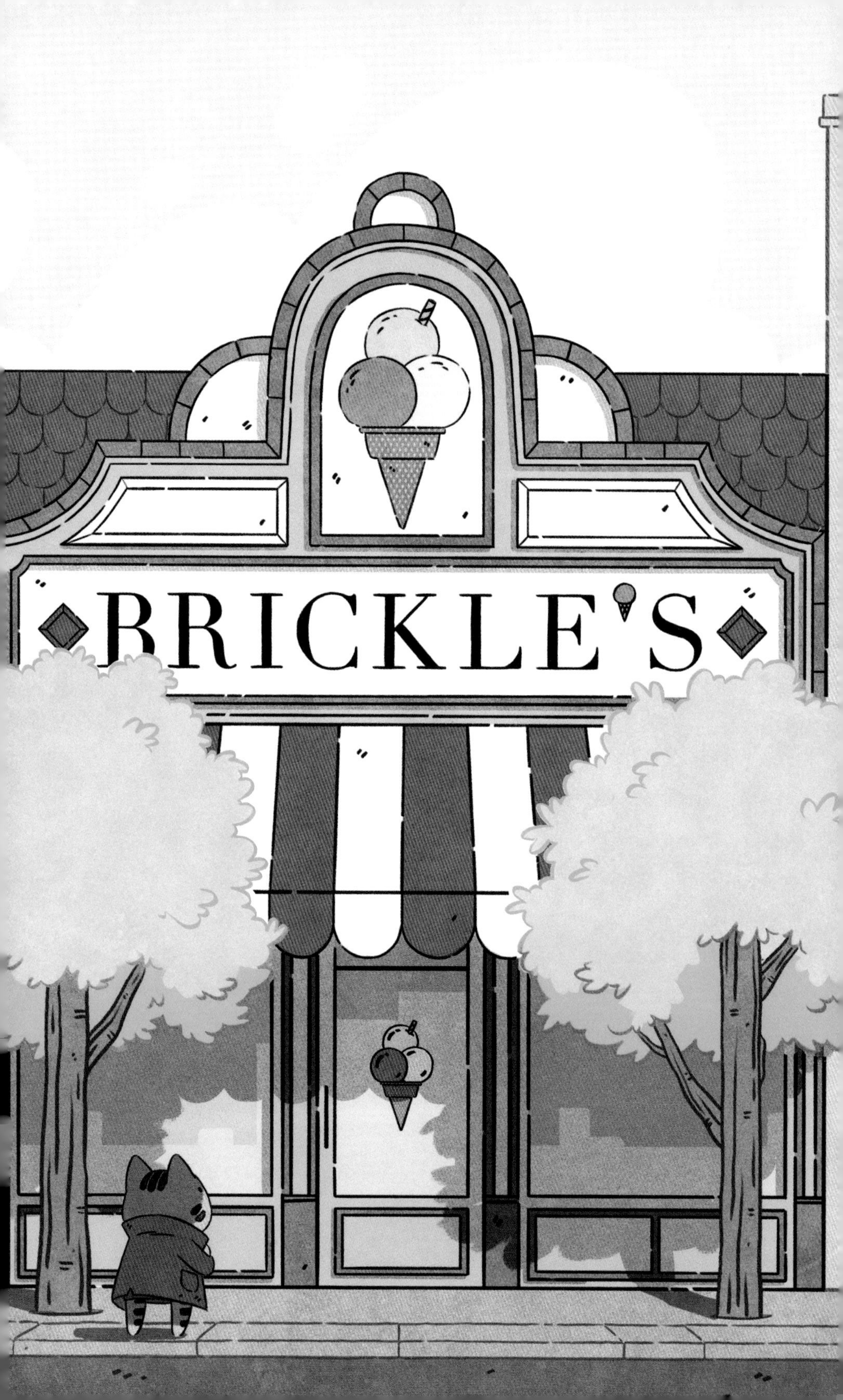
BRICKLE'S

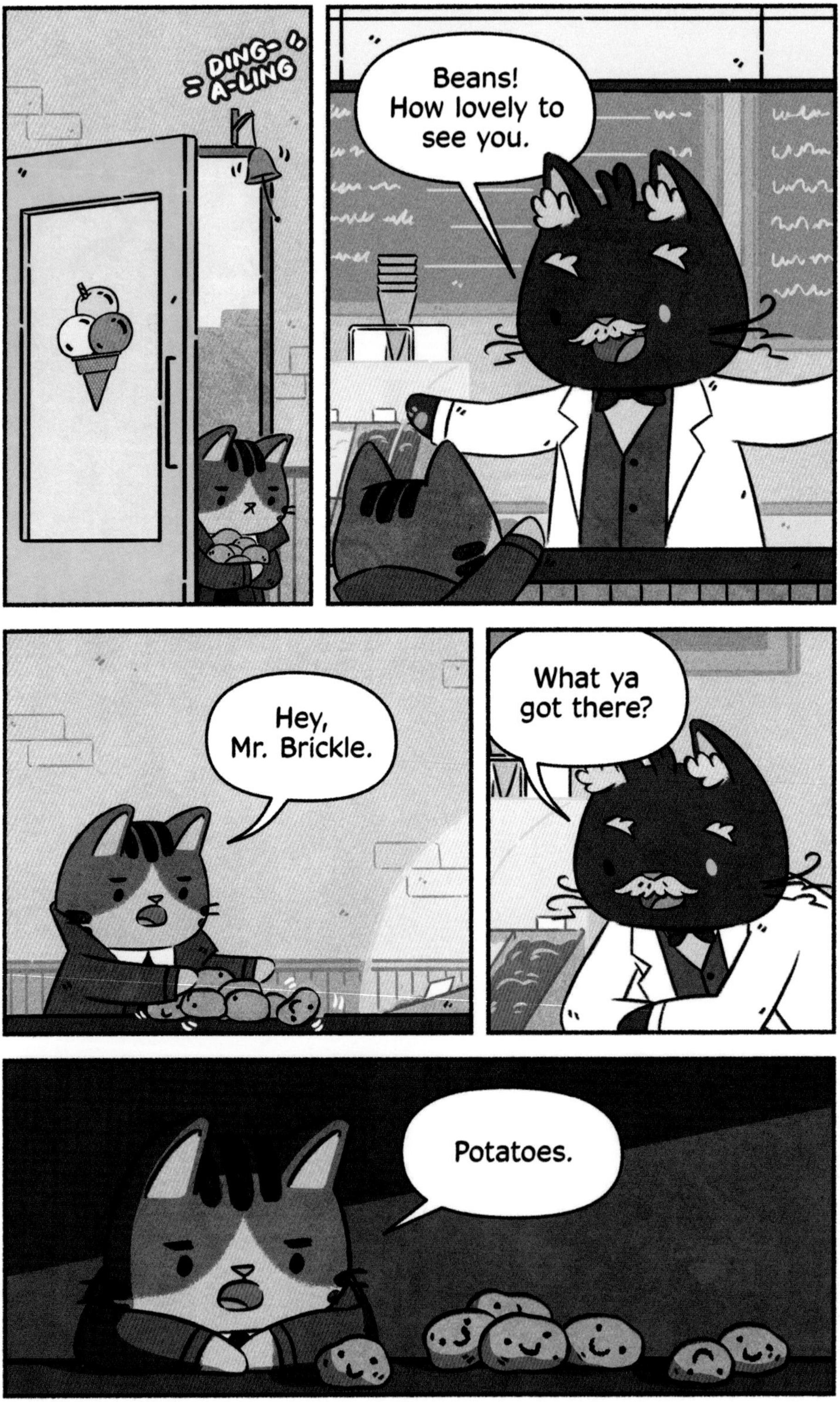
DING-A-LING
Beans! How lovely to see you.
Hey, Mr. Brickle.
What ya got there?
Potatoes.

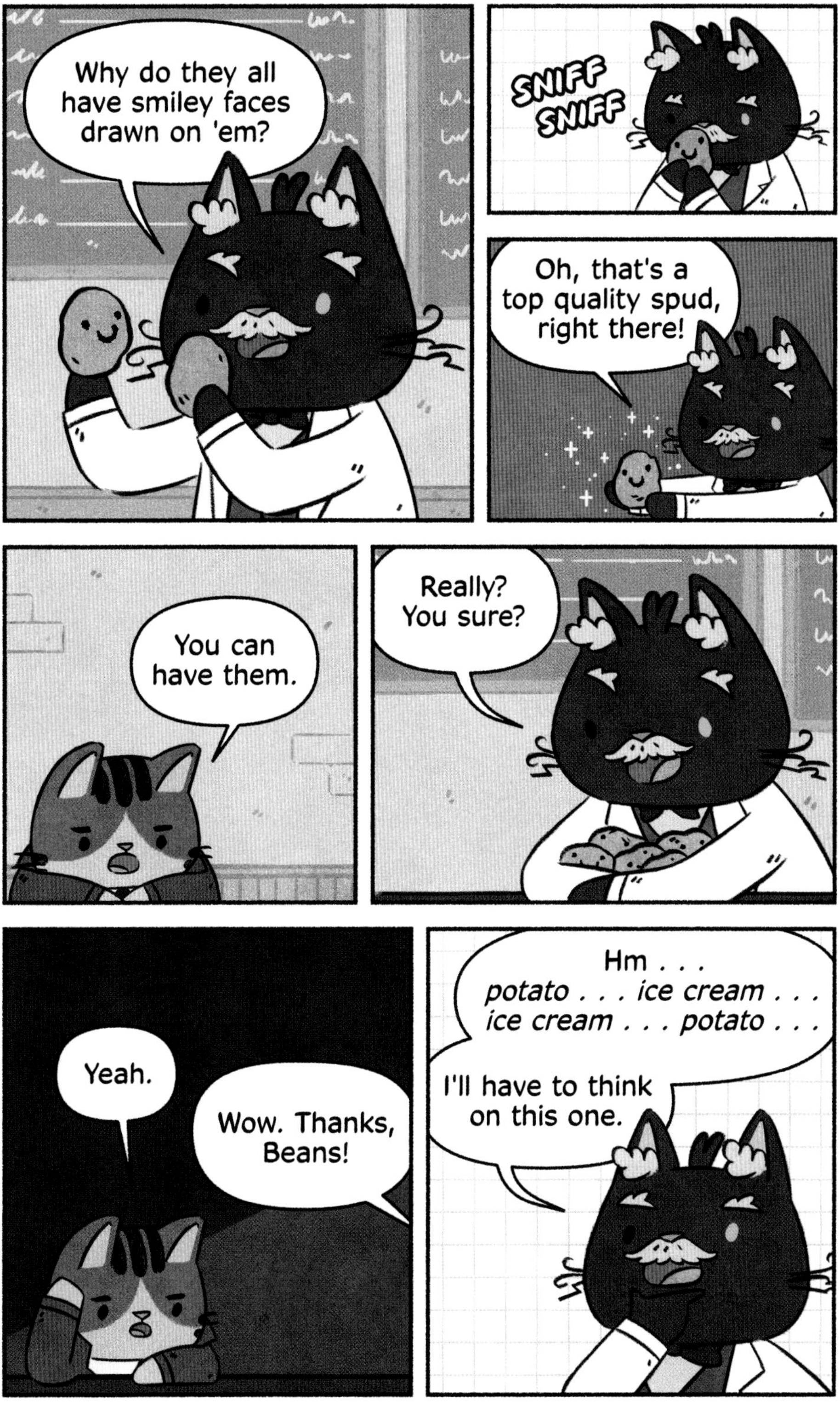
Why do they all have smiley faces drawn on 'em?
SNIFF SNIFF
Oh, that's a top quality spud, right there!
You can have them.
Really? You sure?
Yeah.
Wow. Thanks, Beans!
Hm . . . *potato . . . ice cream . . . ice cream . . . potato . . .*
I'll have to think on this one.

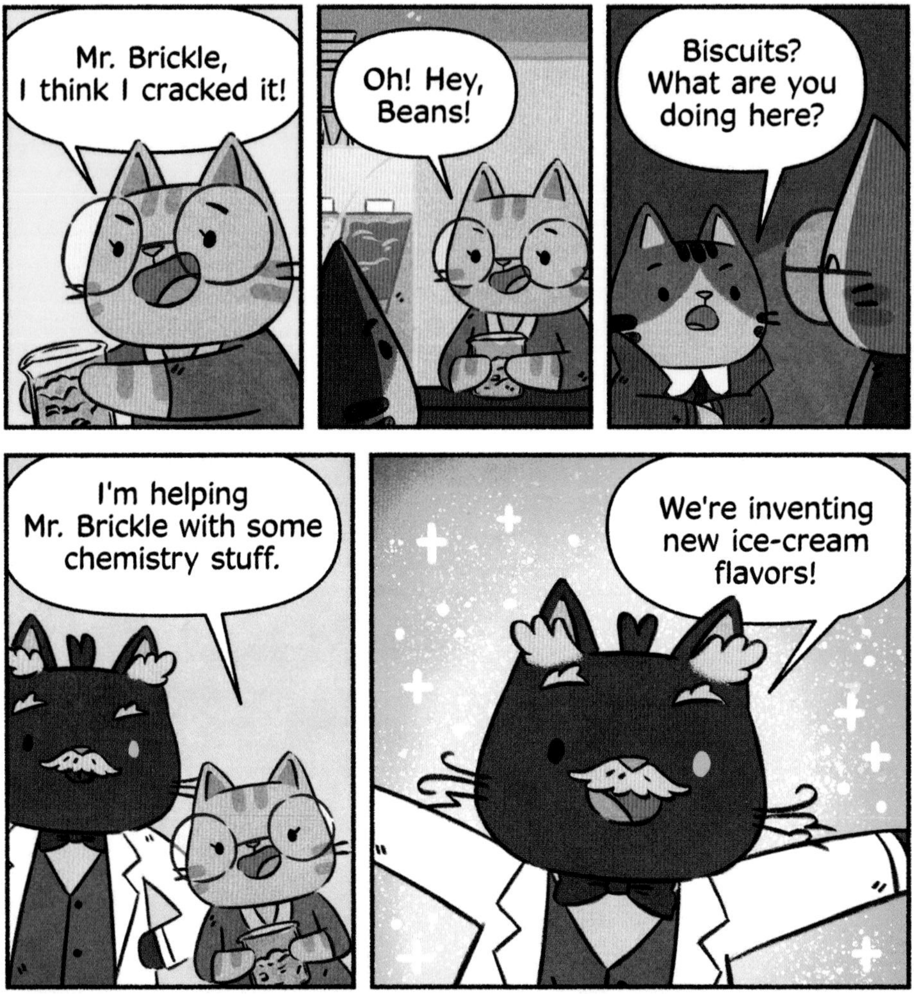
Mr. Brickle,
I think I cracked it!
Oh! Hey,
Beans!
Biscuits?
What are you
doing here?
I'm helping
Mr. Brickle with some
chemistry stuff.
We're inventing
new ice-cream
flavors!

PREVIOUS MR. BRICKLE FLAVORS:

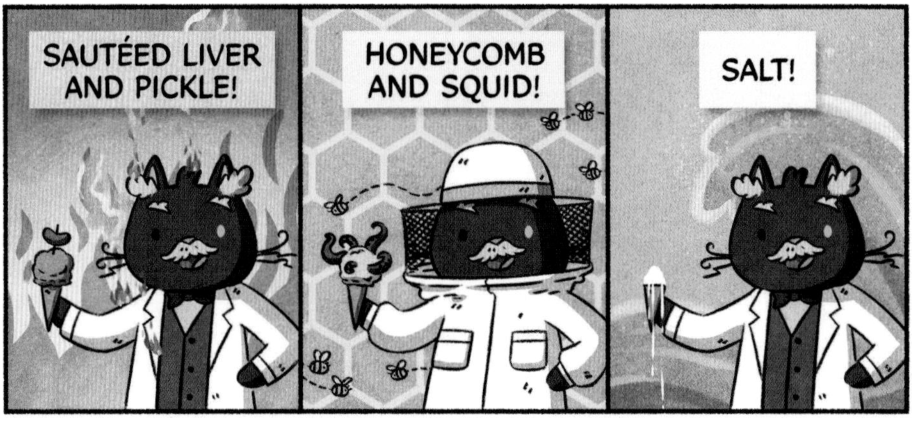
SAUTÉED LIVER
AND PICKLE!
HONEYCOMB
AND SQUID!
SALT!

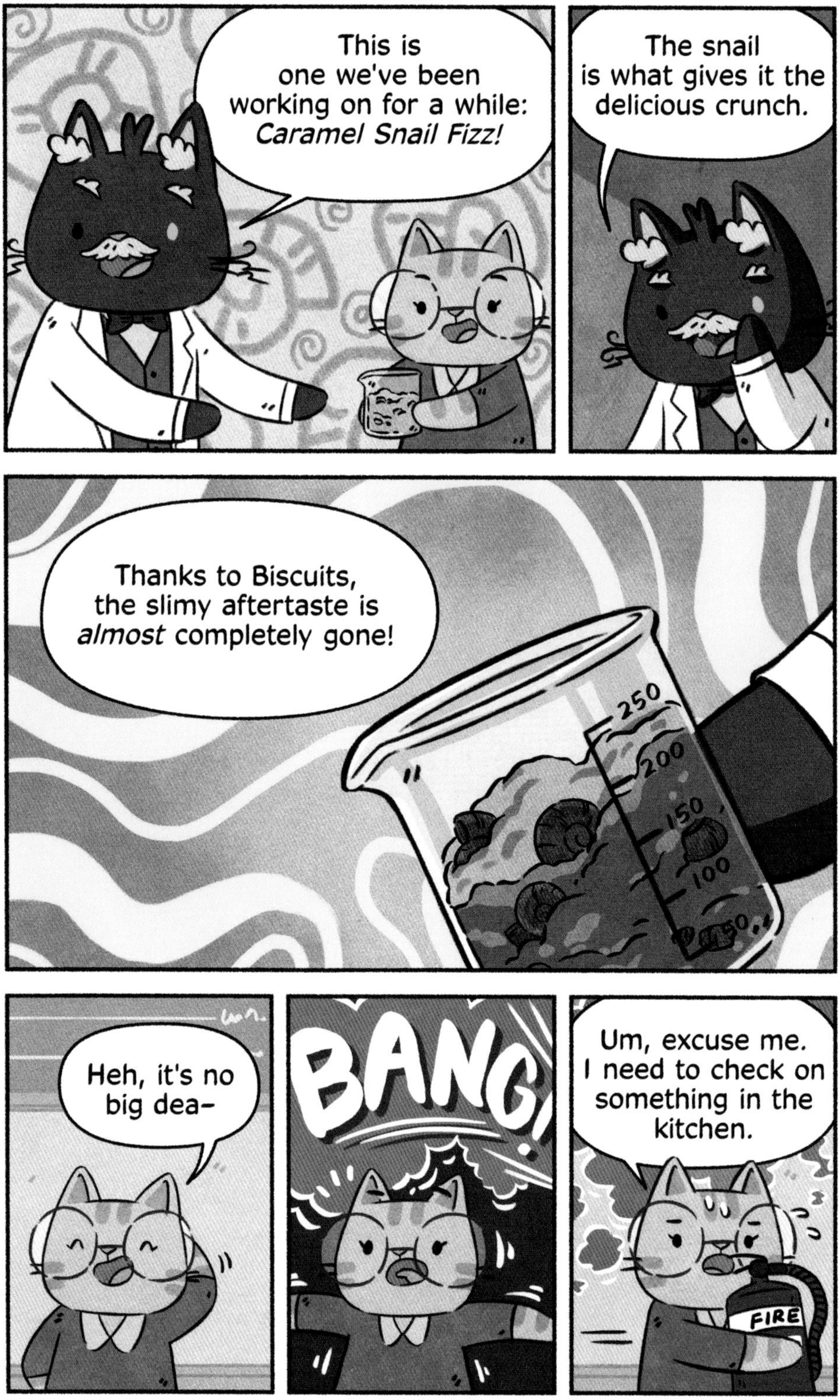
This is one we've been working on for a while: *Caramel Snail Fizz!*
The snail is what gives it the delicious crunch.
Thanks to Biscuits, the slimy aftertaste is *almost* completely gone!
250
200
150
100
50
Heh, it's no big dea-
BANG!
Um, excuse me. I need to check on something in the kitchen.
FIRE

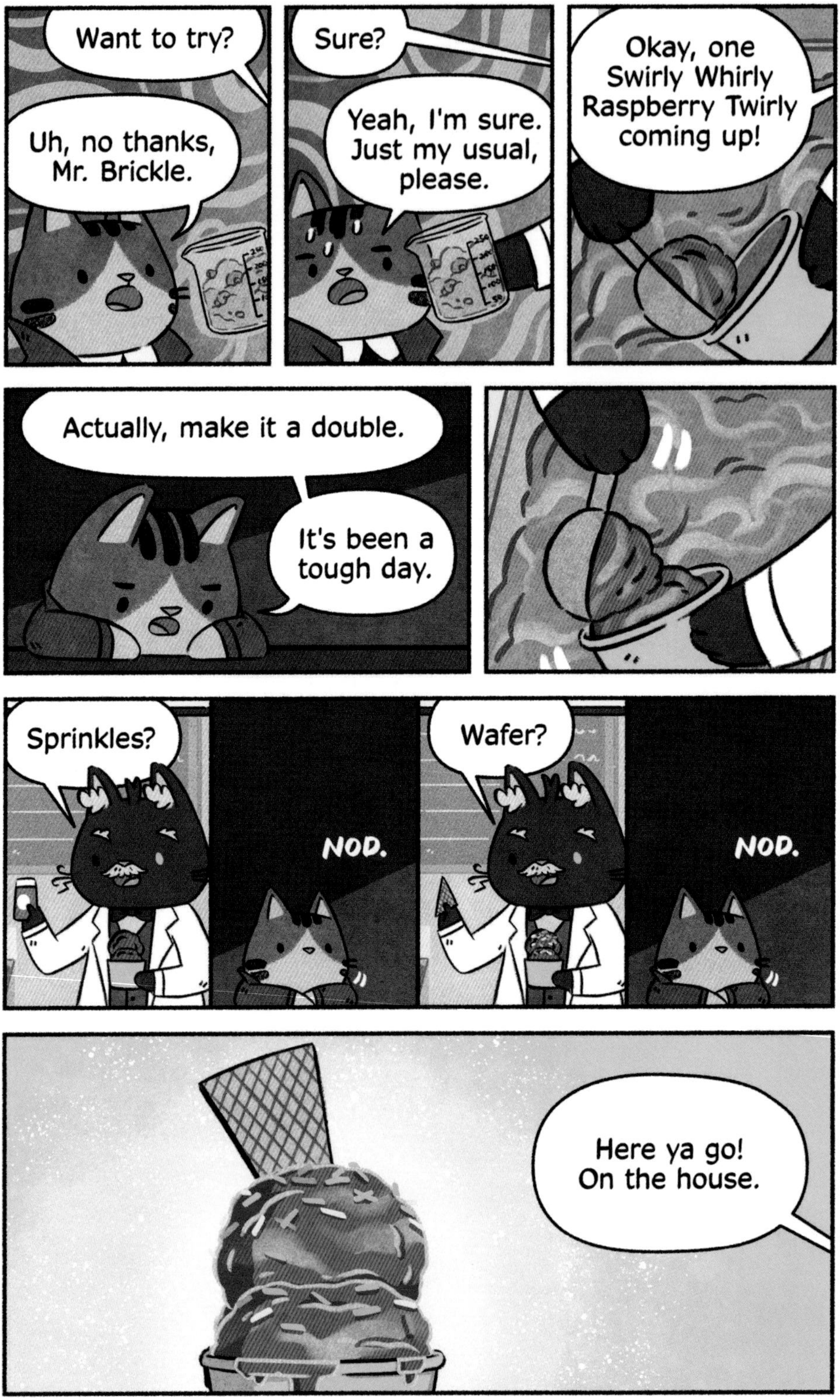
Want to try?
Uh, no thanks, Mr. Brickle.
Sure?
Yeah, I'm sure. Just my usual, please.
Okay, one Swirly Whirly Raspberry Twirly coming up!
Actually, make it a double.
It's been a tough day.
Sprinkles?
NOD.
Wafer?
NOD.
Here ya go! On the house.

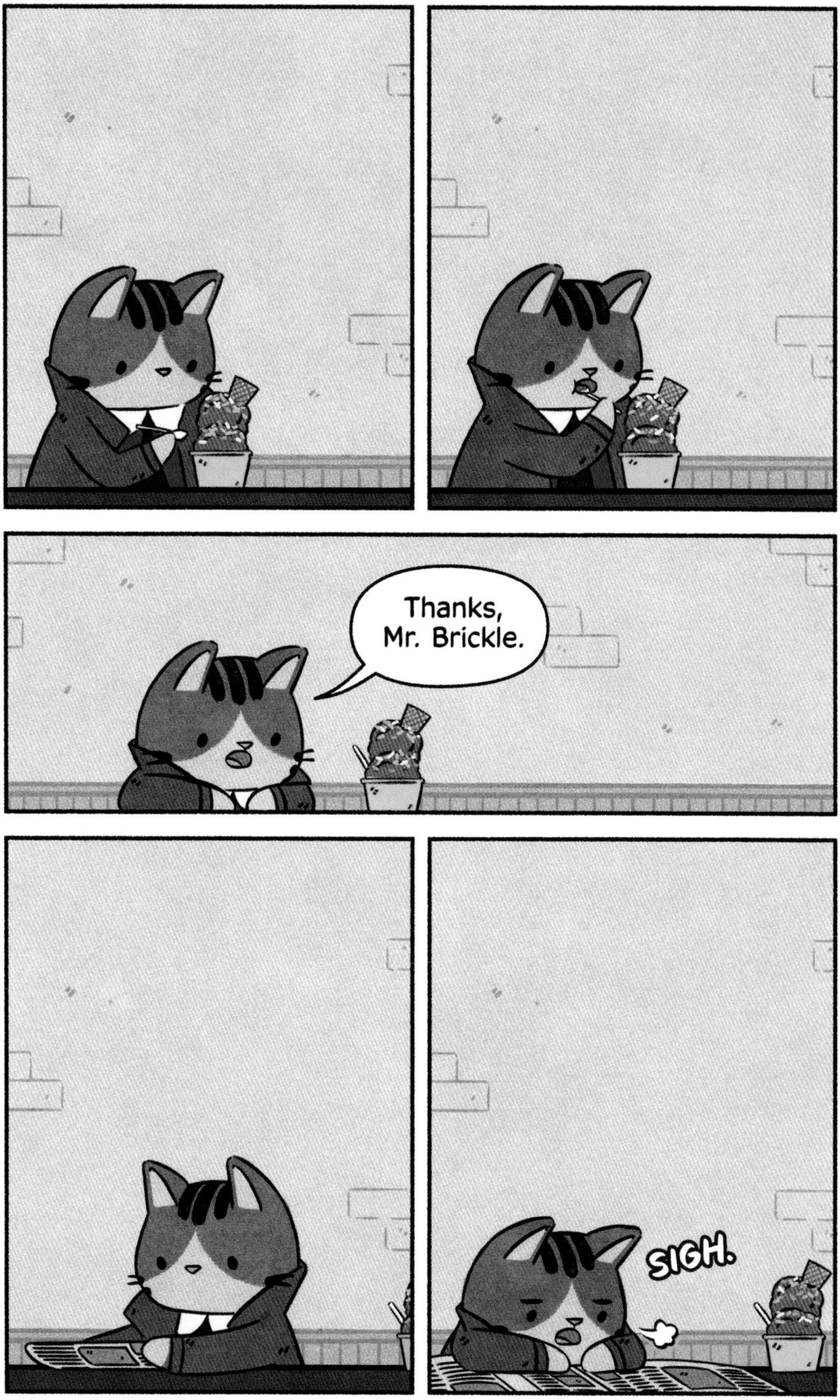
Thanks,
Mr. Brickle.
SIGH.

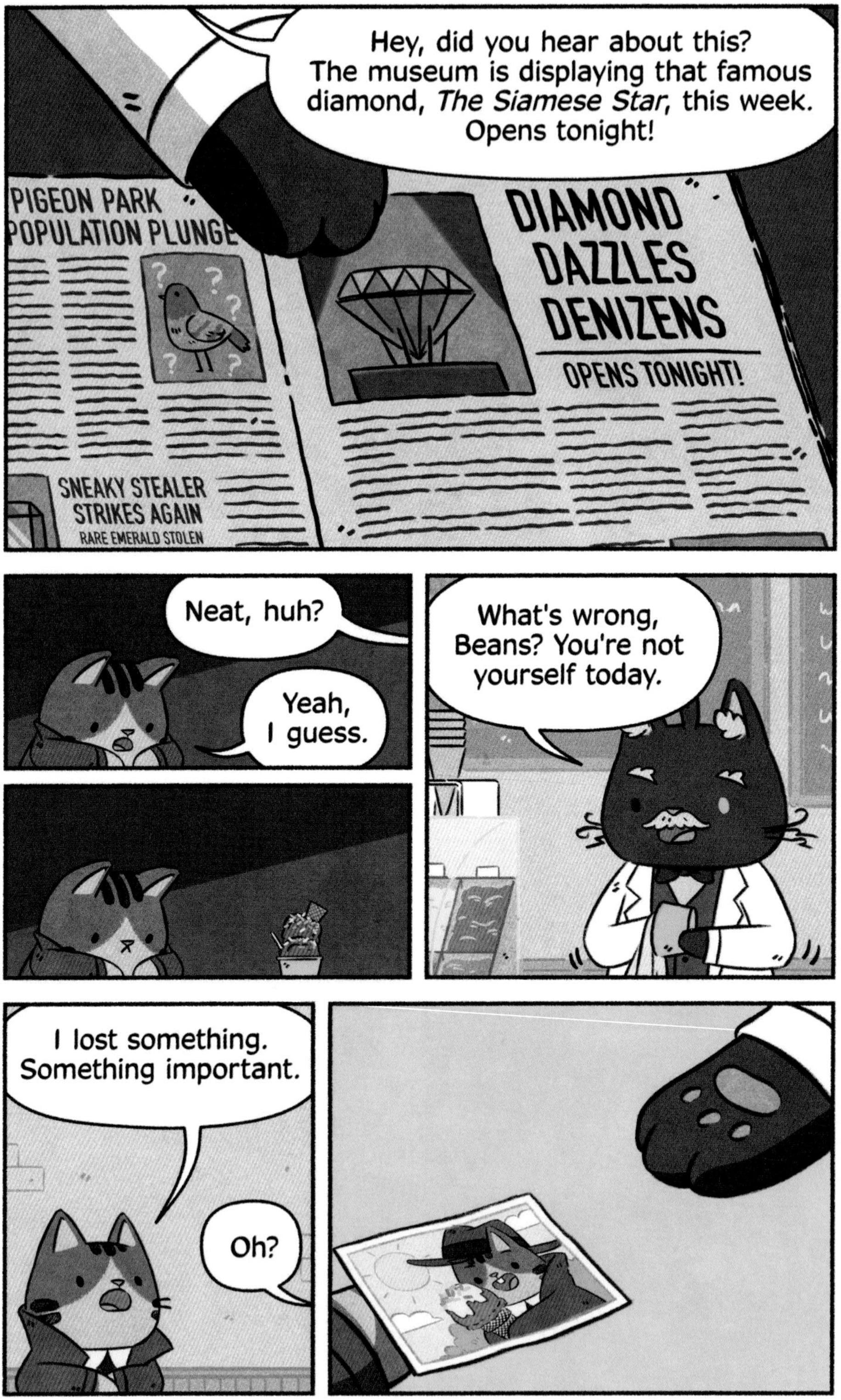

Hey, did you hear about this? The museum is displaying that famous diamond, *The Siamese Star*, this week. Opens tonight!
PIGEON PARK POPULATION PLUNGE
DIAMOND DAZZLES DENIZENS
OPENS TONIGHT!
SNEAKY STEALER STRIKES AGAIN
RARE EMERALD STOLEN
Neat, huh?
Yeah, I guess.
What's wrong, Beans? You're not yourself today.
I lost something. Something important.
Oh?

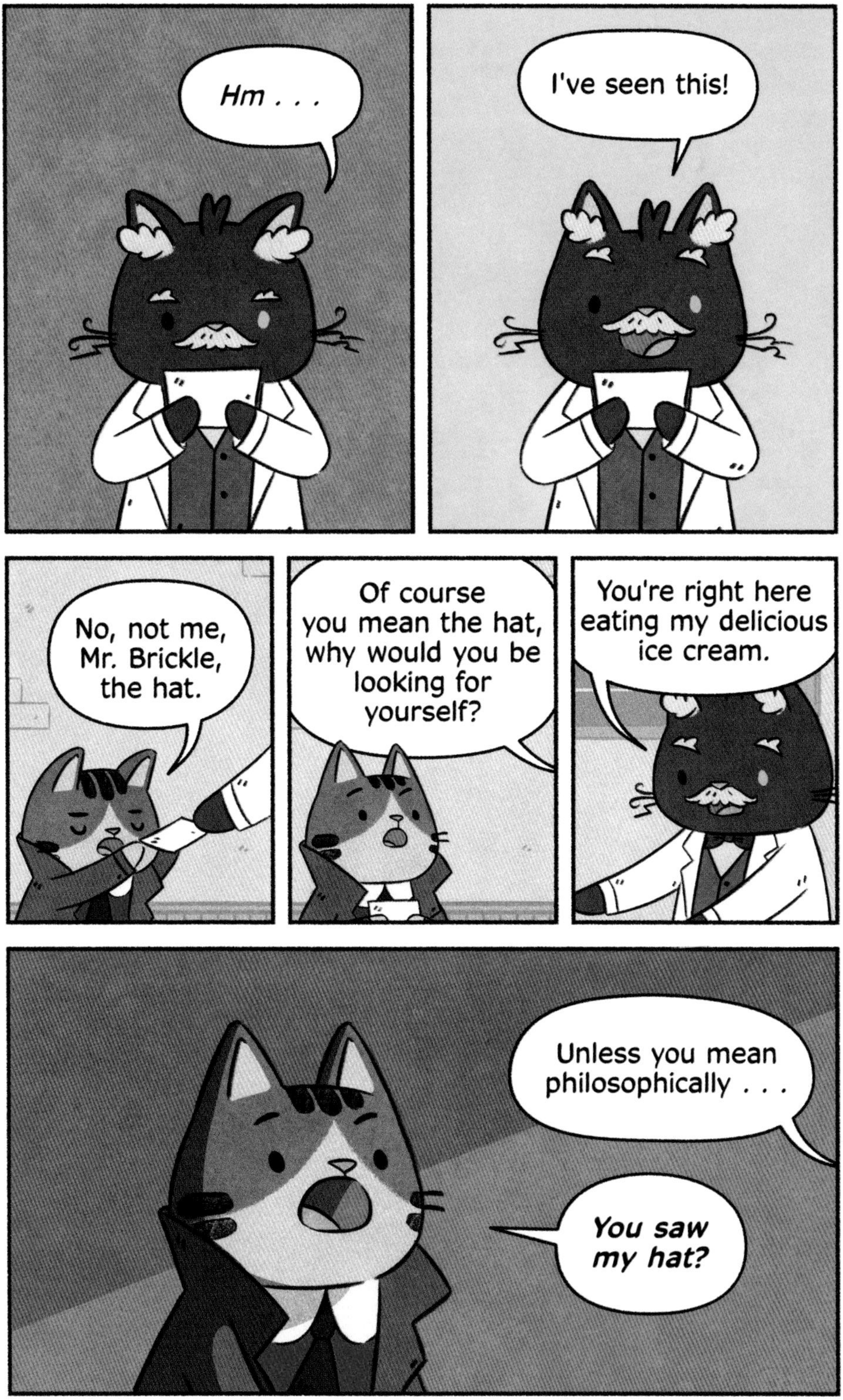
Hm . . .
I've seen this!
No, not me, Mr. Brickle, the hat.
Of course you mean the hat, why would you be looking for yourself?
You're right here eating my delicious ice cream.
Unless you mean philosophically . . .
You saw my hat?

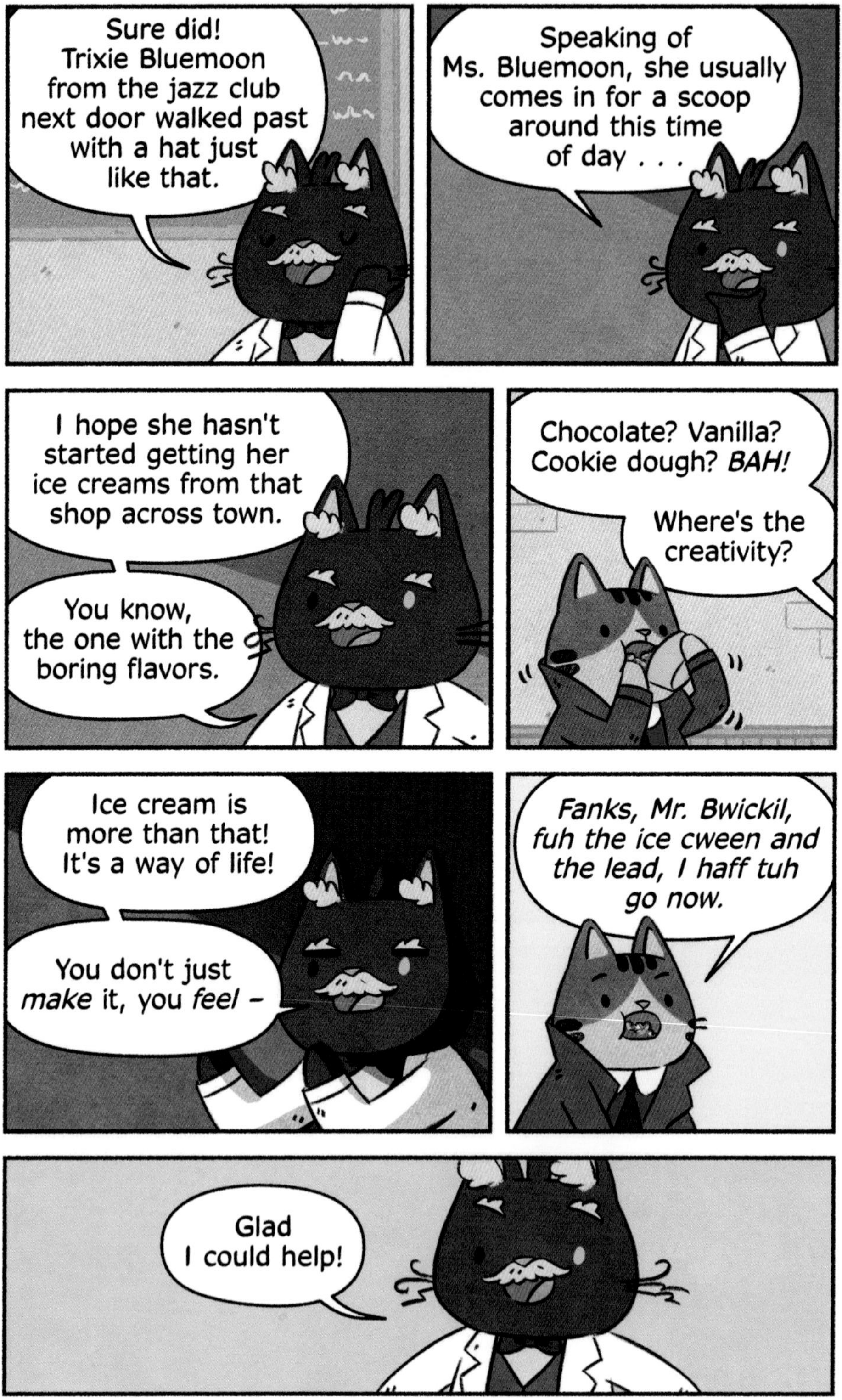
Sure did! Trixie Bluemoon from the jazz club next door walked past with a hat just like that.
Speaking of Ms. Bluemoon, she usually comes in for a scoop around this time of day . . .
I hope she hasn't started getting her ice creams from that shop across town.
You know, the one with the boring flavors.
Chocolate? Vanilla? Cookie dough? *BAH!*
Where's the creativity?
Ice cream is more than that! It's a way of life!
You don't just *make* it, you *feel* –
Fanks, Mr. Bwickil, fuh the ice cween and the lead, I haff tuh go now.
Glad I could help!

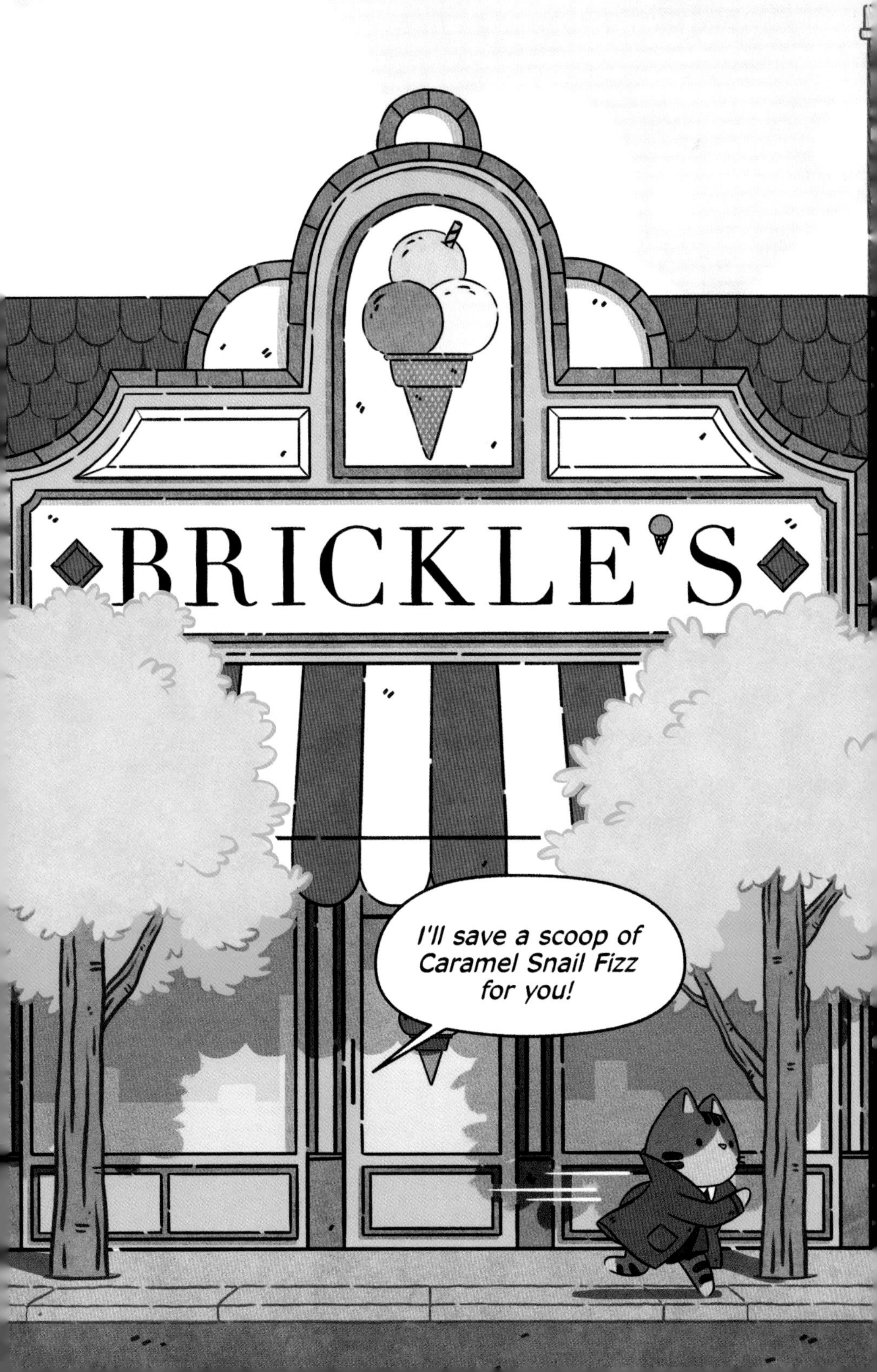
BRICKLE'S
I'll save a scoop of Caramel Snail Fizz for you!

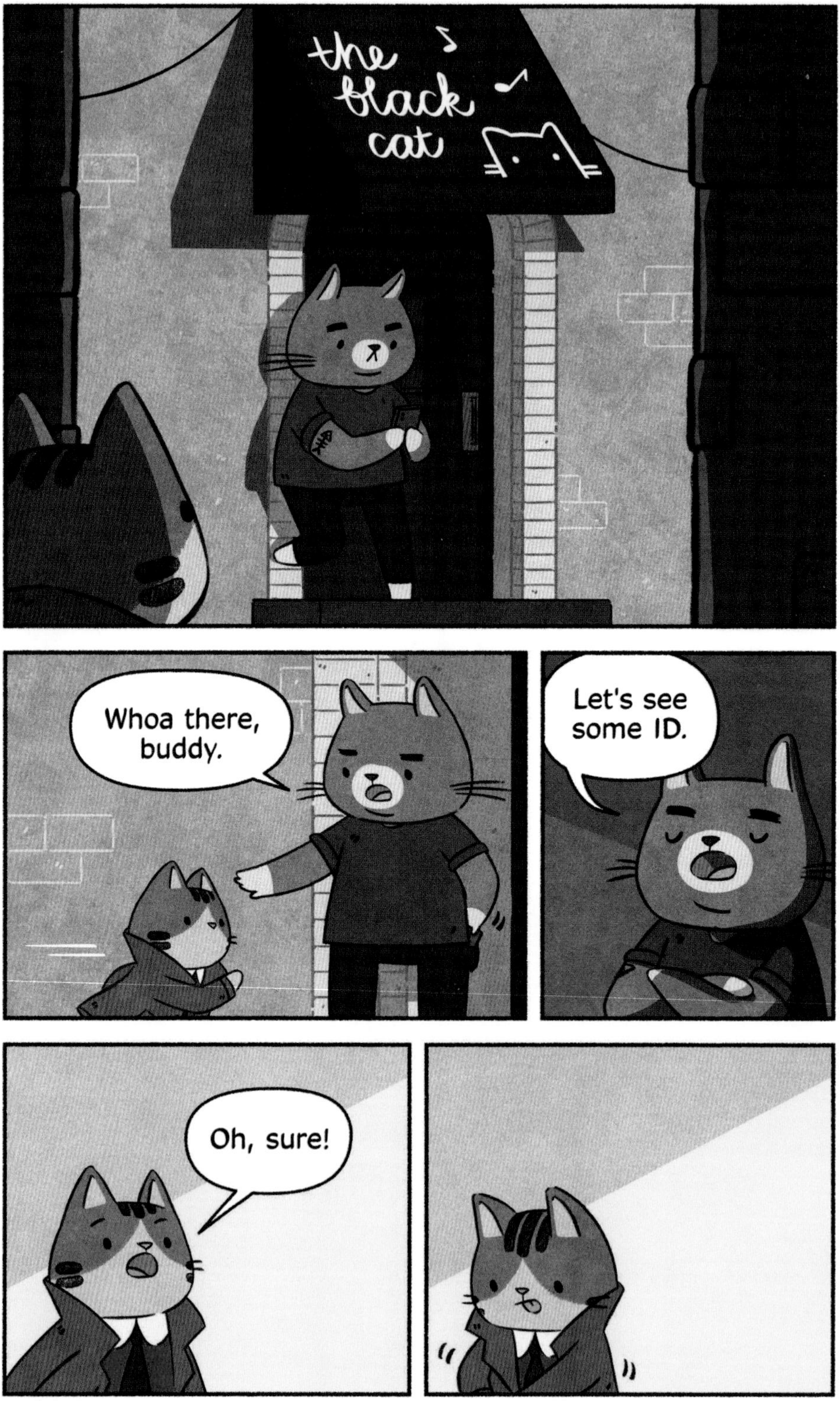
the black cat
Whoa there, buddy.
Let's see some ID.
Oh, sure!

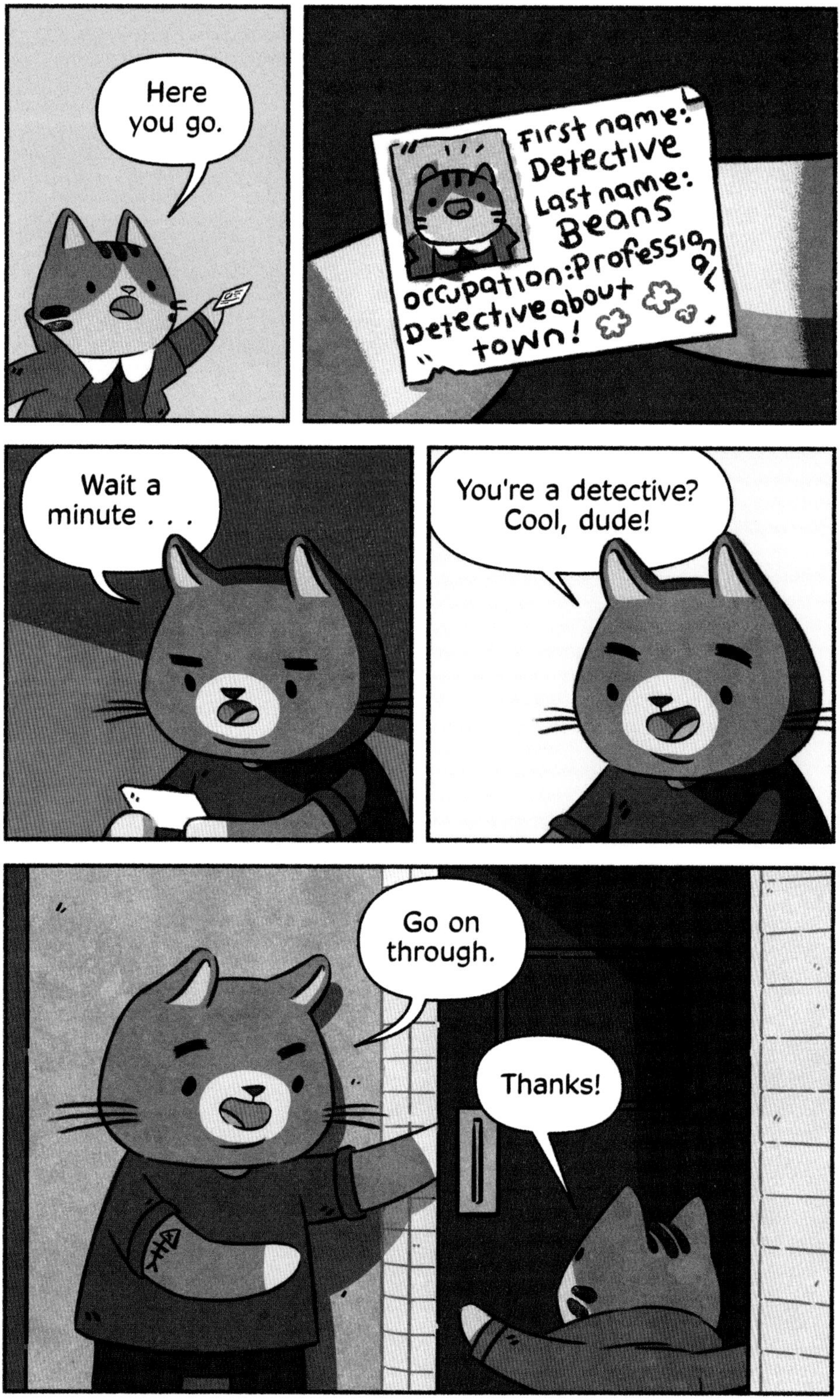

Here you go.
First name: Detective
Last name: Beans
occupation: Professional Detective about town!
Wait a minute . . .
You're a detective? Cool, dude!
Go on through.
Thanks!

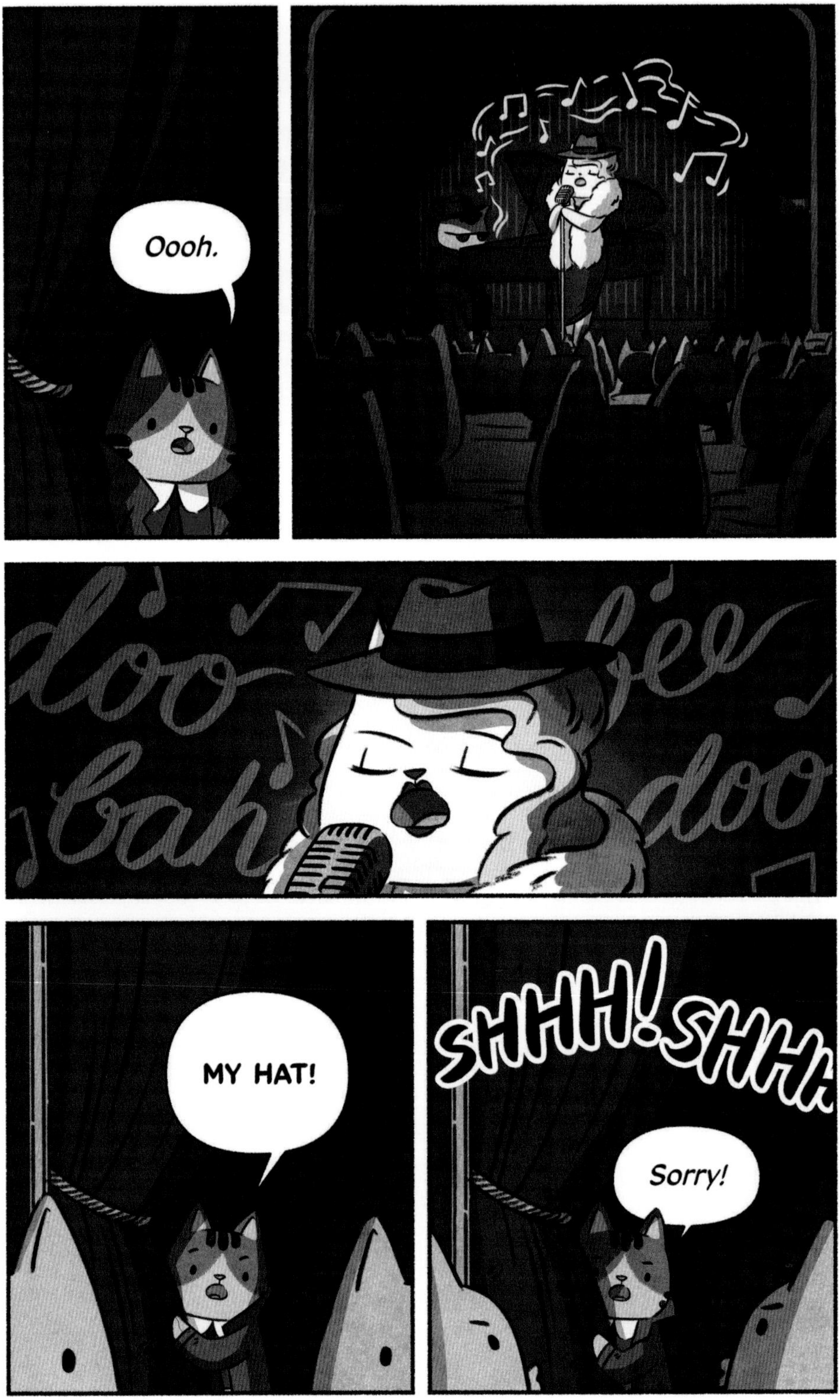
Oooh.
doo bee
bah doo
MY HAT!
SHHH!
Sorry!

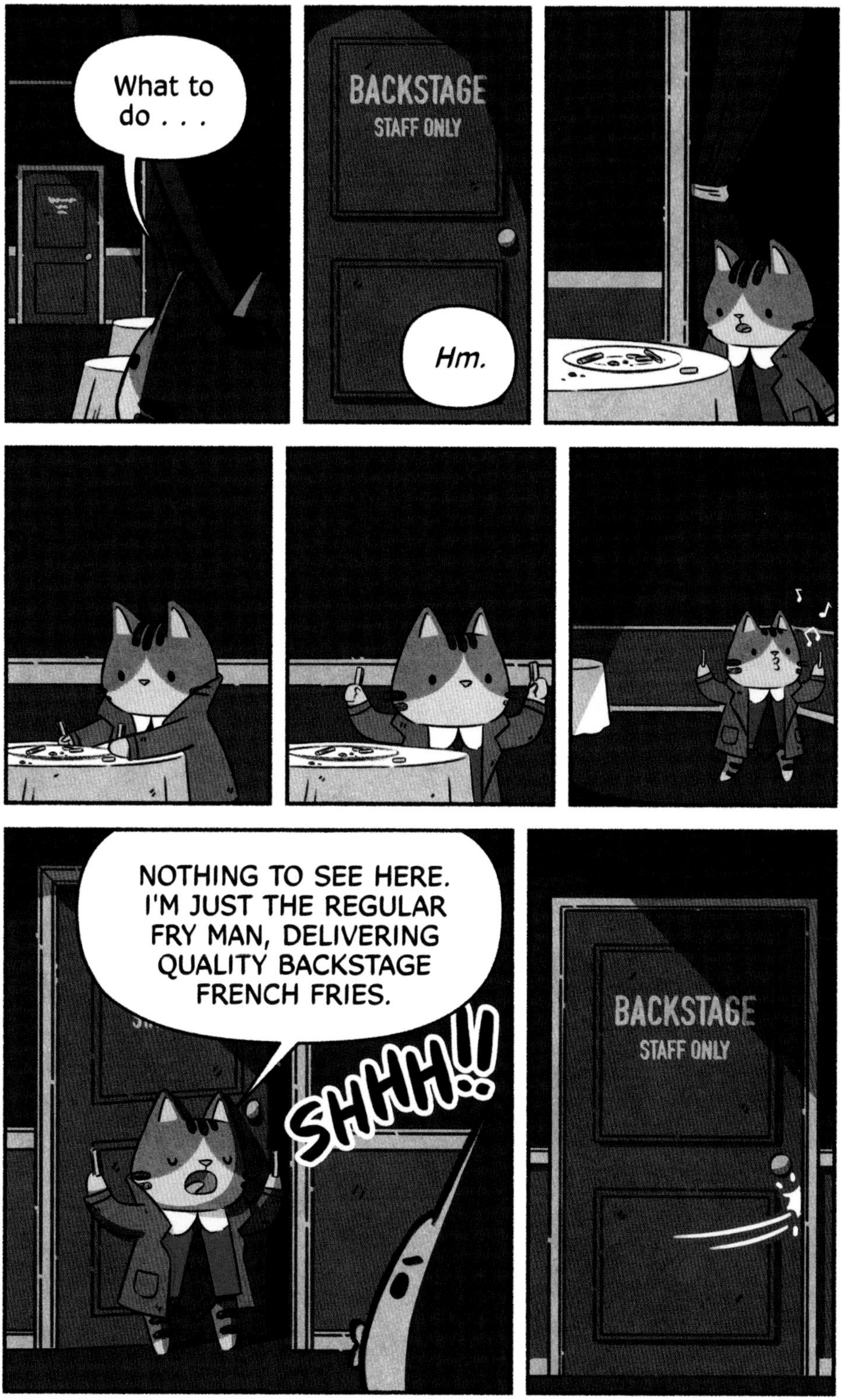
What to do . . .
BACKSTAGE
STAFF ONLY
Hm.
NOTHING TO SEE HERE. I'M JUST THE REGULAR FRY MAN, DELIVERING QUALITY BACKSTAGE FRENCH FRIES.
SHHH!!
BACKSTAGE
STAFF ONLY

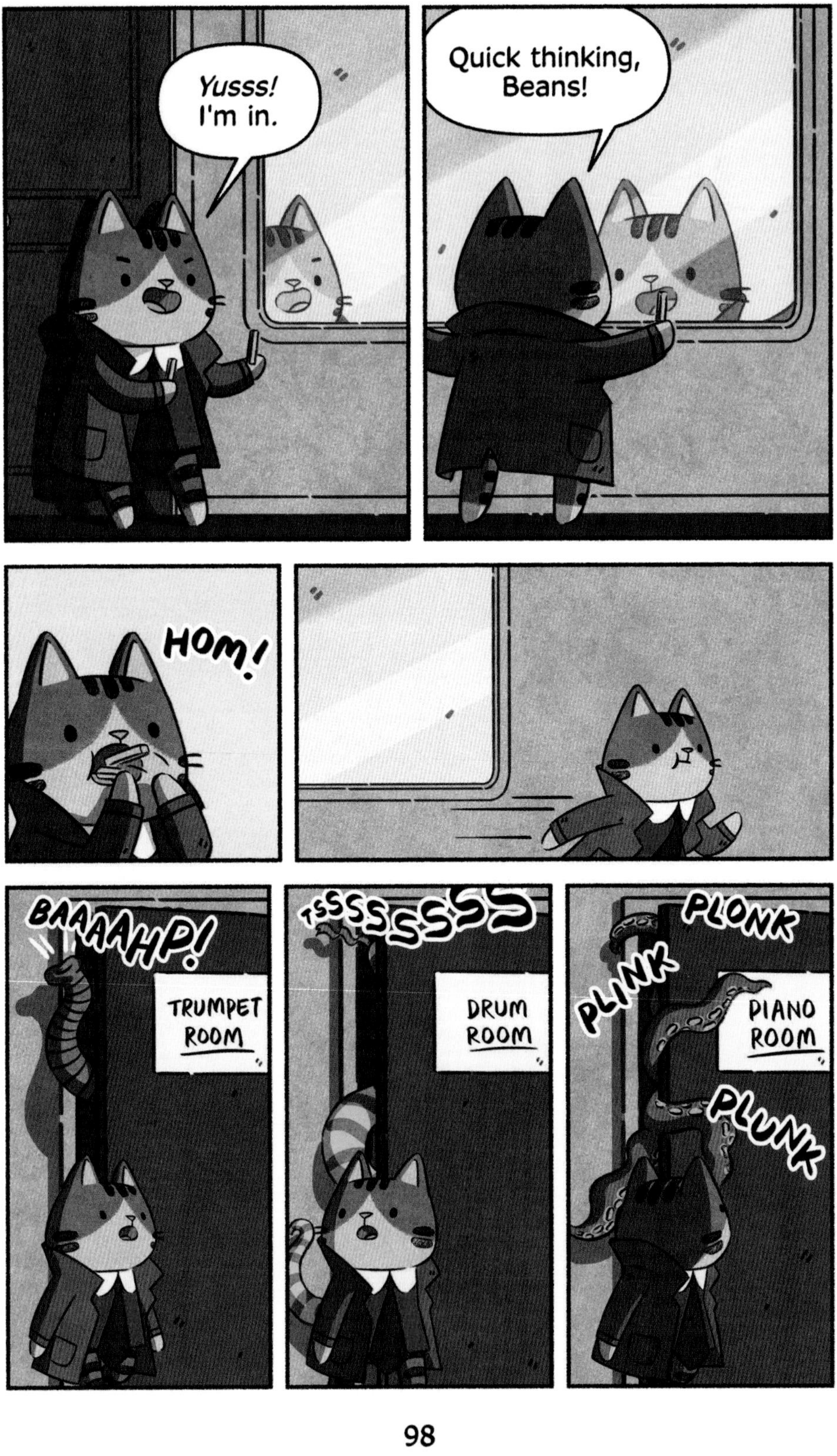
Yusss!
I'm in.
Quick thinking,
Beans!
HOM!
BAAAAHP!
TRUMPET
ROOM
TSSSSSSSSS
DRUM
ROOM
PLONK
PLINK
PIANO
ROOM
PLUNK

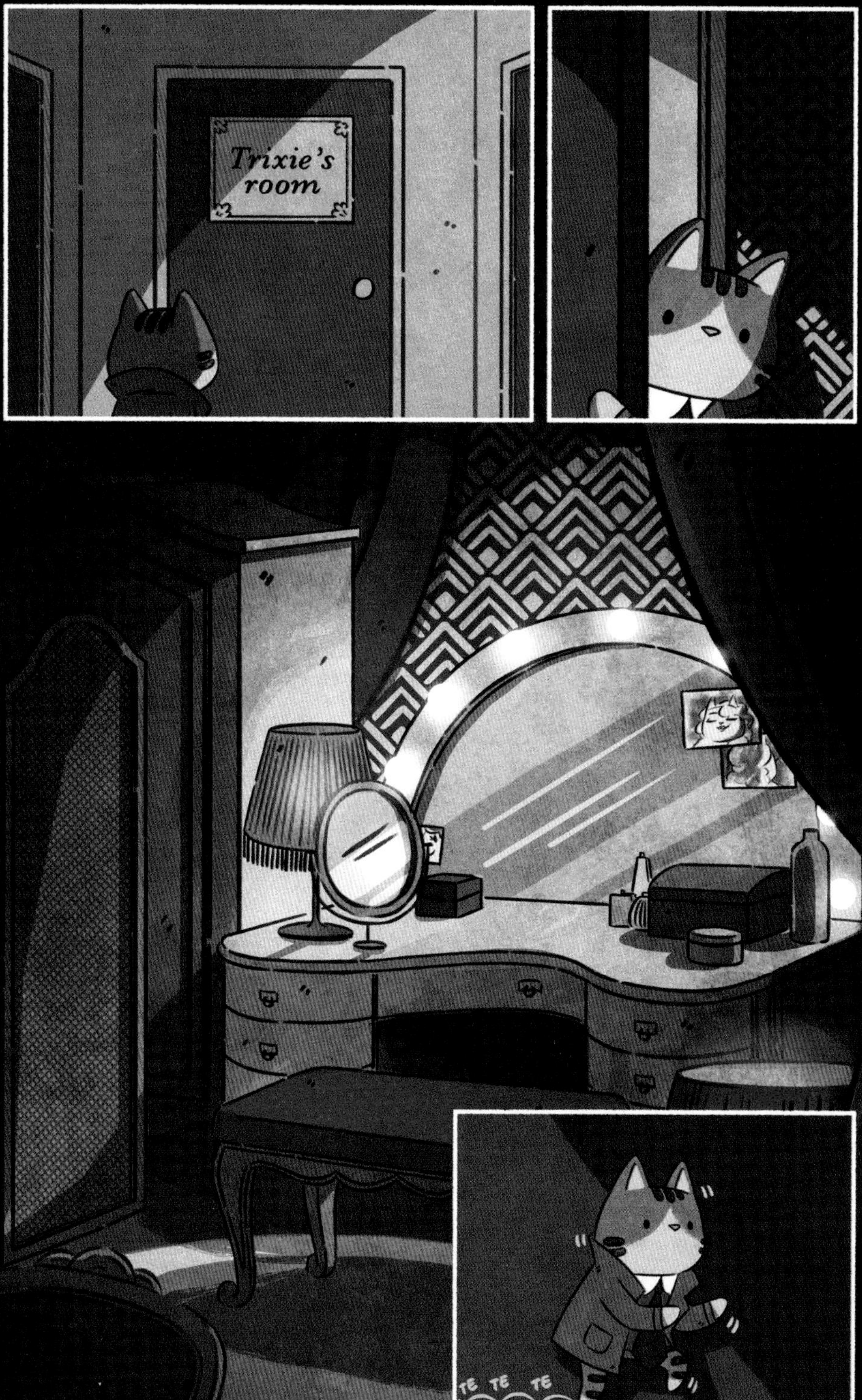
Trixie's room
TE TE TE

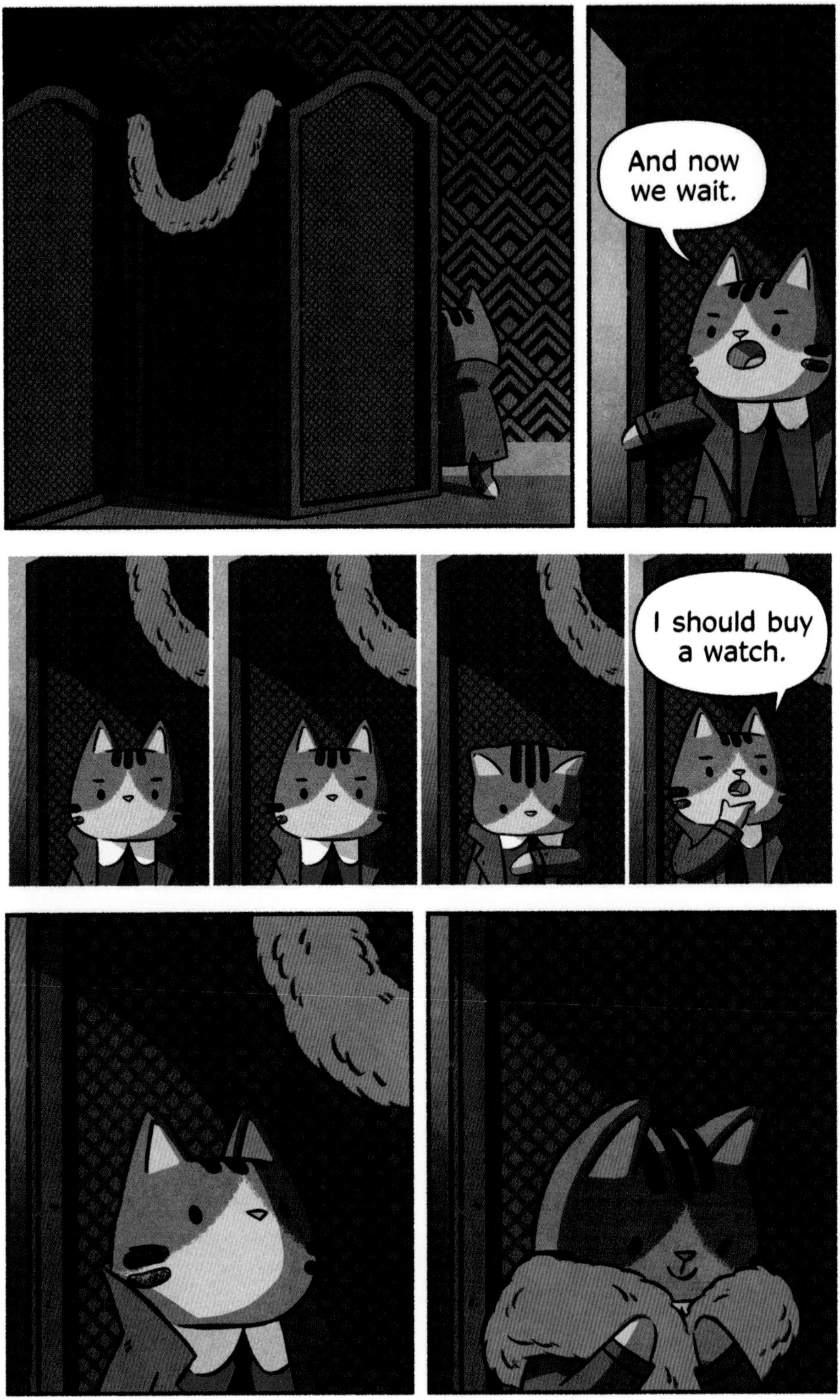
And now we wait.
I should buy a watch.

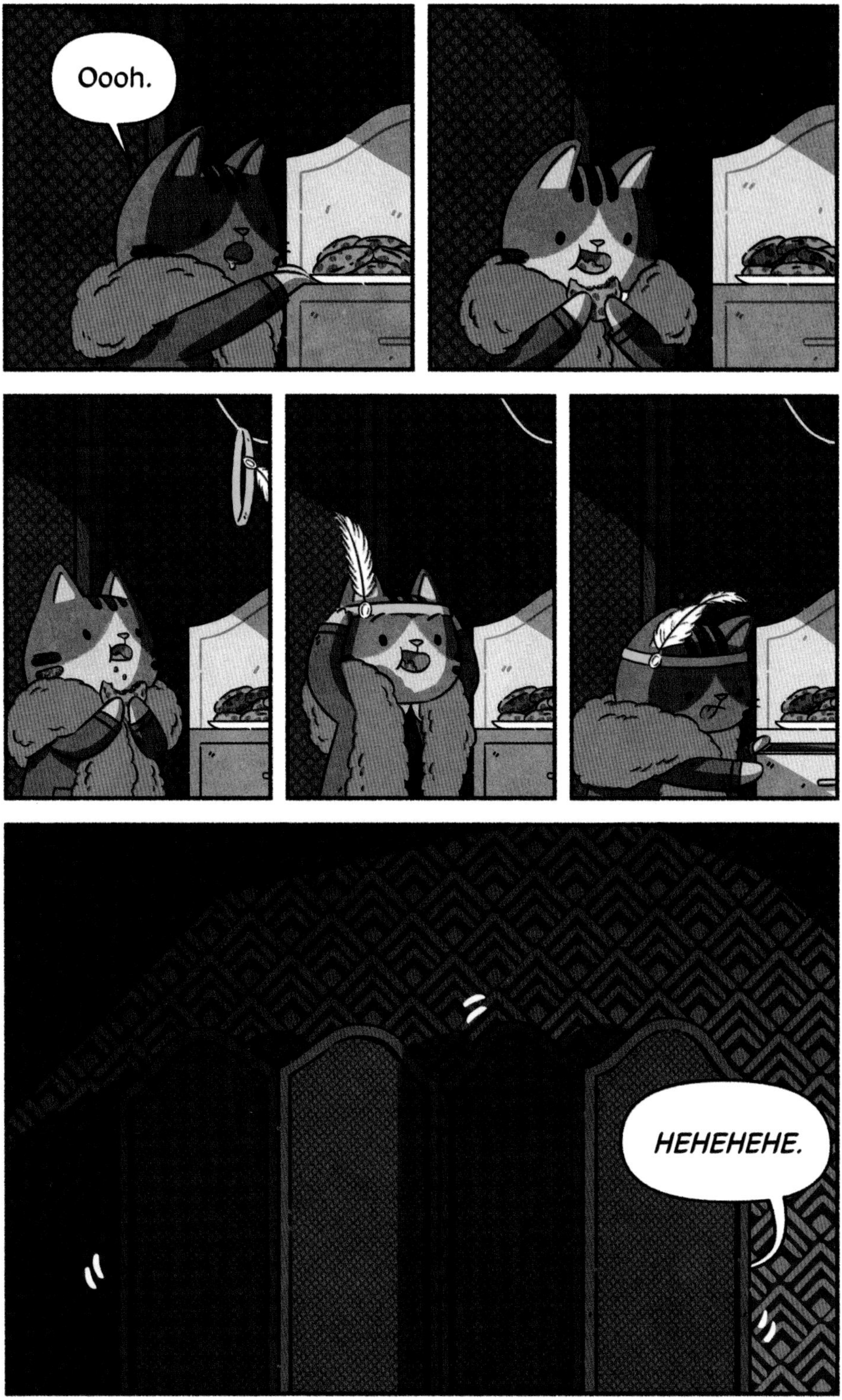
Oooh.
HEHEHEHE.

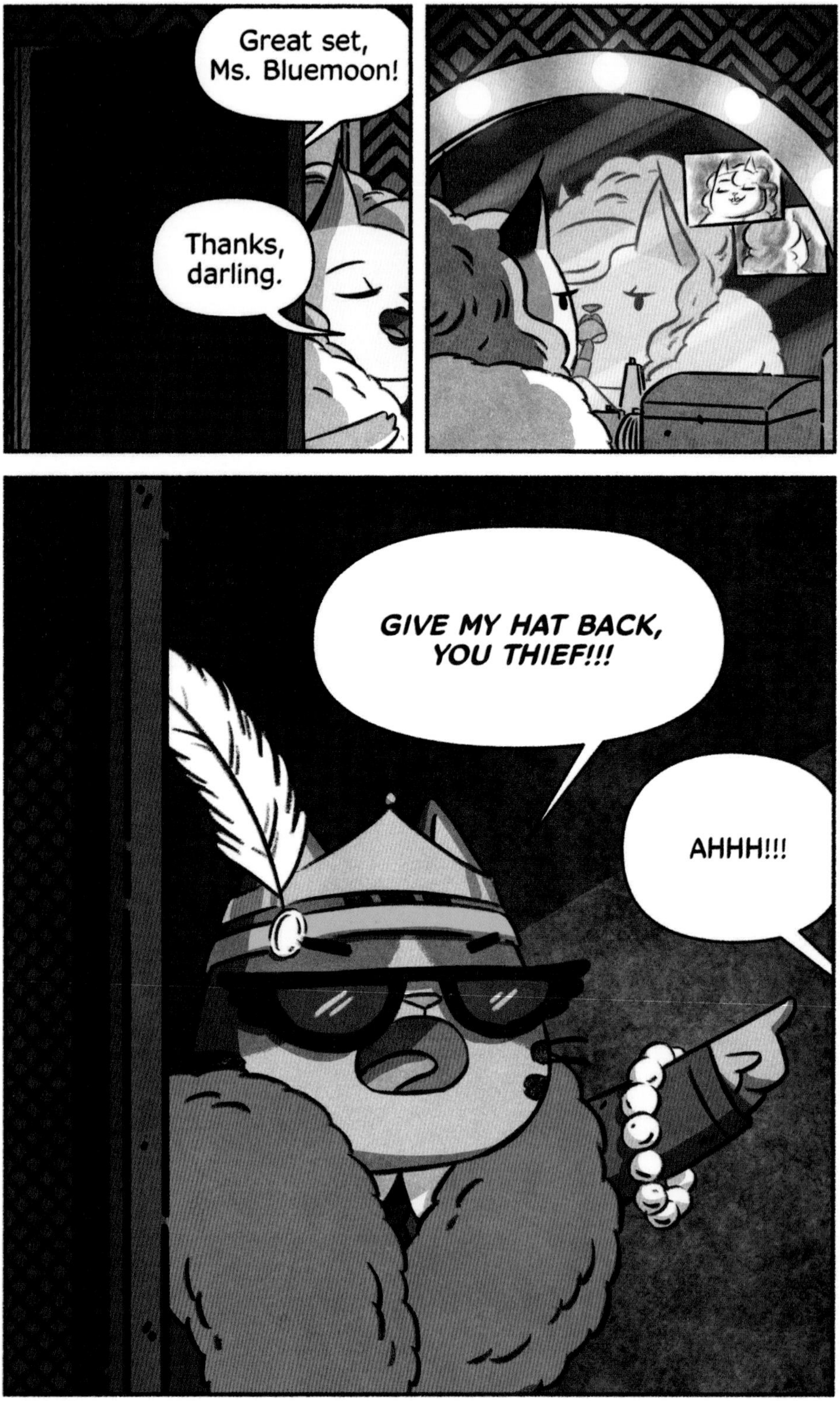

Great set, Ms. Bluemoon!
Thanks, darling.
GIVE MY HAT BACK, YOU THIEF!!!
AHHH!!!

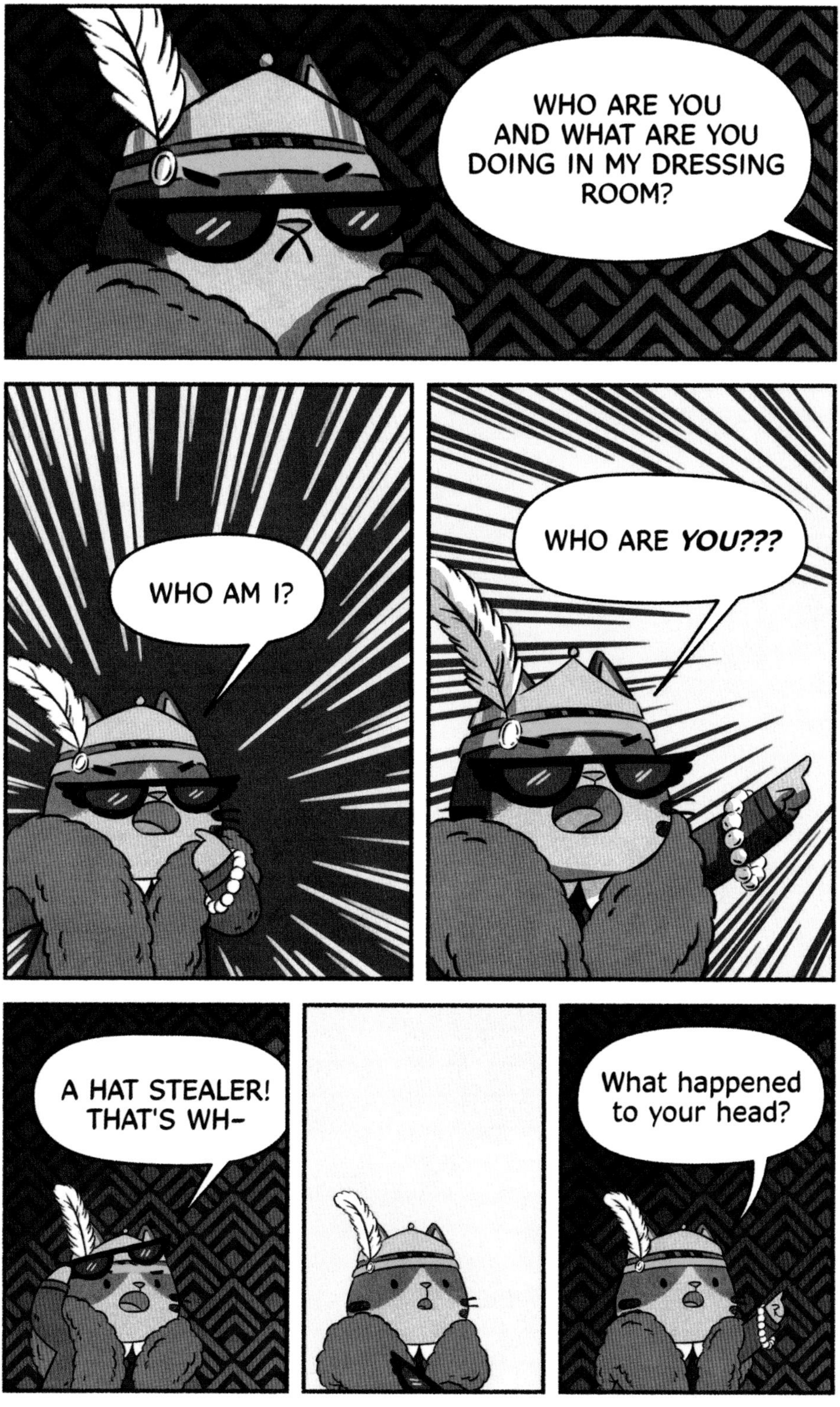
WHO ARE YOU AND WHAT ARE YOU DOING IN MY DRESSING ROOM?
WHO AM I?
WHO ARE *YOU???*
A HAT STEALER! THAT'S WH-
What happened to your head?

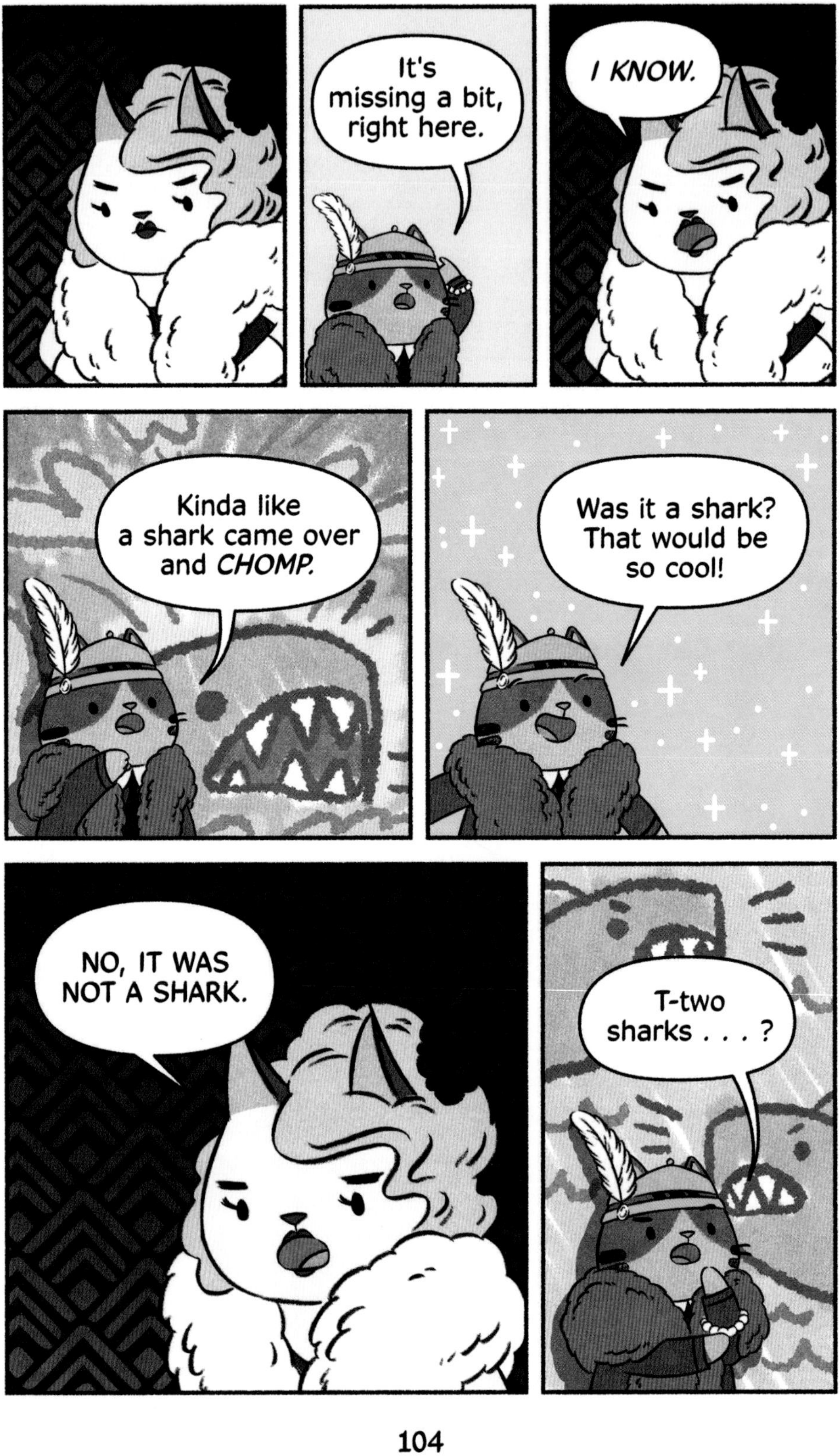
It's missing a bit, right here.
I KNOW.
Kinda like a shark came over and CHOMP.
Was it a shark? That would be so cool!
NO, IT WAS NOT A SHARK.
T-two sharks . . . ?

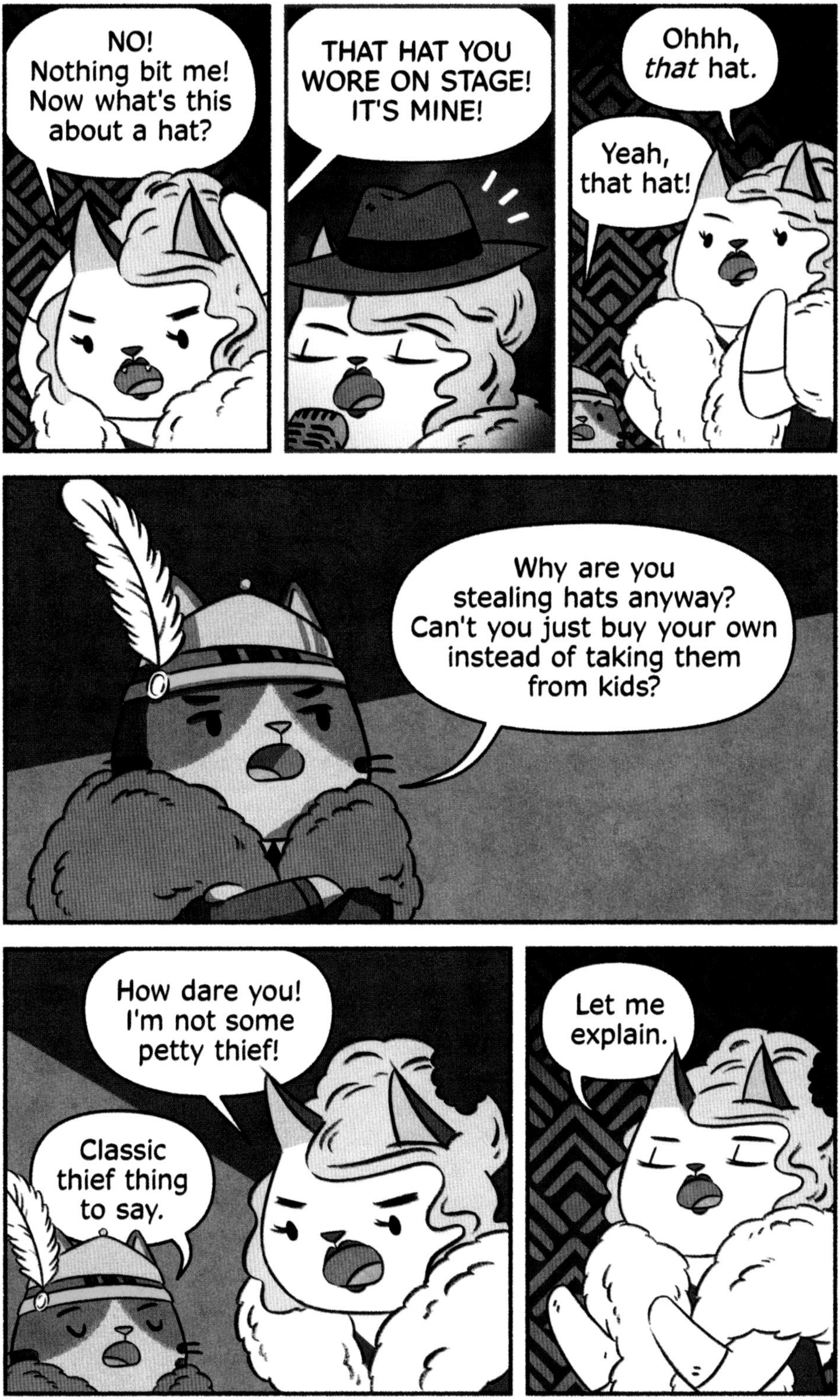
NO! Nothing bit me! Now what's this about a hat?
THAT HAT YOU WORE ON STAGE! IT'S MINE!
Ohhh, *that* hat.
Yeah, that hat!
Why are you stealing hats anyway? Can't you just buy your own instead of taking them from kids?
How dare you! I'm not some petty thief!
Classic thief thing to say.
Let me explain.

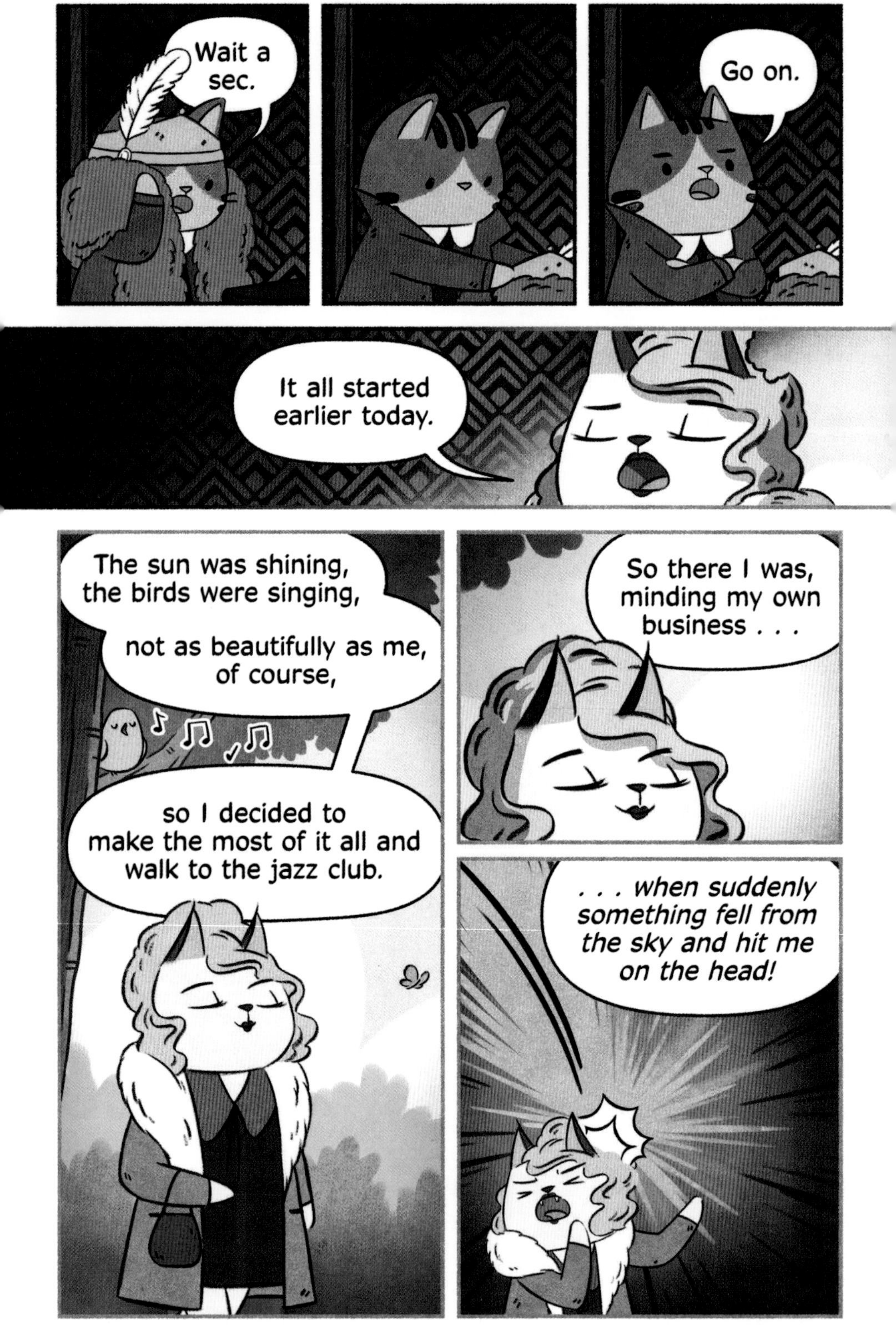
Wait a sec.
Go on.
It all started earlier today.
The sun was shining, the birds were singing,
not as beautifully as me, of course,
so I decided to make the most of it all and walk to the jazz club.
So there I was, minding my own business . . .
. . . when suddenly something fell from the sky and hit me on the head!

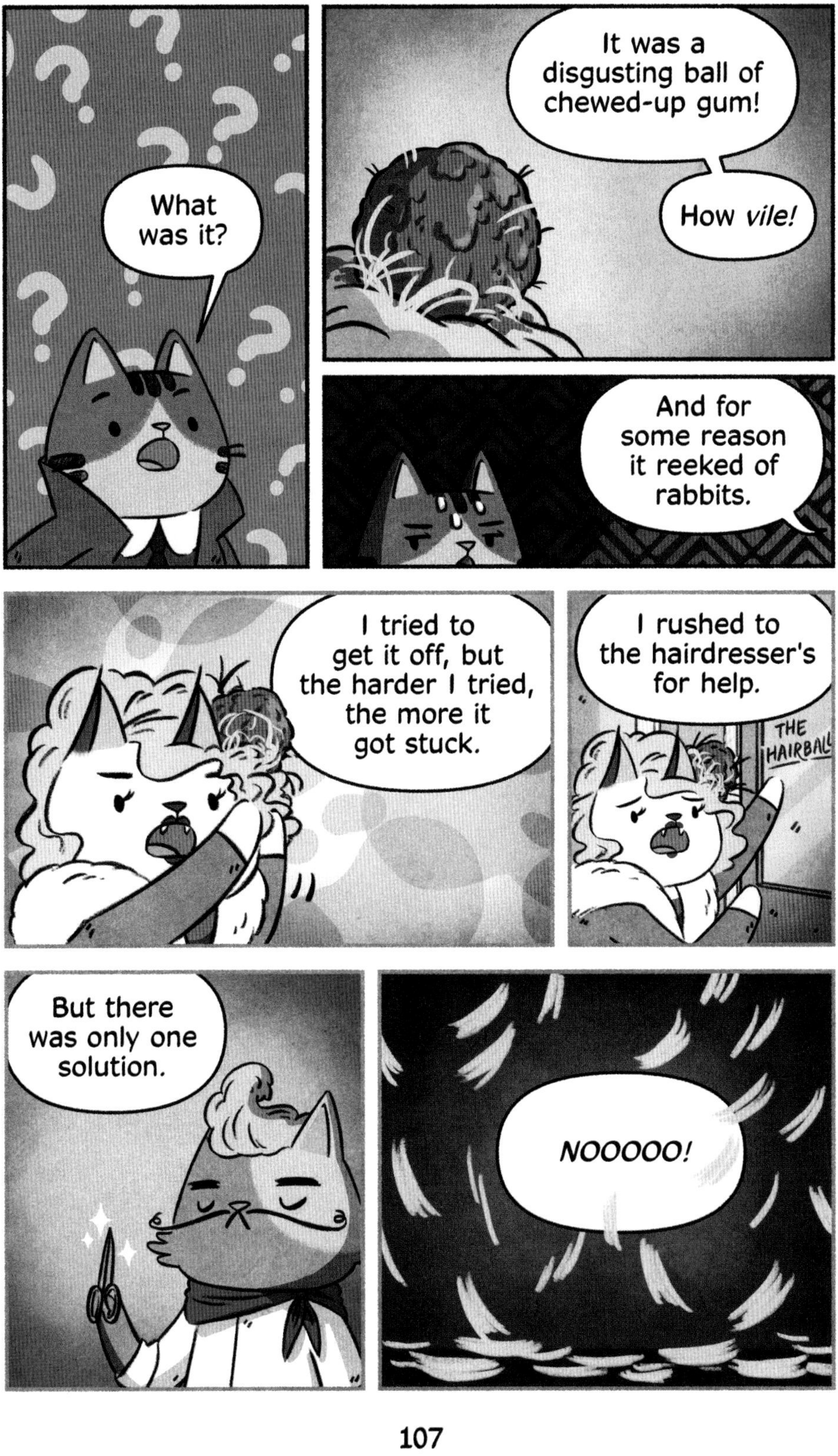
What was it?
It was a disgusting ball of chewed-up gum!
How *vile!*
And for some reason it reeked of rabbits.
I tried to get it off, but the harder I tried, the more it got stuck.
I rushed to the hairdresser's for help.
THE HAIRBALL
But there was only one solution.
NOOOOO!

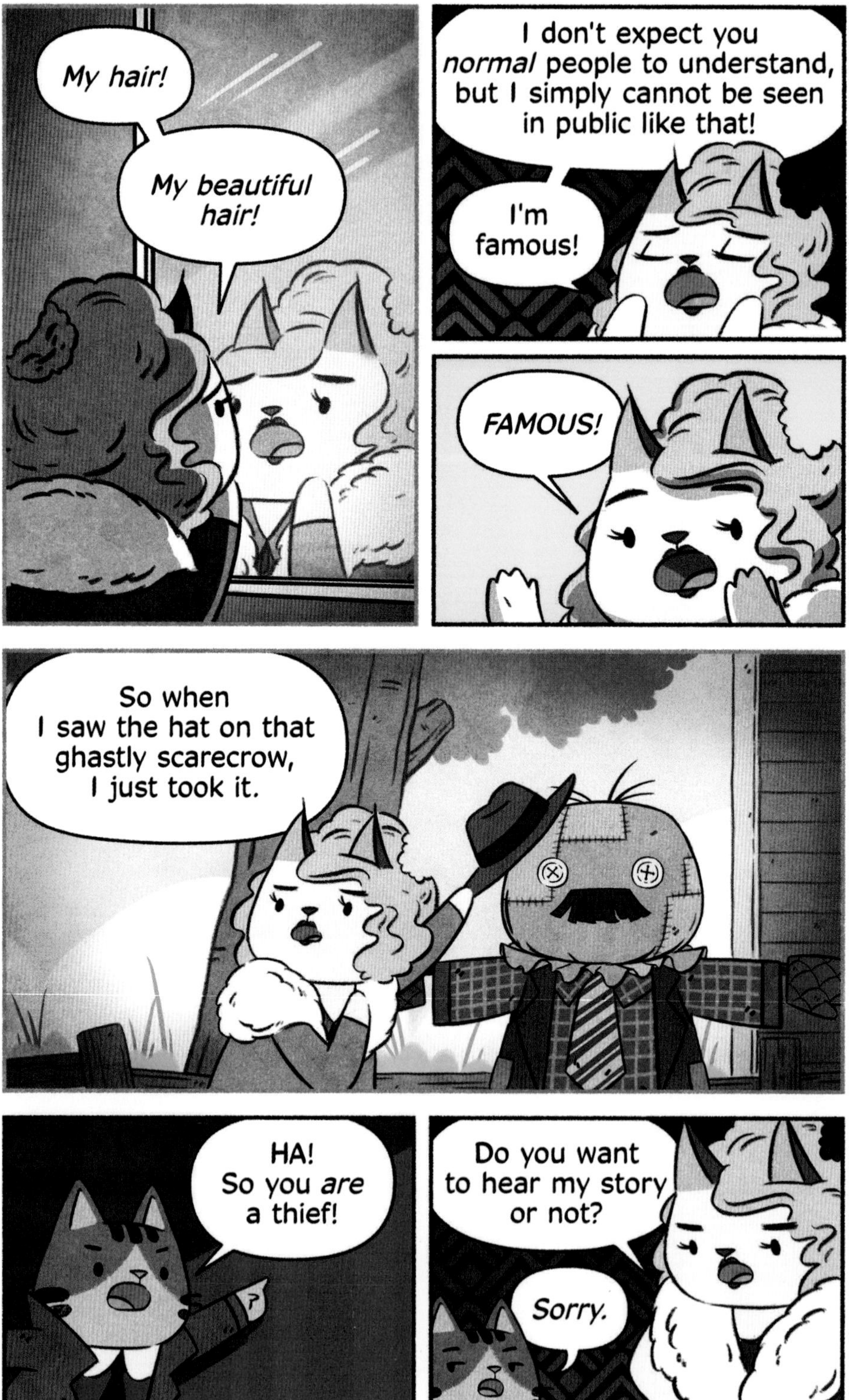
My hair!
My beautiful hair!
I don't expect you *normal* people to understand, but I simply cannot be seen in public like that!
I'm famous!
FAMOUS!
So when I saw the hat on that ghastly scarecrow, I just took it.
HA! So you *are* a thief!
Do you want to hear my story or not?
Sorry.

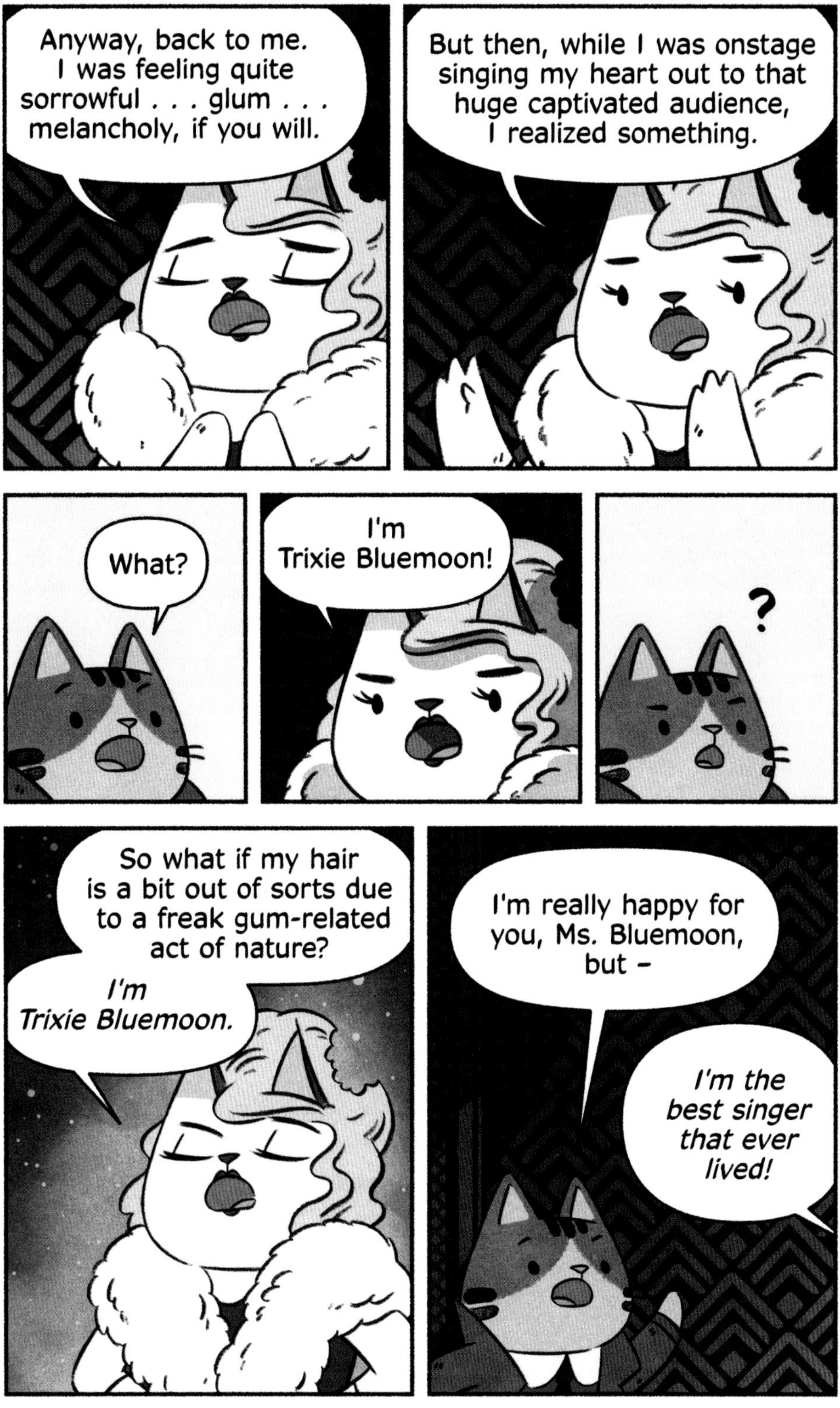
Anyway, back to me. I was feeling quite sorrowful . . . glum . . . melancholy, if you will.
But then, while I was onstage singing my heart out to that huge captivated audience, I realized something.
What?
I'm Trixie Bluemoon!
?
So what if my hair is a bit out of sorts due to a freak gum-related act of nature?
I'm Trixie Bluemoon.
I'm really happy for you, Ms. Bluemoon, but –
I'm the best singer that ever lived!

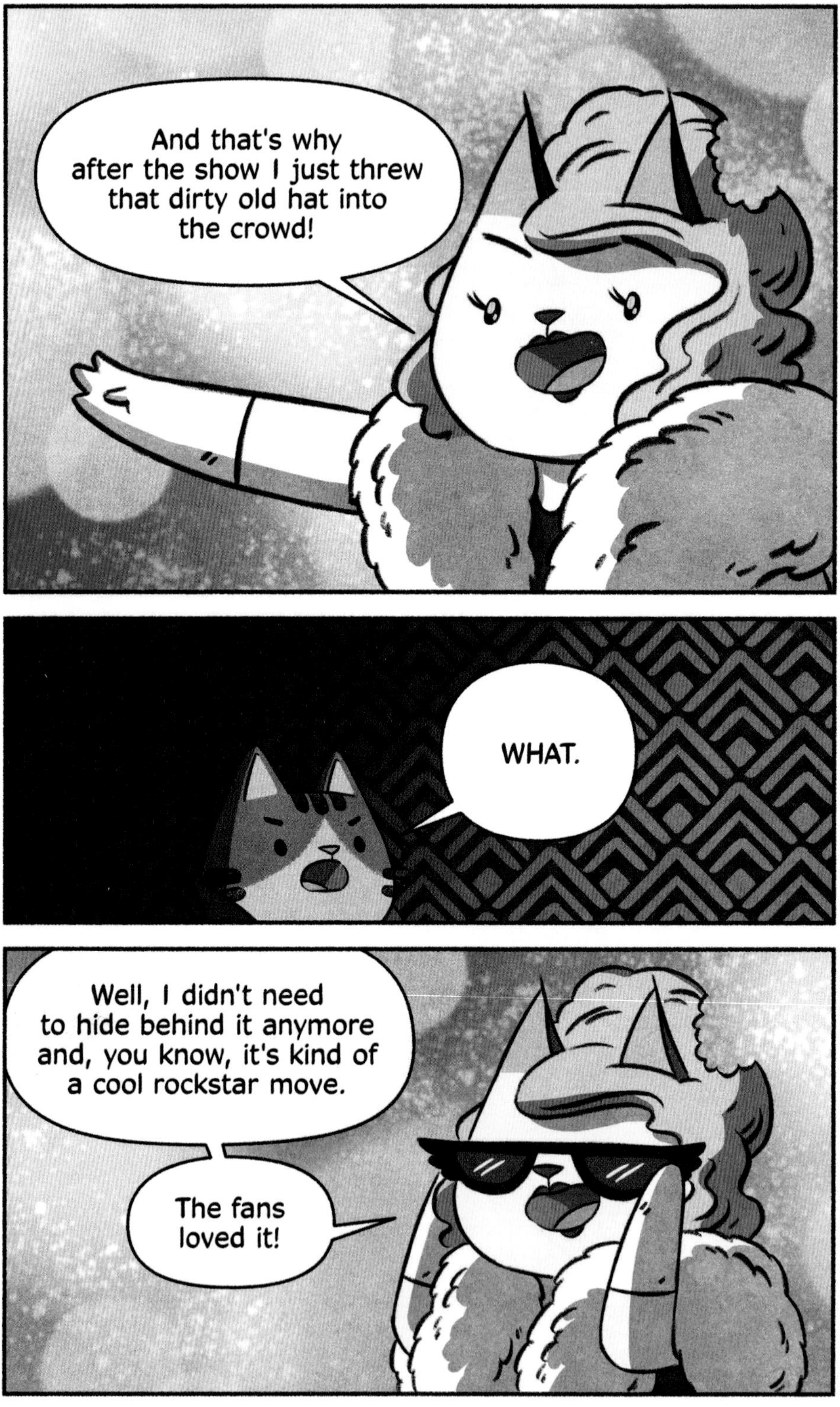
And that's why after the show I just threw that dirty old hat into the crowd!
WHAT.
Well, I didn't need to hide behind it anymore and, you know, it's kind of a cool rockstar move.
The fans loved it!

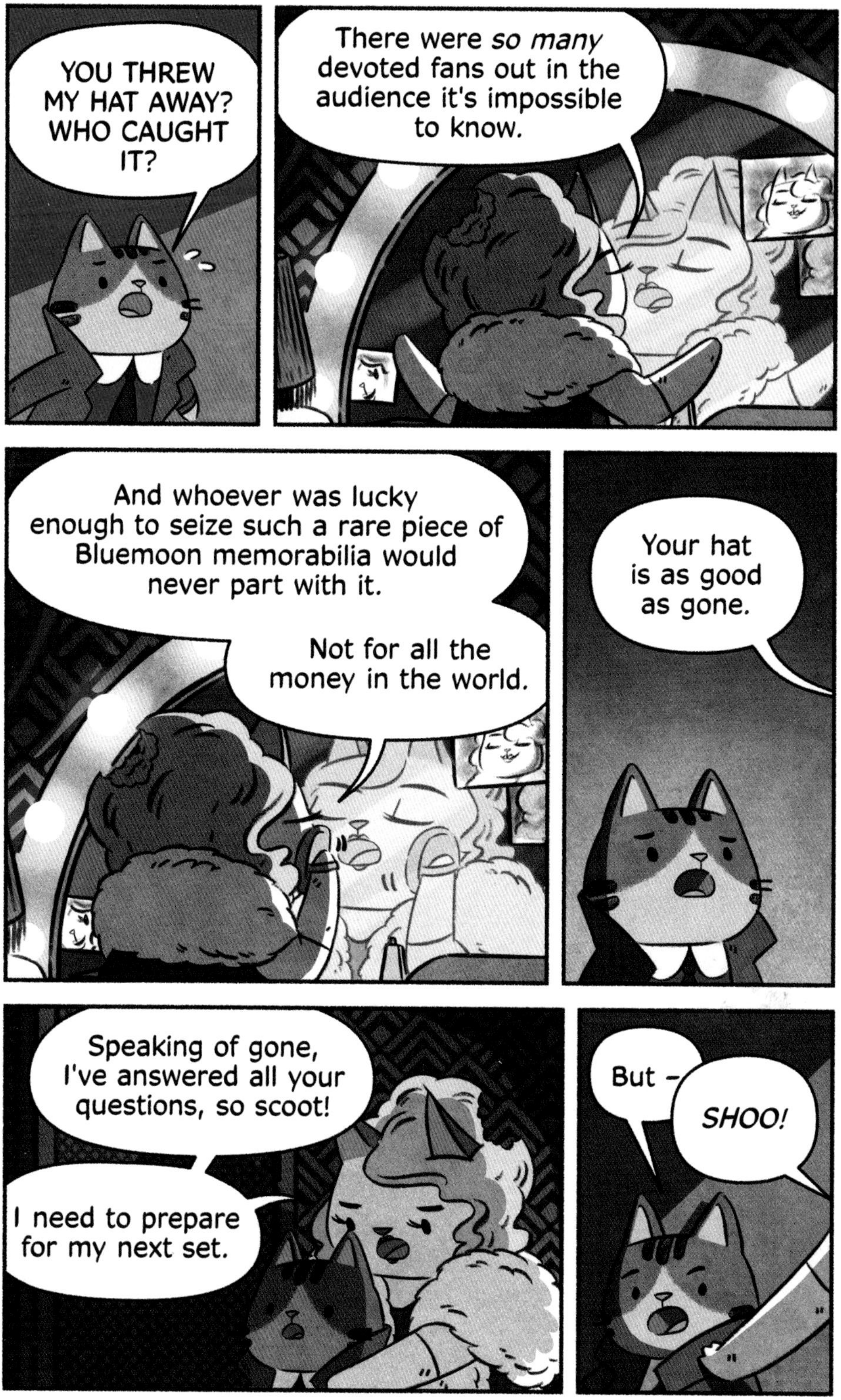

YOU THREW MY HAT AWAY? WHO CAUGHT IT?
There were *so many* devoted fans out in the audience it's impossible to know.
And whoever was lucky enough to seize such a rare piece of Bluemoon memorabilia would never part with it.
Not for all the money in the world.
Your hat is as good as gone.
Speaking of gone, I've answered all your questions, so scoot!
I need to prepare for my next set.
But –
SHOO!

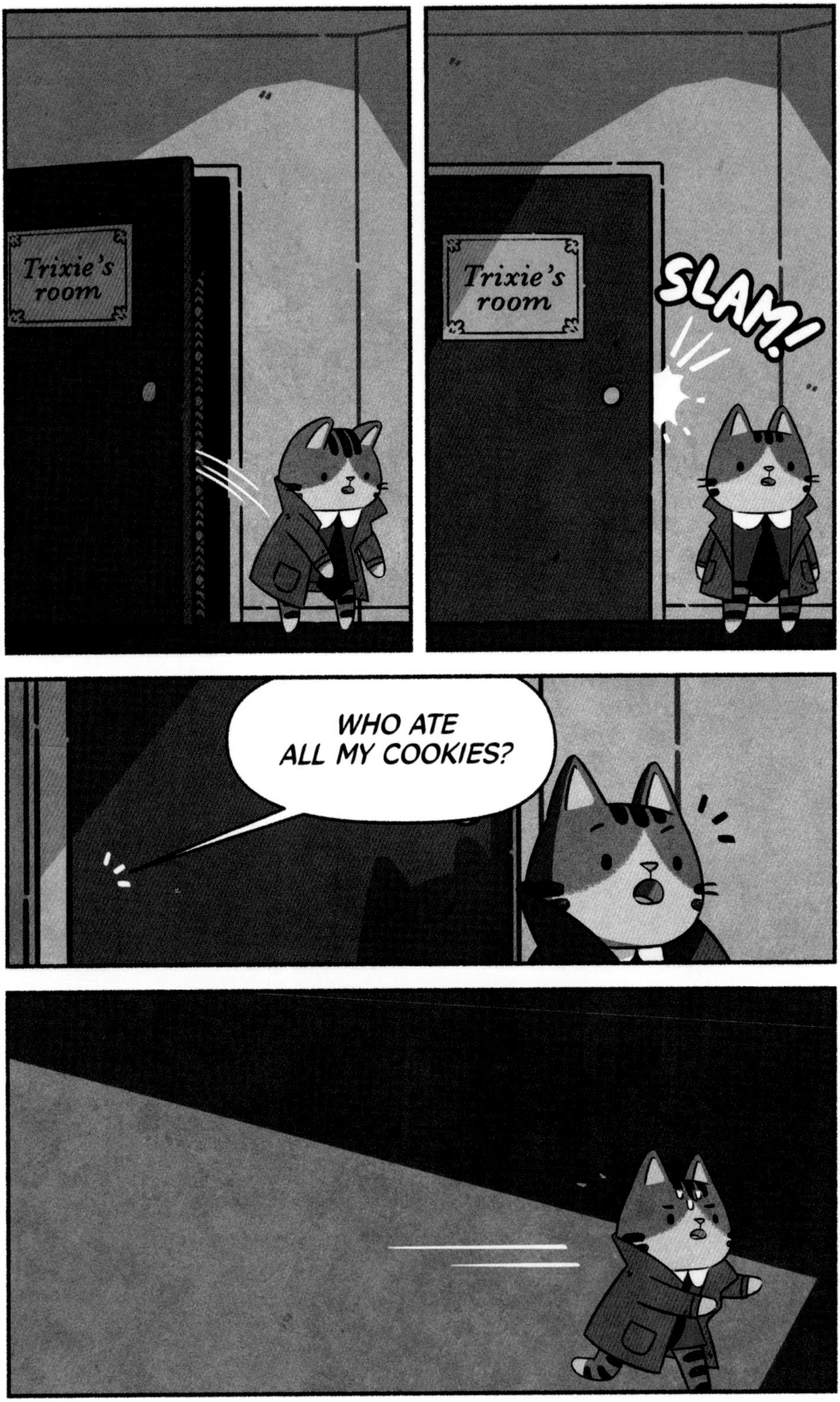
Trixie's room
Trixie's room
SLAM!
WHO ATE ALL MY COOKIES?

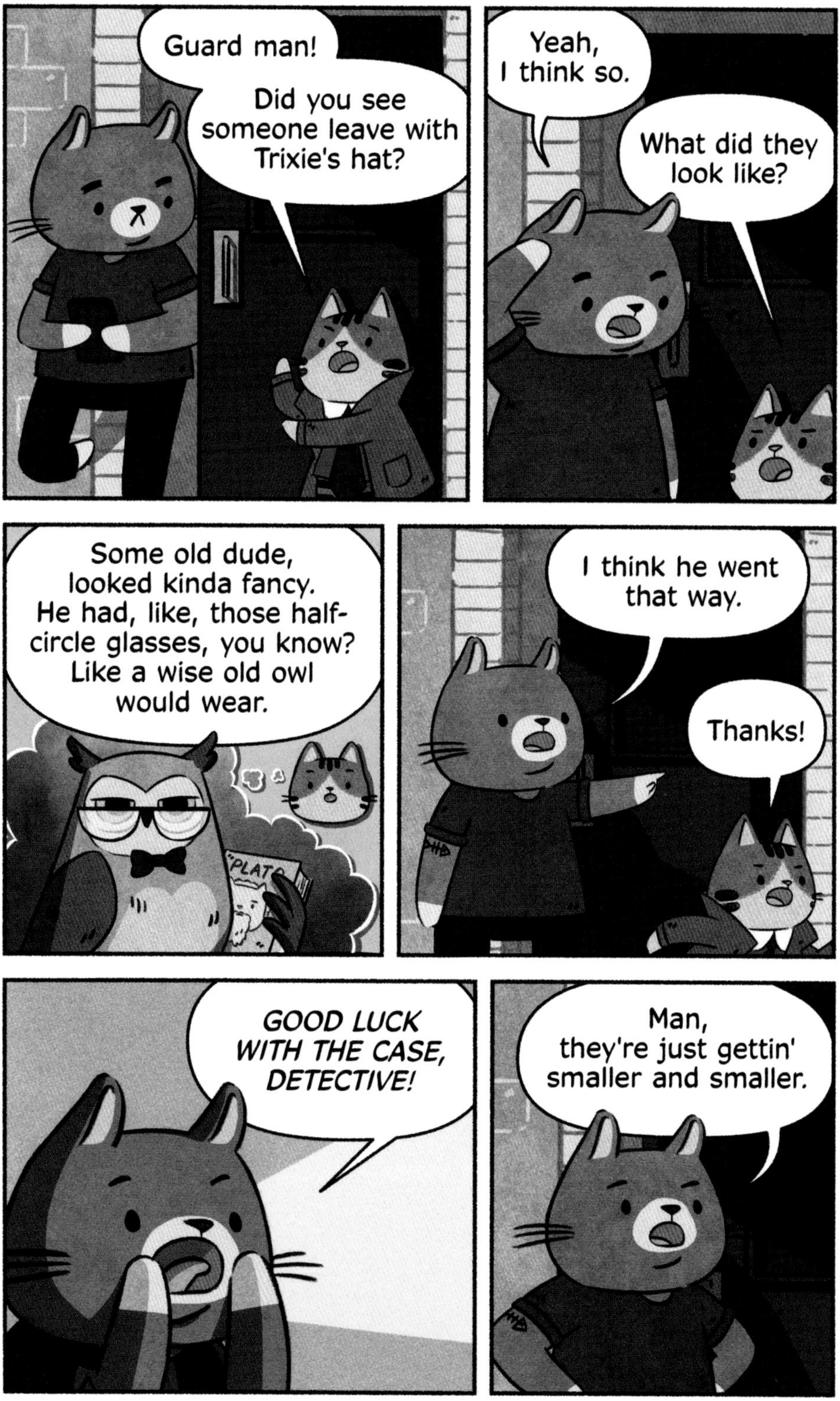
Guard man!
Did you see someone leave with Trixie's hat?
Yeah, I think so.
What did they look like?
Some old dude, looked kinda fancy. He had, like, those half-circle glasses, you know? Like a wise old owl would wear.
"PLATO
I think he went that way.
Thanks!
GOOD LUCK WITH THE CASE, DETECTIVE!
Man, they're just gettin' smaller and smaller.

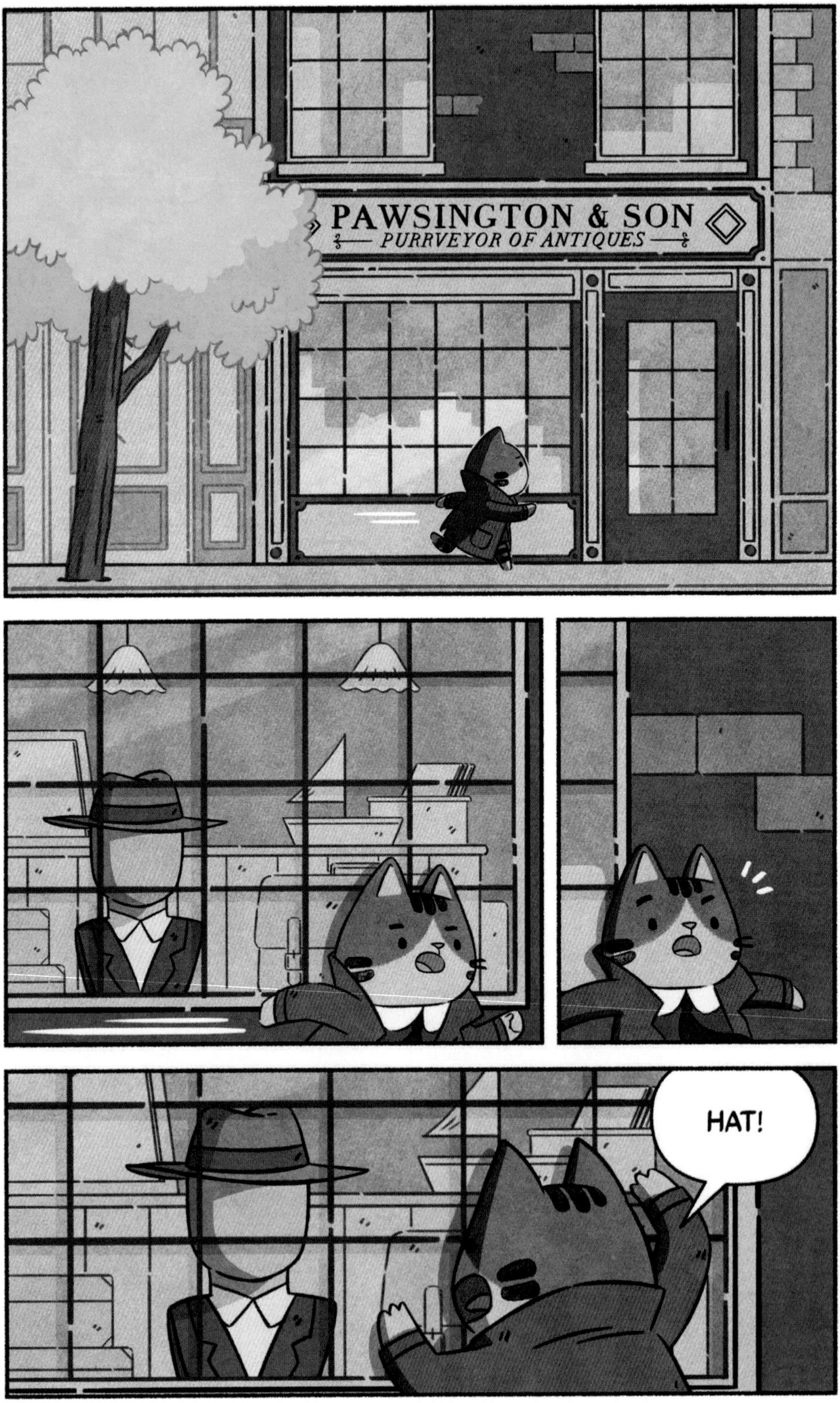
PAWSINGTON & SON
PURRVEYOR OF ANTIQUES
HAT!

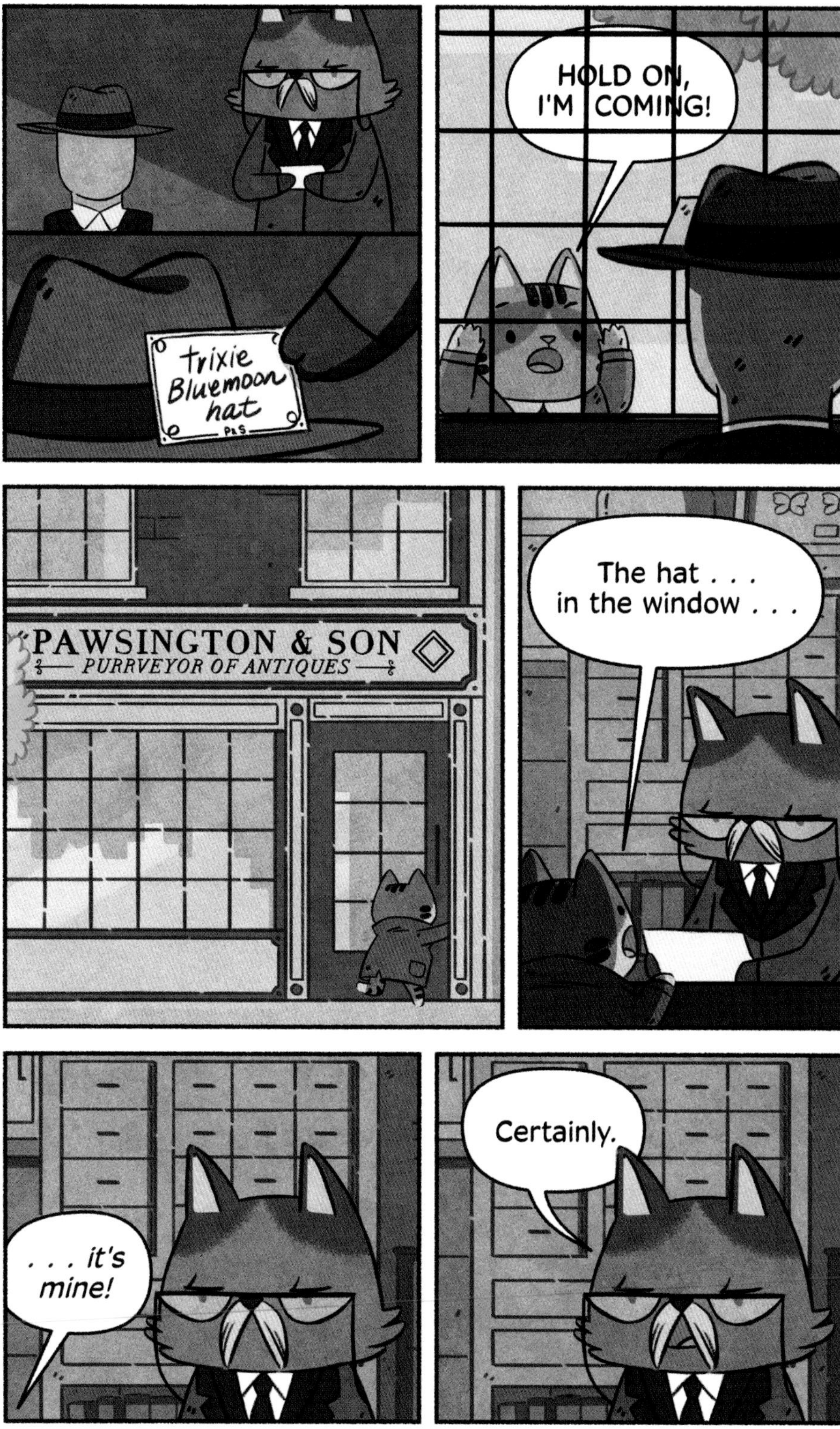

trixie Bluemoon hat
P&S
HOLD ON, I'M COMING!
PAWSINGTON & SON
PURRVEYOR OF ANTIQUES
The hat . . . in the window . . .
. . . it's mine!
Certainly.

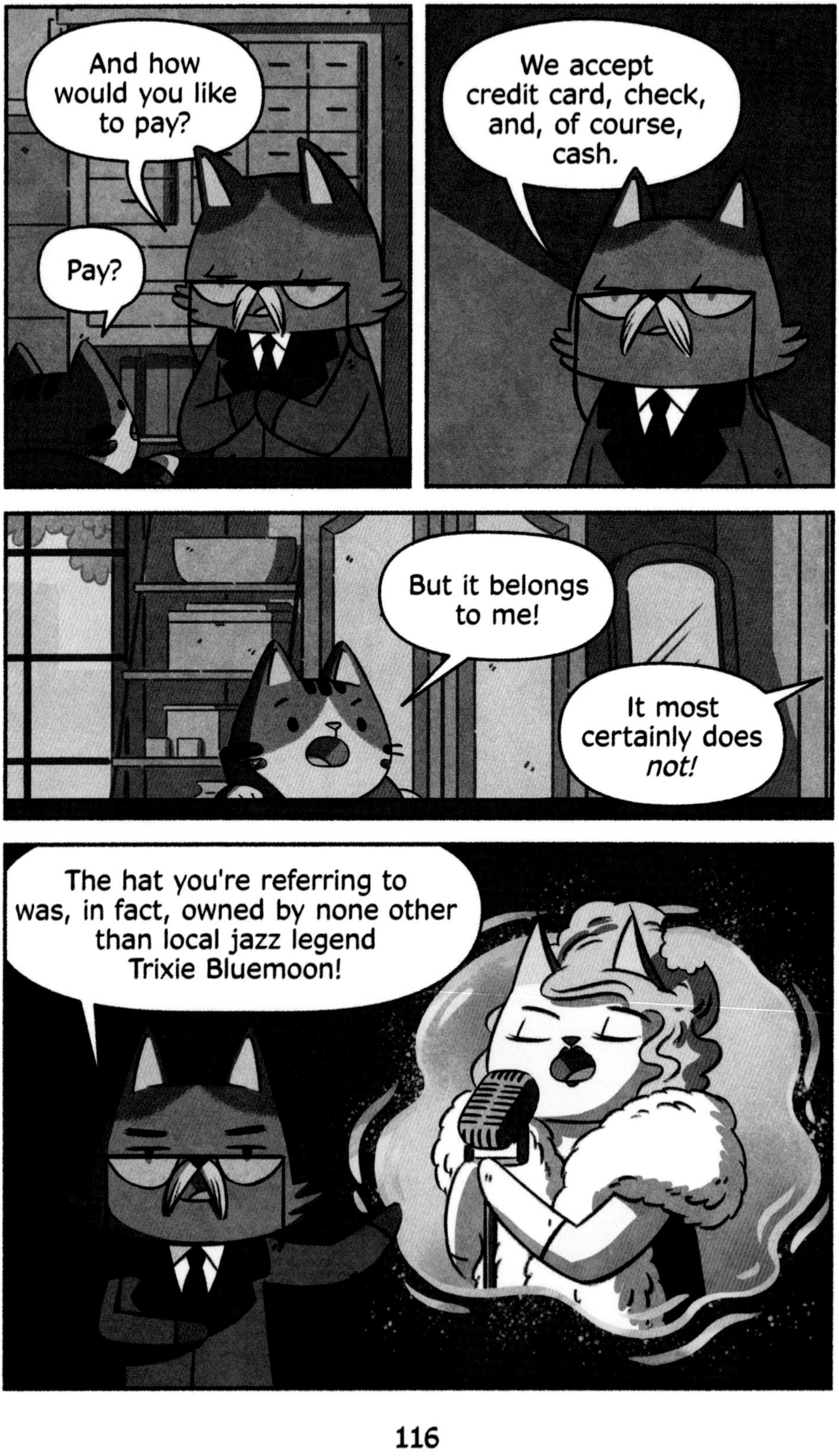
And how would you like to pay?
Pay?
We accept credit card, check, and, of course, cash.
But it belongs to me!
It most certainly does *not!*
The hat you're referring to was, in fact, owned by none other than local jazz legend Trixie Bluemoon!

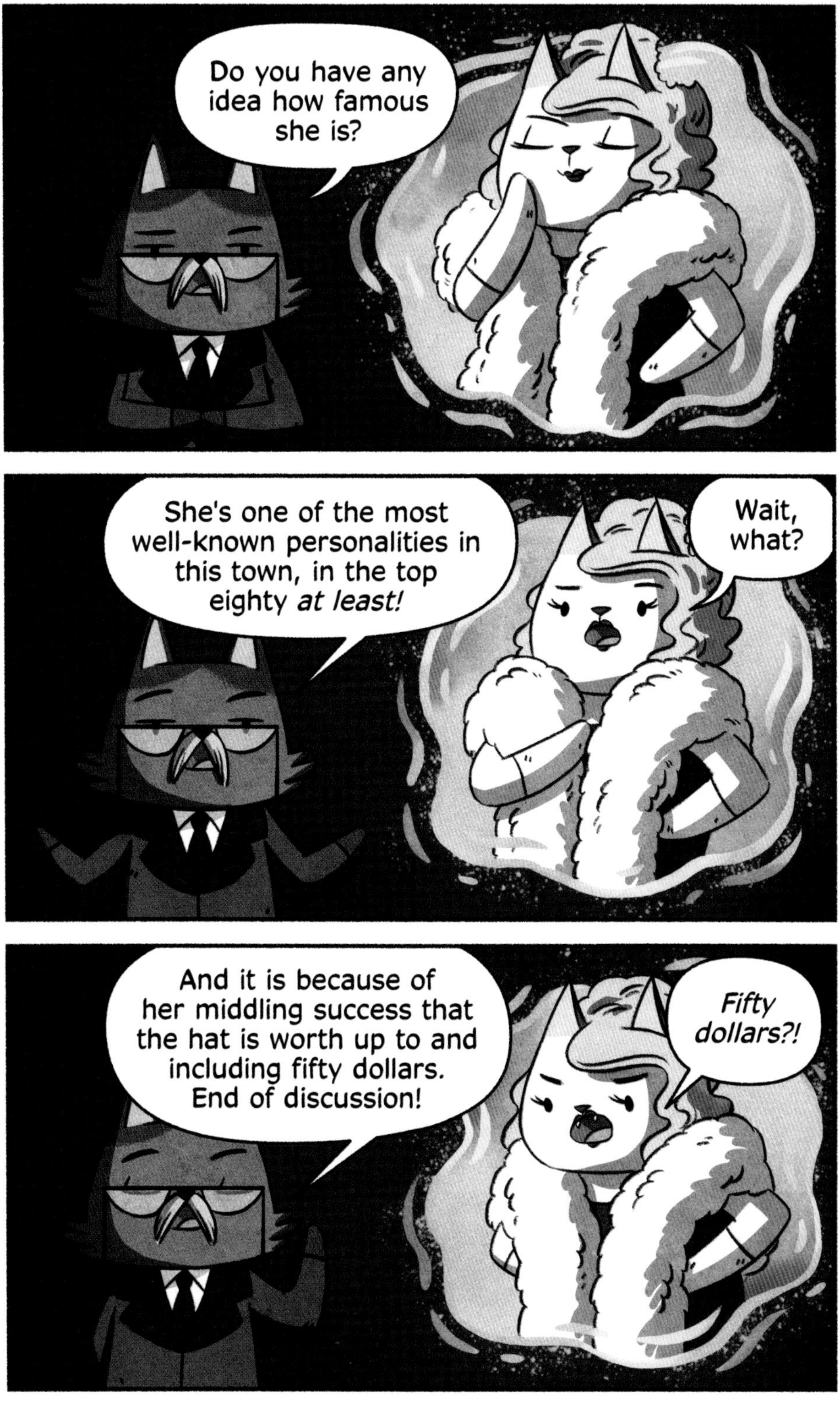
Do you have any idea how famous she is?
She's one of the most well-known personalities in this town, in the top eighty *at least!*
Wait, what?
And it is because of her middling success that the hat is worth up to and including fifty dollars. End of discussion!
Fifty dollars?!

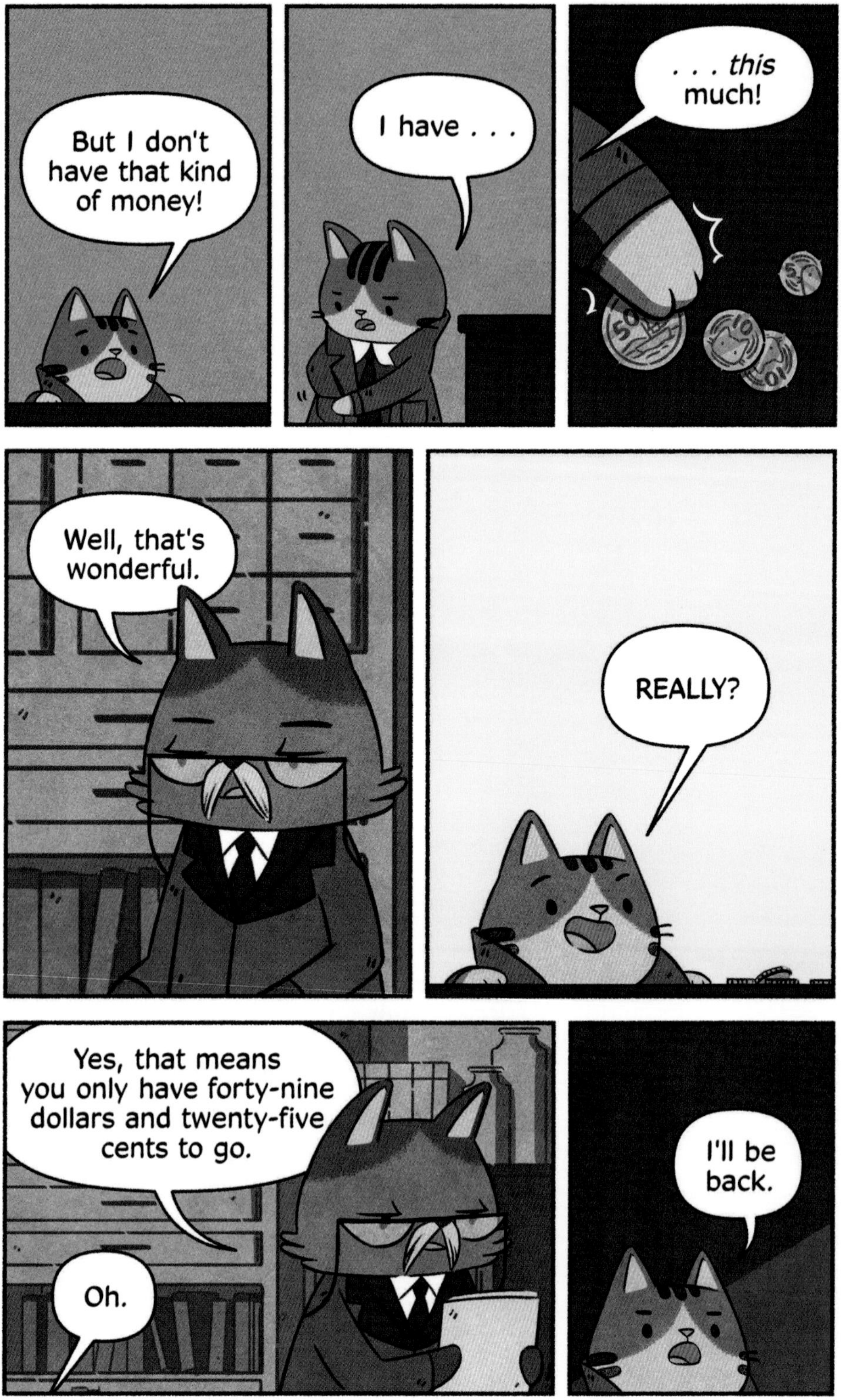
But I don't have that kind of money!
I have . . .
. . . *this* much!
Well, that's wonderful.
REALLY?
Yes, that means you only have forty-nine dollars and twenty-five cents to go.
Oh.
I'll be back.

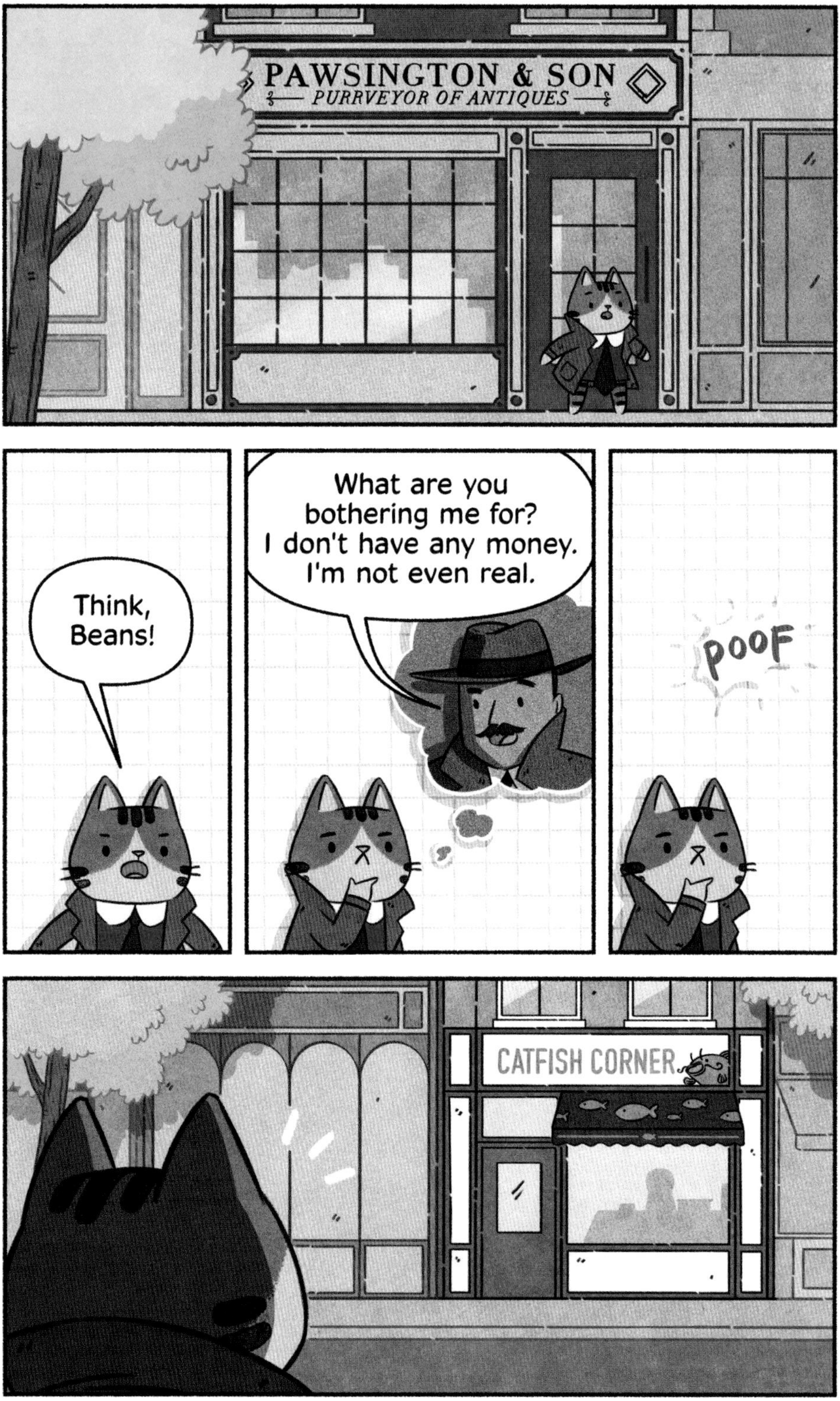
PAWSINGTON & SON
PURRVEYOR OF ANTIQUES
Think, Beans!
What are you bothering me for? I don't have any money. I'm not even real.
POOF
CATFISH CORNER

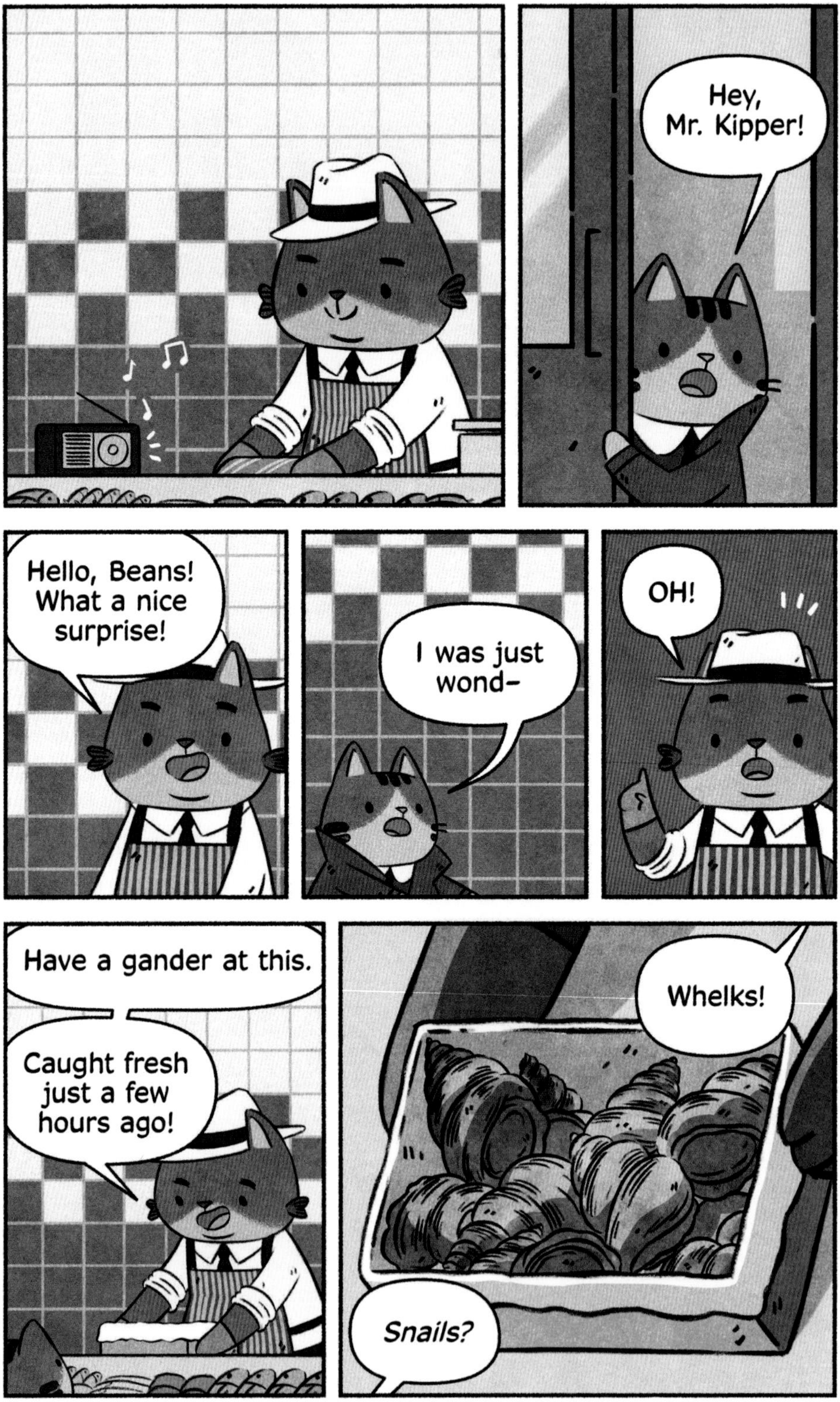
Hey,
Mr. Kipper!
Hello, Beans!
What a nice
surprise!
I was just
wond-
OH!
Have a gander at this.
Caught fresh
just a few
hours ago!
Whelks!
Snails?

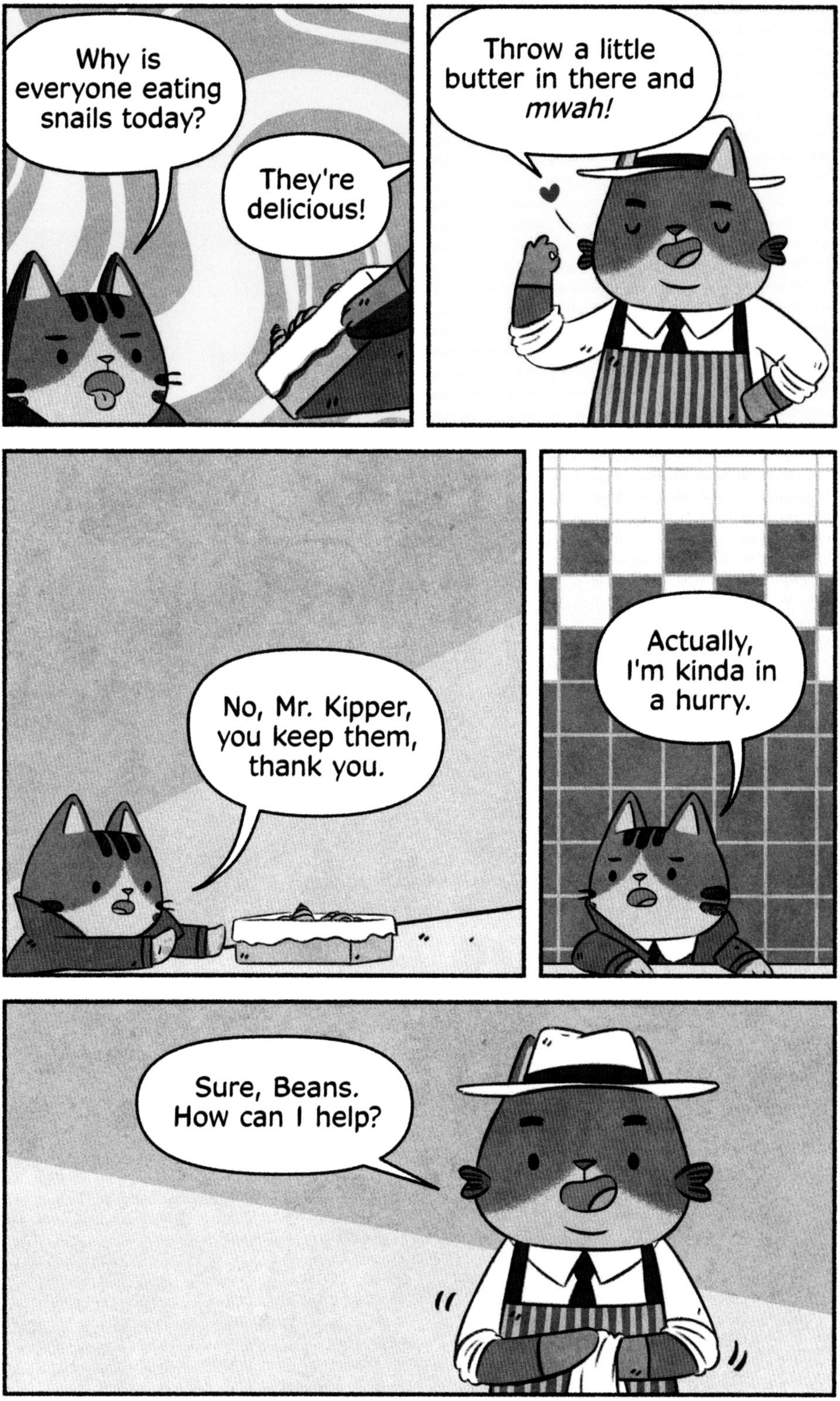
Why is everyone eating snails today?
They're delicious!
Throw a little butter in there and *mwah!*
No, Mr. Kipper, you keep them, thank you.
Actually, I'm kinda in a hurry.
Sure, Beans. How can I help?

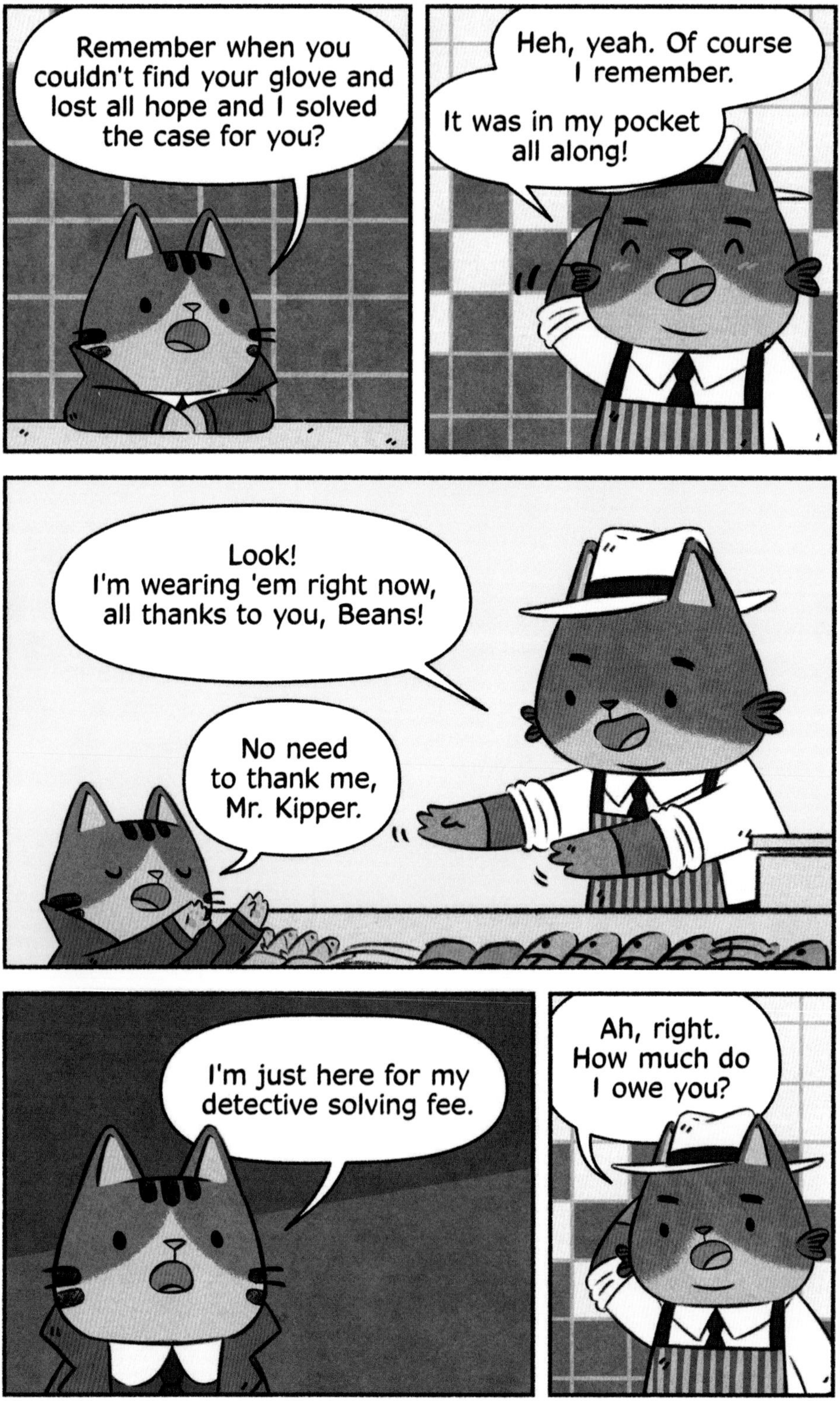

Remember when you couldn't find your glove and lost all hope and I solved the case for you?
Heh, yeah. Of course I remember.
It was in my pocket all along!
Look! I'm wearing 'em right now, all thanks to you, Beans!
No need to thank me, Mr. Kipper.
I'm just here for my detective solving fee.
Ah, right. How much do I owe you?

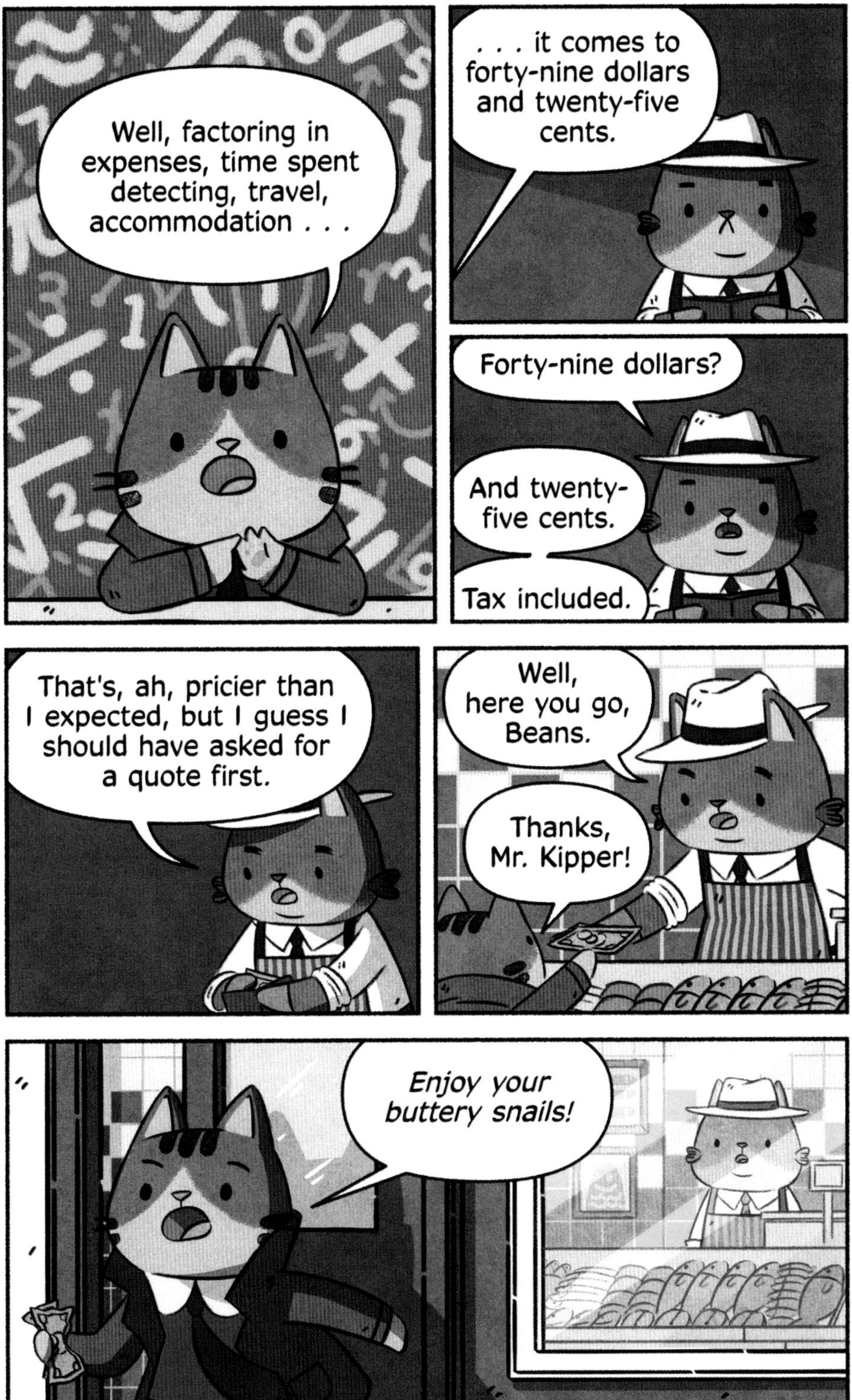
Well, factoring in expenses, time spent detecting, travel, accommodation . . .
. . . it comes to forty-nine dollars and twenty-five cents.
Forty-nine dollars?
And twenty-five cents.
Tax included.
That's, ah, pricier than I expected, but I guess I should have asked for a quote first.
Well, here you go, Beans.
Thanks, Mr. Kipper!
Enjoy your buttery snails!

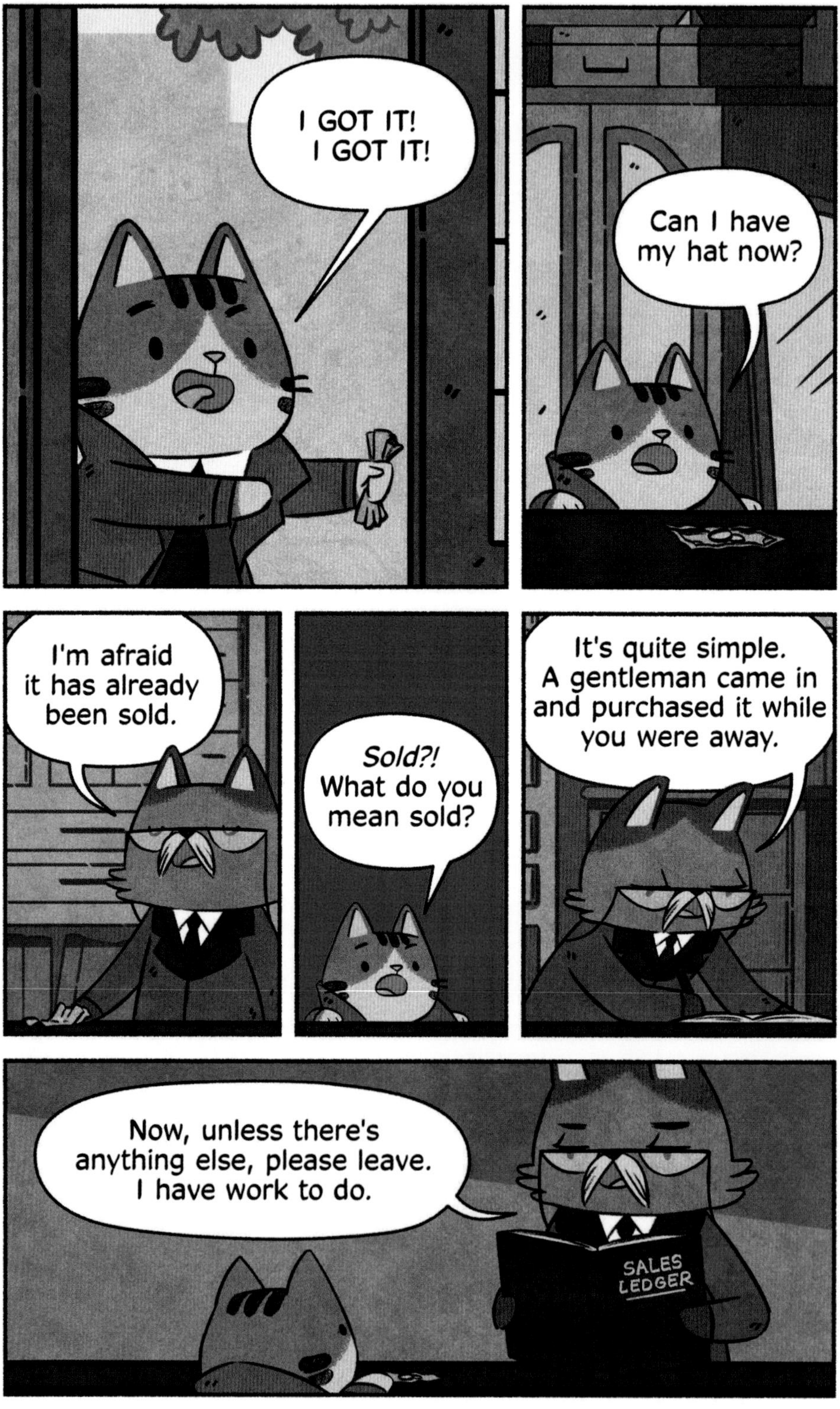
I GOT IT! I GOT IT!
Can I have my hat now?
I'm afraid it has already been sold.
Sold?! What do you mean sold?
It's quite simple. A gentleman came in and purchased it while you were away.
Now, unless there's anything else, please leave. I have work to do.
SALES LEDGER

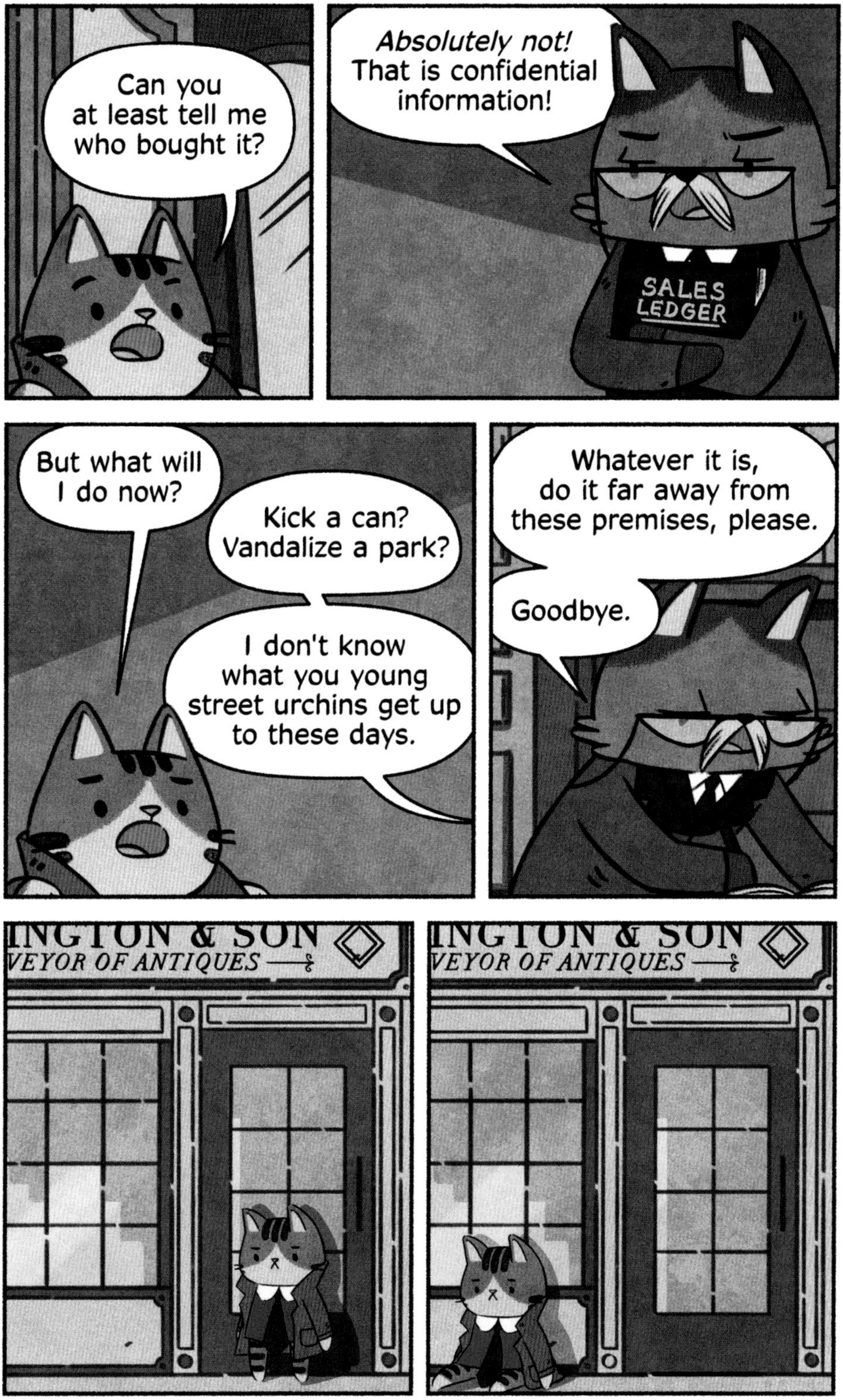
Can you at least tell me who bought it?
Absolutely not! That is confidential information!
SALES LEDGER
But what will I do now?
Kick a can? Vandalize a park?
I don't know what you young street urchins get up to these days.
Whatever it is, do it far away from these premises, please.
Goodbye.
INGTON & SON
VEYOR OF ANTIQUES
INGTON & SON
VEYOR OF ANTIQUES

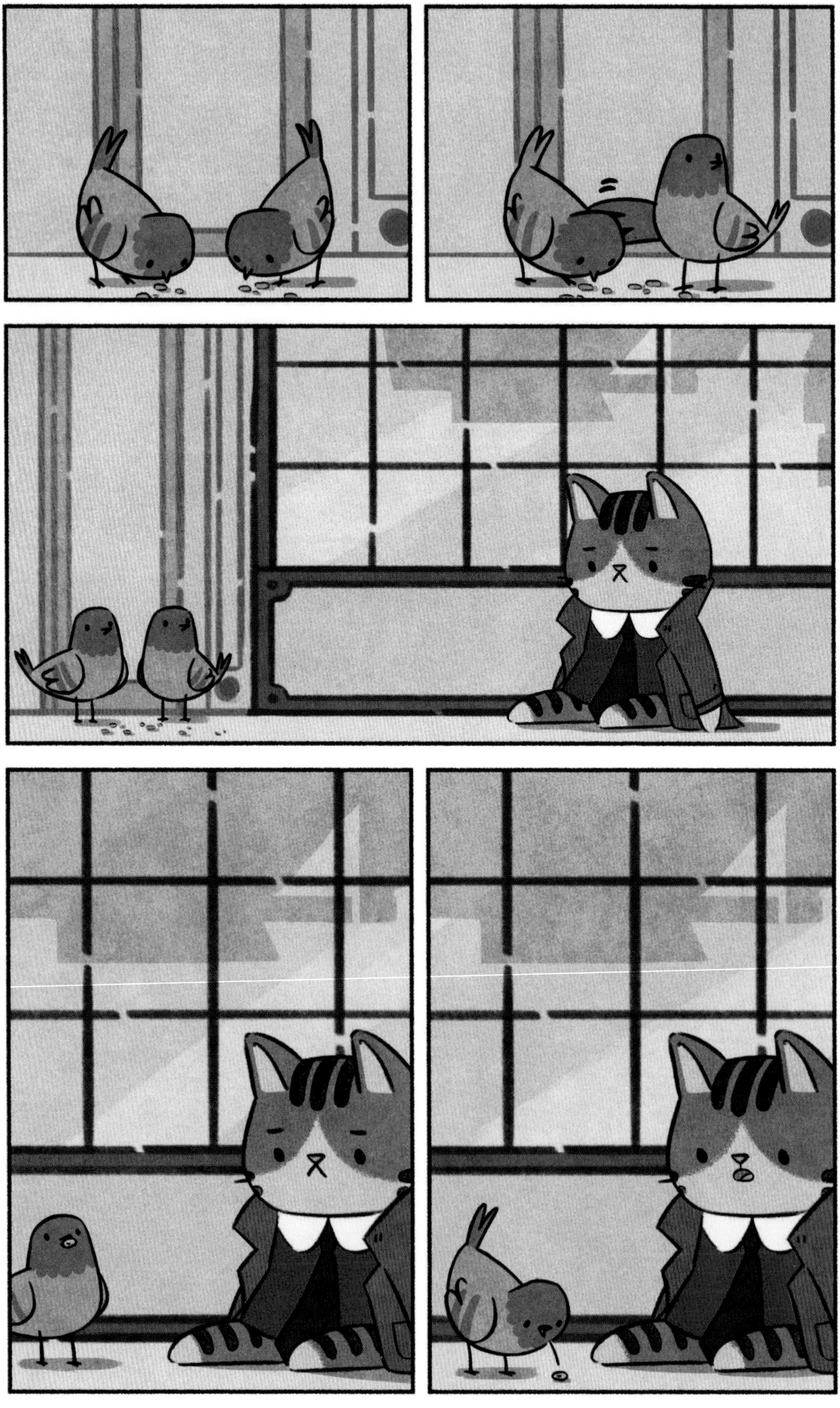

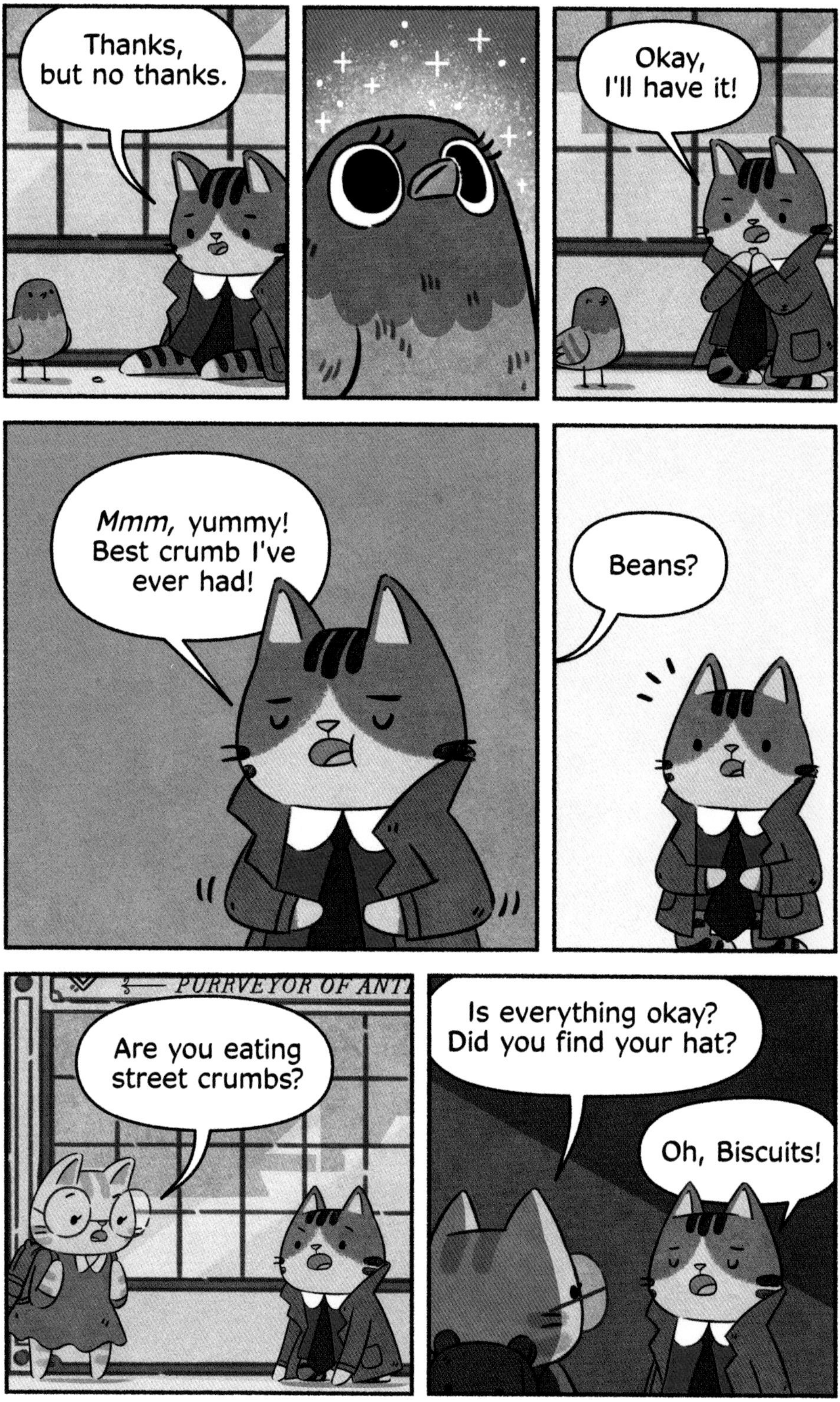
Thanks, but no thanks.
Okay, I'll have it!
Mmm, yummy! Best crumb I've ever had!
Beans?
PURRVEYOR OF ANT
Are you eating street crumbs?
Is everything okay? Did you find your hat?
Oh, Biscuits!

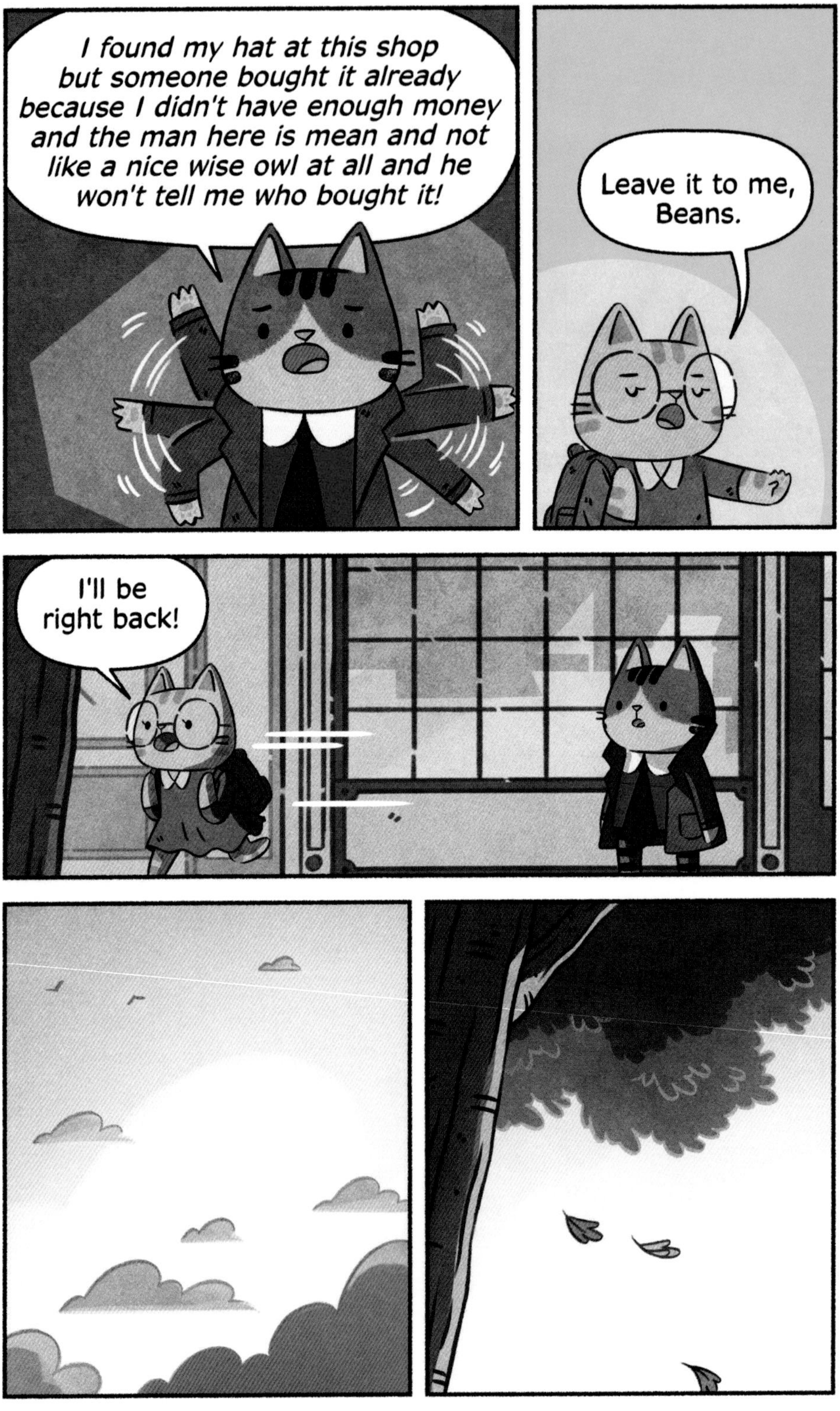

I found my hat at this shop but someone bought it already because I didn't have enough money and the man here is mean and not like a nice wise owl at all and he won't tell me who bought it!
Leave it to me, Beans.
I'll be right back!

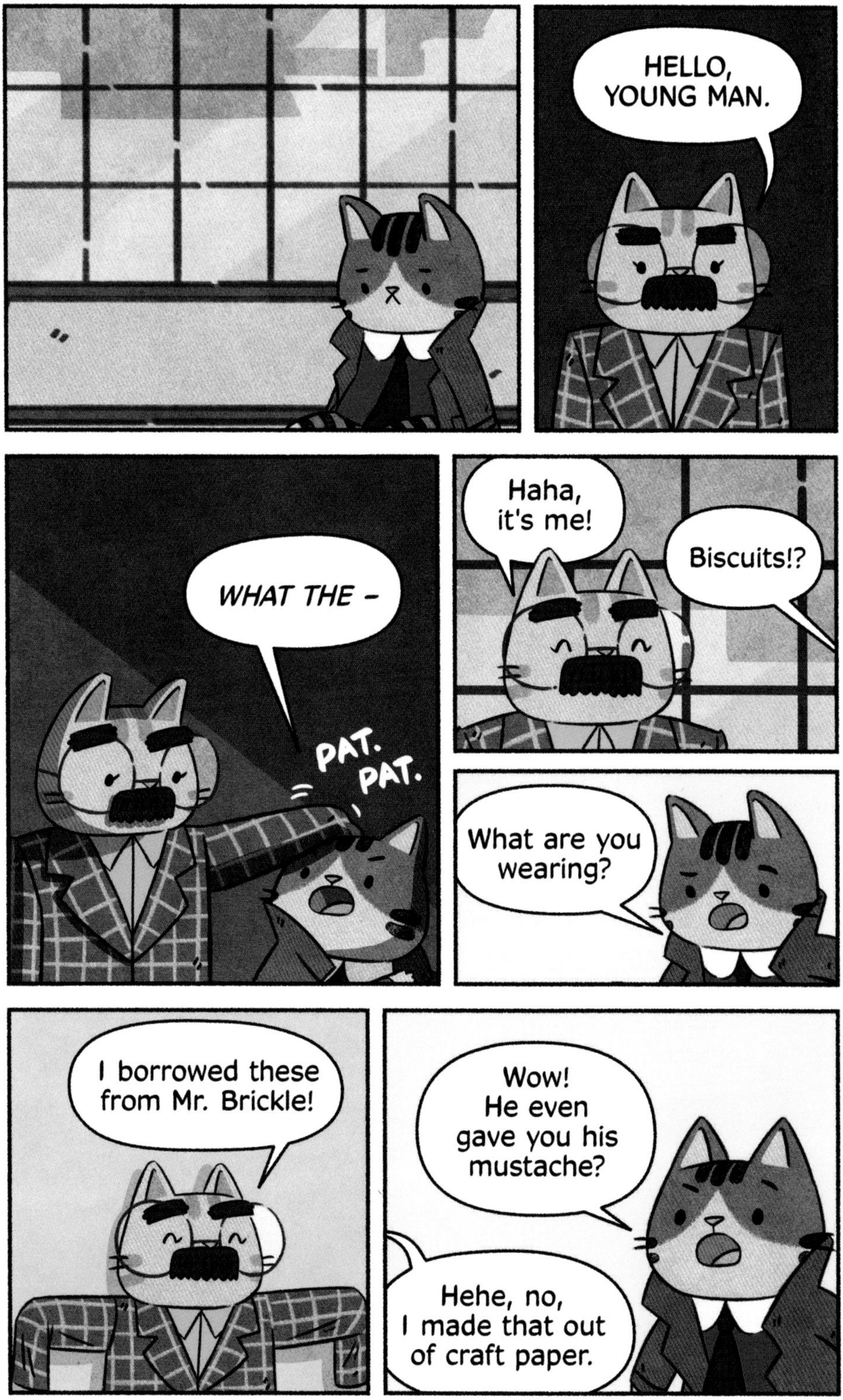
HELLO, YOUNG MAN.
WHAT THE –
PAT. PAT.
Haha, it's me!
Biscuits!?
What are you wearing?
I borrowed these from Mr. Brickle!
Wow! He even gave you his mustache?
Hehe, no, I made that out of craft paper.

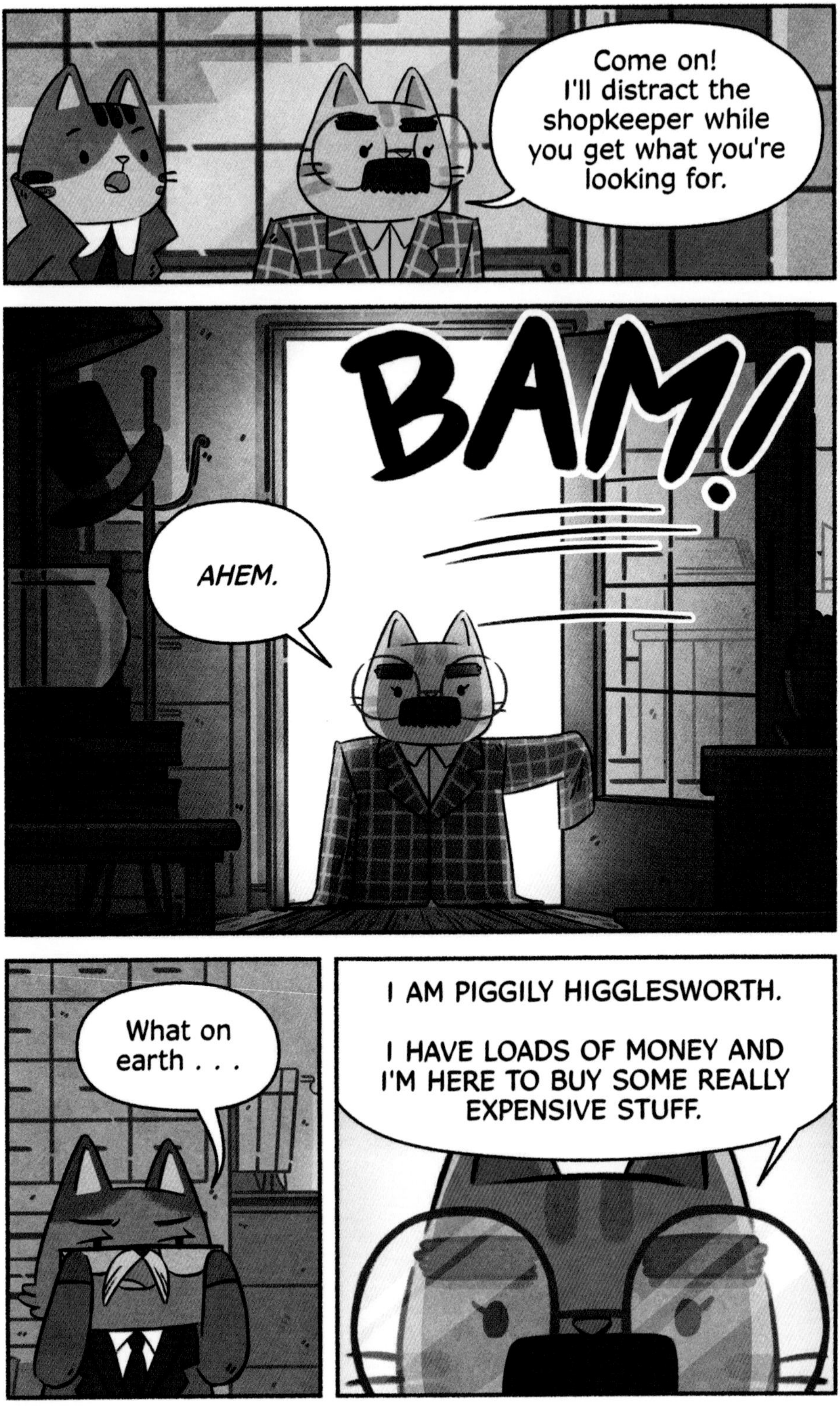
Come on! I'll distract the shopkeeper while you get what you're looking for.
BAM!
AHEM.
What on earth . . .
I AM PIGGILY HIGGLESWORTH.
I HAVE LOADS OF MONEY AND I'M HERE TO BUY SOME REALLY EXPENSIVE STUFF.

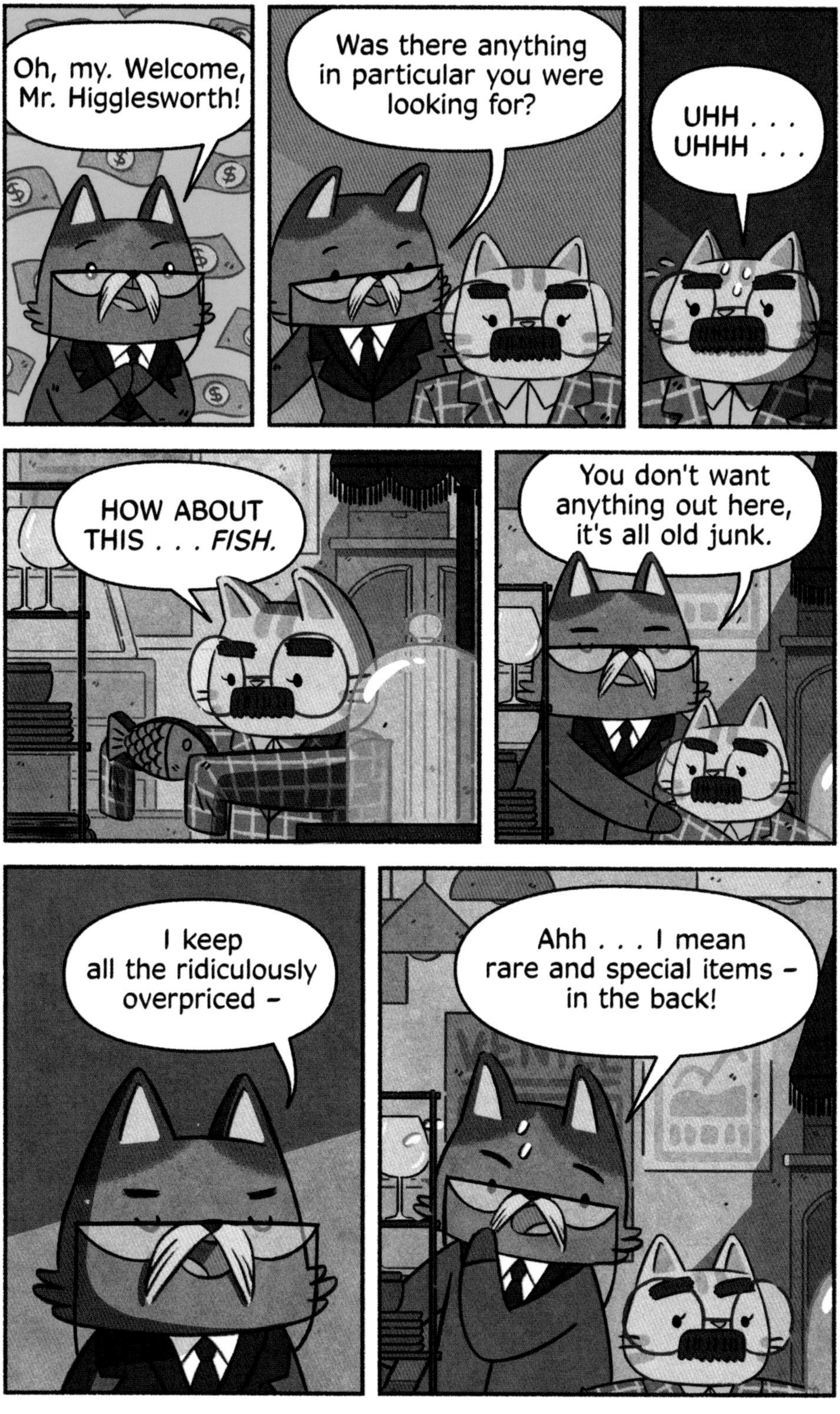
Oh, my. Welcome, Mr. Higglesworth!
Was there anything in particular you were looking for?
UHH . . . UHHH . . .
HOW ABOUT THIS . . . *FISH.*
You don't want anything out here, it's all old junk.
I keep all the ridiculously overpriced –
Ahh . . . I mean rare and special items – in the back!

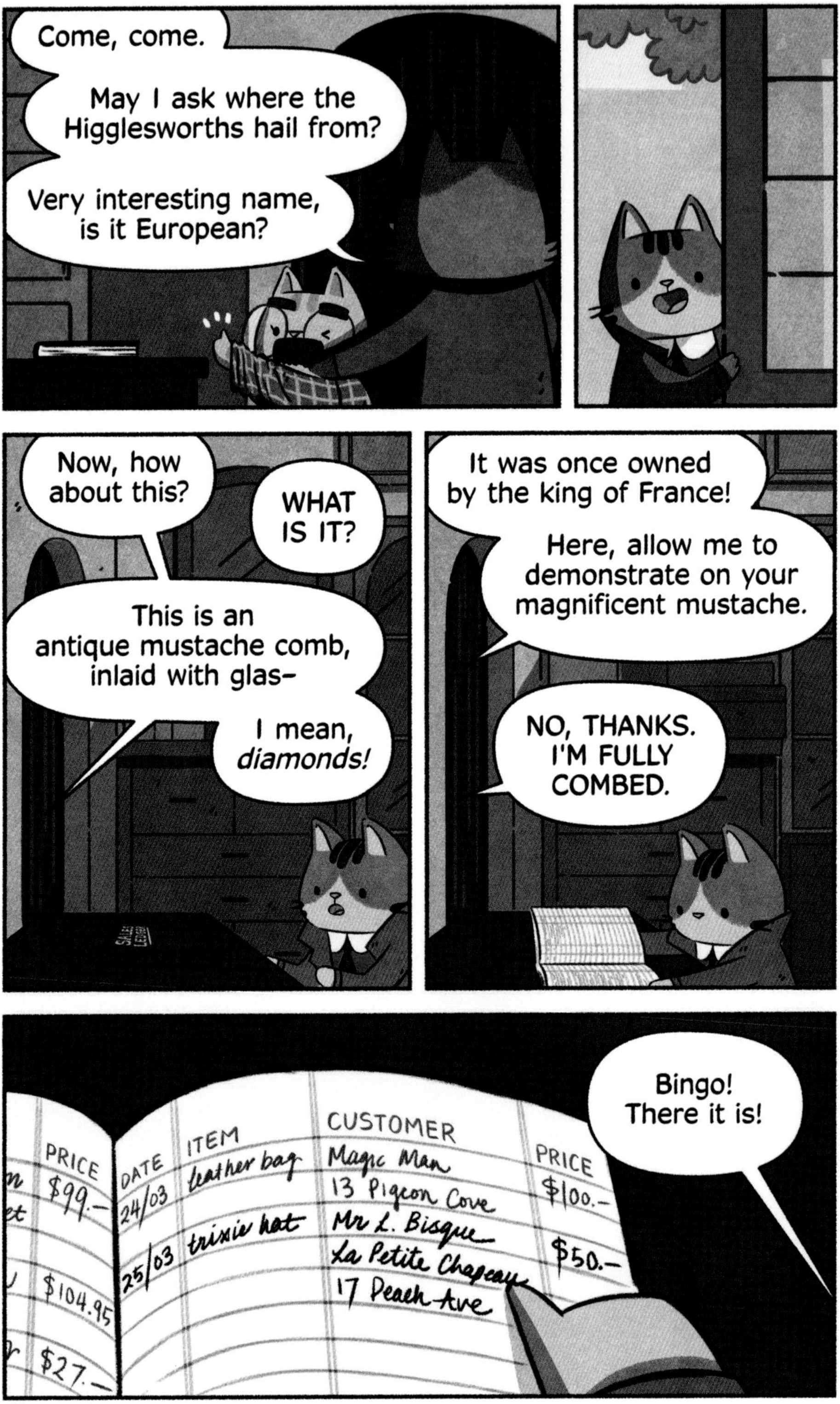
Come, come.
May I ask where the Higglesworths hail from?
Very interesting name, is it European?
Now, how about this?
WHAT IS IT?
This is an antique mustache comb, inlaid with glas–
I mean, *diamonds!*
It was once owned by the king of France!
Here, allow me to demonstrate on your magnificent mustache.
NO, THANKS. I'M FULLY COMBED.
PRICE
$99.–
$104.95
$27.–
DATE
ITEM
CUSTOMER
PRICE
24/03
leather bag
Magic Man
13 Pigeon Cove
$100.–
25/03
trixie hat
Mr L. Bisque
La Petite Chapeau
17 Peach Ave
$50.–
Bingo! There it is!

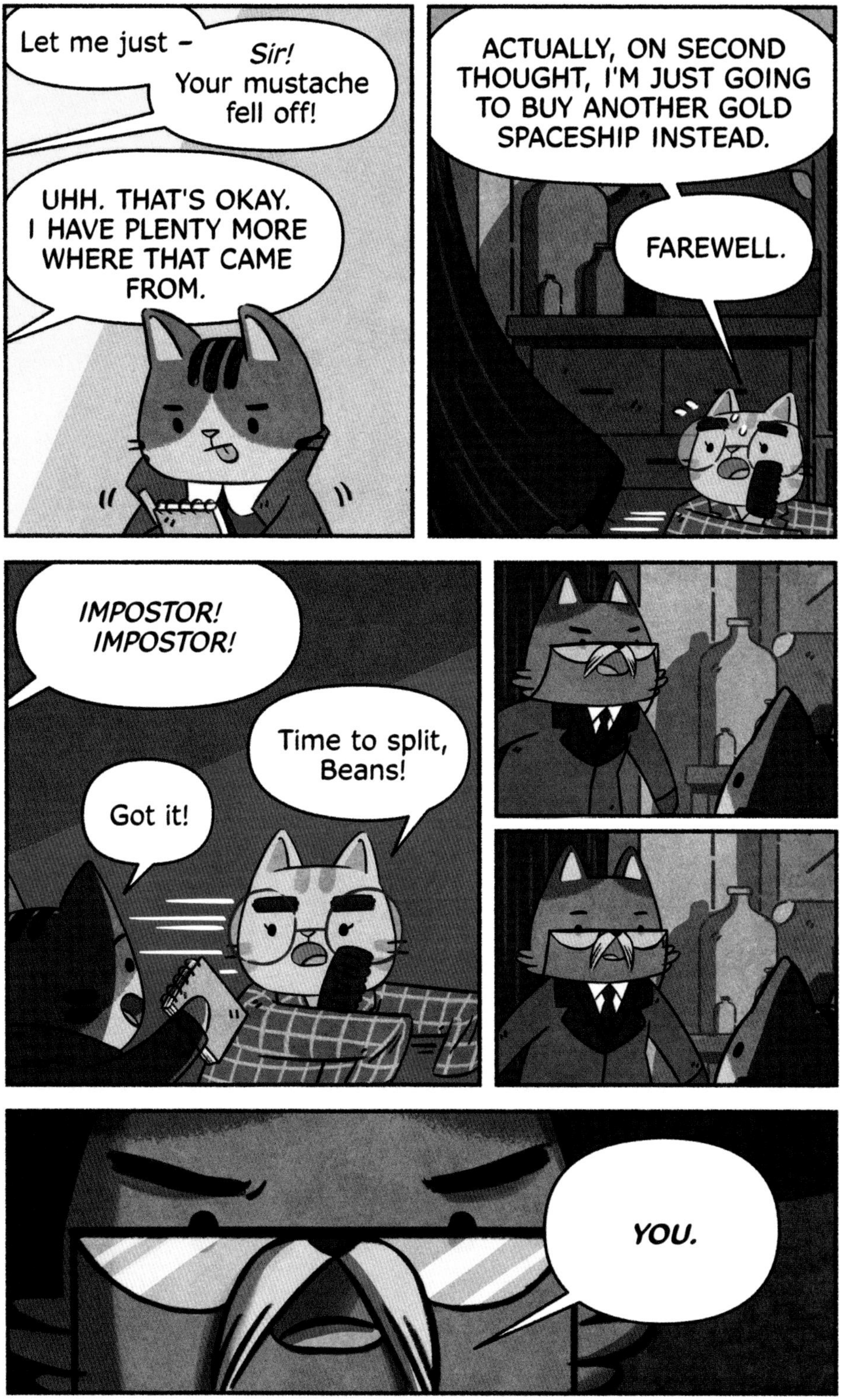
Let me just –
Sir! Your mustache fell off!
UHH. THAT'S OKAY. I HAVE PLENTY MORE WHERE THAT CAME FROM.
ACTUALLY, ON SECOND THOUGHT, I'M JUST GOING TO BUY ANOTHER GOLD SPACESHIP INSTEAD.
FAREWELL.
IMPOSTOR! IMPOSTOR!
Time to split, Beans!
Got it!
YOU.

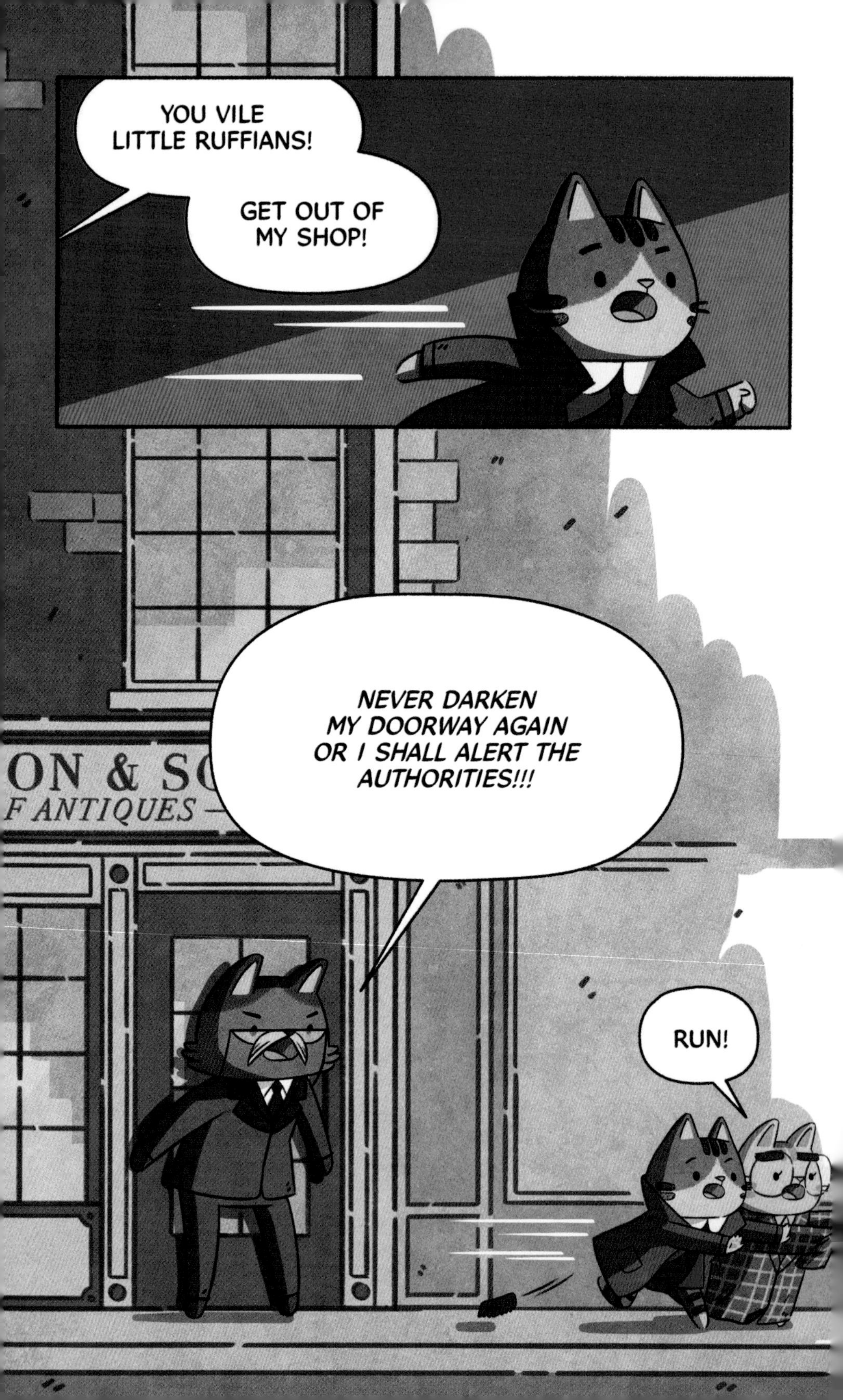
YOU VILE LITTLE RUFFIANS!
GET OUT OF MY SHOP!
ON & SO
F ANTIQUES
NEVER DARKEN MY DOORWAY AGAIN OR I SHALL ALERT THE AUTHORITIES!!!
RUN!

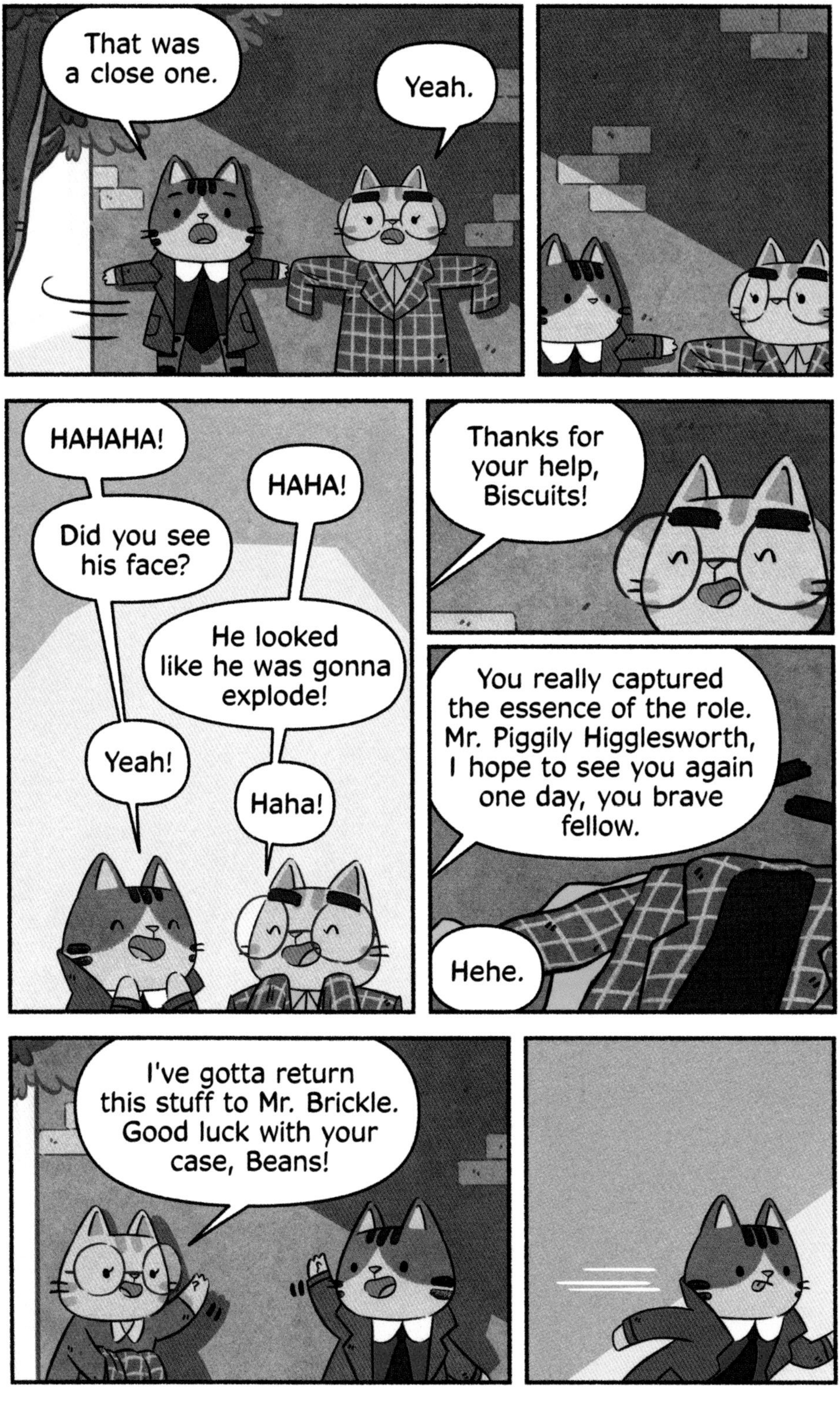
That was a close one.
Yeah.
HAHAHA!
Did you see his face?
HAHA!
He looked like he was gonna explode!
Yeah!
Haha!
Thanks for your help, Biscuits!
You really captured the essence of the role. Mr. Piggily Higglesworth, I hope to see you again one day, you brave fellow.
Hehe.
I've gotta return this stuff to Mr. Brickle. Good luck with your case, Beans!

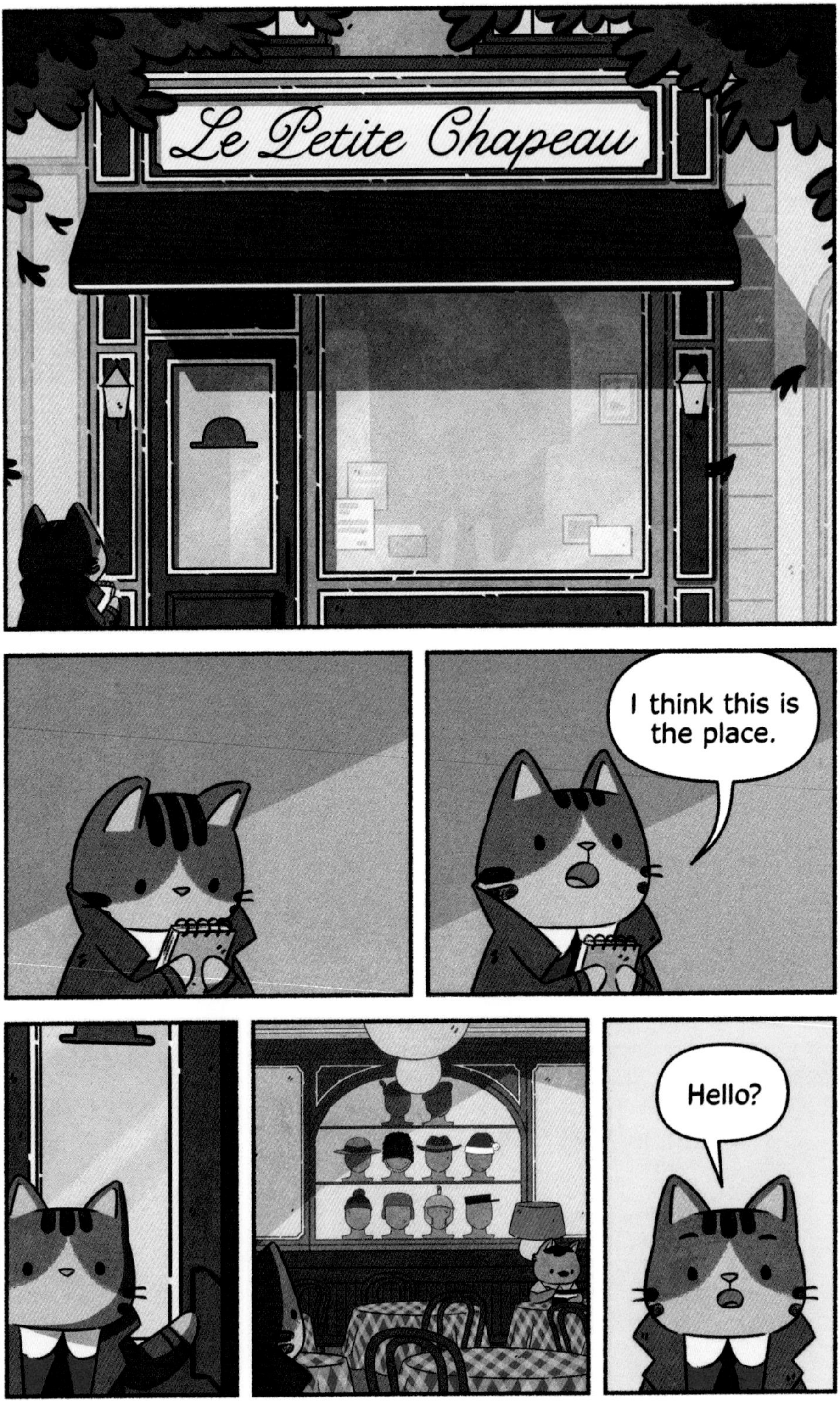
Le Petite Chapeau
I think this is the place.
Hello?

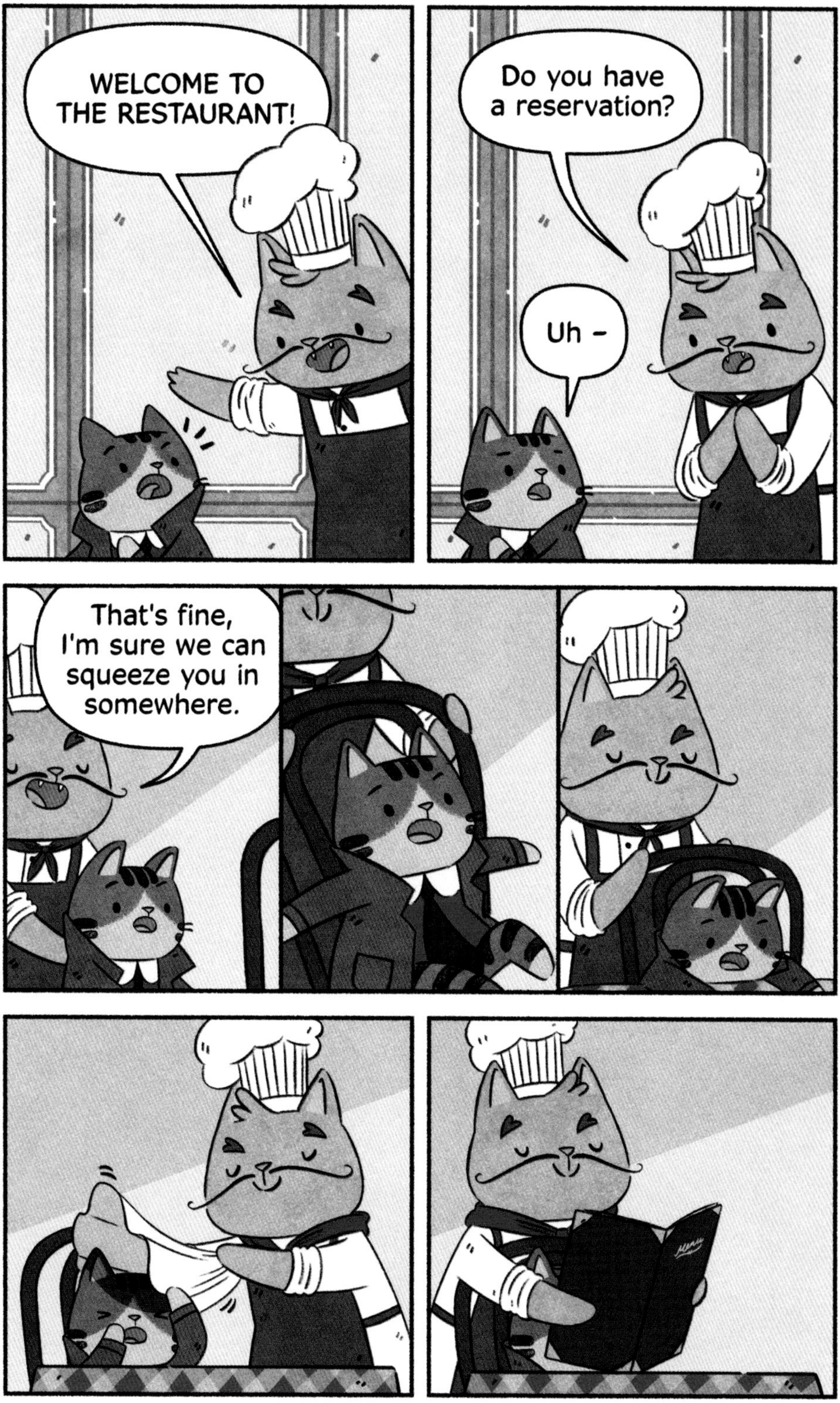
WELCOME TO THE RESTAURANT!
Do you have a reservation?
Uh -
That's fine, I'm sure we can squeeze you in somewhere.

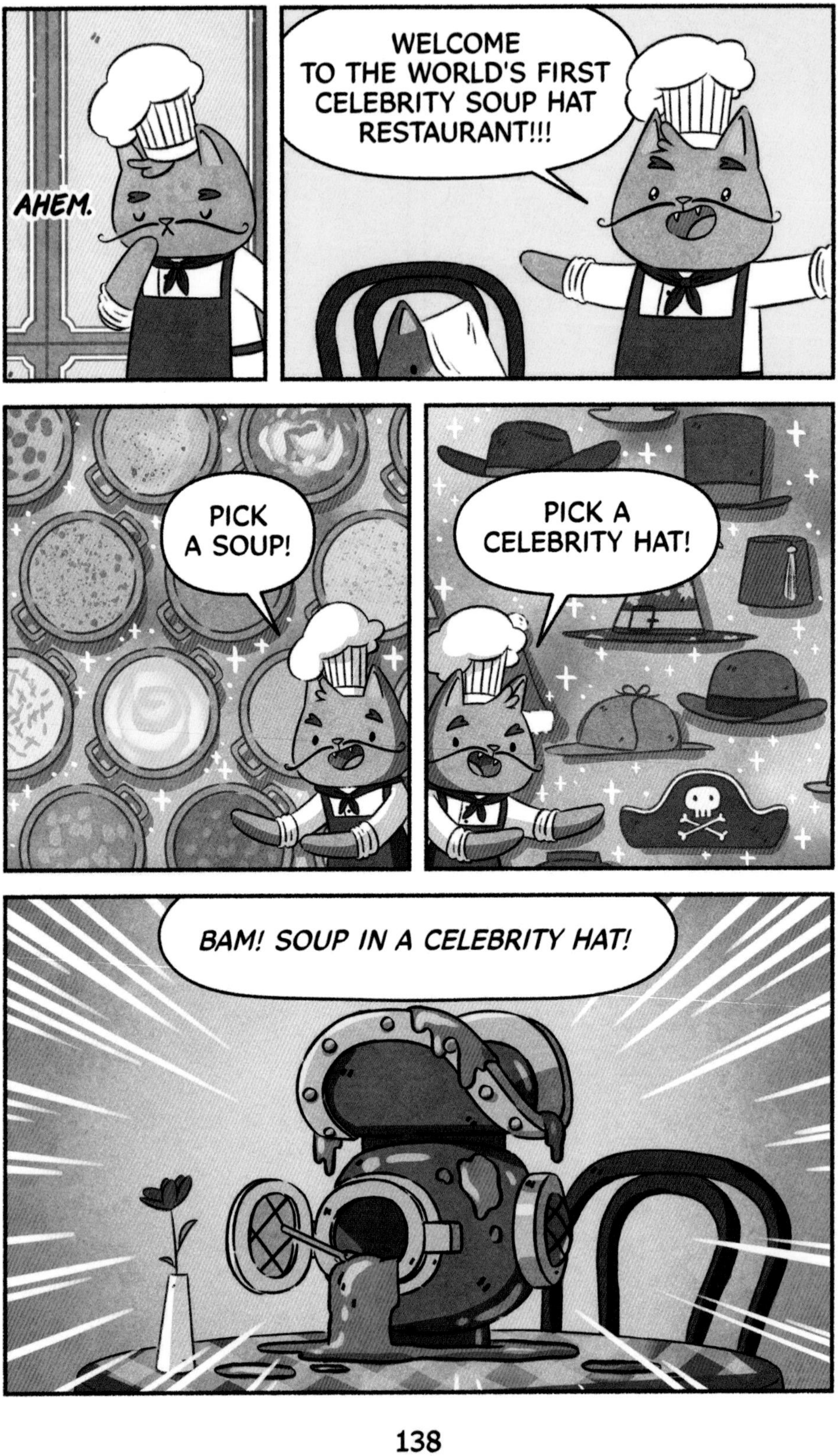
AHEM.
WELCOME TO THE WORLD'S FIRST CELEBRITY SOUP HAT RESTAURANT!!!
PICK A SOUP!
PICK A CELEBRITY HAT!
BAM! SOUP IN A CELEBRITY HAT!

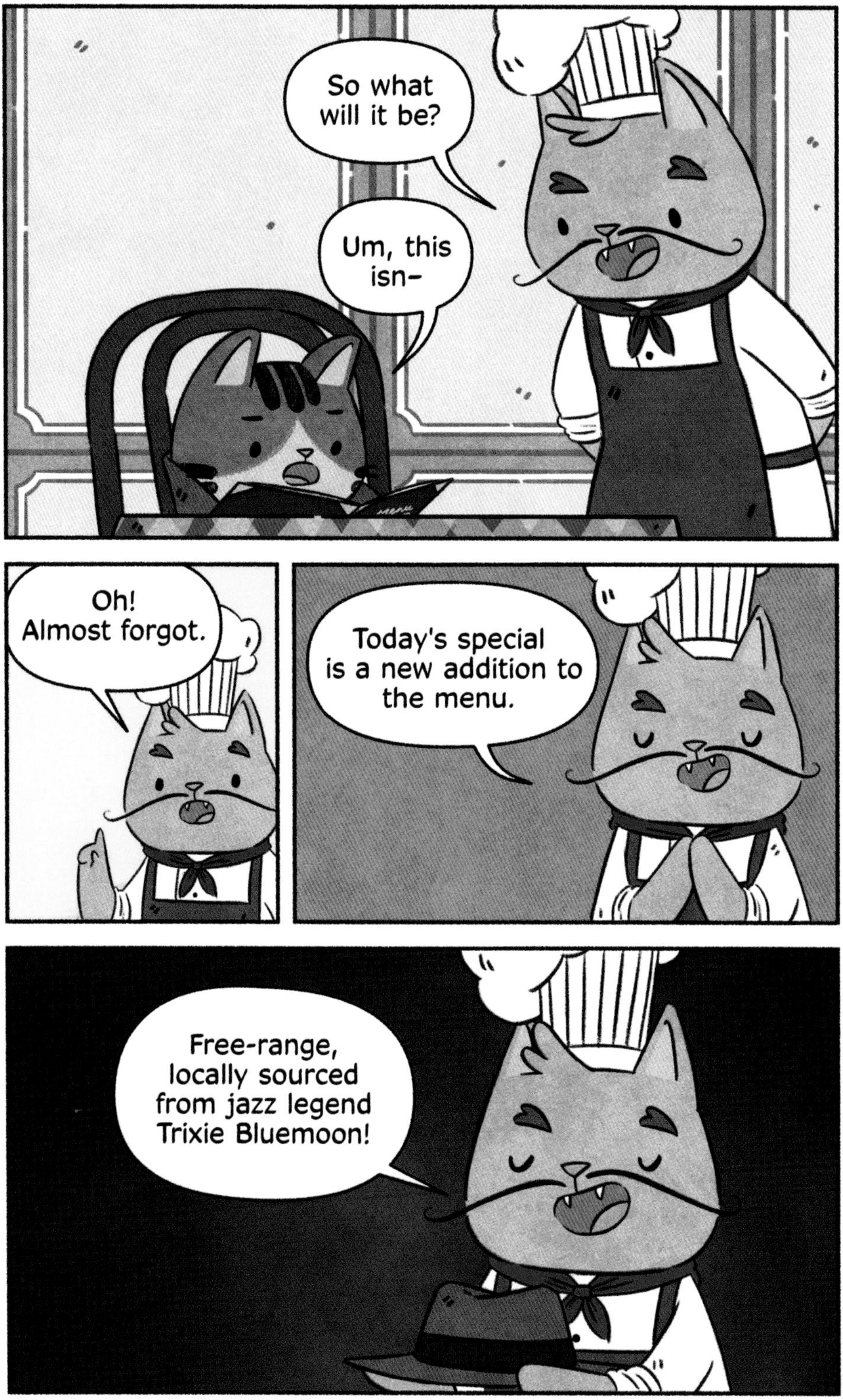
So what will it be?
Um, this isn–
Oh! Almost forgot.
Today's special is a new addition to the menu.
Free-range, locally sourced from jazz legend Trixie Bluemoon!

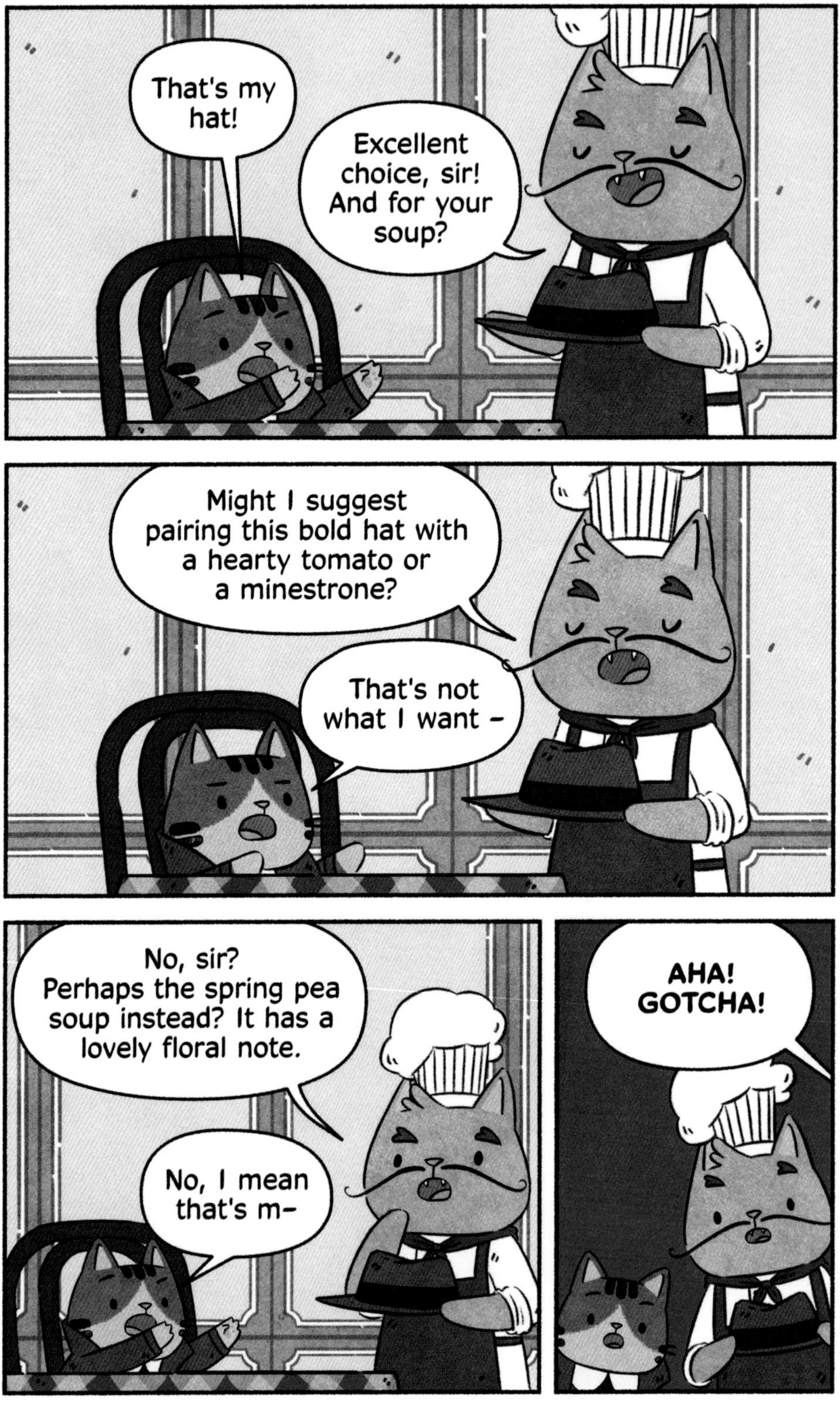

That's my hat!
Excellent choice, sir! And for your soup?
Might I suggest pairing this bold hat with a hearty tomato or a minestrone?
That's not what I want –
No, sir? Perhaps the spring pea soup instead? It has a lovely floral note.
No, I mean that's m–
AHA! GOTCHA!

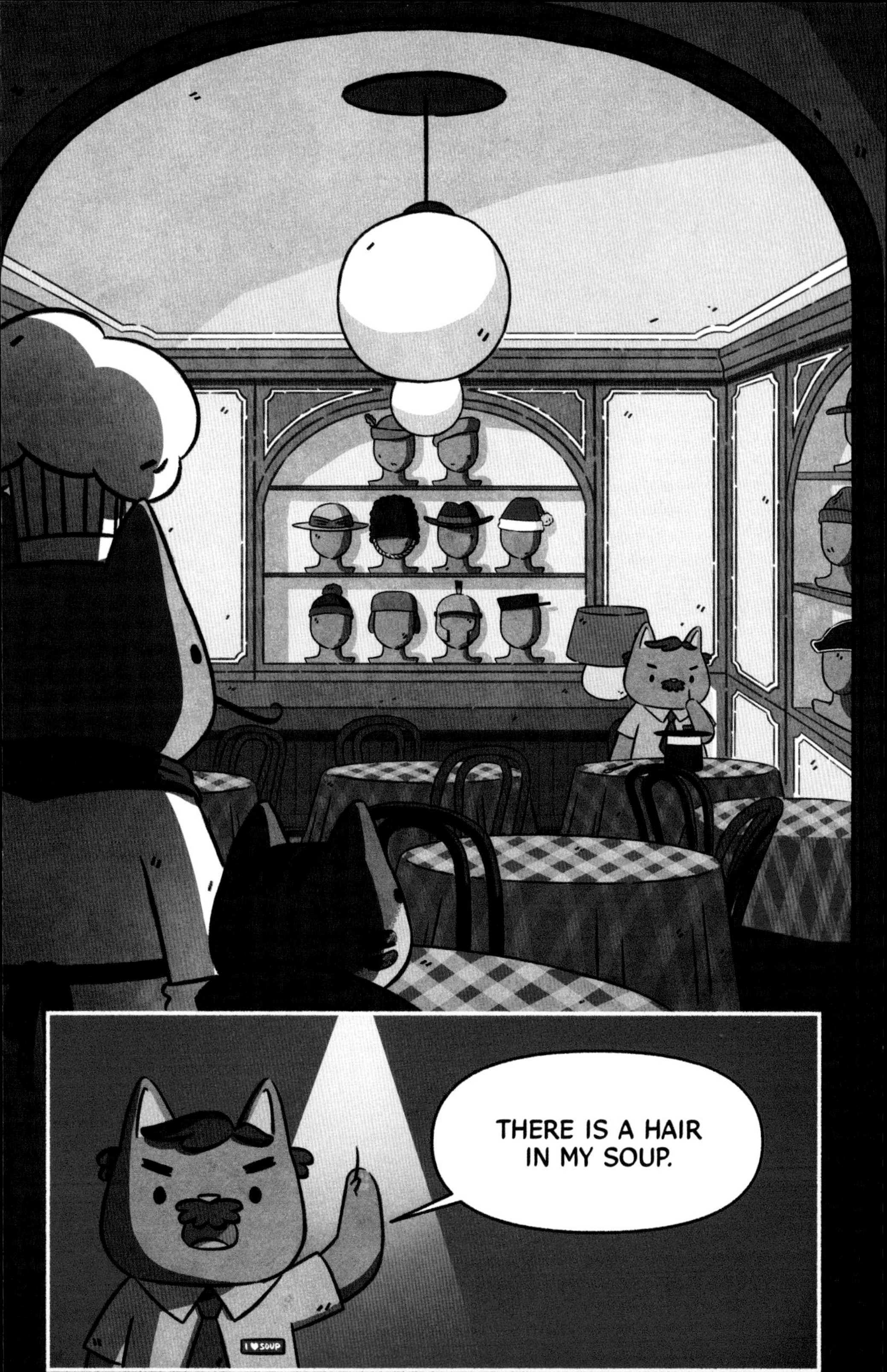
THERE IS A HAIR IN MY SOUP.
I ♥ SOUP

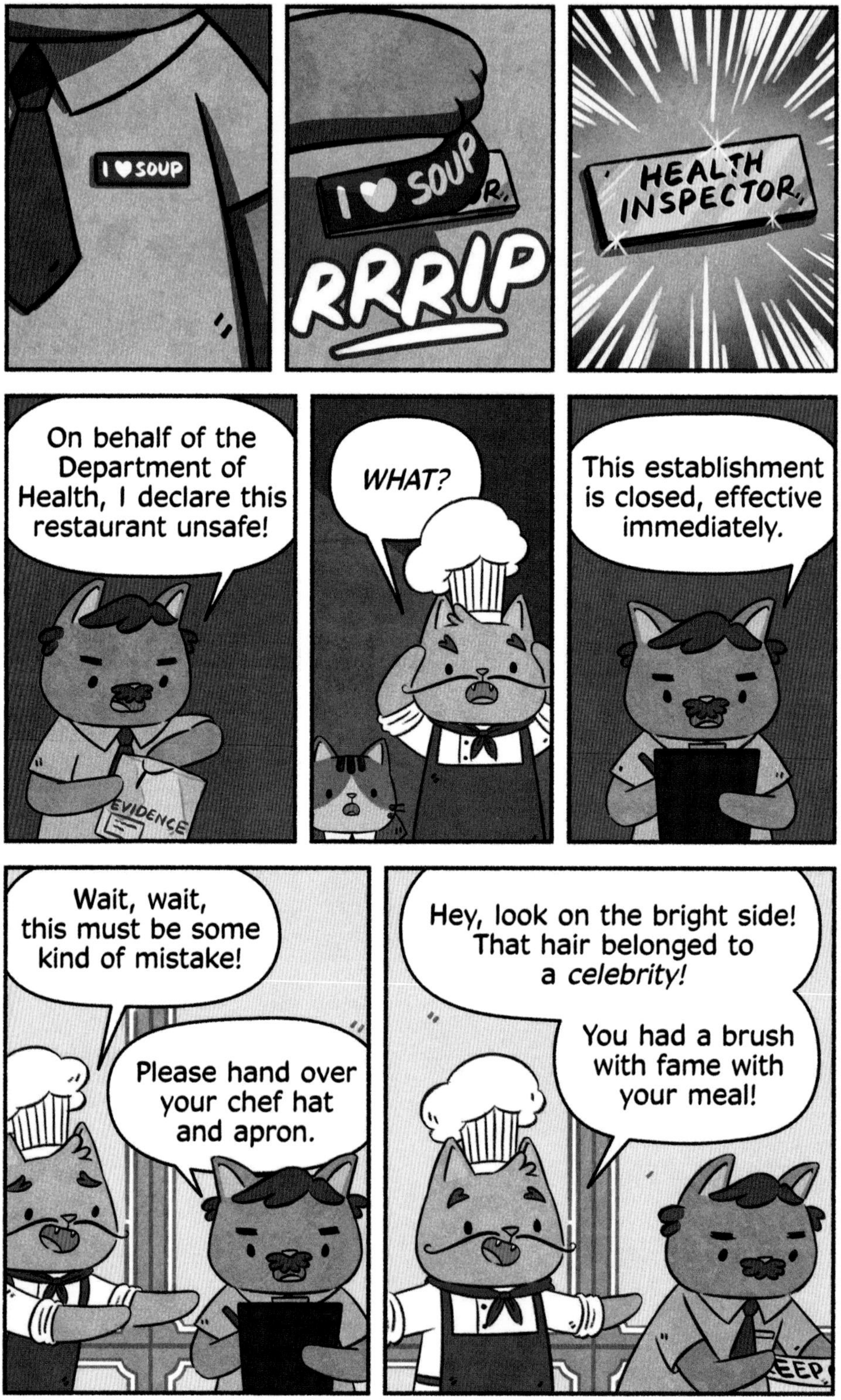
I ♥ SOUP
I ♥ SOUP
RRRIP
HEALTH INSPECTOR
On behalf of the Department of Health, I declare this restaurant unsafe!
EVIDENCE
WHAT?
This establishment is closed, effective immediately.
Wait, wait, this must be some kind of mistake!
Please hand over your chef hat and apron.
Hey, look on the bright side! That hair belonged to a *celebrity!*
You had a brush with fame with your meal!

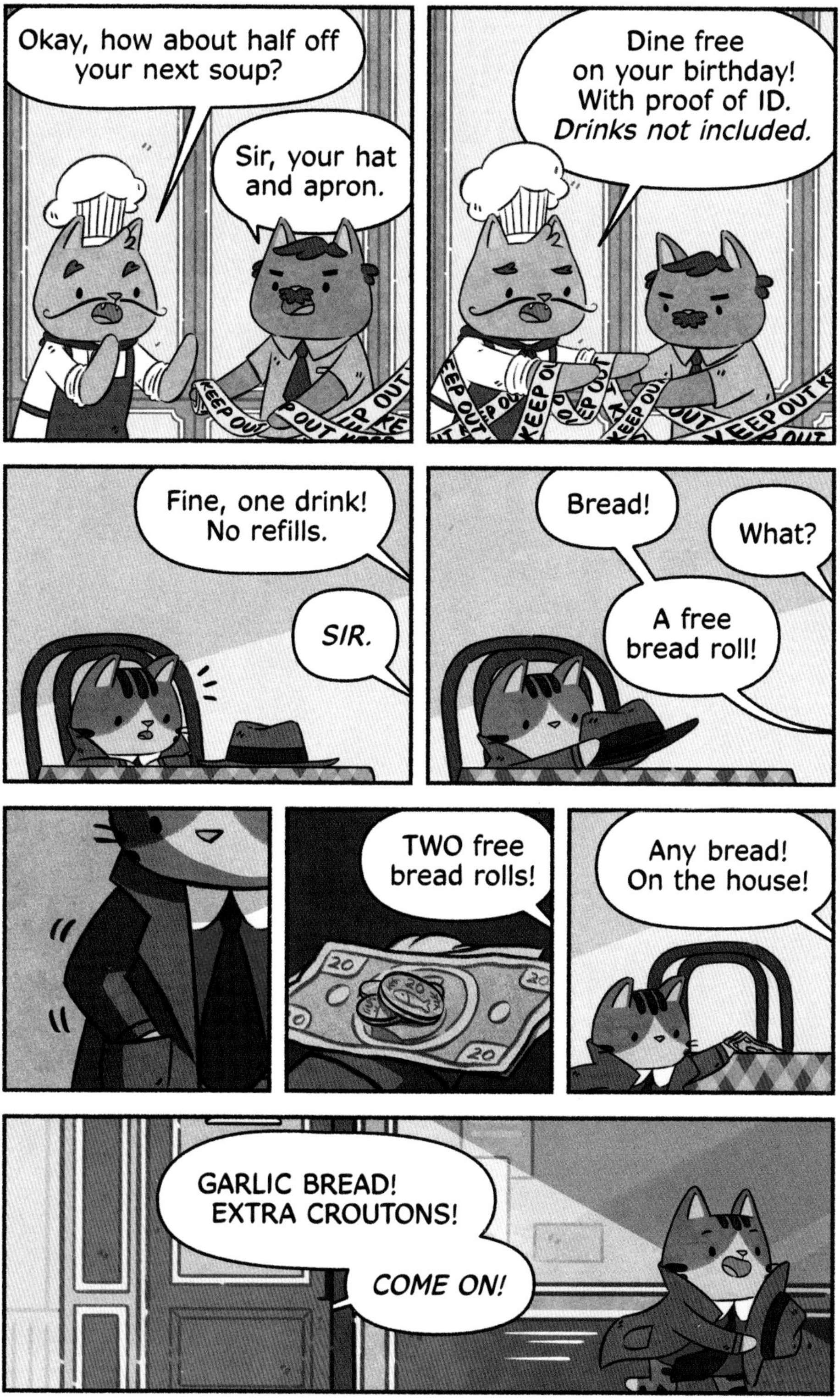

Okay, how about half off your next soup?
Sir, your hat and apron.
Dine free on your birthday! With proof of ID. *Drinks not included.*
KEEP OUT
Fine, one drink! No refills.
SIR.
Bread!
What?
A free bread roll!
TWO free bread rolls!
20
Any bread! On the house!
GARLIC BREAD! EXTRA CROUTONS!
COME ON!

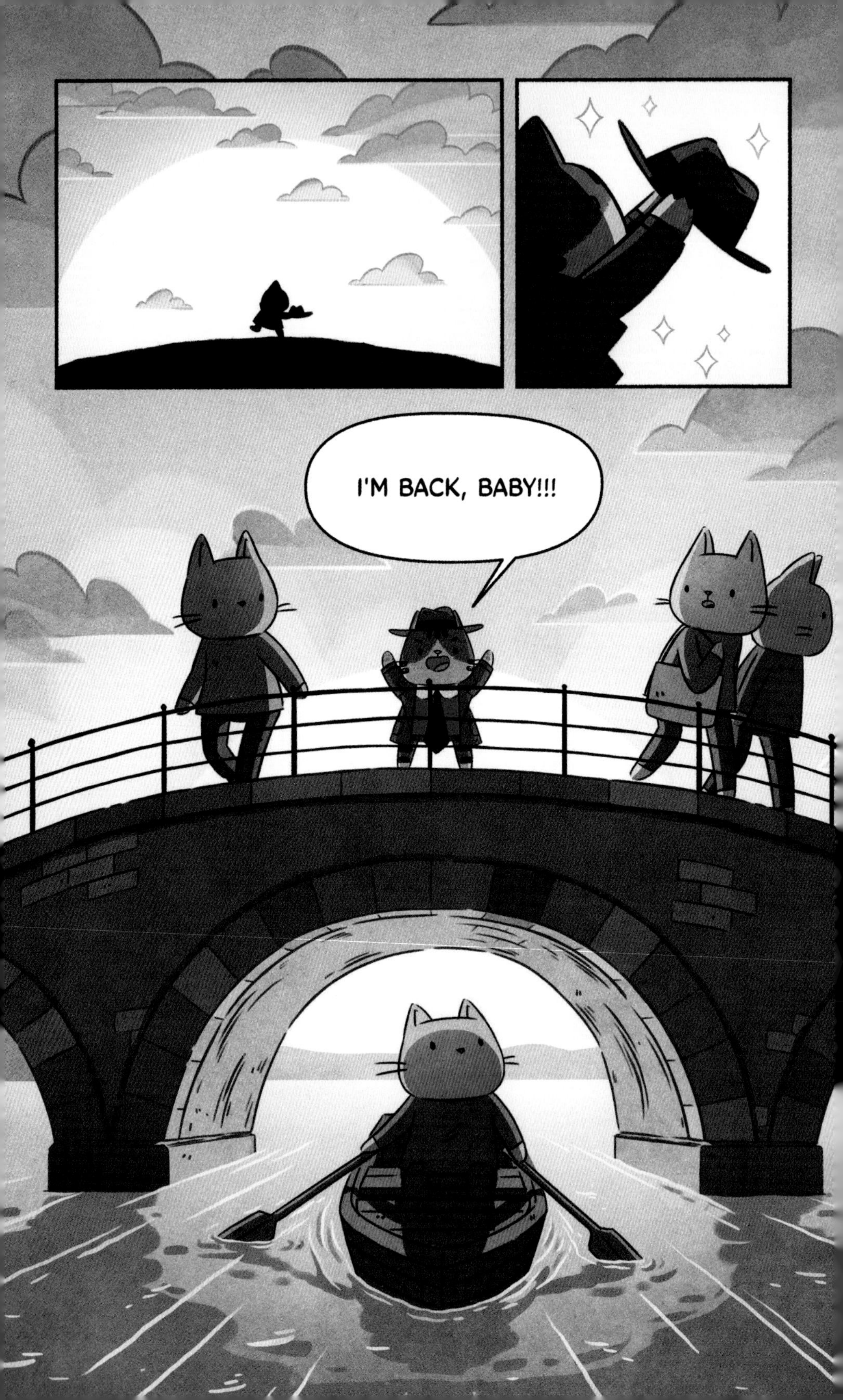
I'M BACK, BABY!!!

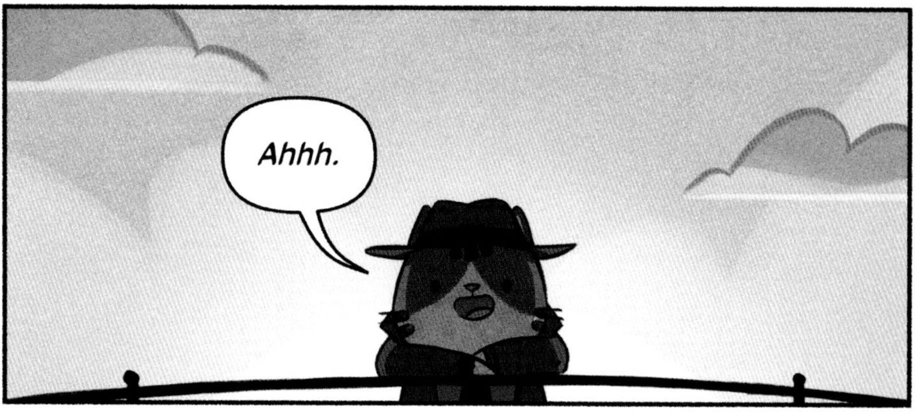
Ahhh.

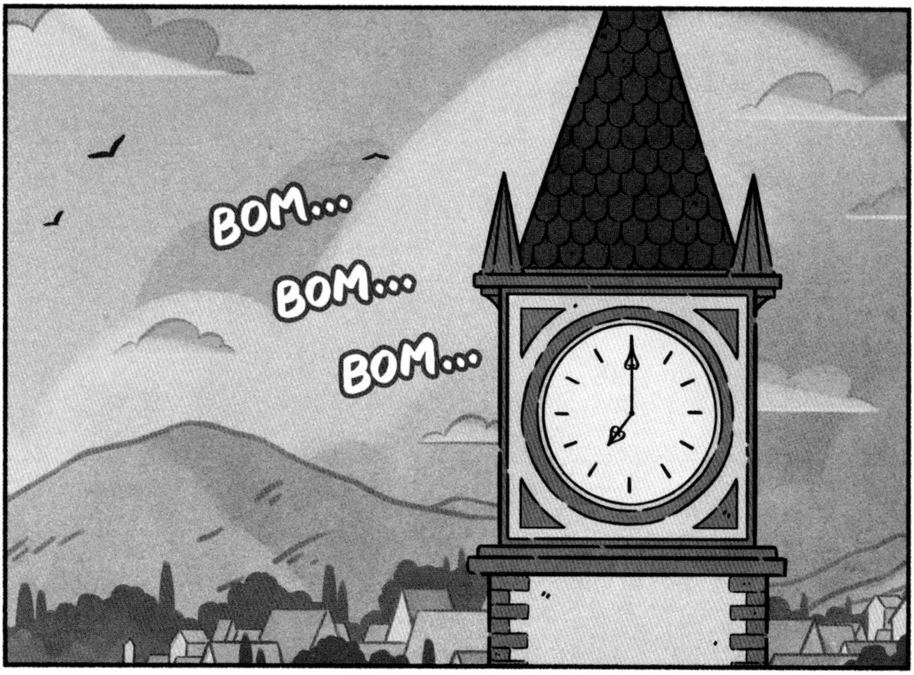
BOM...
BOM...
BOM...

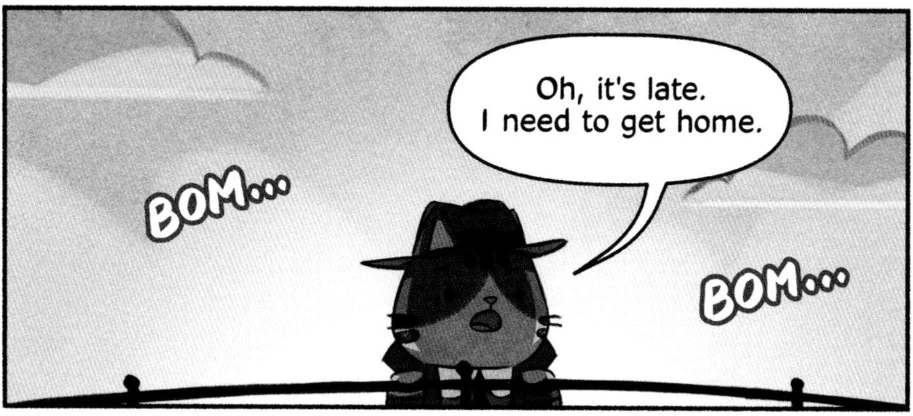
Oh, it's late.
I need to get home.
BOM...
BOM...

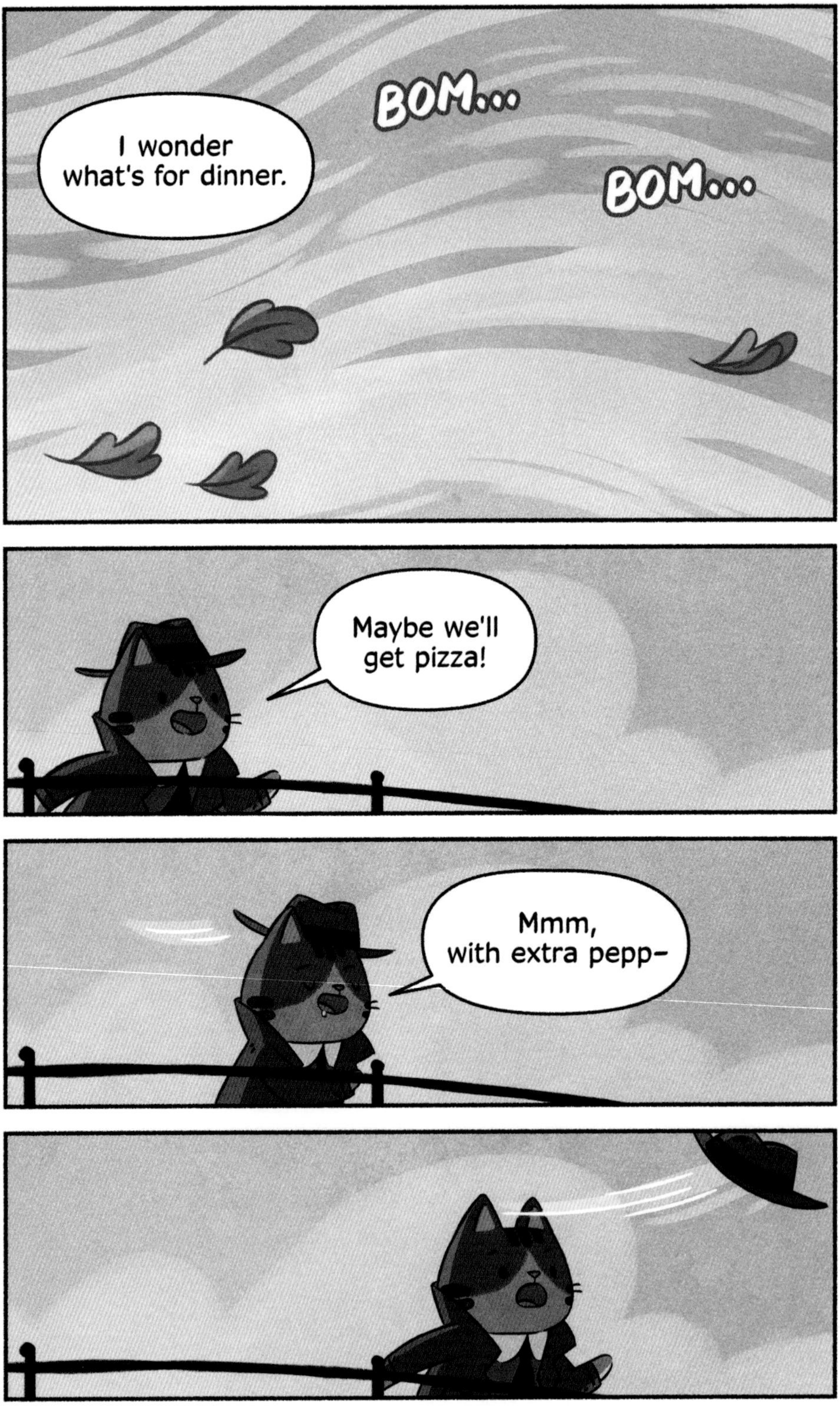
I wonder what's for dinner.
BOM...
BOM...
Maybe we'll get pizza!
Mmm, with extra pepp-

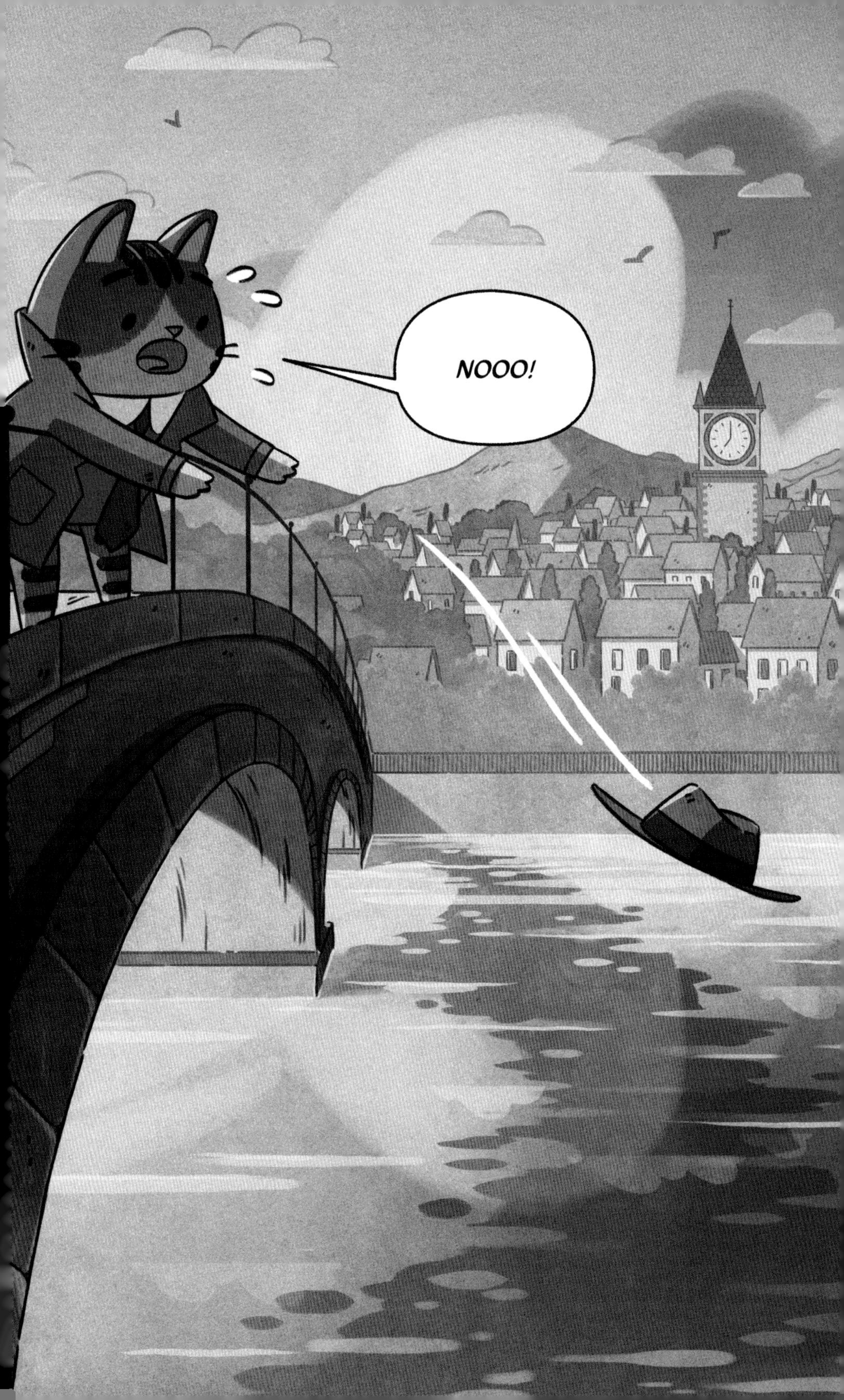
NOOO!

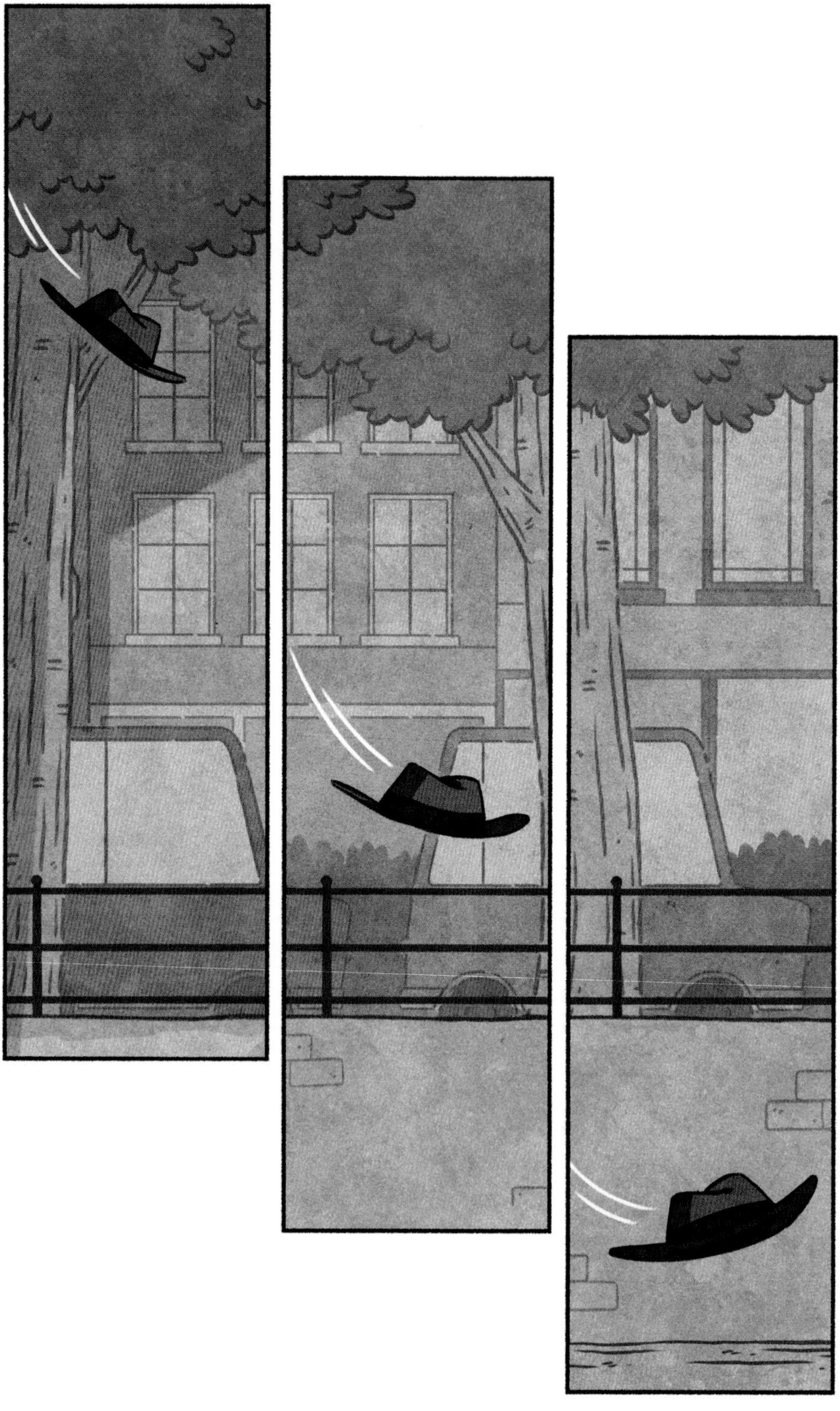

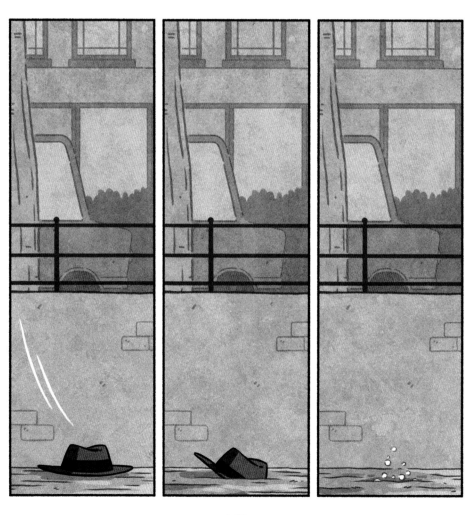

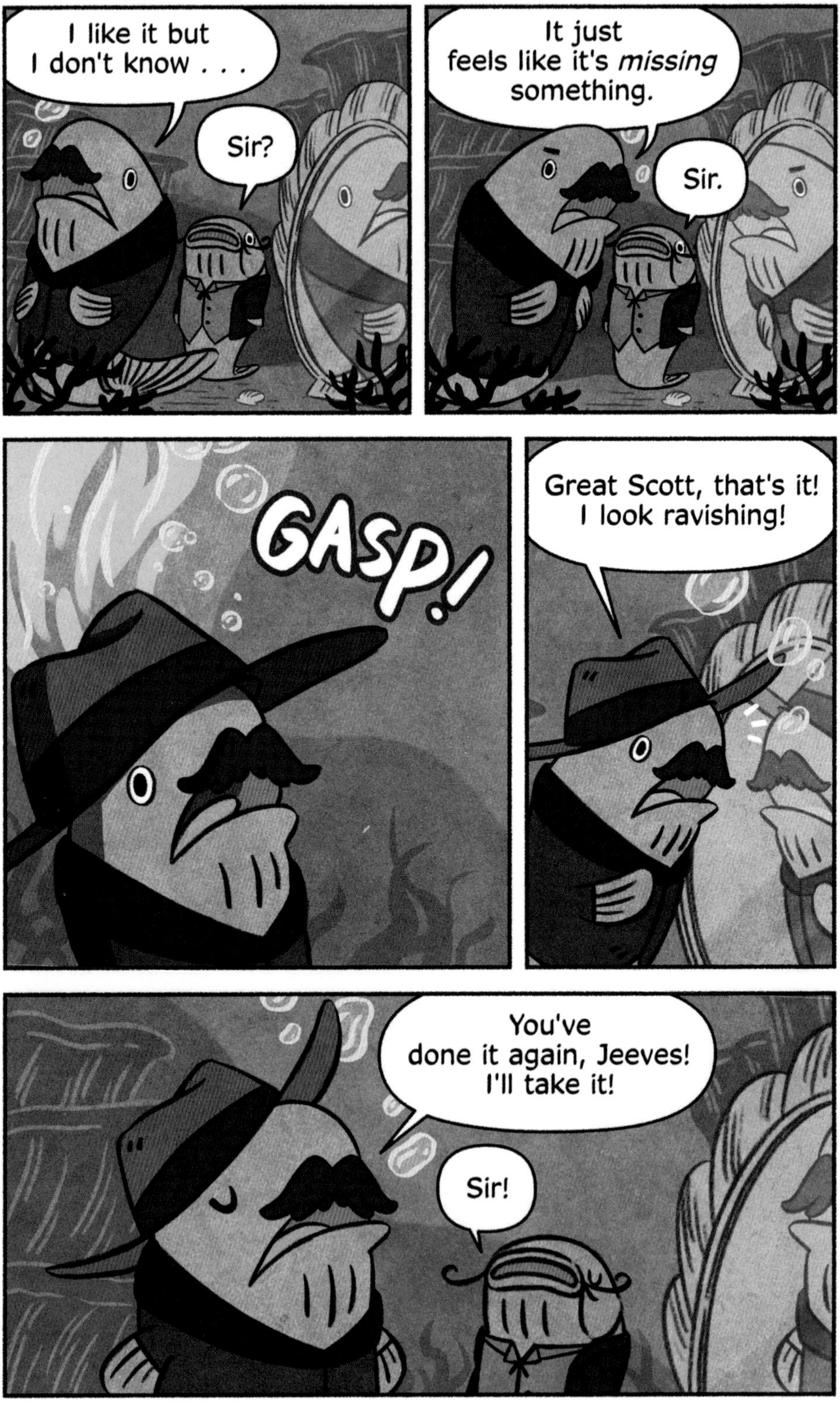
I like it but
I don't know . . .
Sir?
It just feels like it's *missing* something.
Sir.
GASP!
Great Scott, that's it! I look ravishing!
You've done it again, Jeeves! I'll take it!
Sir!

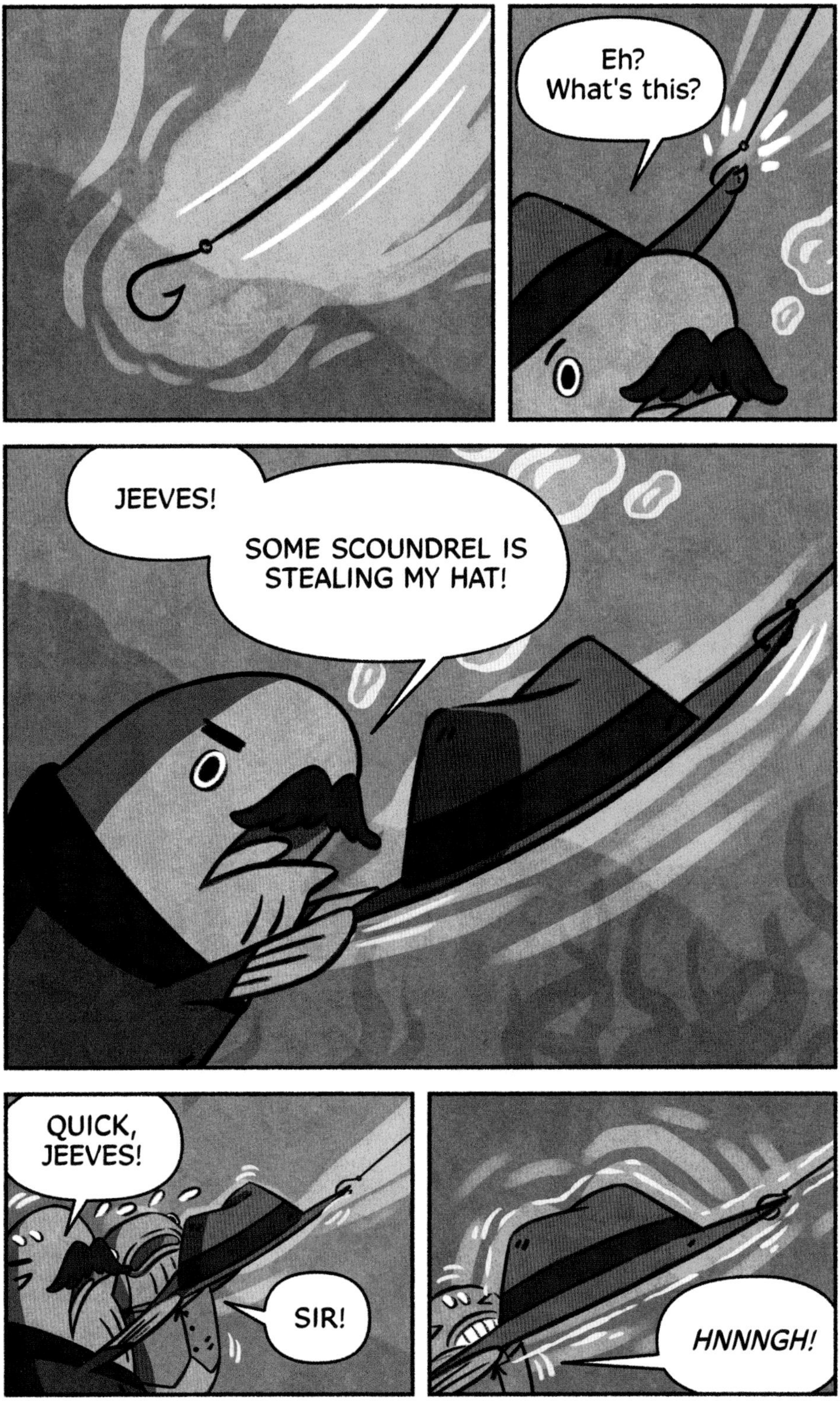
Eh?
What's this?
JEEVES!
SOME SCOUNDREL IS STEALING MY HAT!
QUICK, JEEVES!
SIR!
HNNNGH!

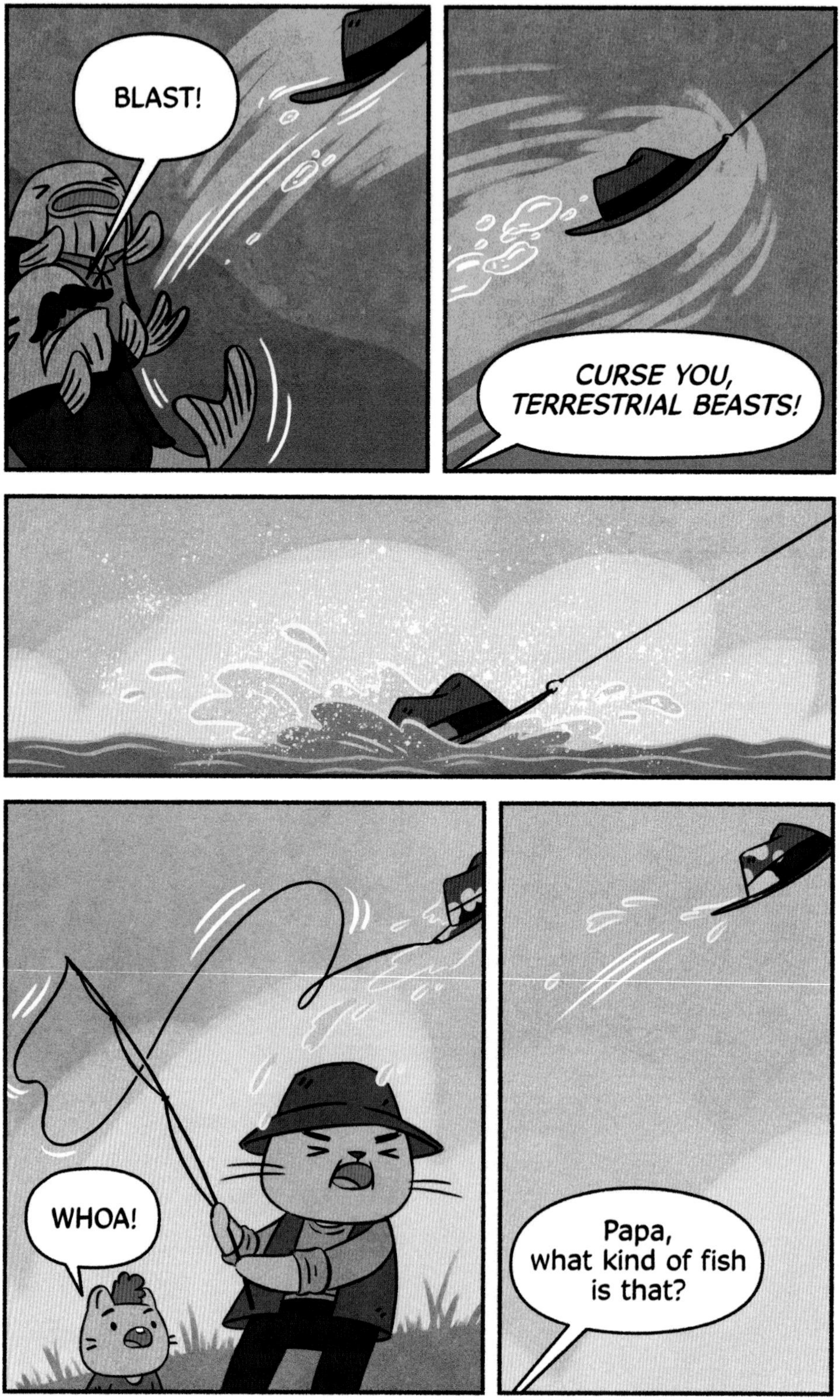
BLAST!
CURSE YOU, TERRESTRIAL BEASTS!
WHOA!
Papa, what kind of fish is that?

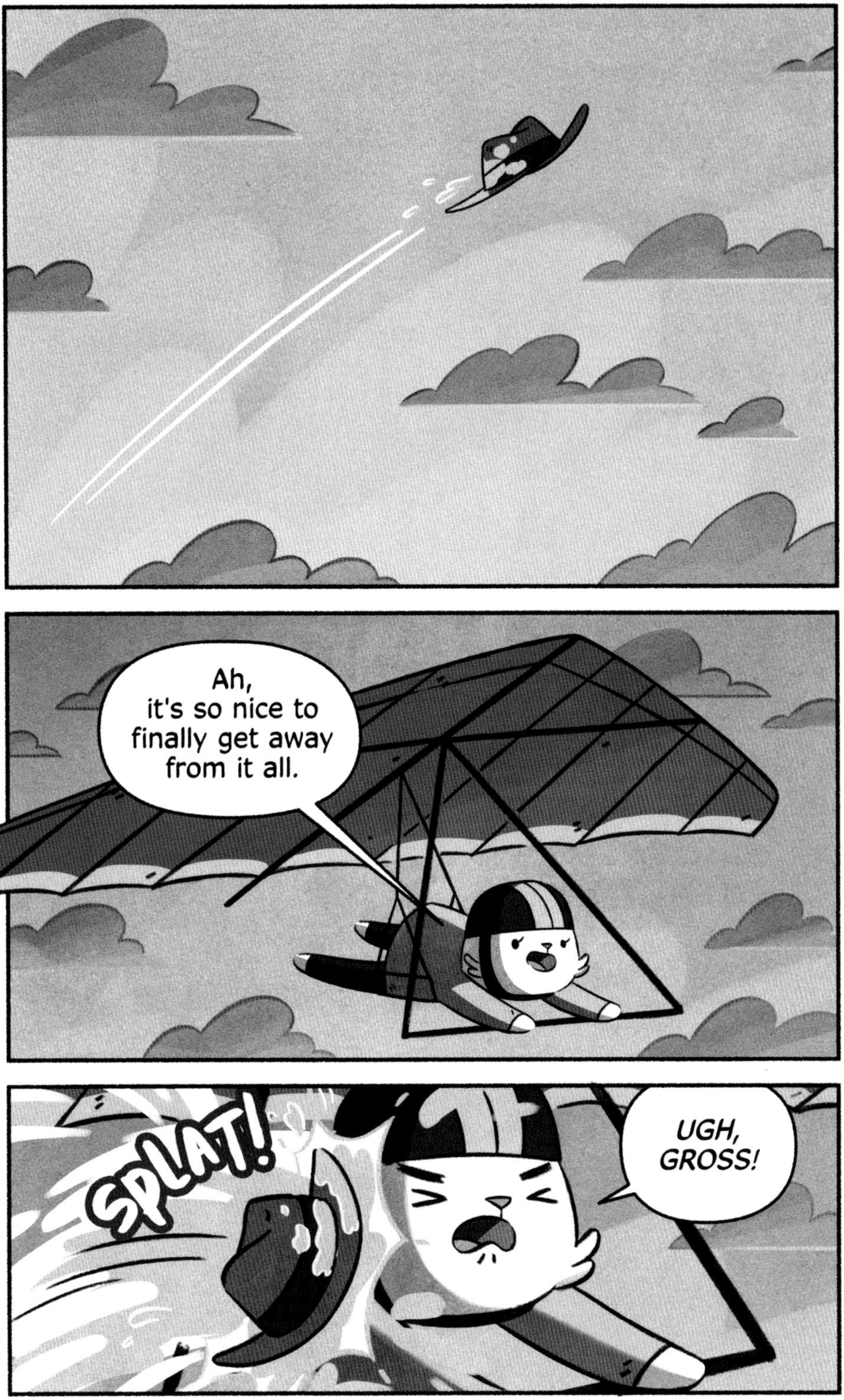
Ah,
it's so nice to finally get away from it all.
SPLAT!
UGH, GROSS!

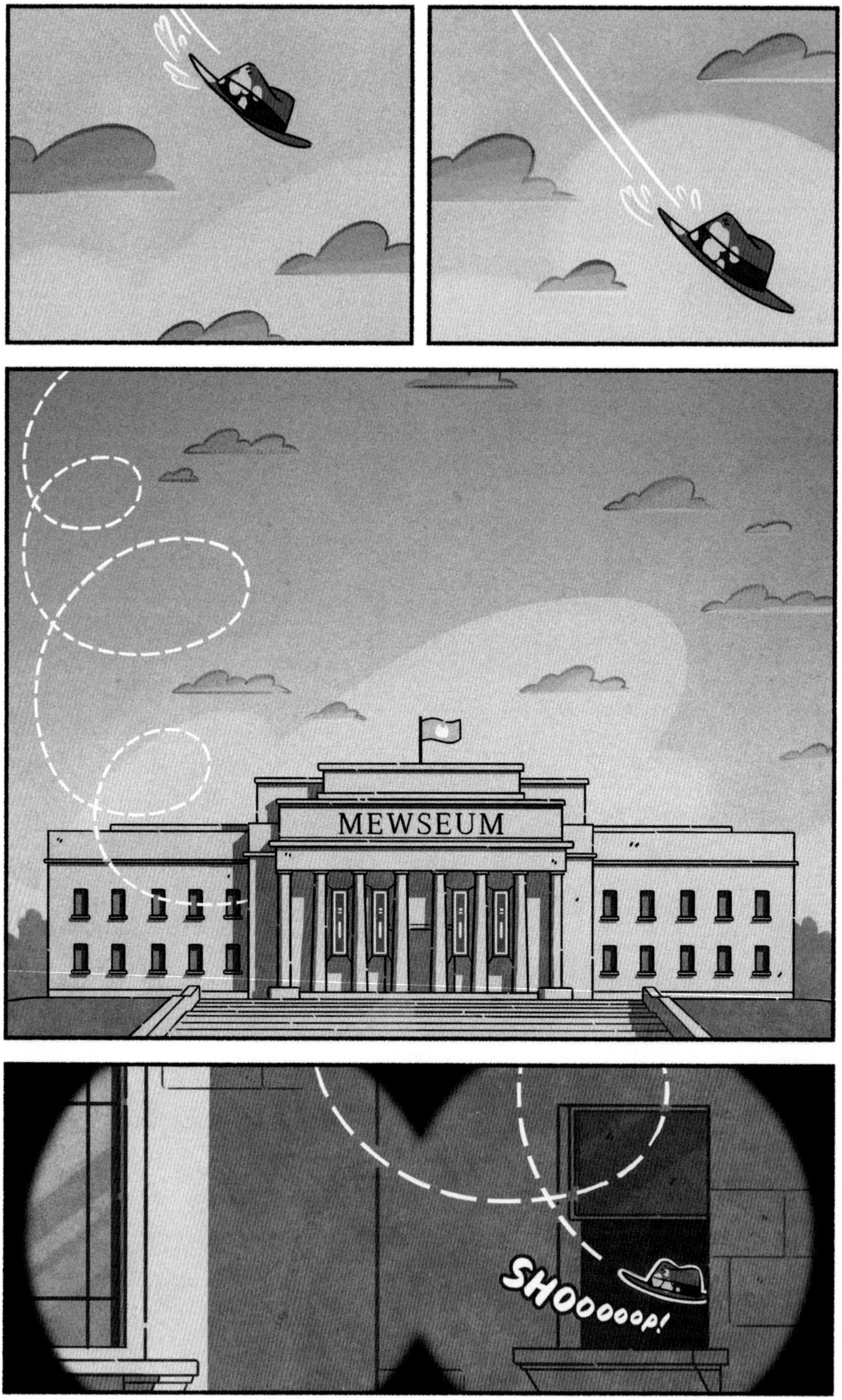
MEWSEUM
SHOOOOOP!

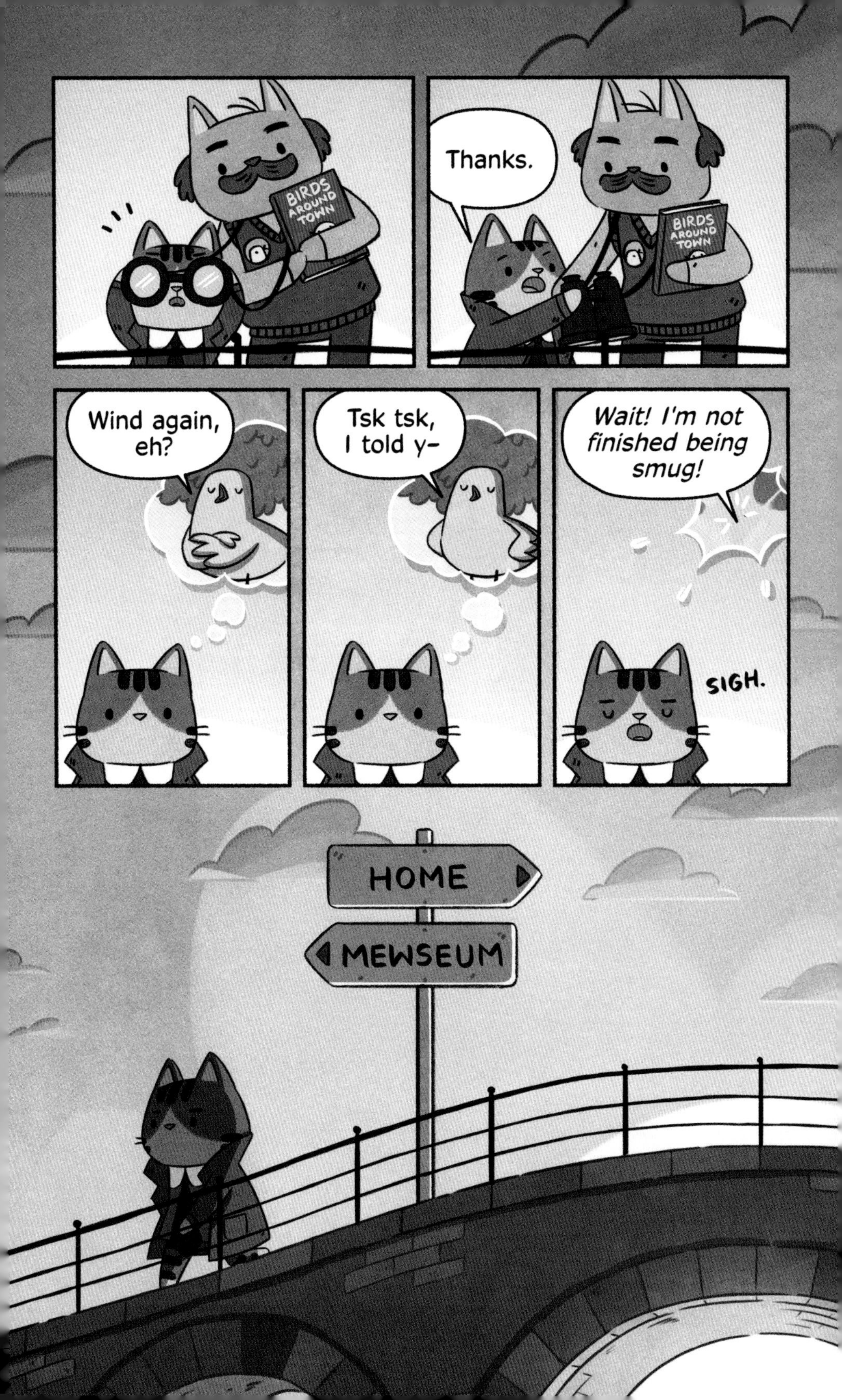
BIRDS AROUND TOWN
Thanks.
BIRDS AROUND TOWN
Wind again, eh?
Tsk tsk, I told y-
Wait! I'm not finished being smug!
SIGH.
HOME
MEWSEUM

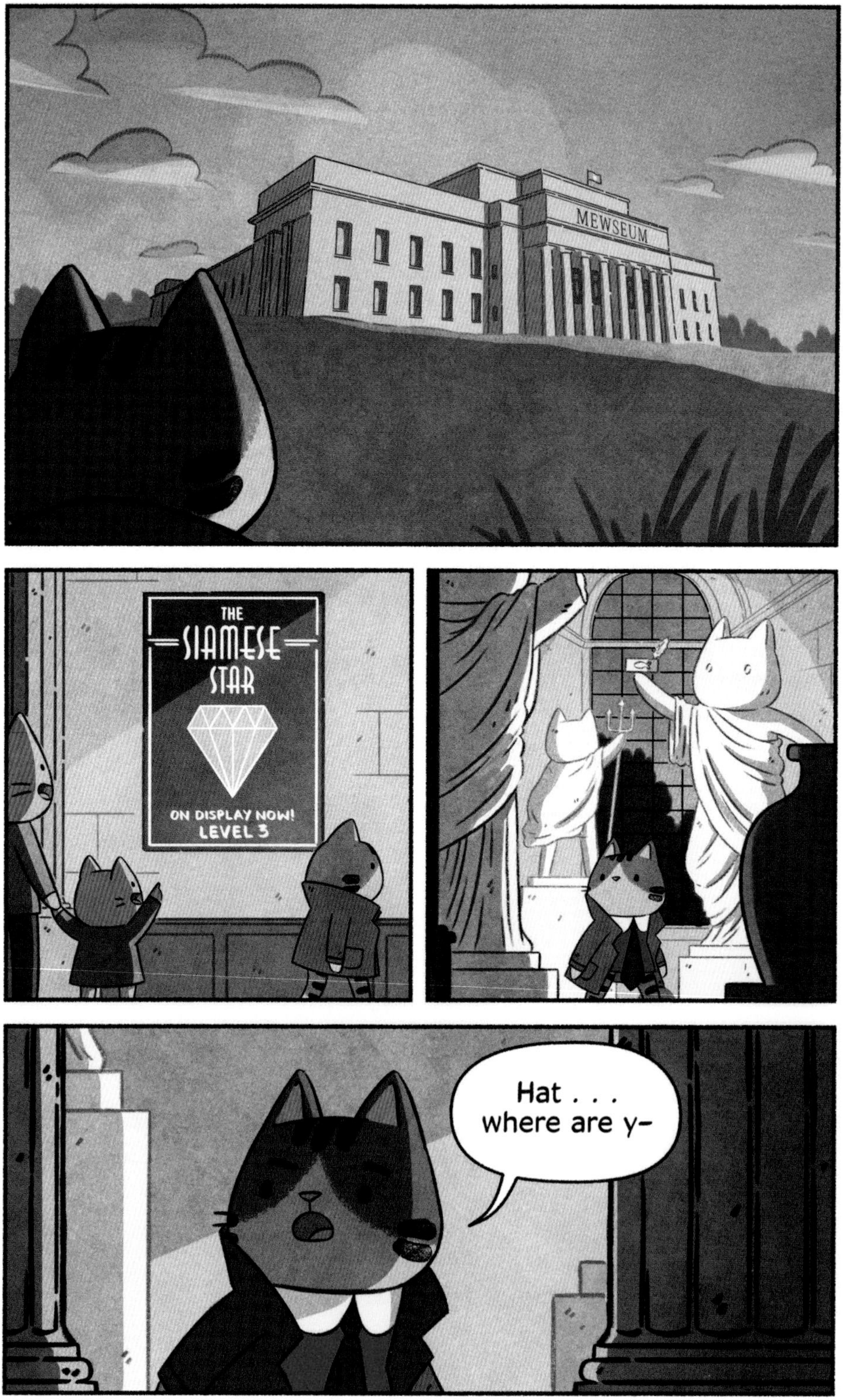
MEWSEUM
THE SIAMESE STAR
ON DISPLAY NOW!
LEVEL 3
Hat . . .
where are y-

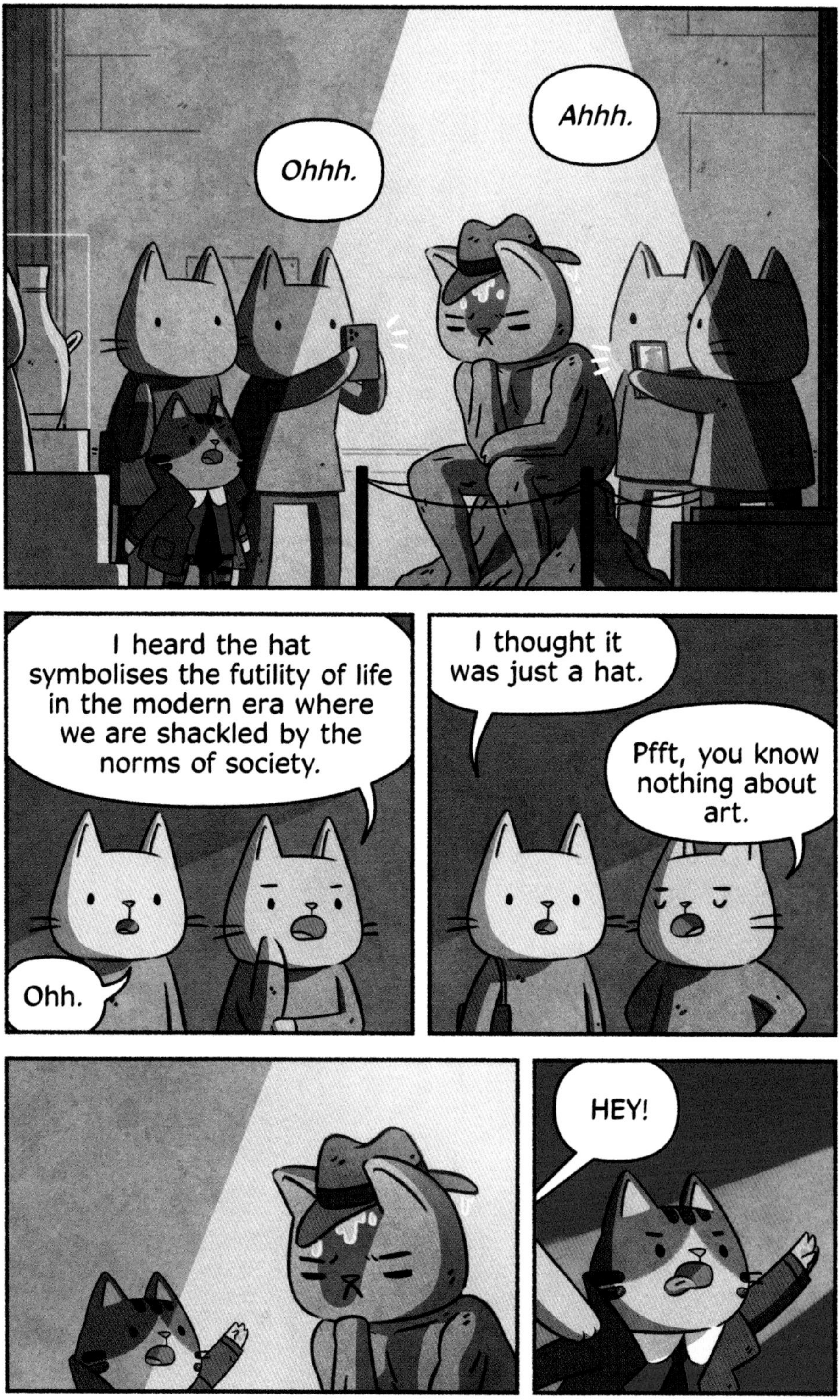

Ohhh.
Ahhh.
I heard the hat symbolises the futility of life in the modern era where we are shackled by the norms of society.
Ohh.
I thought it was just a hat.
Pfft, you know nothing about art.
HEY!

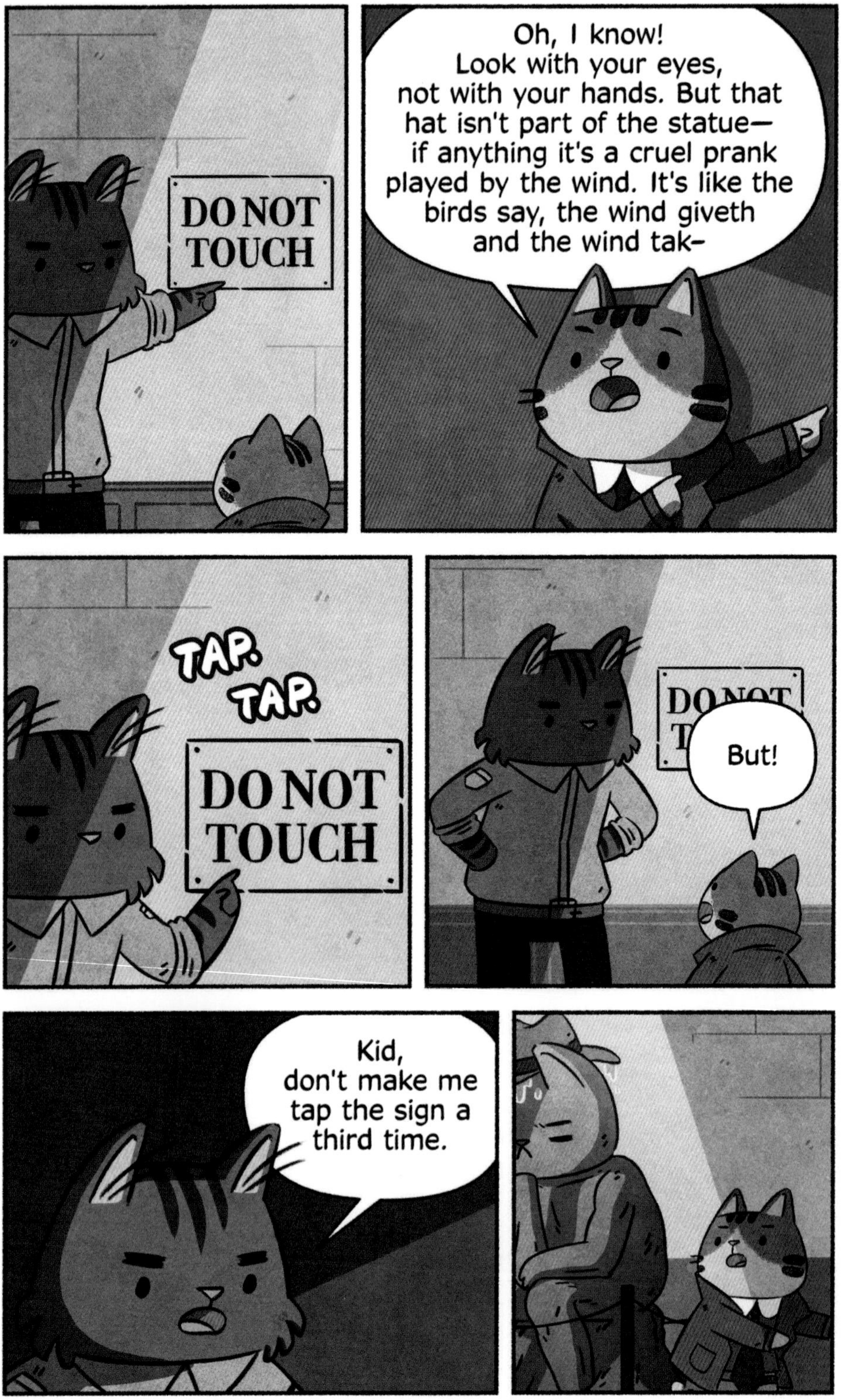
DO NOT TOUCH
Oh, I know! Look with your eyes, not with your hands. But that hat isn't part of the statue— if anything it's a cruel prank played by the wind. It's like the birds say, the wind giveth and the wind tak–
TAP. TAP.
DO NOT TOUCH
But!
Kid, don't make me tap the sign a third time.

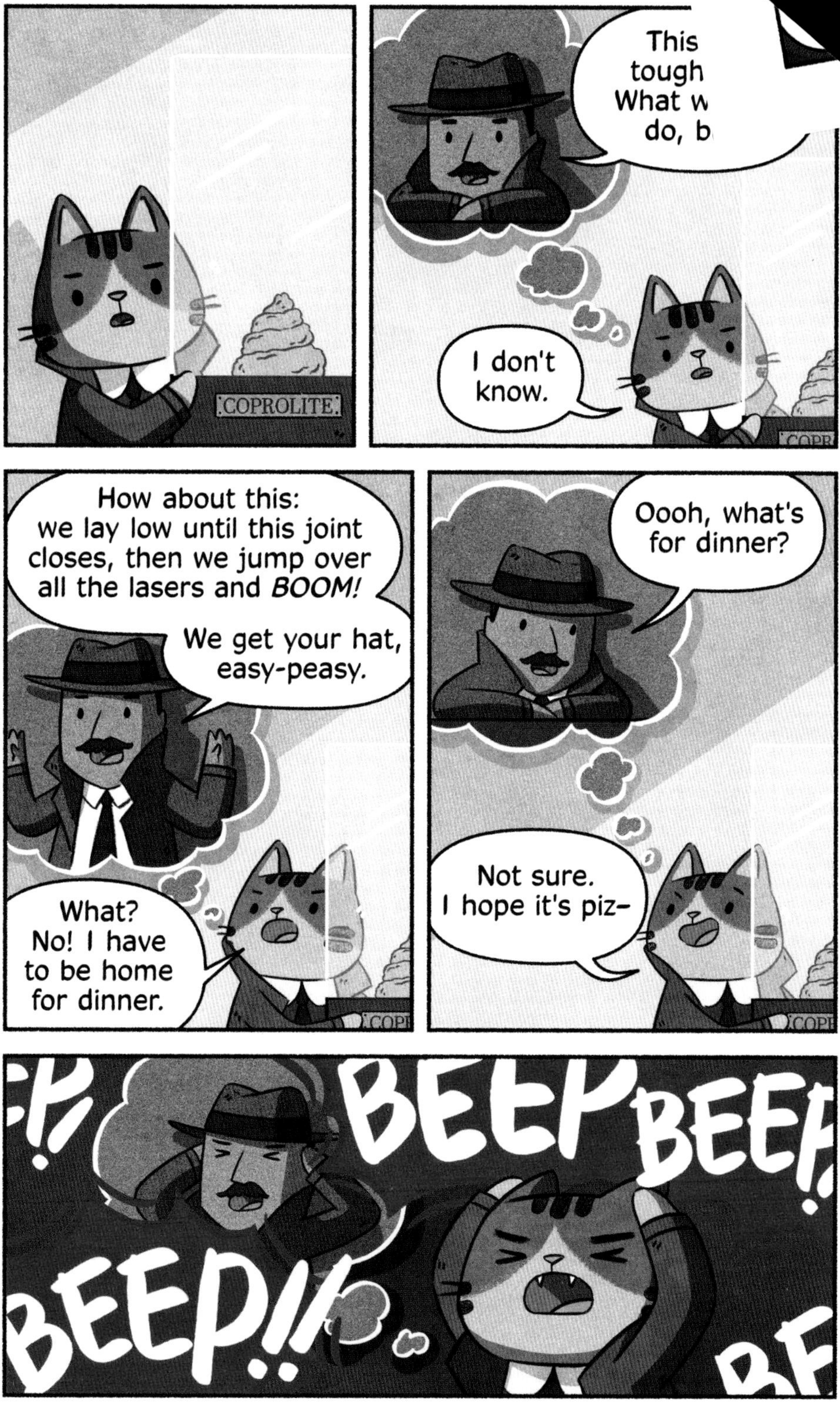
COPROLITE
This
tough
What w
do, b
I don't know.
How about this: we lay low until this joint closes, then we jump over all the lasers and *BOOM!*
We get your hat, easy-peasy.
What? No! I have to be home for dinner.
Oooh, what's for dinner?
Not sure. I hope it's piz–
BEEP
BEEP!!

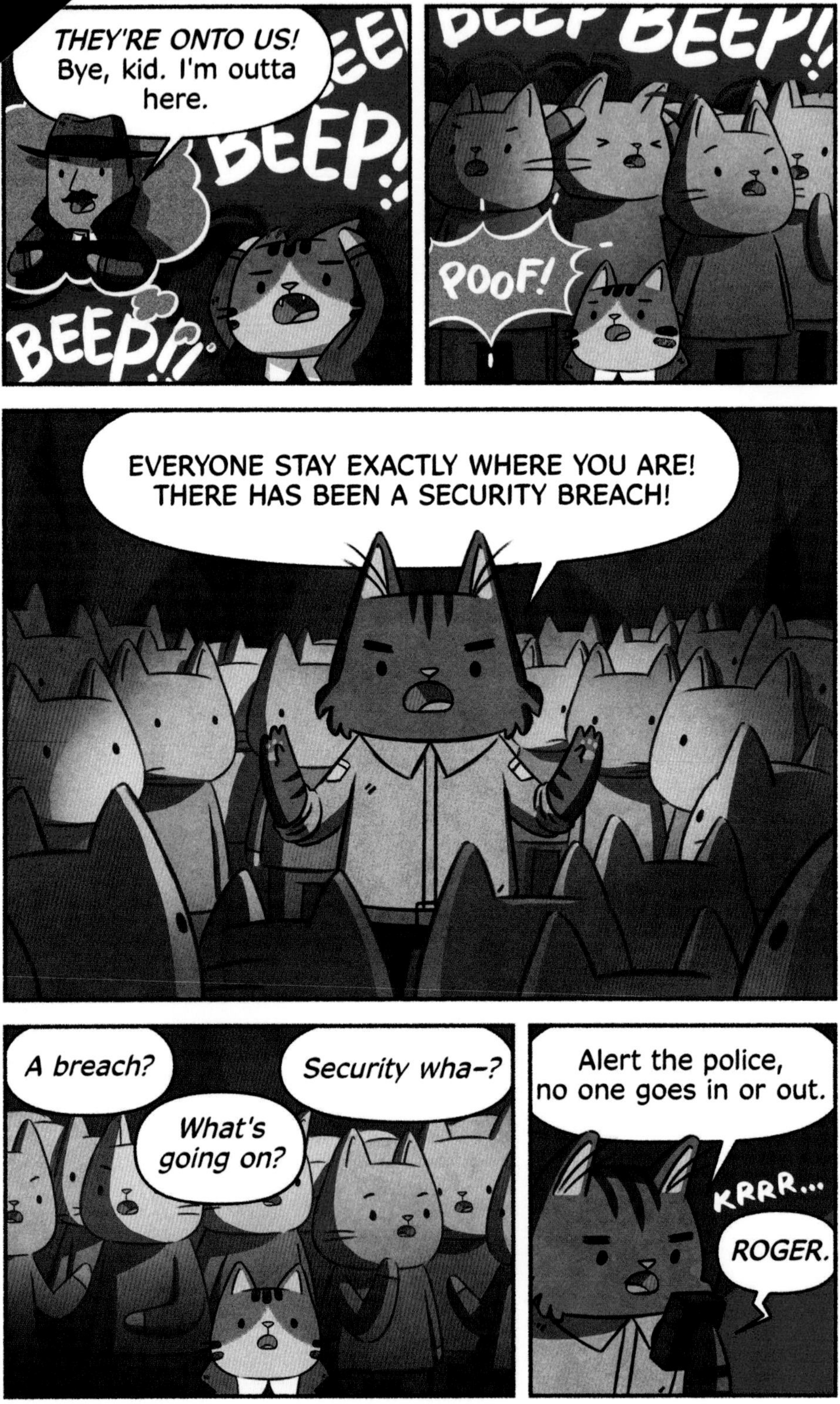
THEY'RE ONTO US!
Bye, kid. I'm outta here.
BEEP!!
BEEP!!
BEEP BEEP!!
POOF!
EVERYONE STAY EXACTLY WHERE YOU ARE!
THERE HAS BEEN A SECURITY BREACH!
A breach?
What's going on?
Security wha-?
Alert the police, no one goes in or out.
KRRR...
ROGER.

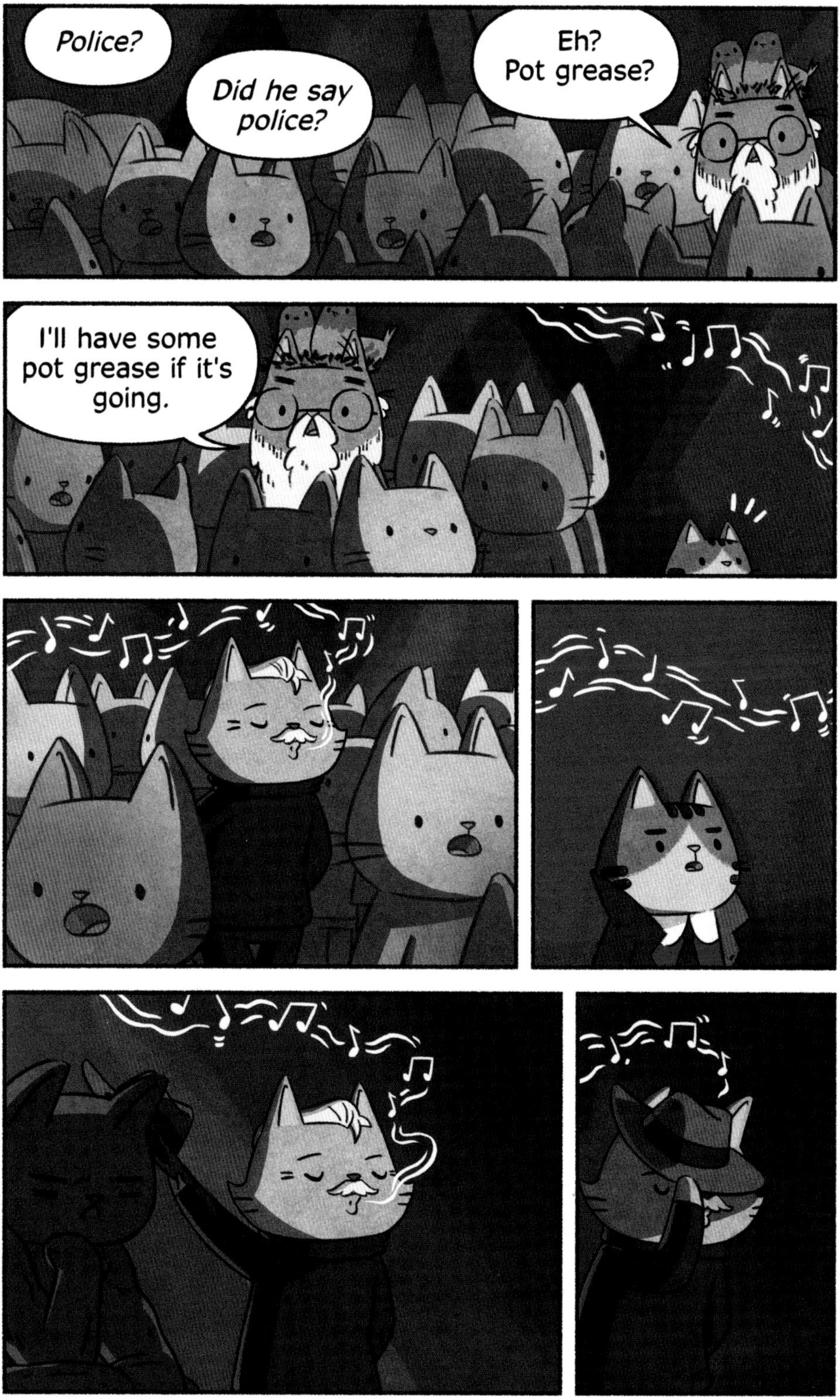
Police?
Did he say police?
Eh? Pot grease?
I'll have some pot grease if it's going.

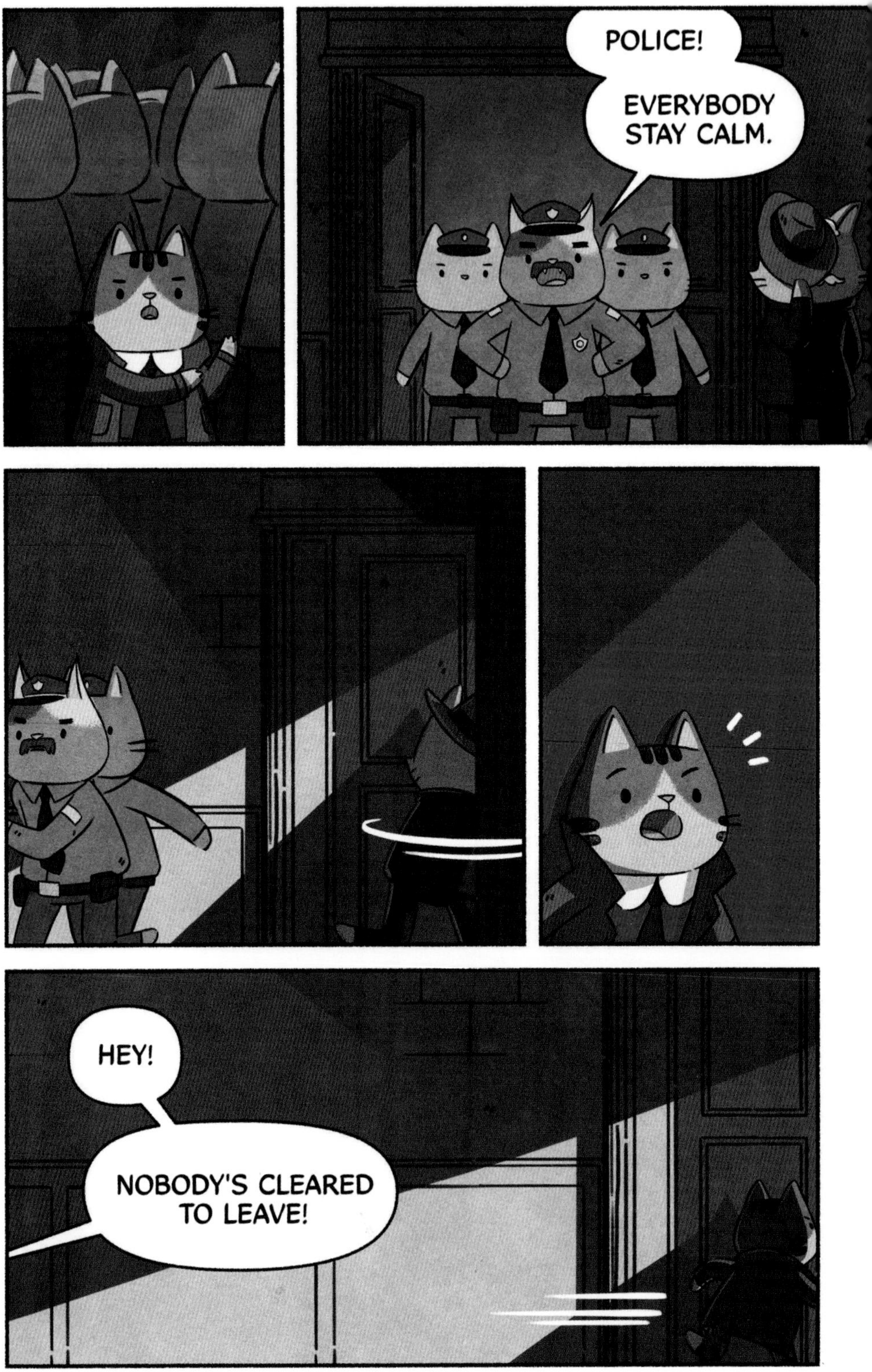
POLICE!
EVERYBODY STAY CALM.
HEY!
NOBODY'S CLEARED TO LEAVE!

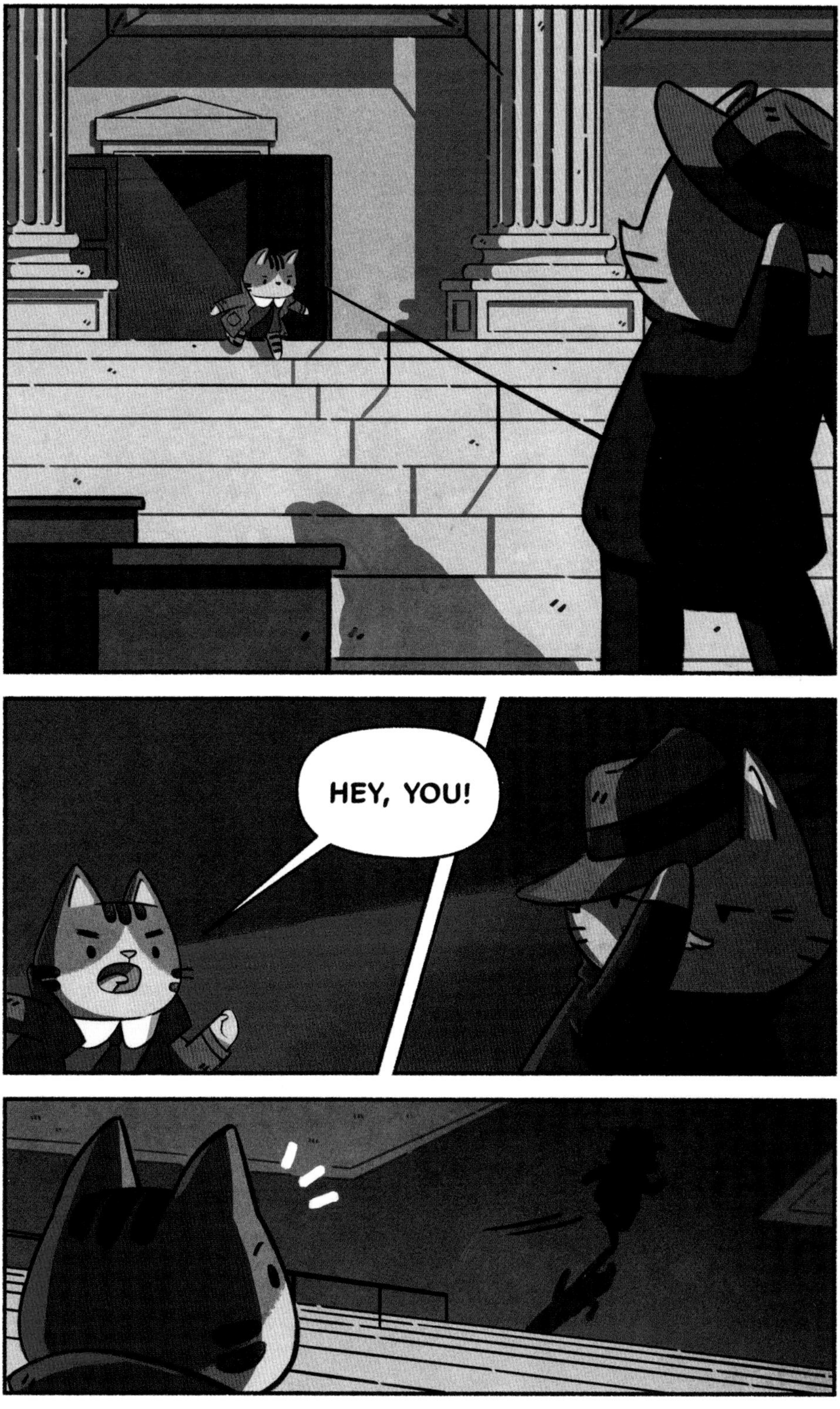
HEY, YOU!

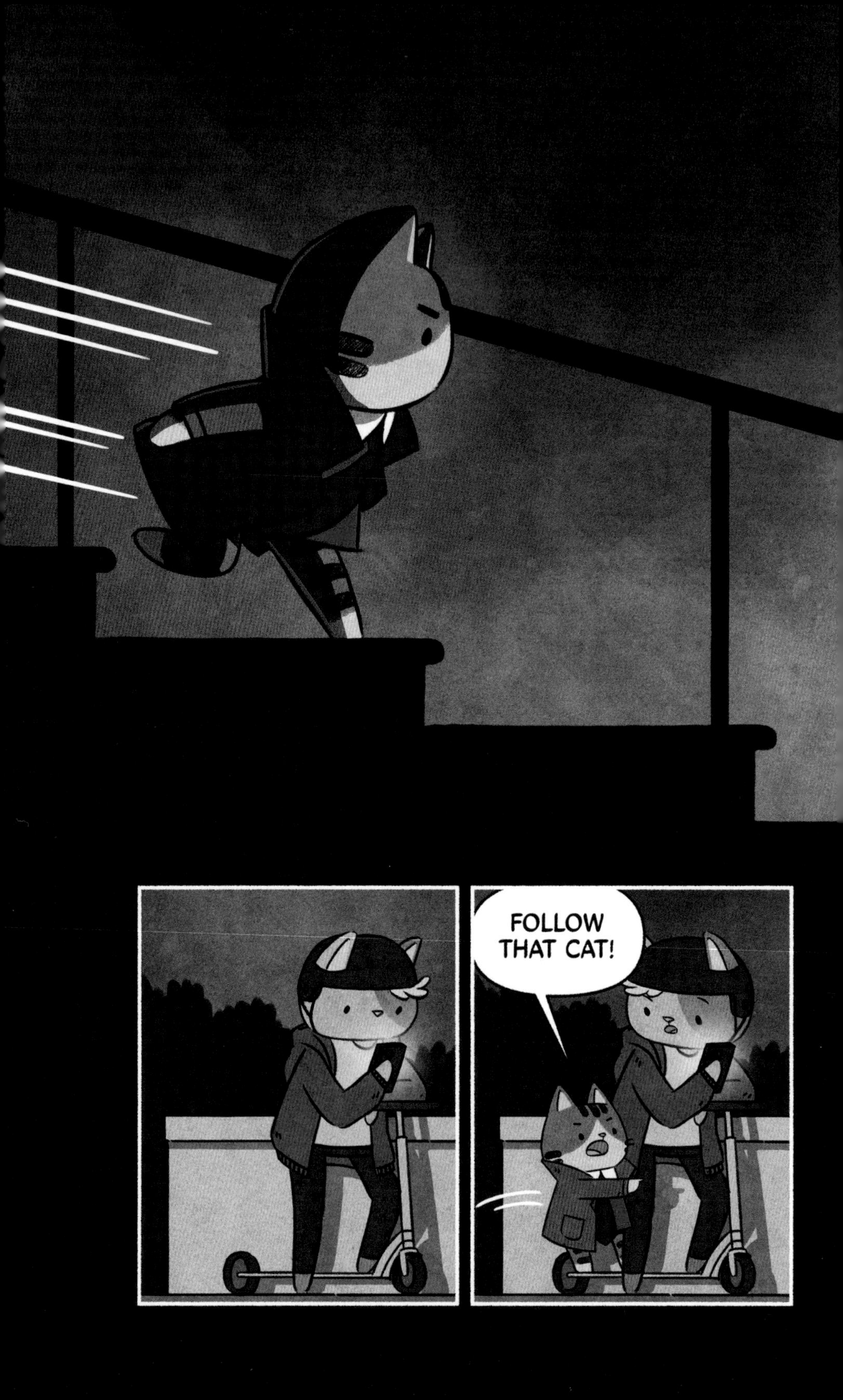
FOLLOW THAT CAT!

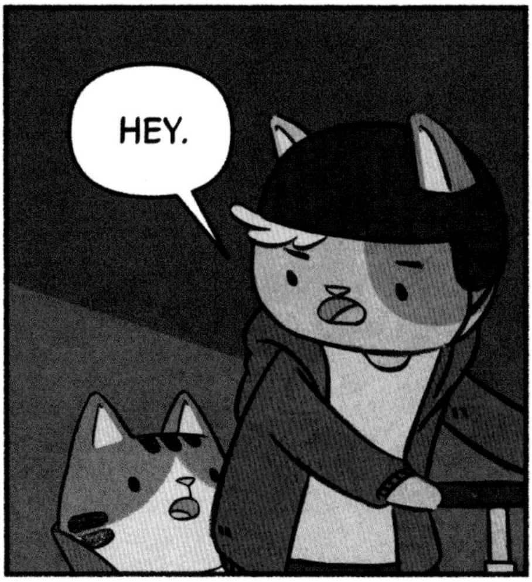
HEY.

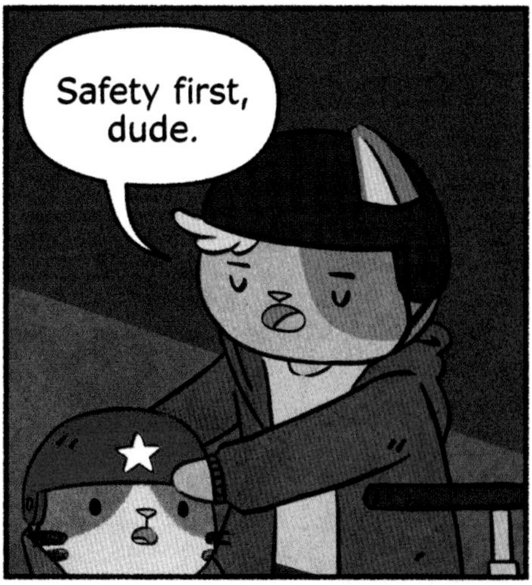
Safety first,
dude.

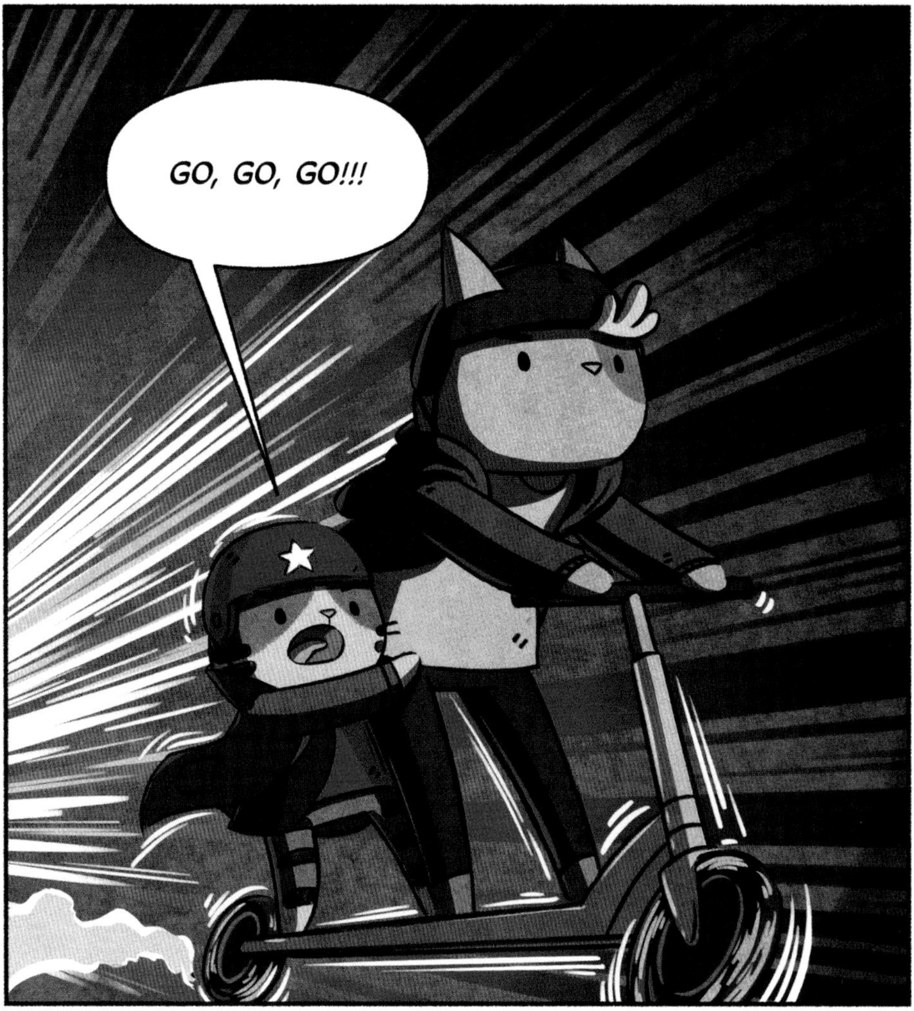
GO, GO, GO!!!

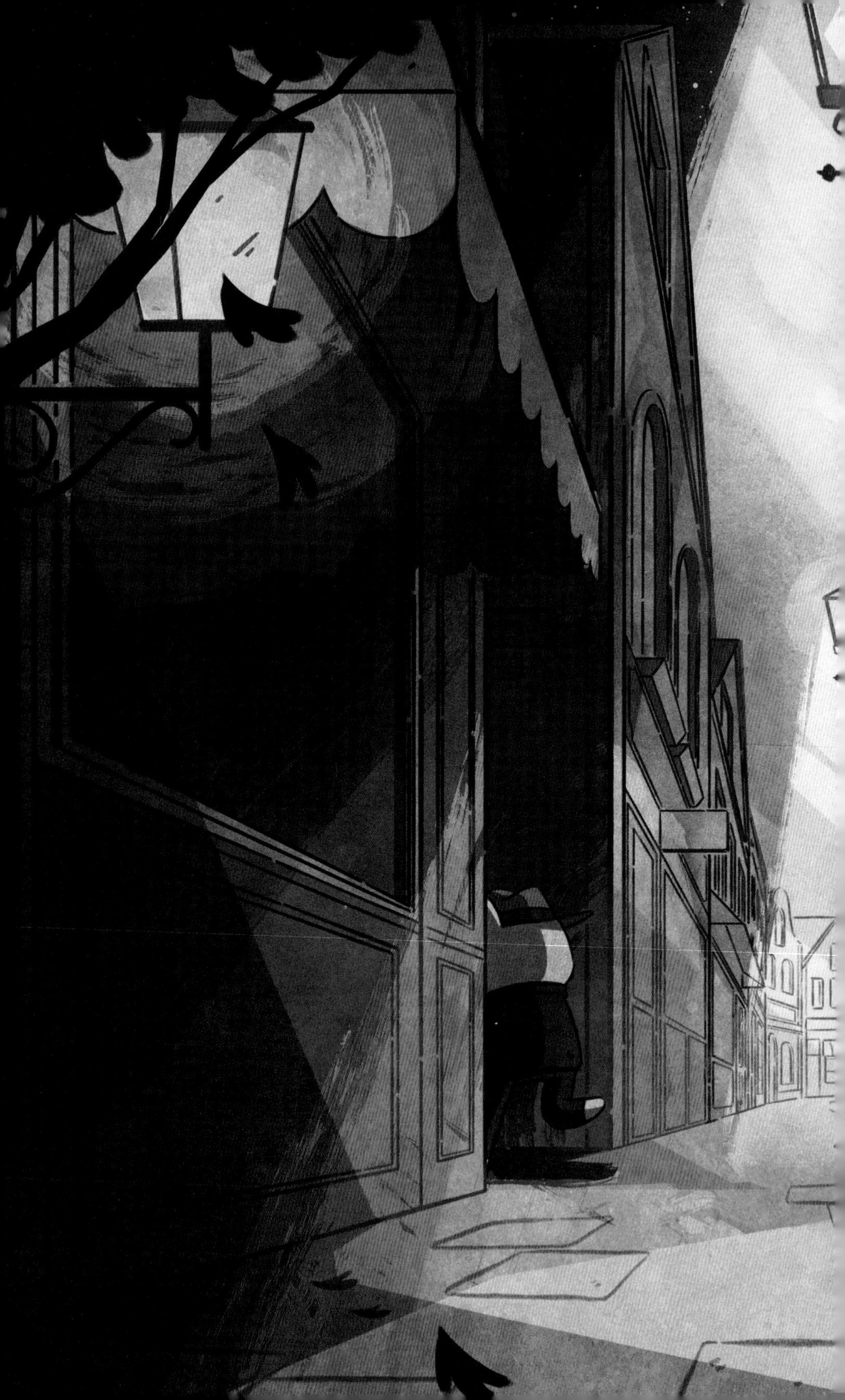

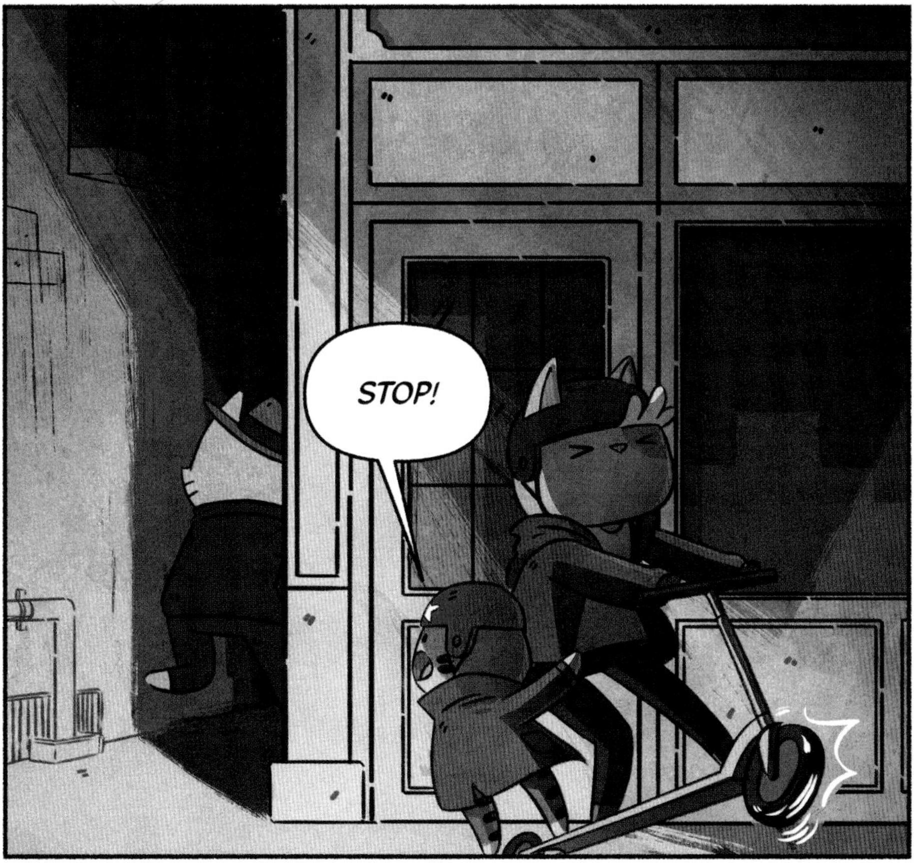
STOP!

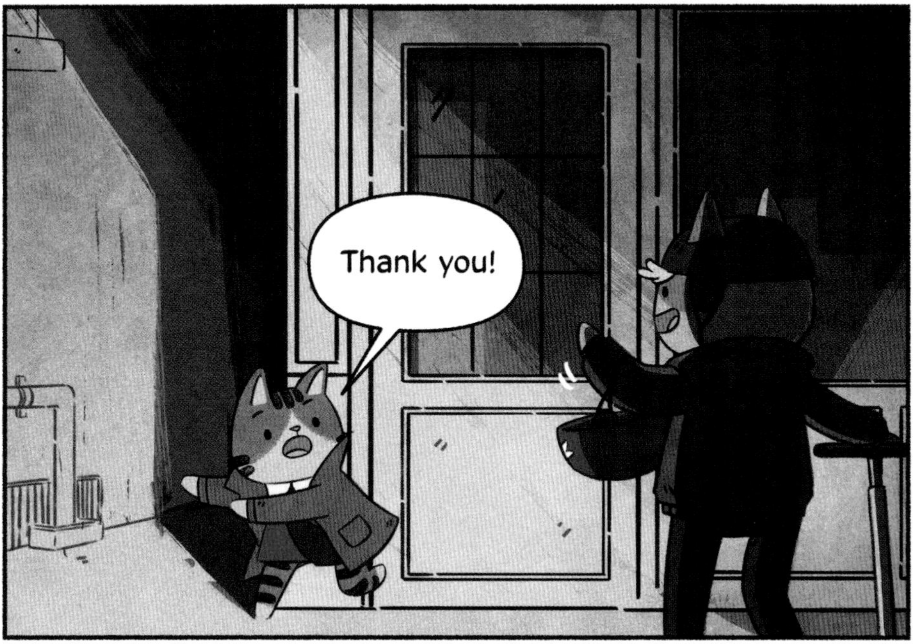
Thank you!

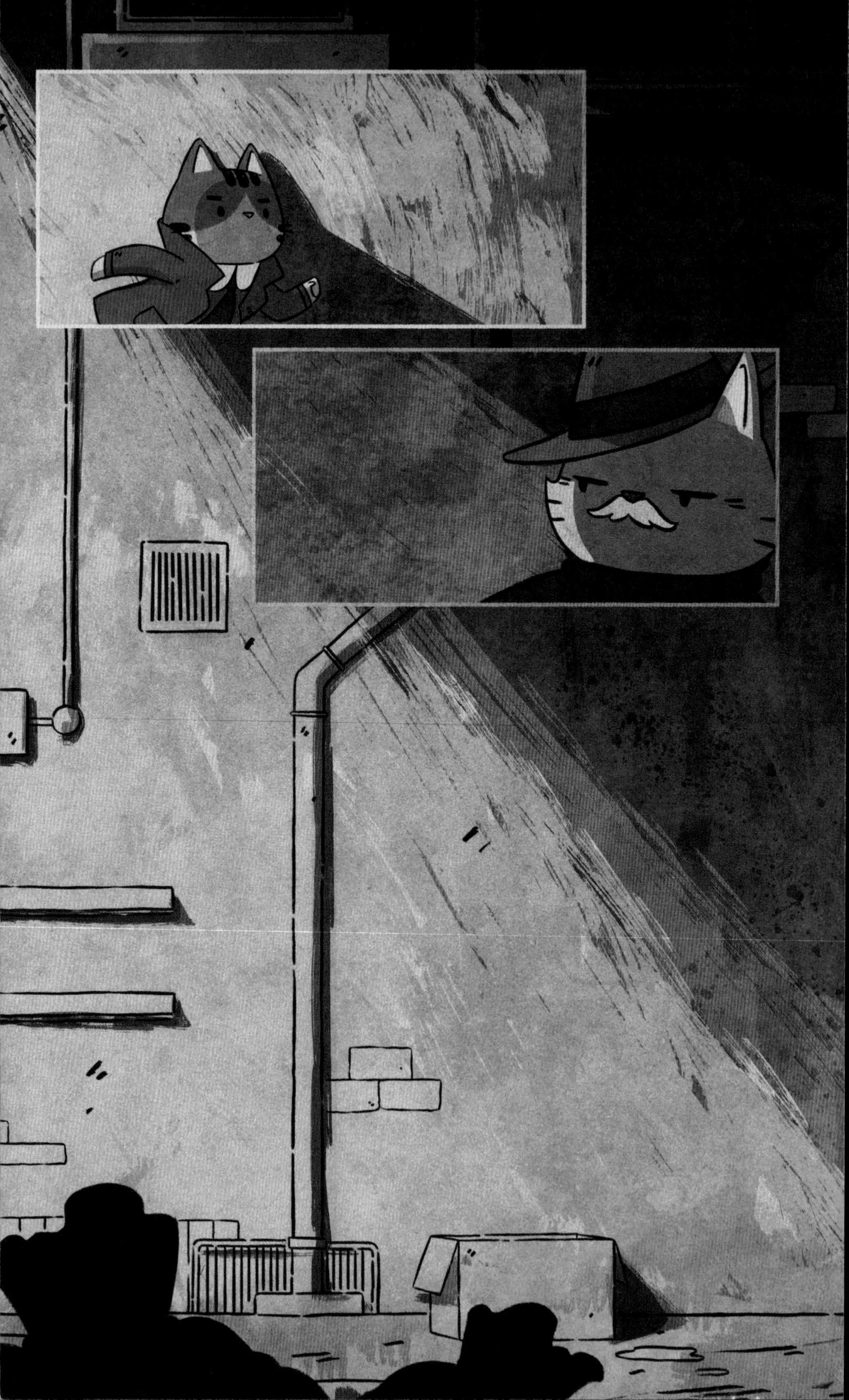

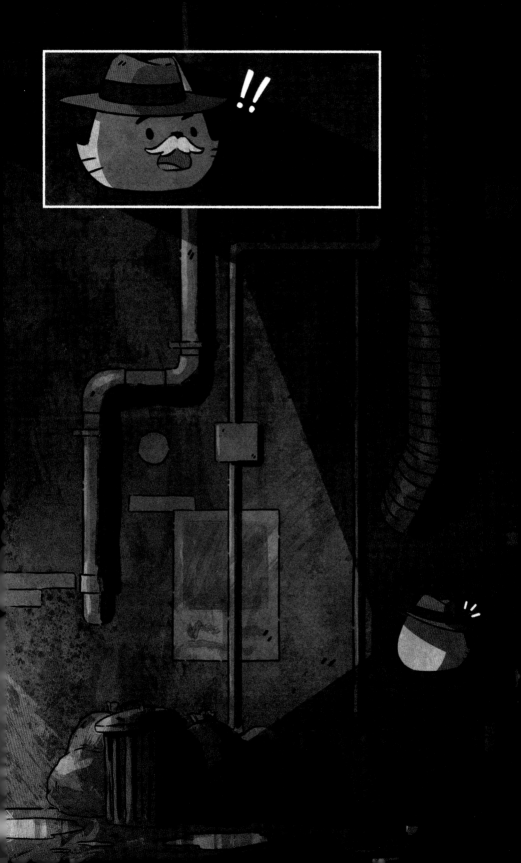

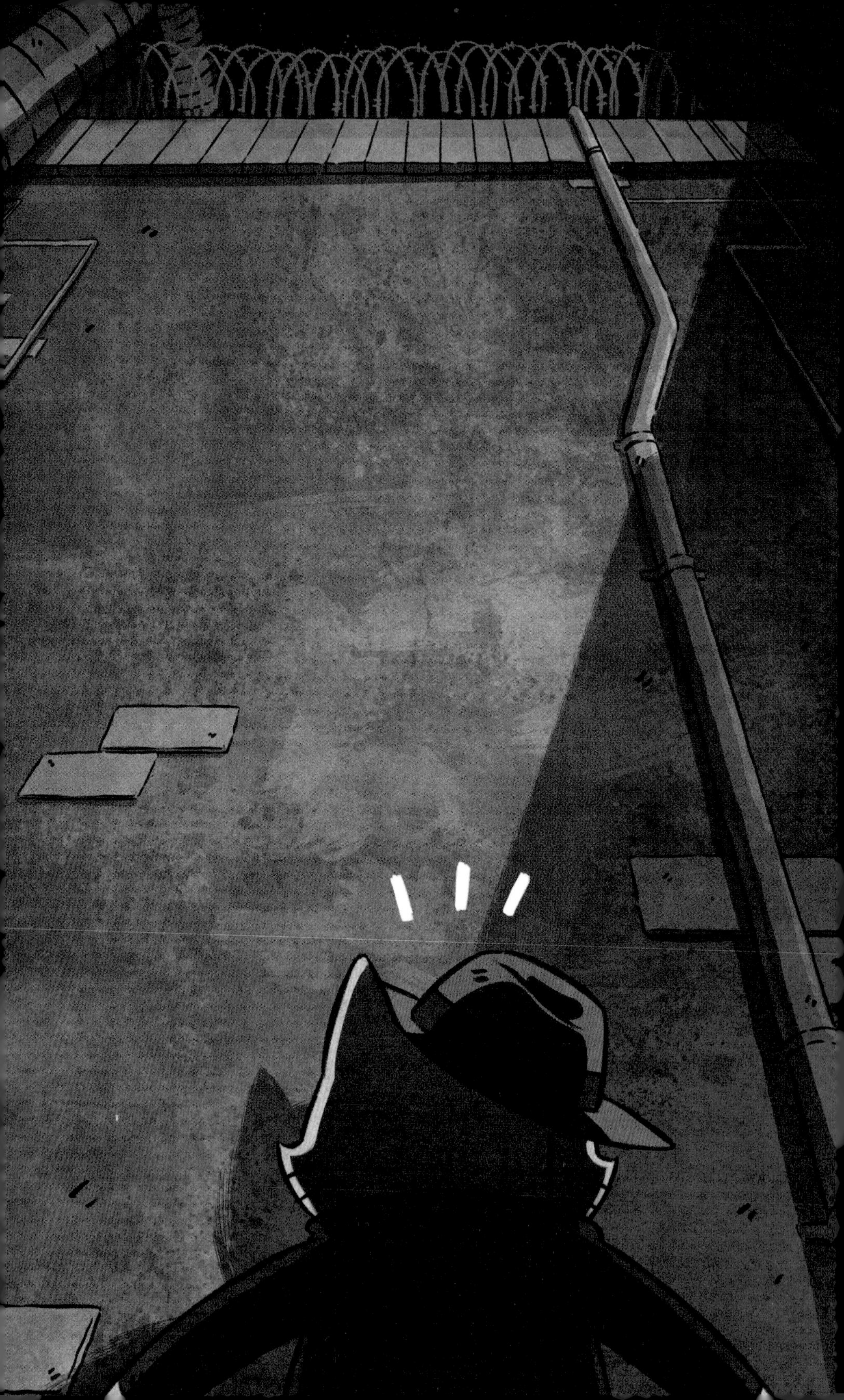

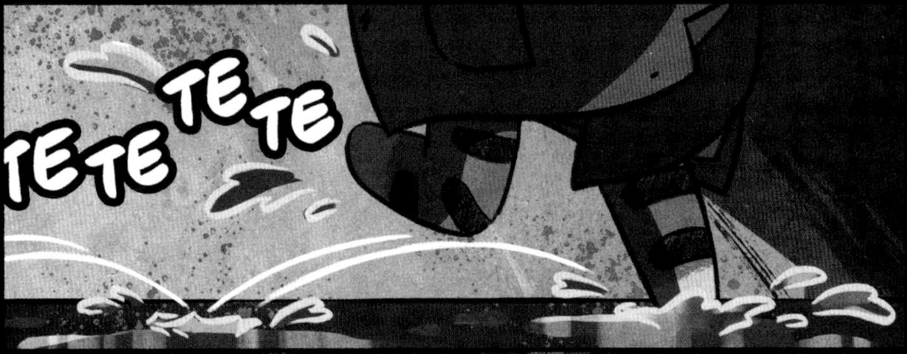
TE TE TE TE
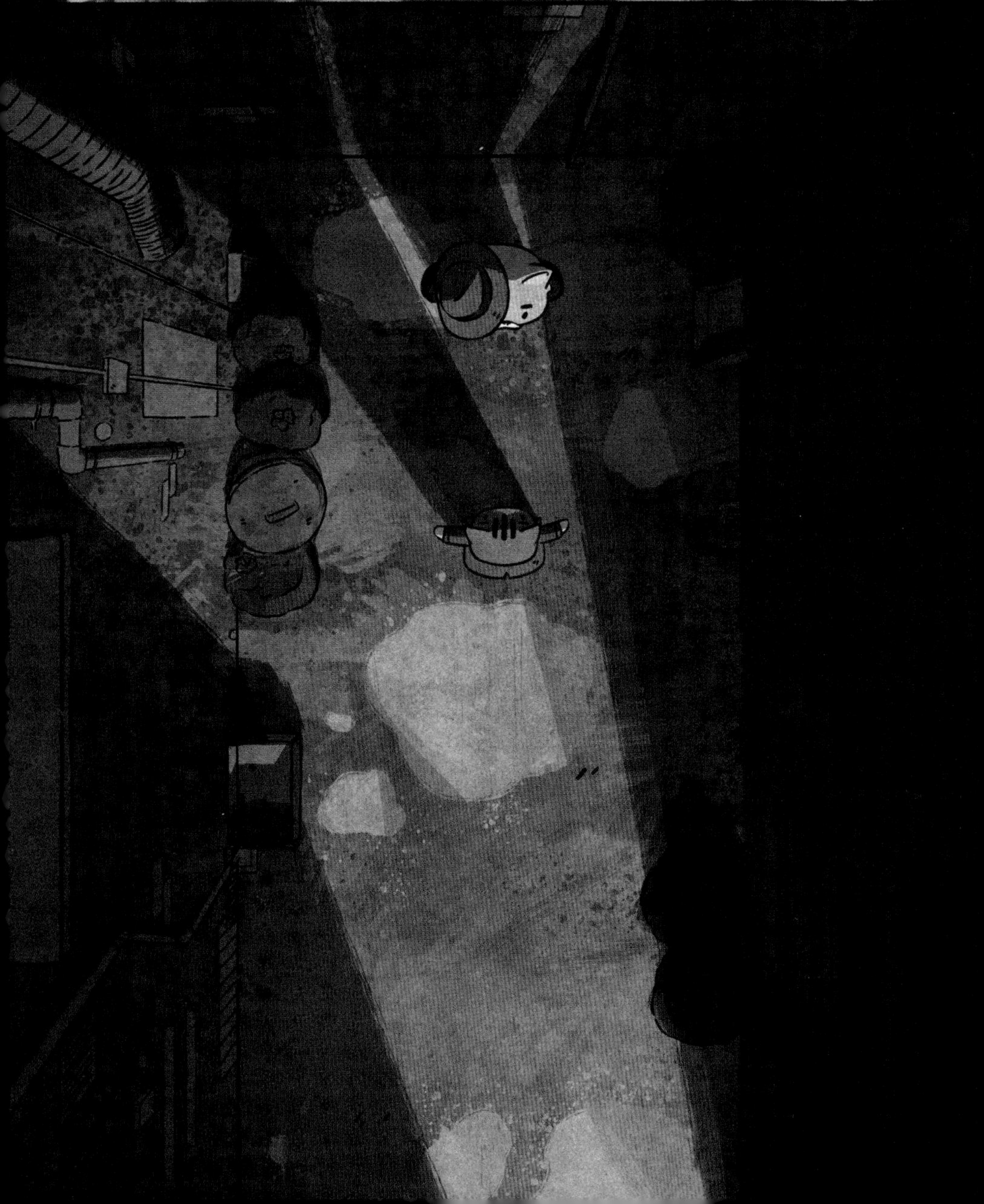

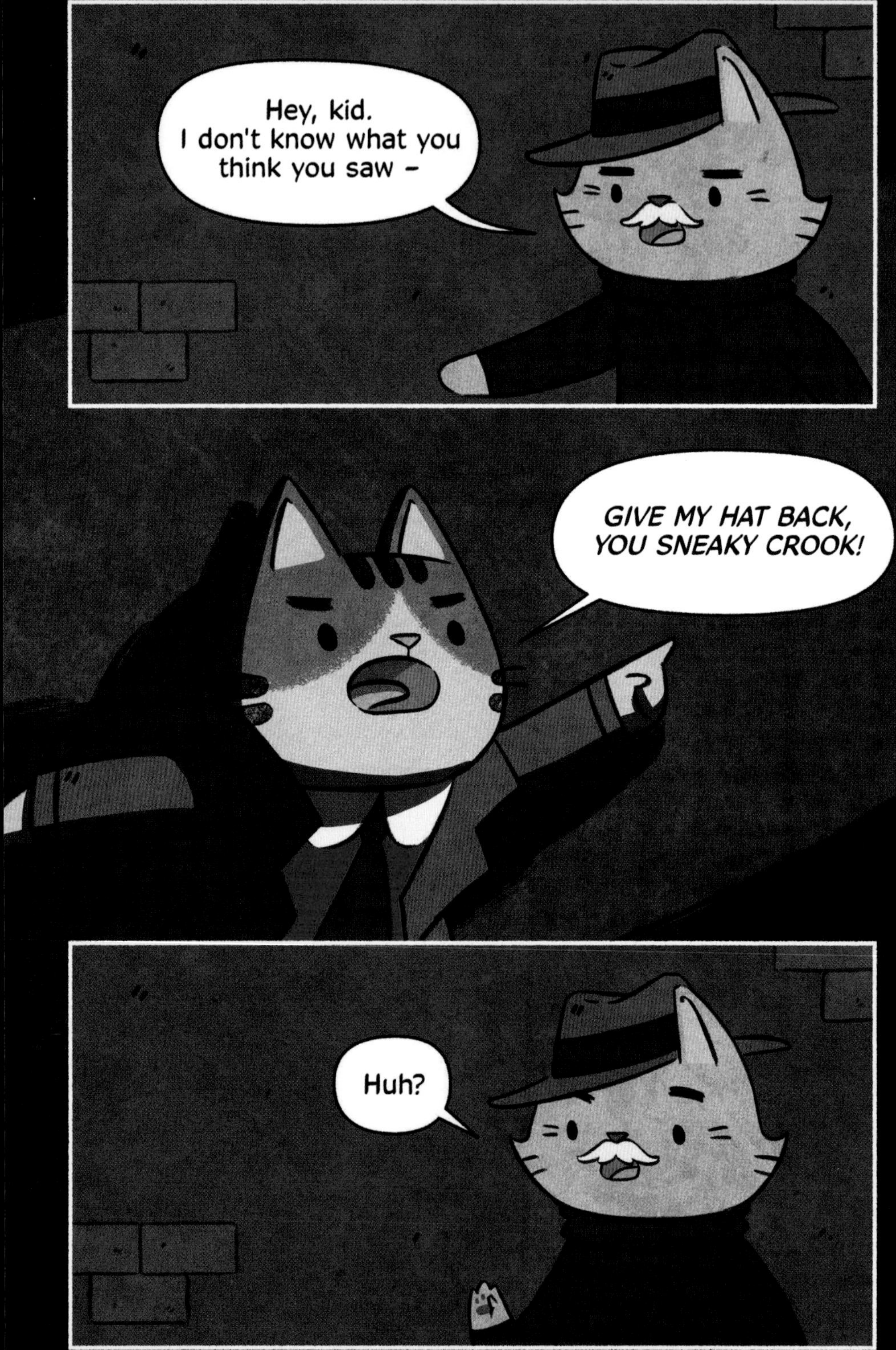
Hey, kid.
I don't know what you think you saw -
GIVE MY HAT BACK, YOU SNEAKY CROOK!
Huh?

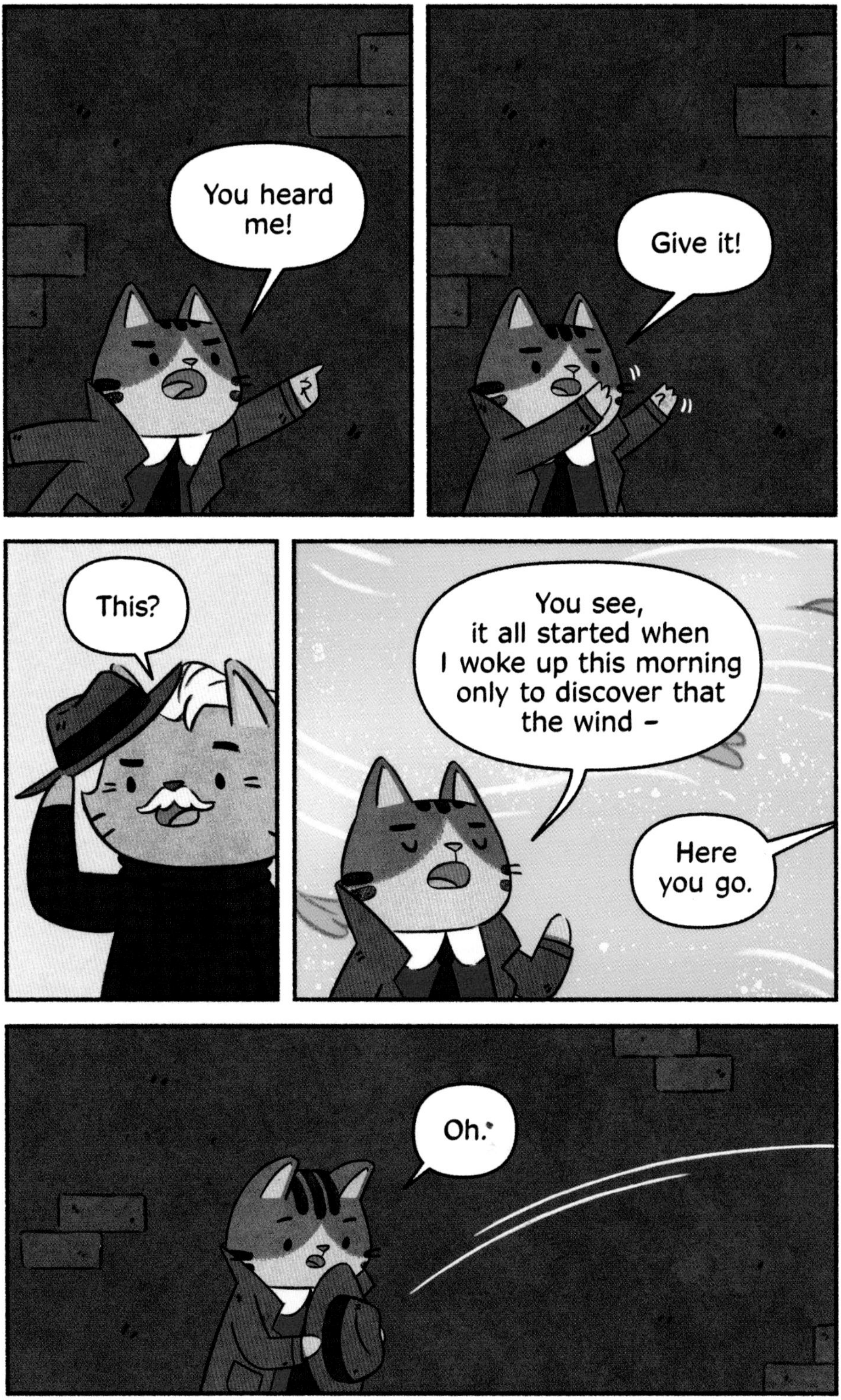
You heard me!
Give it!
This?
You see, it all started when I woke up this morning only to discover that the wind –
Here you go.
Oh.

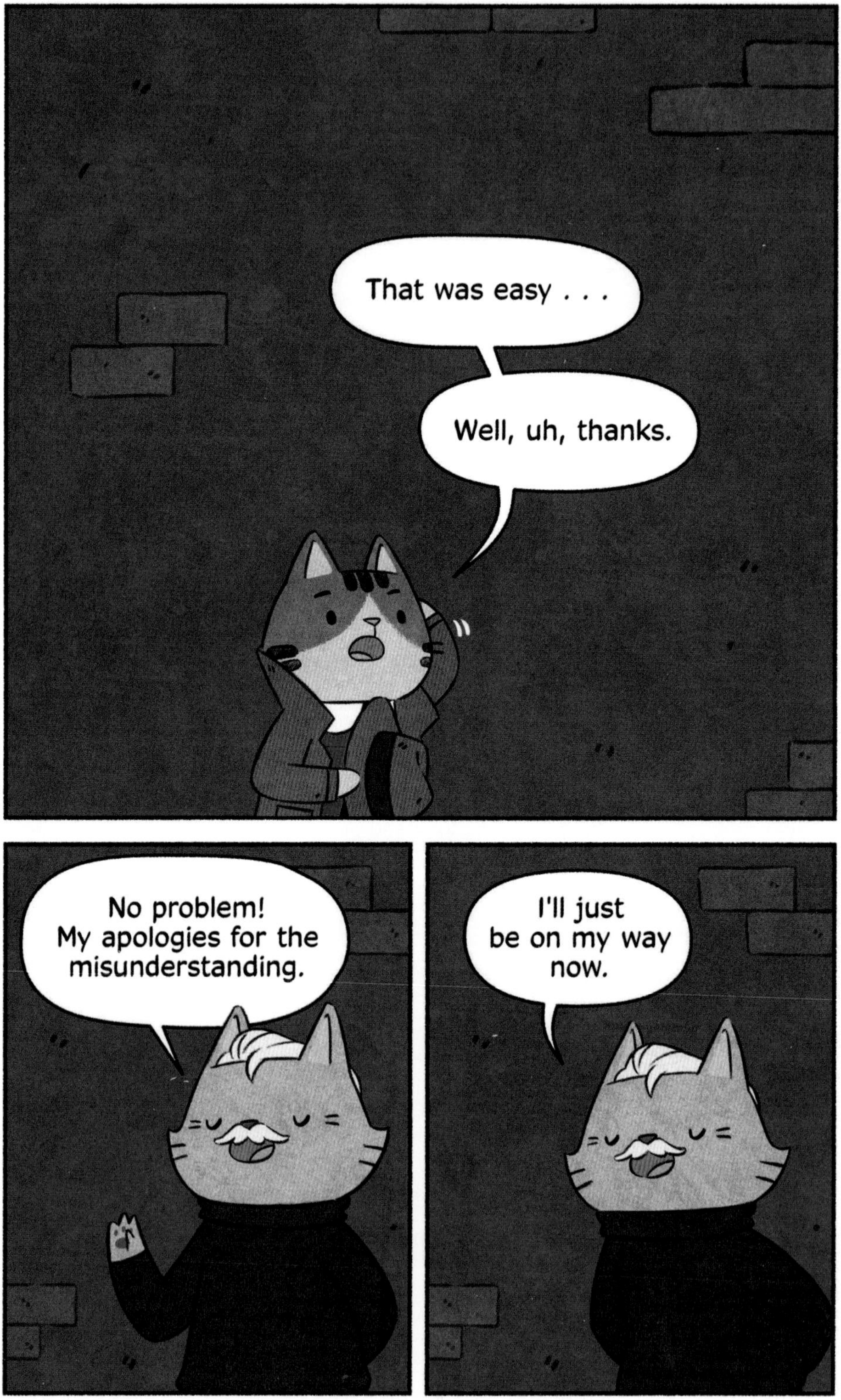
That was easy . . .
Well, uh, thanks.
No problem! My apologies for the misunderstanding.
I'll just be on my way now.

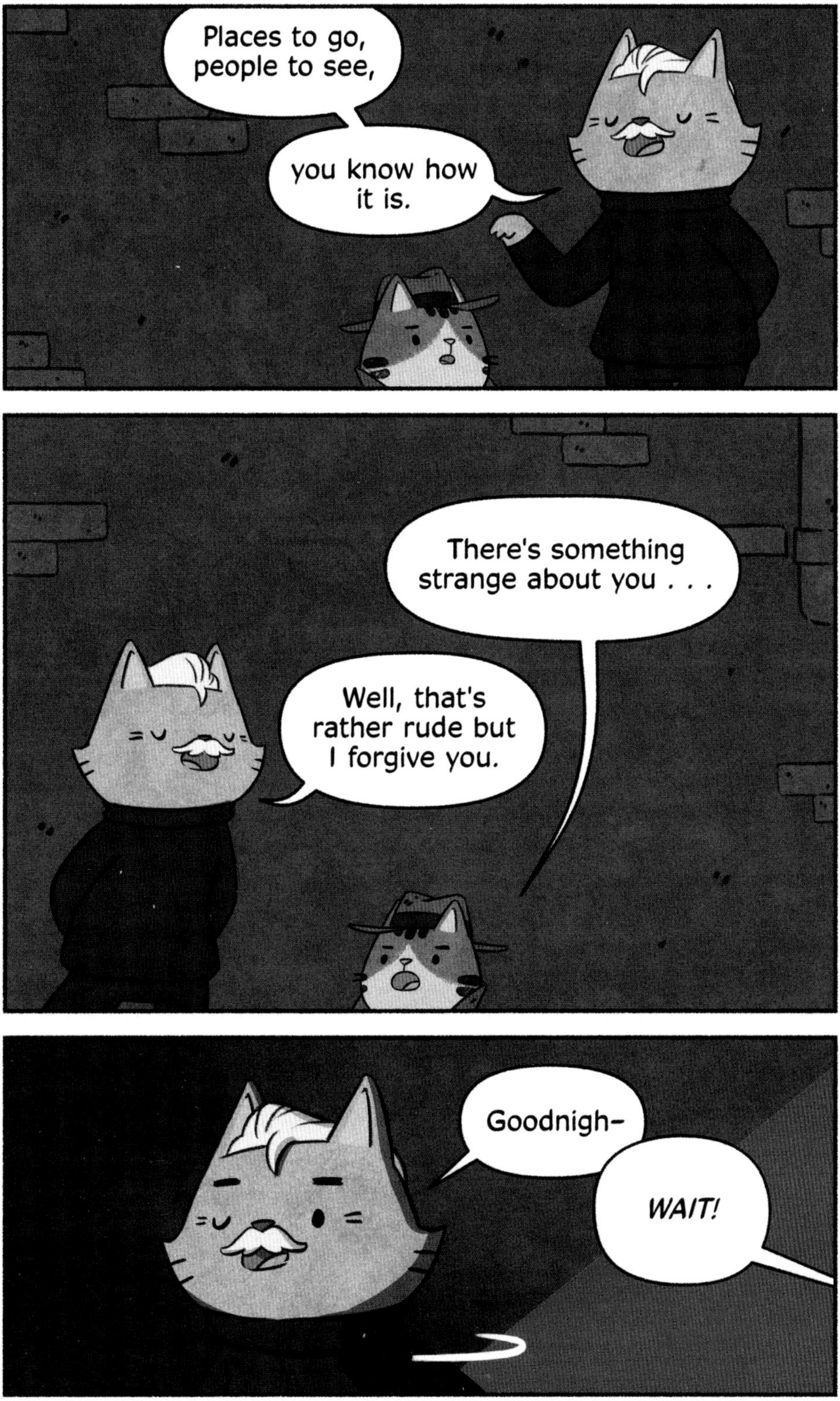
Places to go, people to see,
you know how it is.
There's something strange about you . . .
Well, that's rather rude but I forgive you.
Goodnigh-
WAIT!

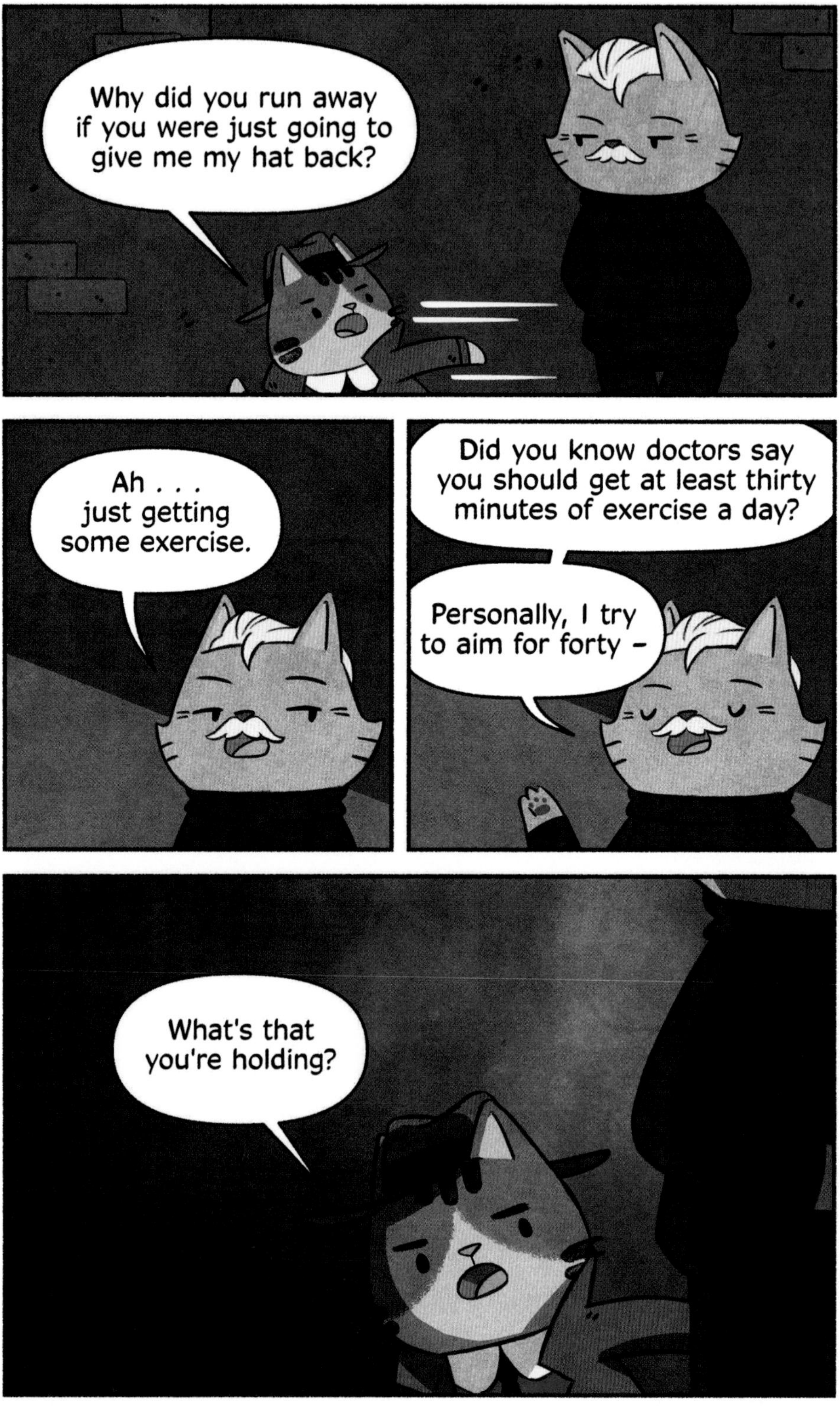
Why did you run away if you were just going to give me my hat back?
Ah . . . just getting some exercise.
Did you know doctors say you should get at least thirty minutes of exercise a day?
Personally, I try to aim for forty –
What's that you're holding?

Hm?
Oh, nothing, see?
See?

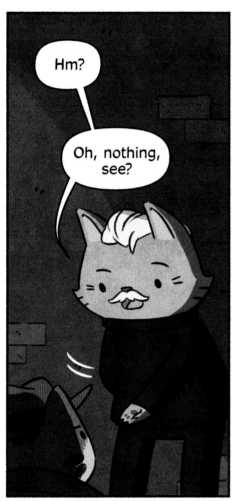

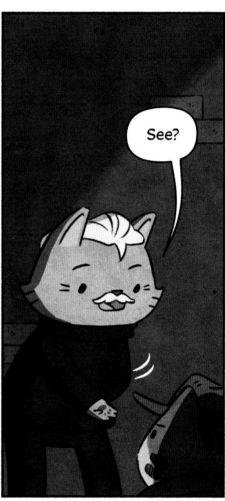

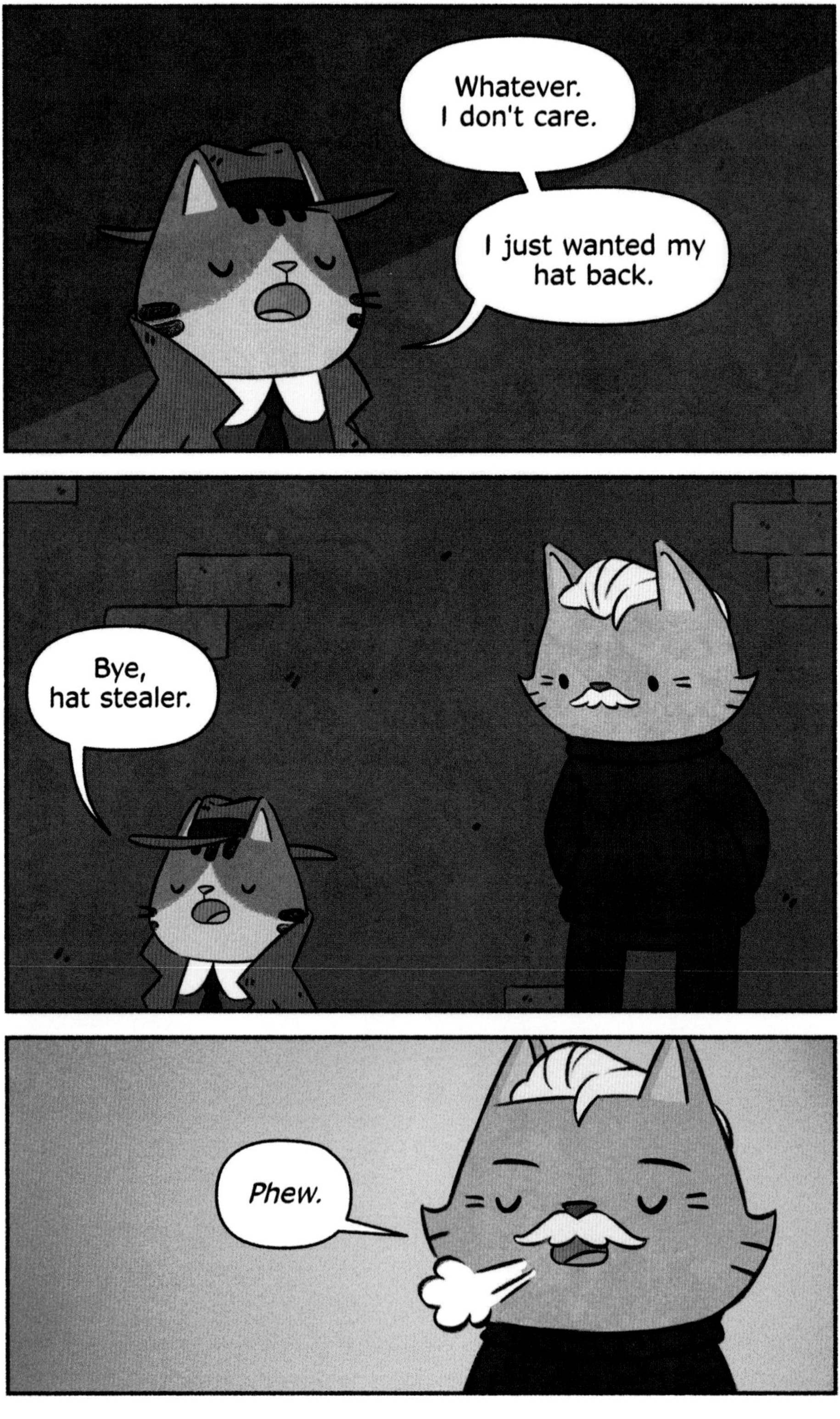
Whatever. I don't care.
I just wanted my hat back.
Bye, hat stealer.
Phew.

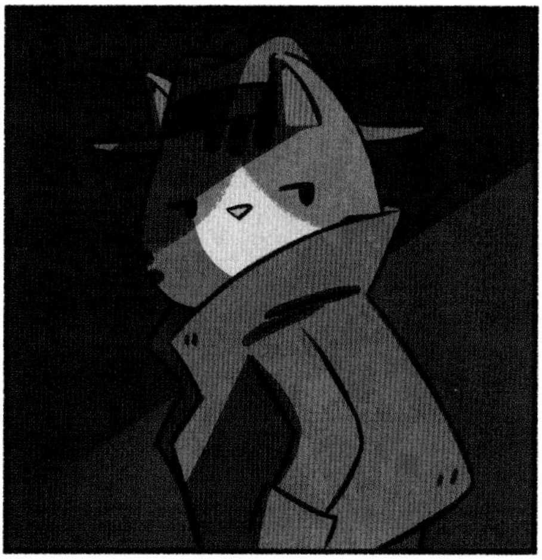

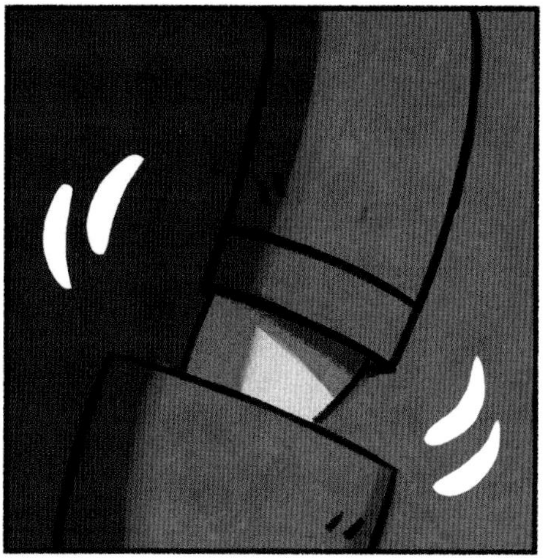

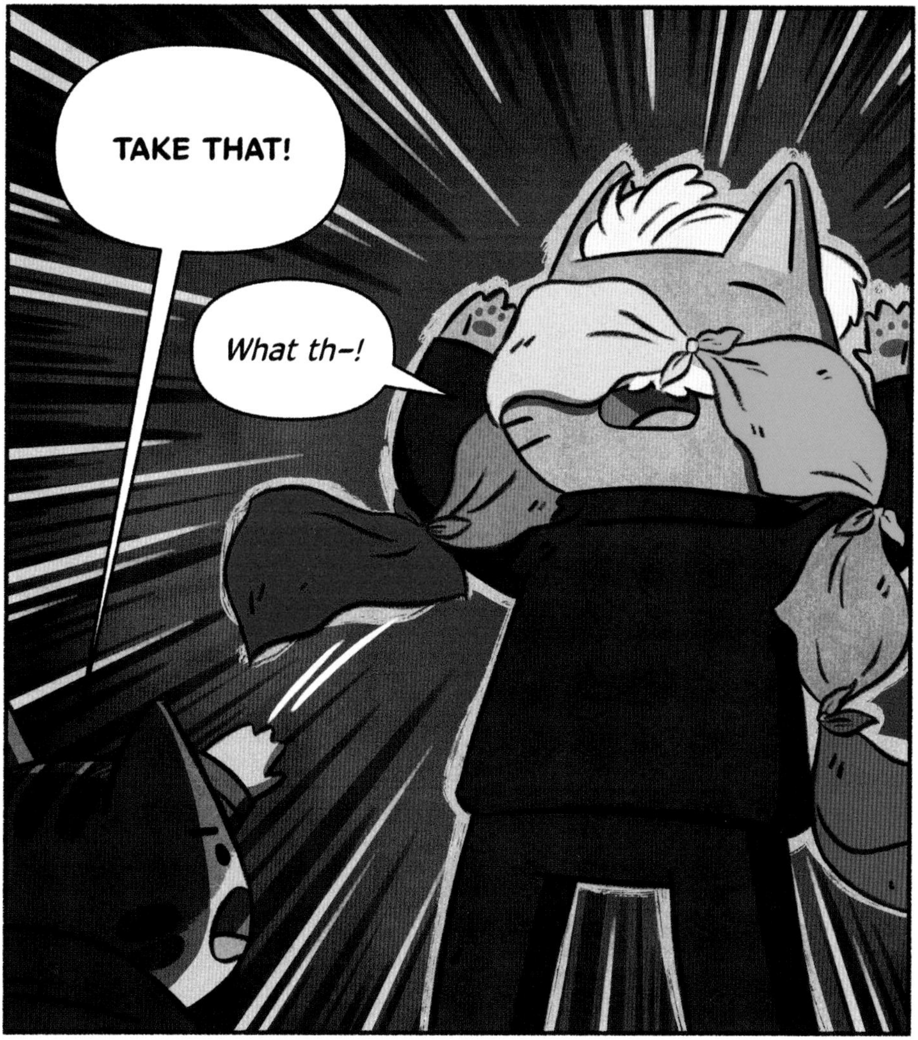
TAKE THAT!
What th-!

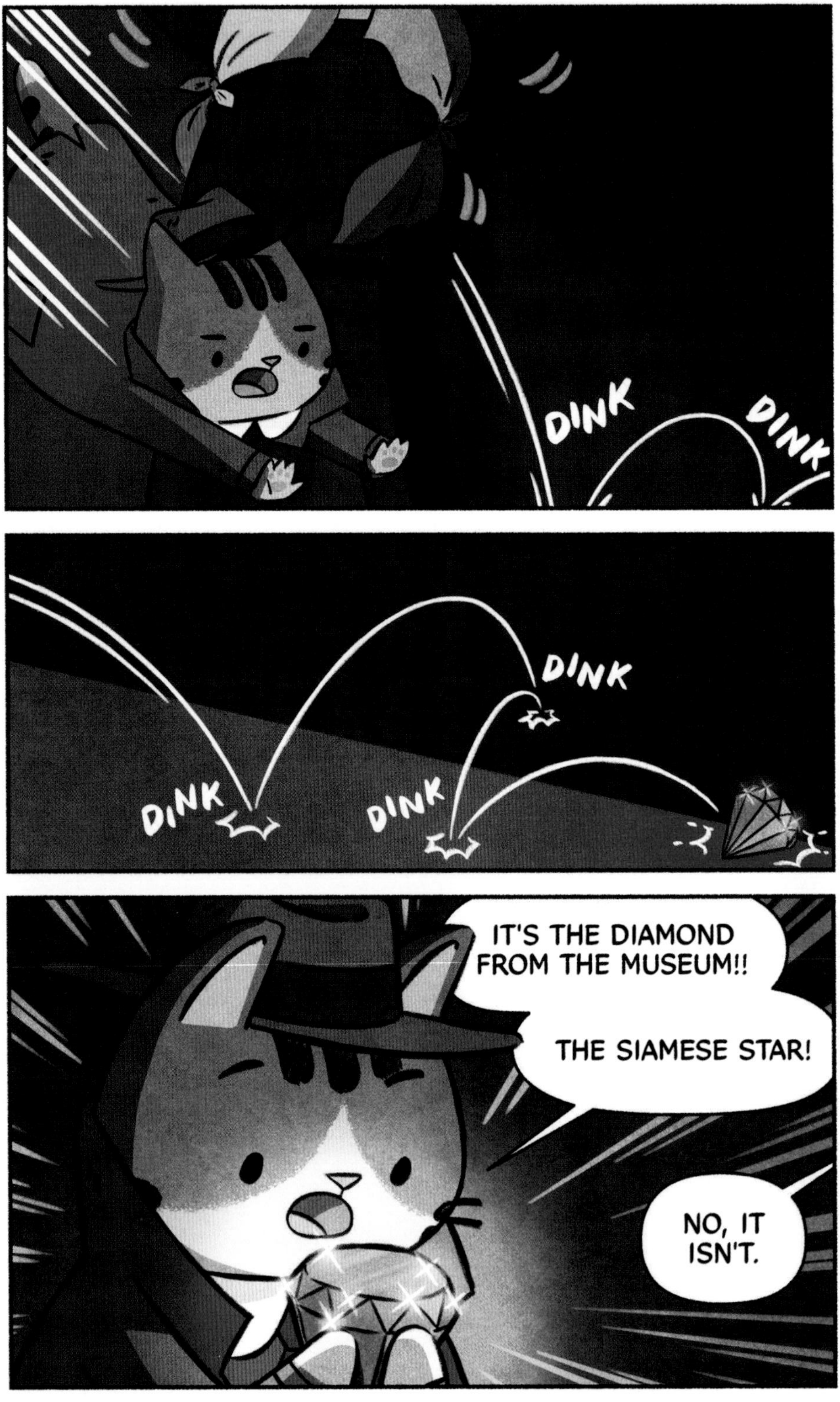
DINK
DINK
DINK
DINK
DINK
IT'S THE DIAMOND FROM THE MUSEUM!!
THE SIAMESE STAR!
NO, IT ISN'T.

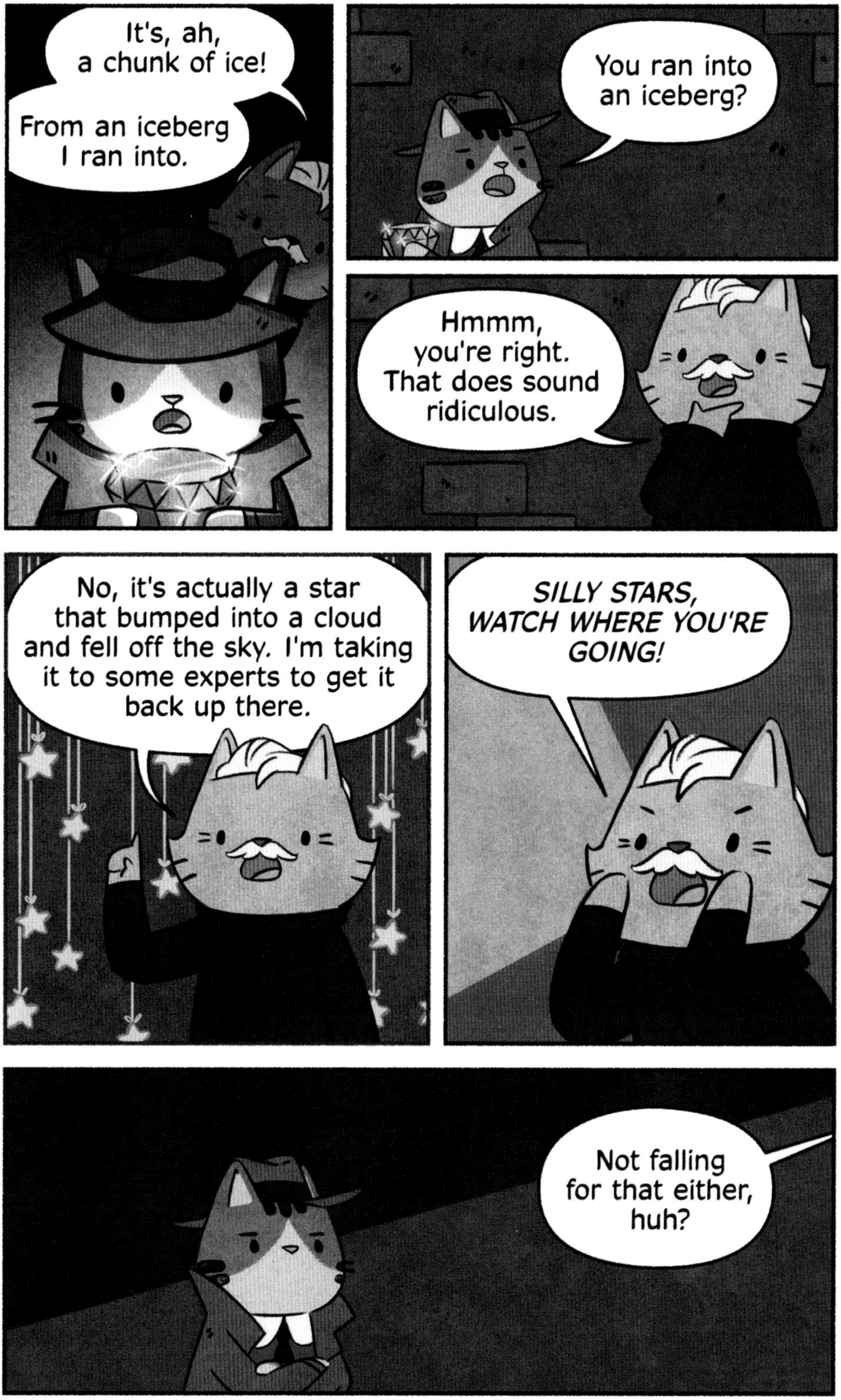
It's, ah, a chunk of ice!
From an iceberg I ran into.
You ran into an iceberg?
Hmmm, you're right. That does sound ridiculous.
No, it's actually a star that bumped into a cloud and fell off the sky. I'm taking it to some experts to get it back up there.
SILLY STARS, WATCH WHERE YOU'RE GOING!
Not falling for that either, huh?

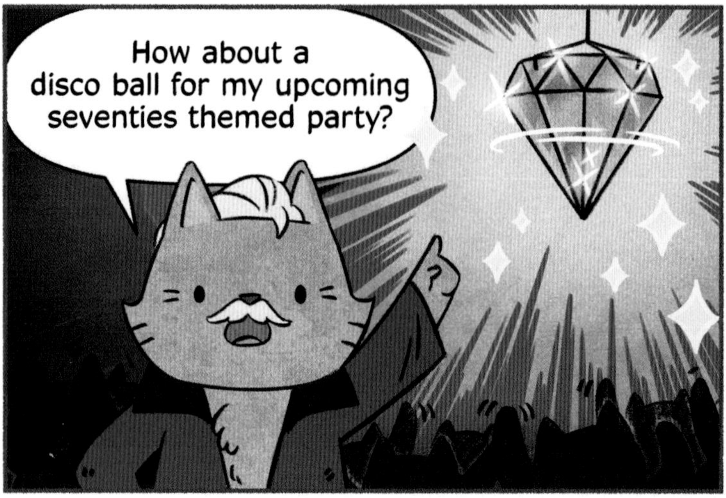
How about a disco ball for my upcoming seventies themed party?

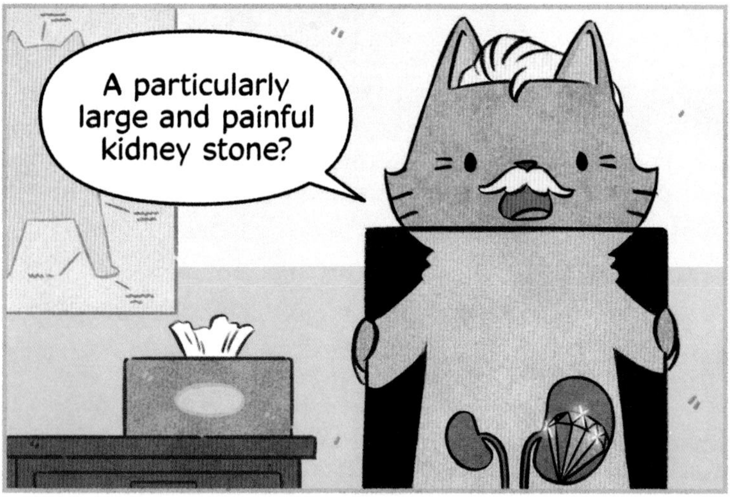
A particularly large and painful kidney stone?

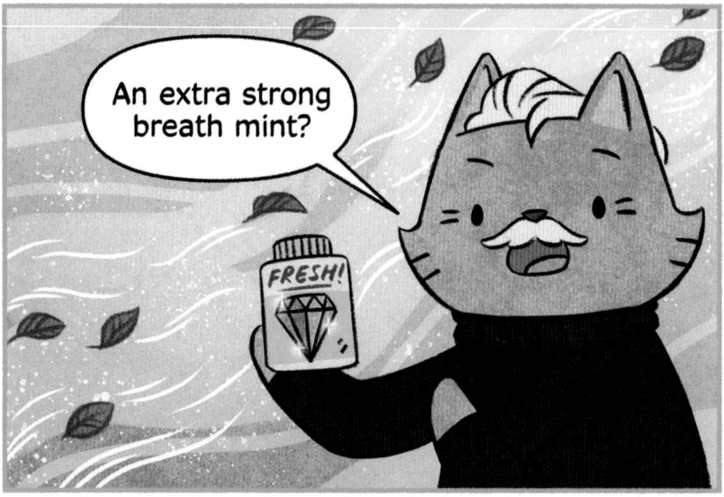
An extra strong breath mint?
FRESH!

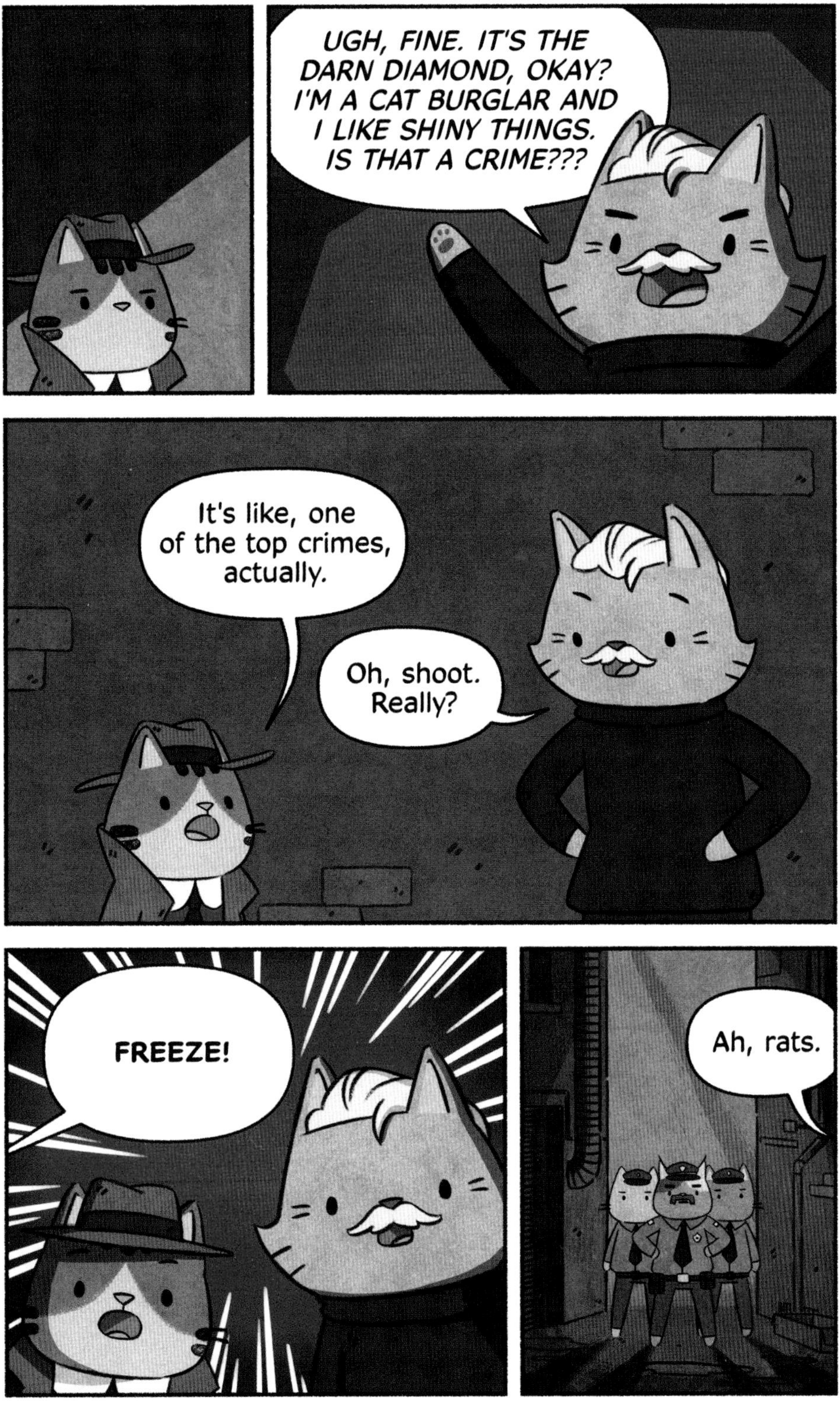
UGH, FINE. IT'S THE DARN DIAMOND, OKAY? I'M A CAT BURGLAR AND I LIKE SHINY THINGS. IS THAT A CRIME???
It's like, one of the top crimes, actually.
Oh, shoot. Really?
FREEZE!
Ah, rats.

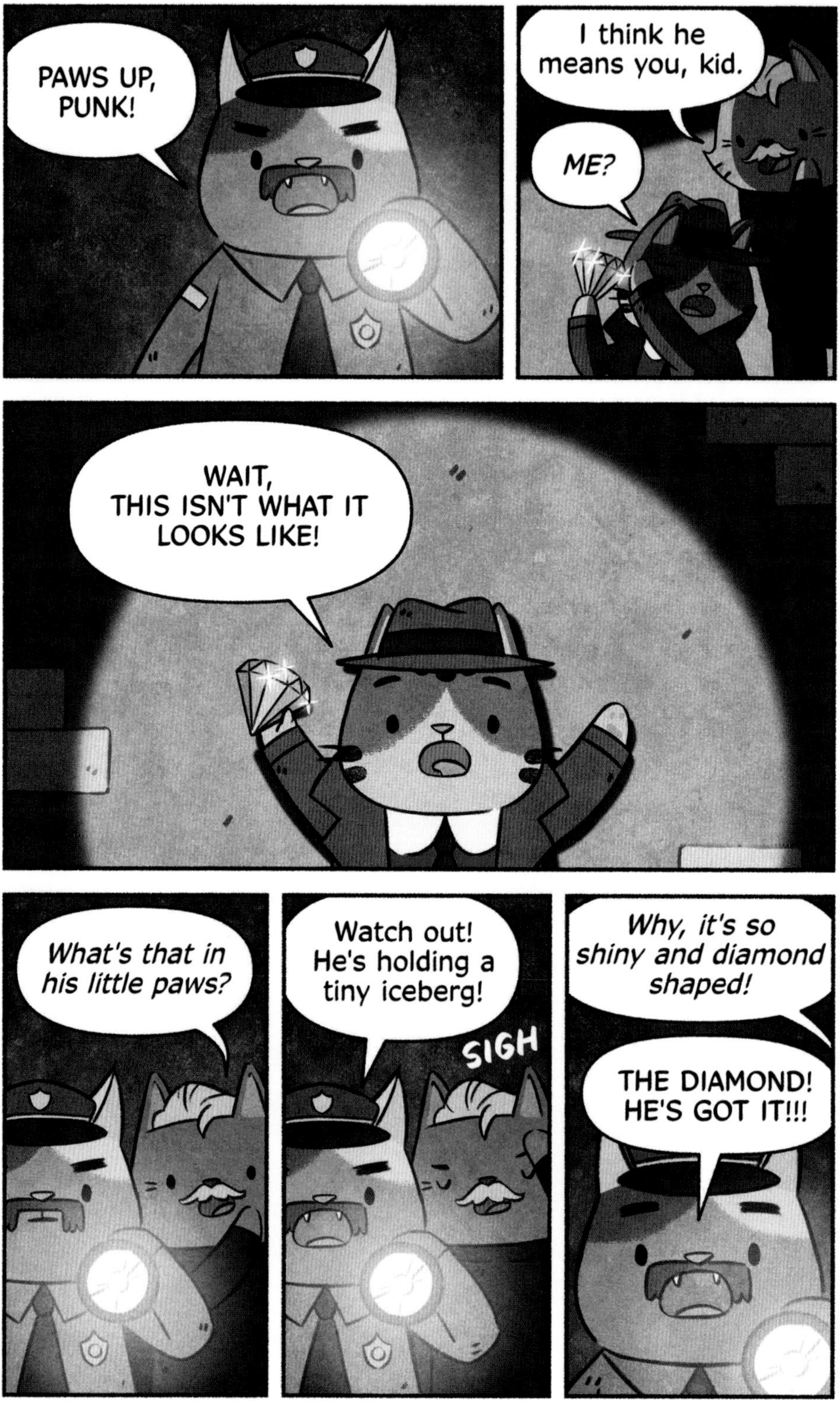
PAWS UP, PUNK!
I think he means you, kid.
ME?
WAIT, THIS ISN'T WHAT IT LOOKS LIKE!
What's that in his little paws?
Watch out! He's holding a tiny iceberg!
SIGH
Why, it's so shiny and diamond shaped!
THE DIAMOND! HE'S GOT IT!!!

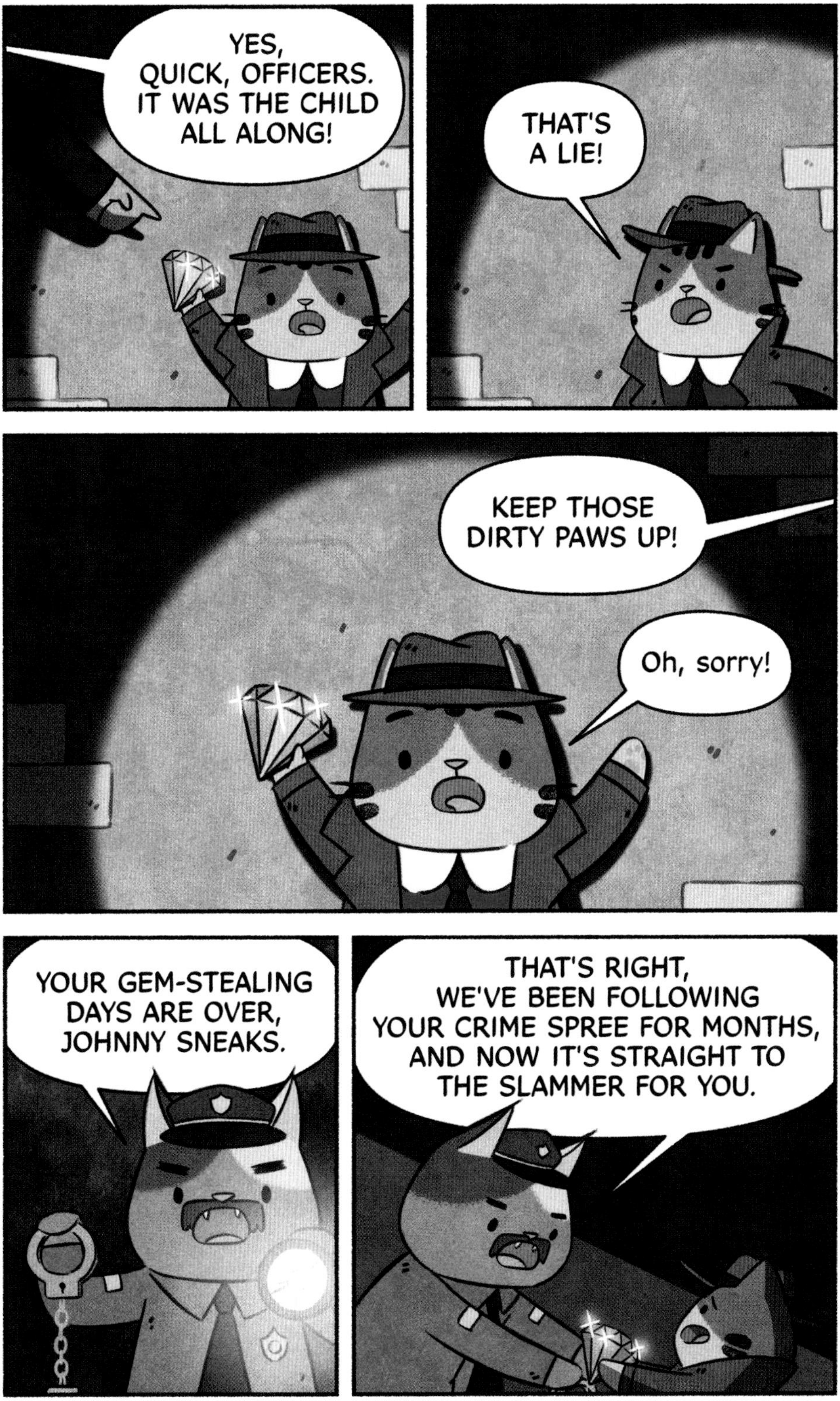

YES, QUICK, OFFICERS. IT WAS THE CHILD ALL ALONG!
THAT'S A LIE!
KEEP THOSE DIRTY PAWS UP!
Oh, sorry!
YOUR GEM-STEALING DAYS ARE OVER, JOHNNY SNEAKS.
THAT'S RIGHT, WE'VE BEEN FOLLOWING YOUR CRIME SPREE FOR MONTHS, AND NOW IT'S STRAIGHT TO THE SLAMMER FOR YOU.

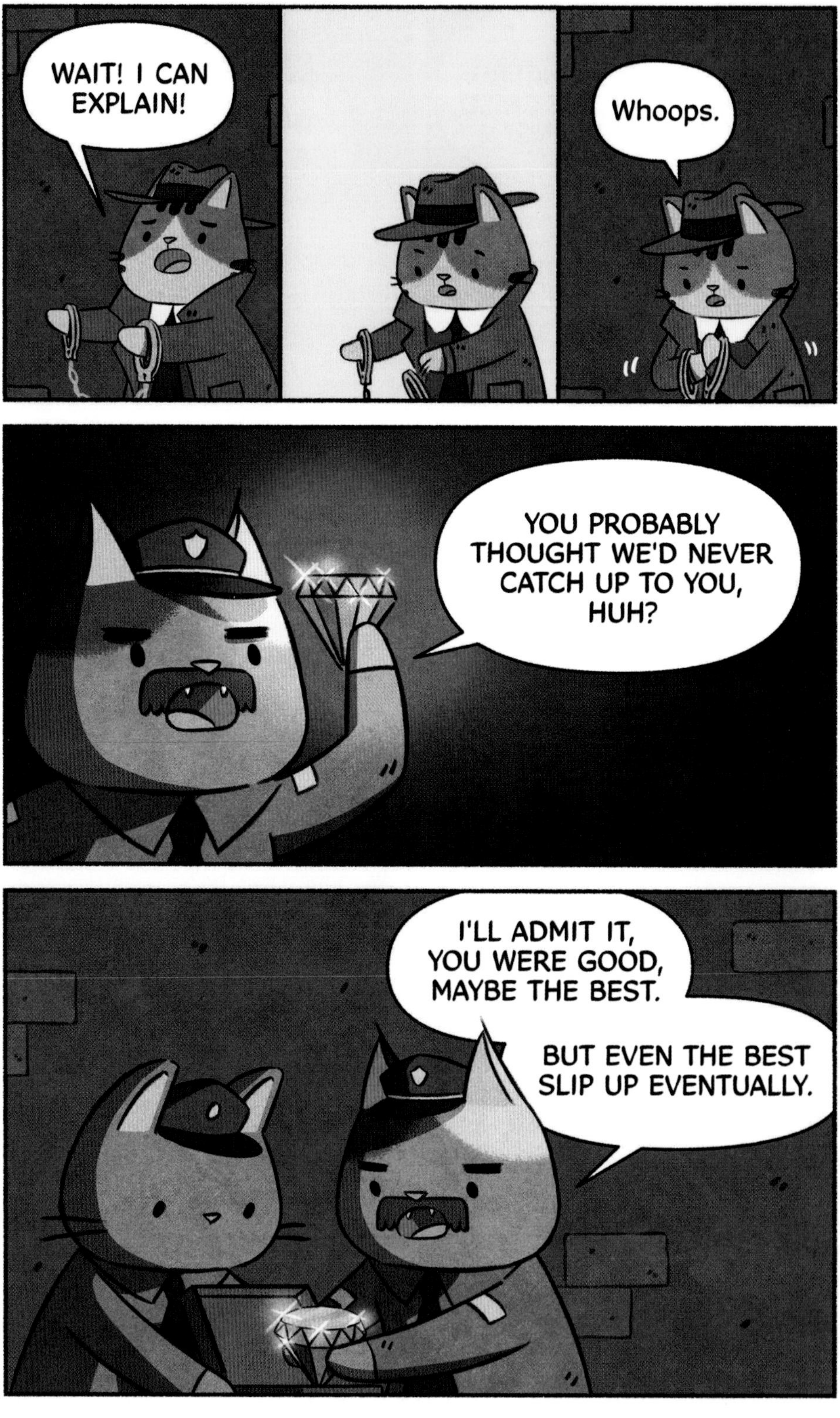
WAIT! I CAN EXPLAIN!
Whoops.
YOU PROBABLY THOUGHT WE'D NEVER CATCH UP TO YOU, HUH?
I'LL ADMIT IT, YOU WERE GOOD, MAYBE THE BEST.
BUT EVEN THE BEST SLIP UP EVENTUALLY.

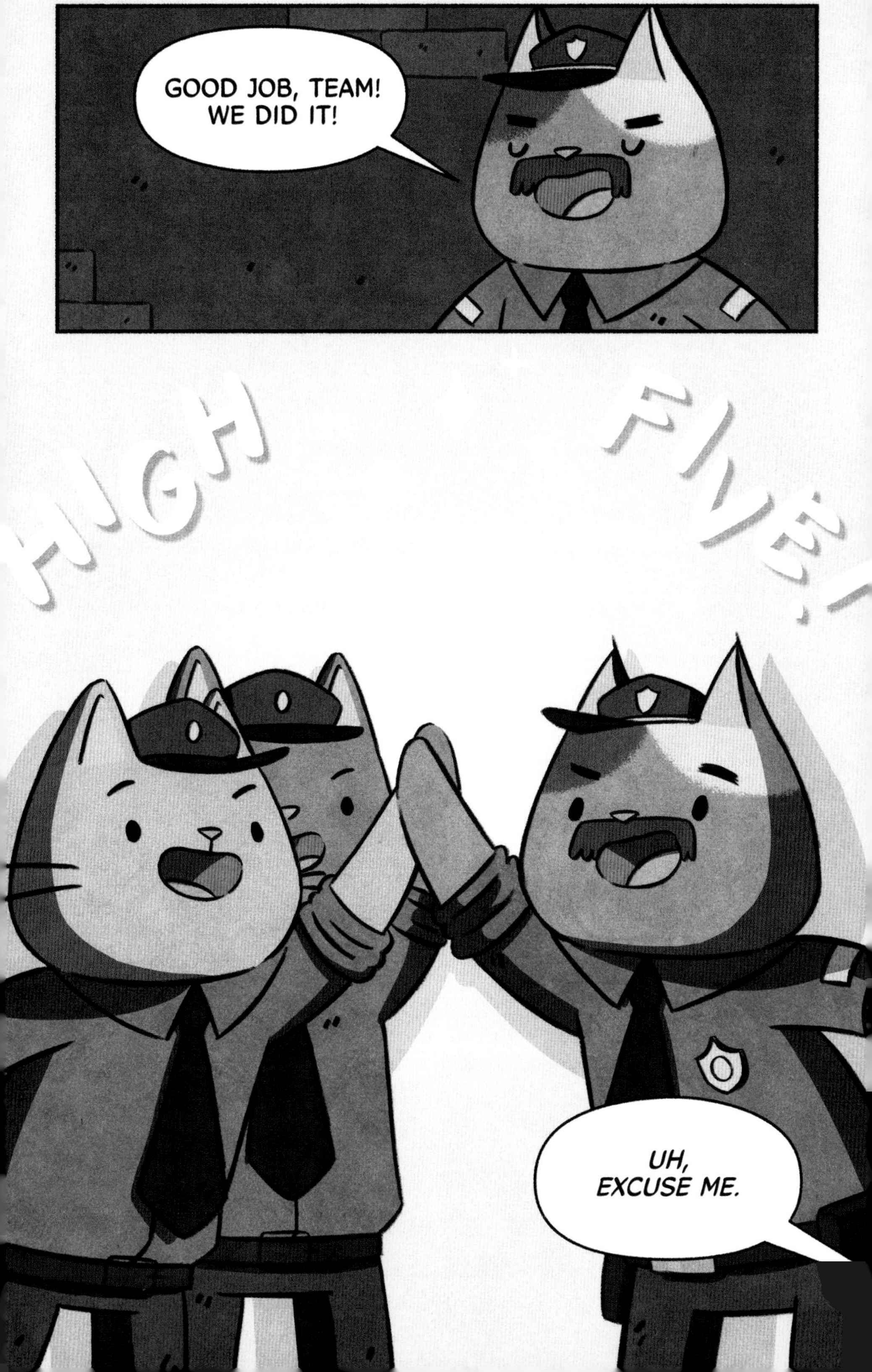
GOOD JOB, TEAM! WE DID IT!
HIGH FIVE!
UH, EXCUSE ME.

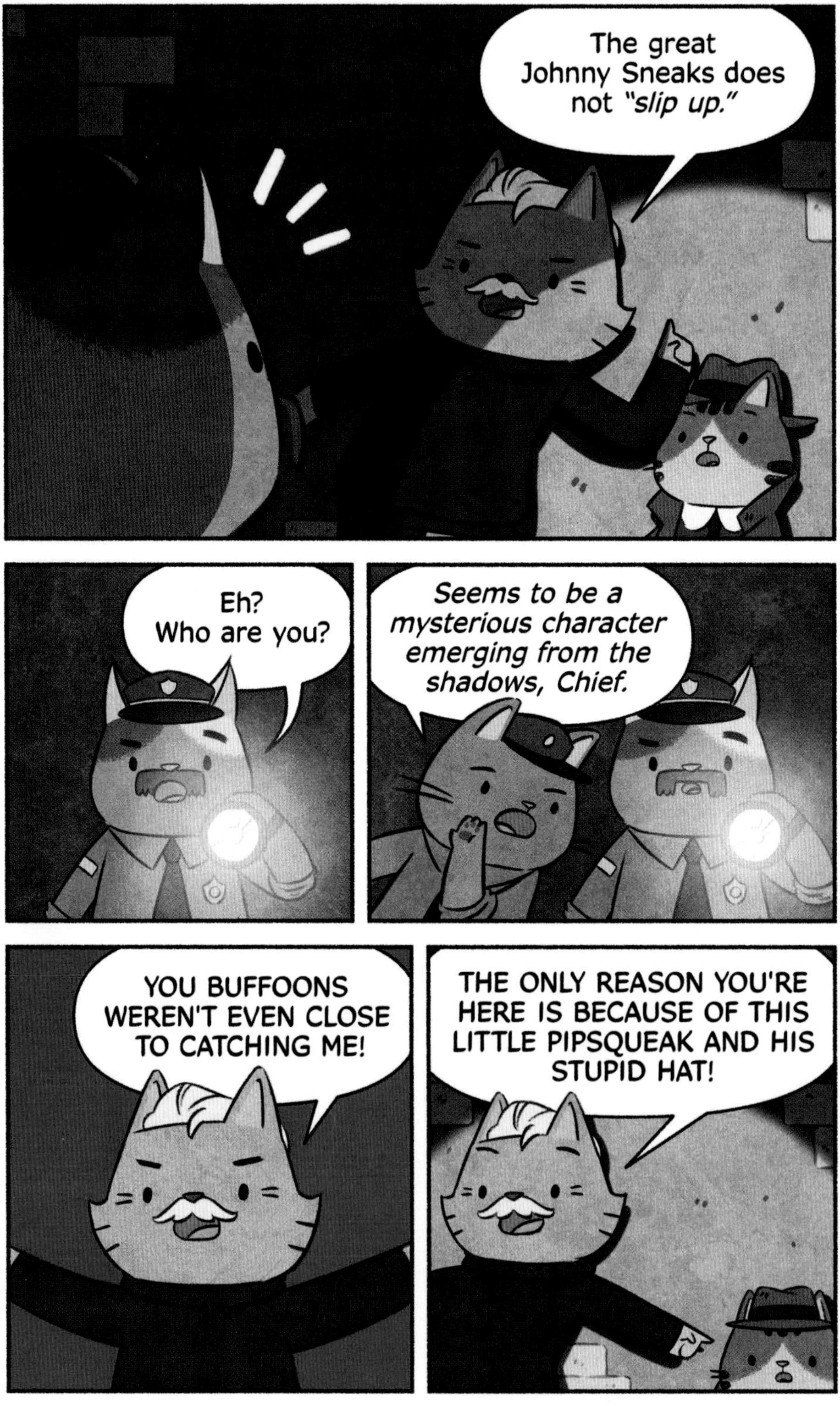
The great Johnny Sneaks does not *"slip up."*
Eh? Who are you?
Seems to be a mysterious character emerging from the shadows, Chief.
YOU BUFFOONS WEREN'T EVEN CLOSE TO CATCHING ME!
THE ONLY REASON YOU'RE HERE IS BECAUSE OF THIS LITTLE PIPSQUEAK AND HIS STUPID HAT!

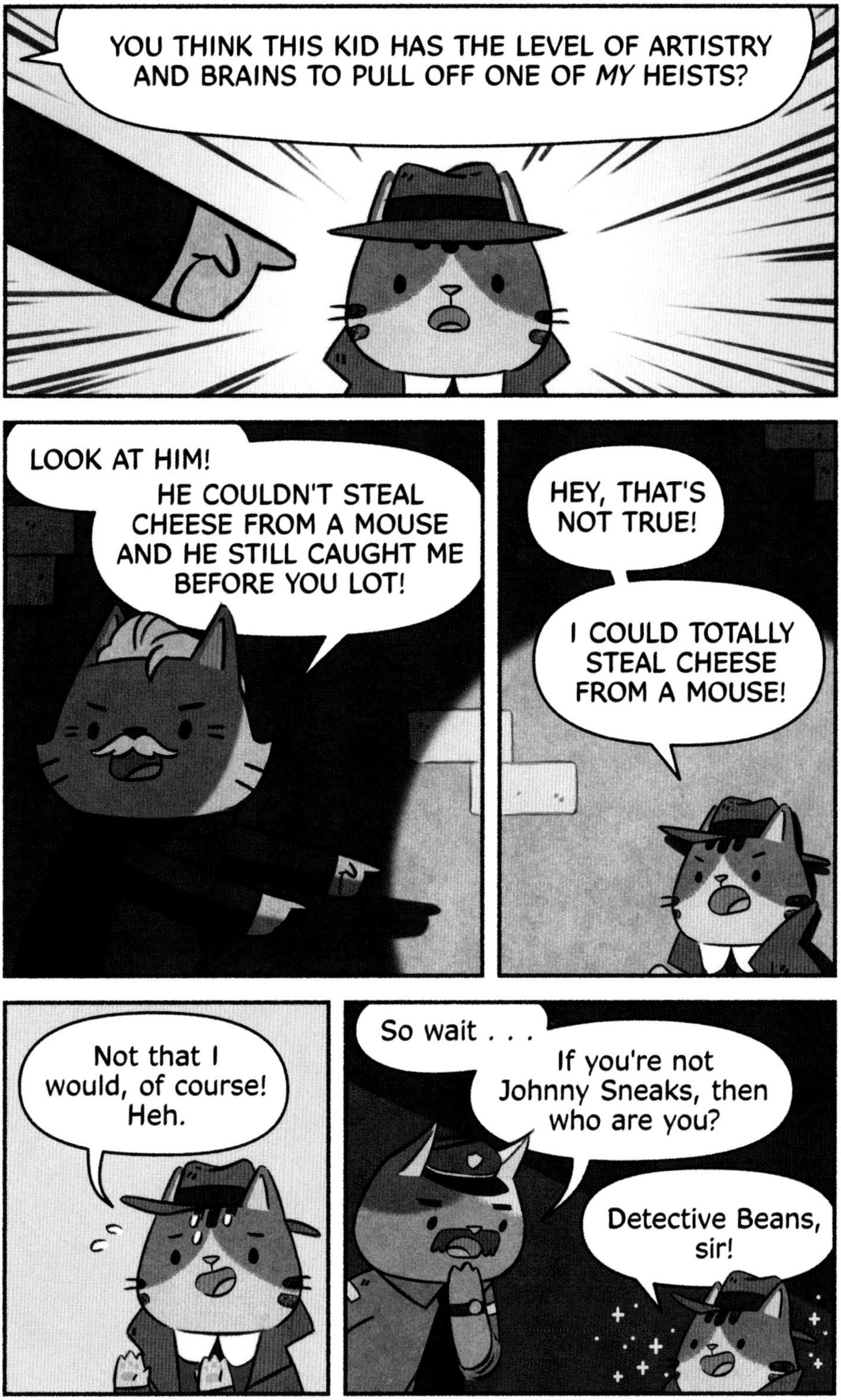
YOU THINK THIS KID HAS THE LEVEL OF ARTISTRY AND BRAINS TO PULL OFF ONE OF *MY* HEISTS?
LOOK AT HIM!
HE COULDN'T STEAL CHEESE FROM A MOUSE AND HE STILL CAUGHT ME BEFORE YOU LOT!
HEY, THAT'S NOT TRUE!
I COULD TOTALLY STEAL CHEESE FROM A MOUSE!
Not that I would, of course! Heh.
So wait . . .
If you're not Johnny Sneaks, then who are you?
Detective Beans, sir!

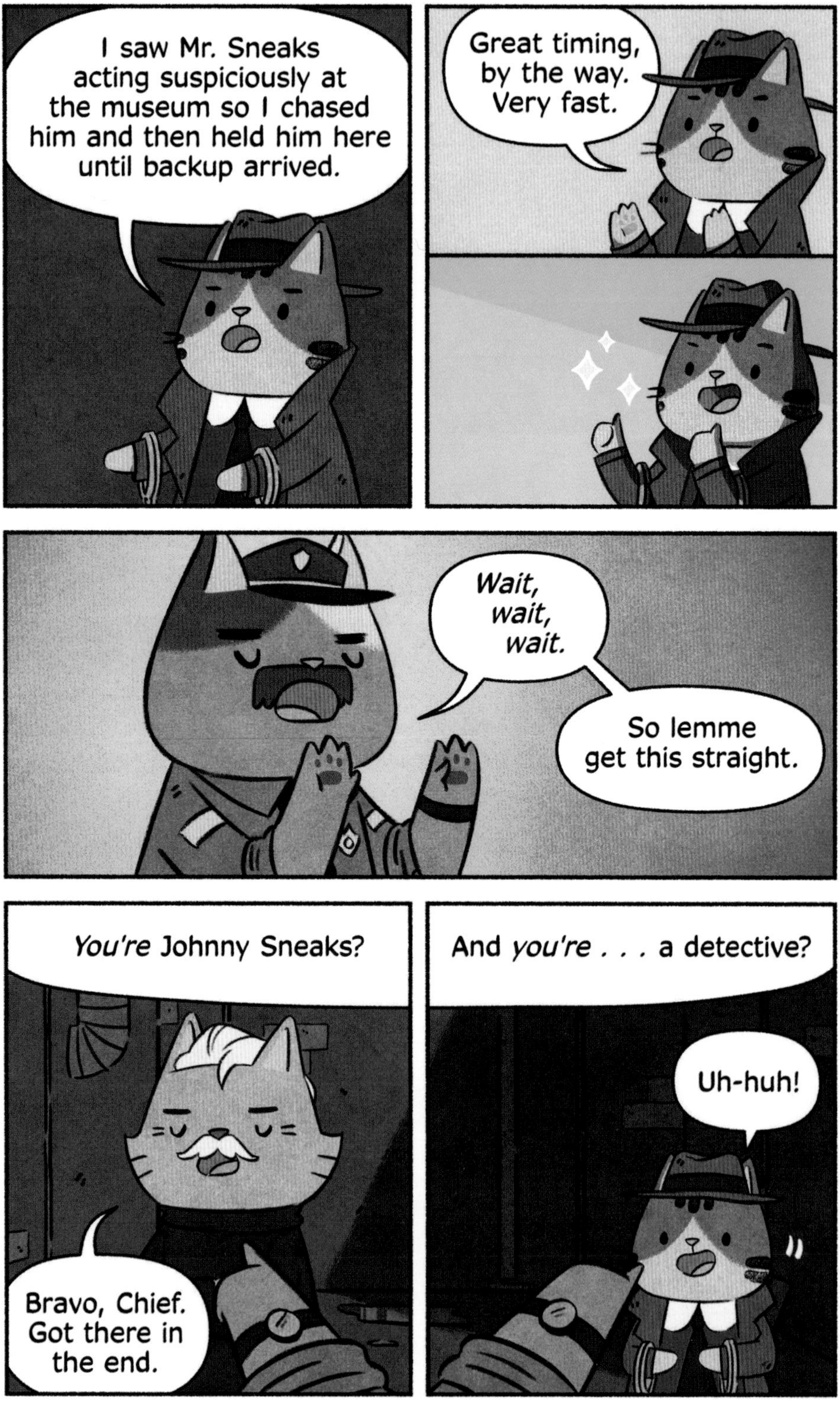
I saw Mr. Sneaks acting suspiciously at the museum so I chased him and then held him here until backup arrived.
Great timing, by the way. Very fast.
Wait, wait, wait.
So lemme get this straight.
You're Johnny Sneaks?
Bravo, Chief. Got there in the end.
And *you're* . . . a detective?
Uh-huh!

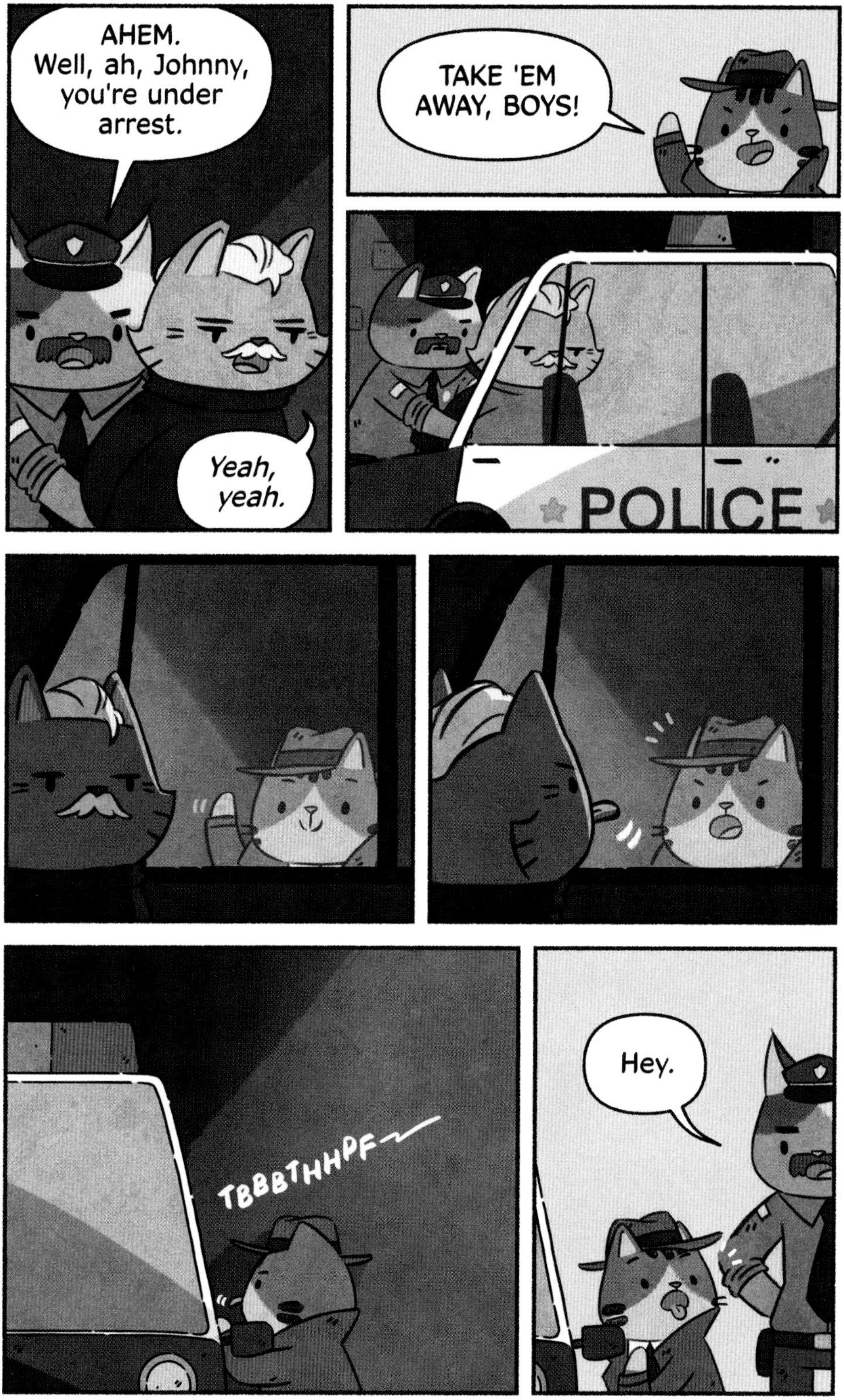
AHEM. Well, ah, Johnny, you're under arrest.
Yeah, yeah.
TAKE 'EM AWAY, BOYS!
POLICE
TBBBTHHPF
Hey.

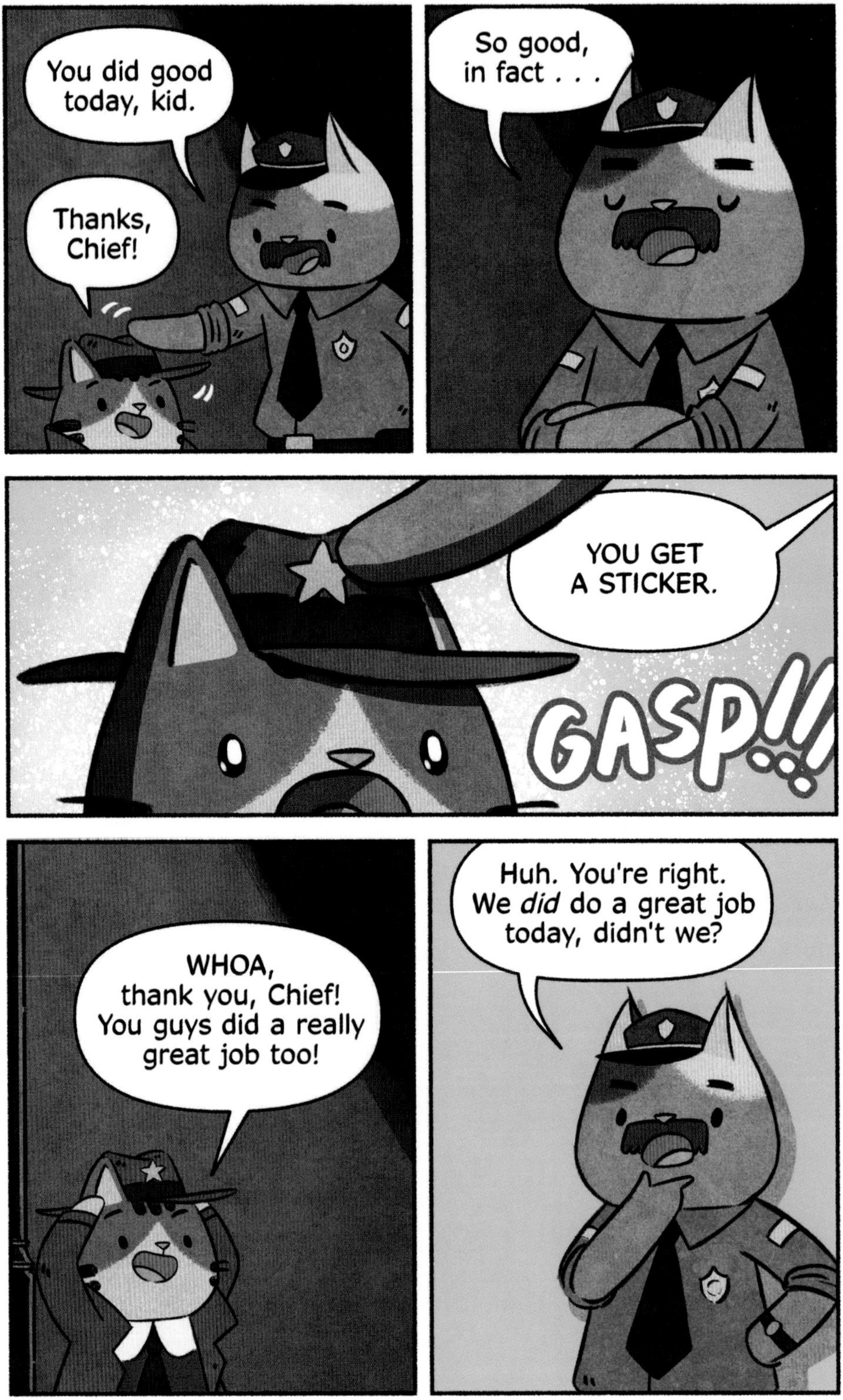
You did good today, kid.
Thanks, Chief!
So good, in fact . . .
YOU GET A STICKER.
GASP!!
WHOA, thank you, Chief! You guys did a really great job too!
Huh. You're right. We *did* do a great job today, didn't we?

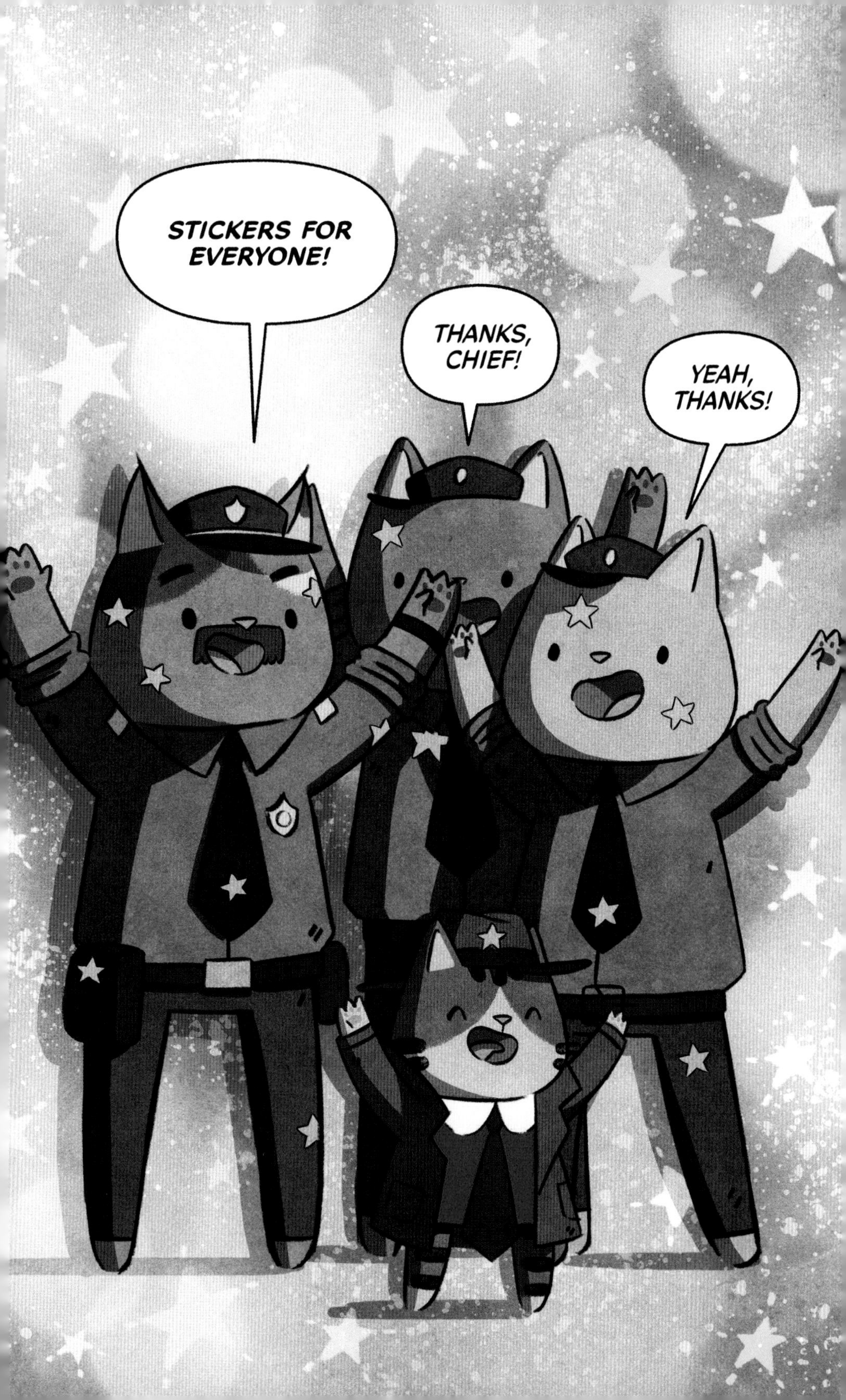
STICKERS FOR EVERYONE!
THANKS, CHIEF!
YEAH, THANKS!

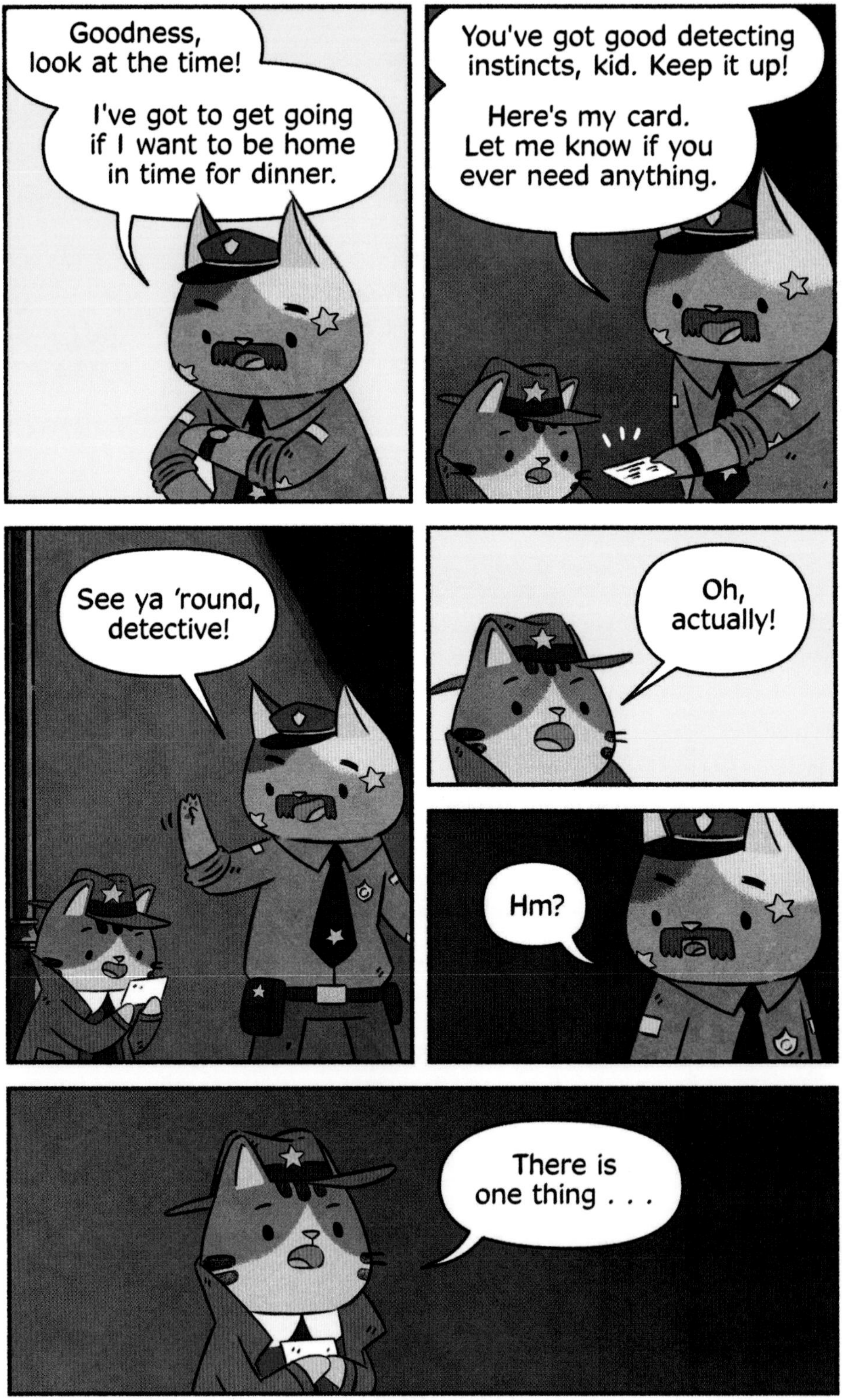
Goodness, look at the time!
I've got to get going if I want to be home in time for dinner.
You've got good detecting instincts, kid. Keep it up!
Here's my card. Let me know if you ever need anything.
See ya 'round, detective!
Oh, actually!
Hm?
There is one thing . . .

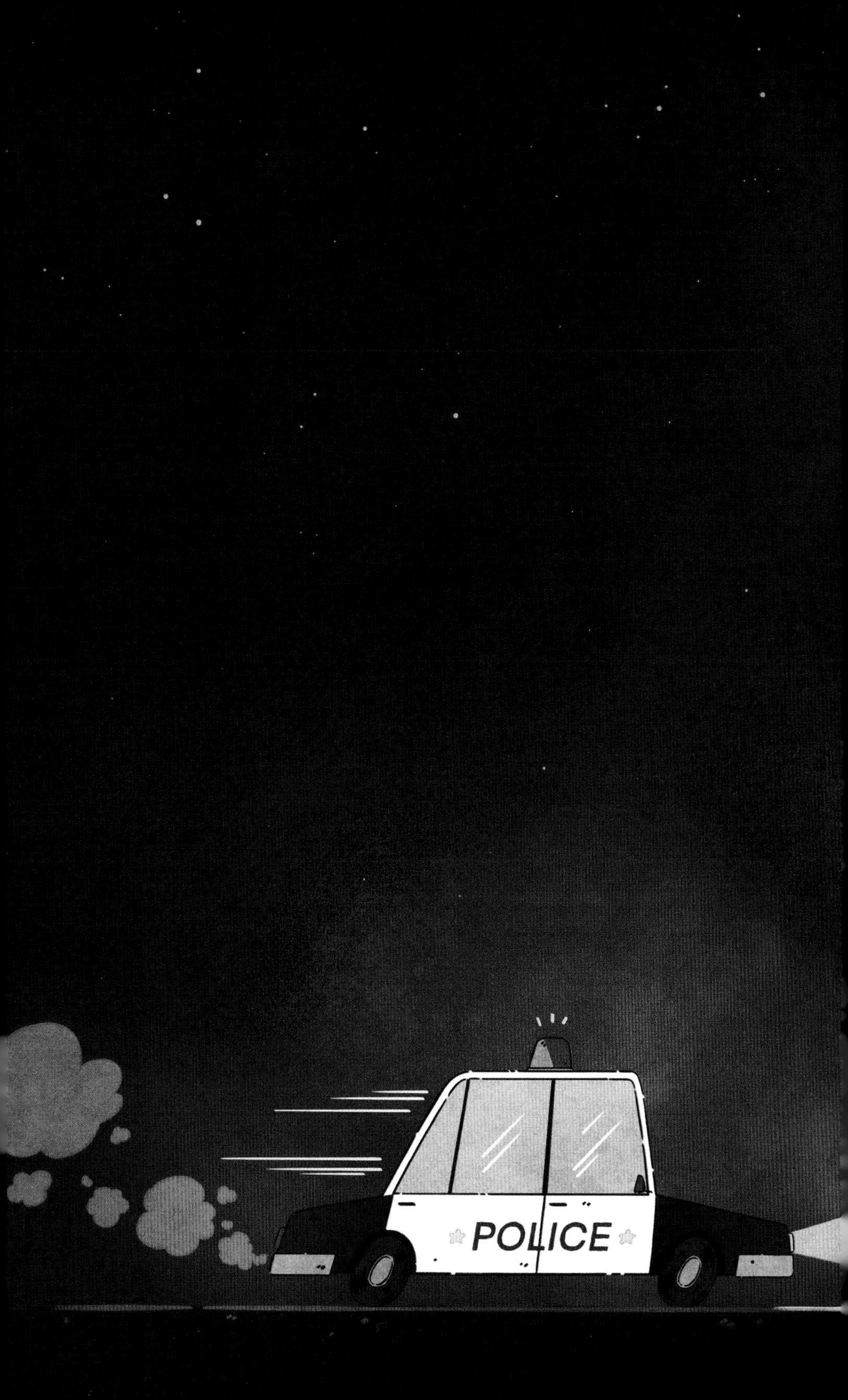
POLICE

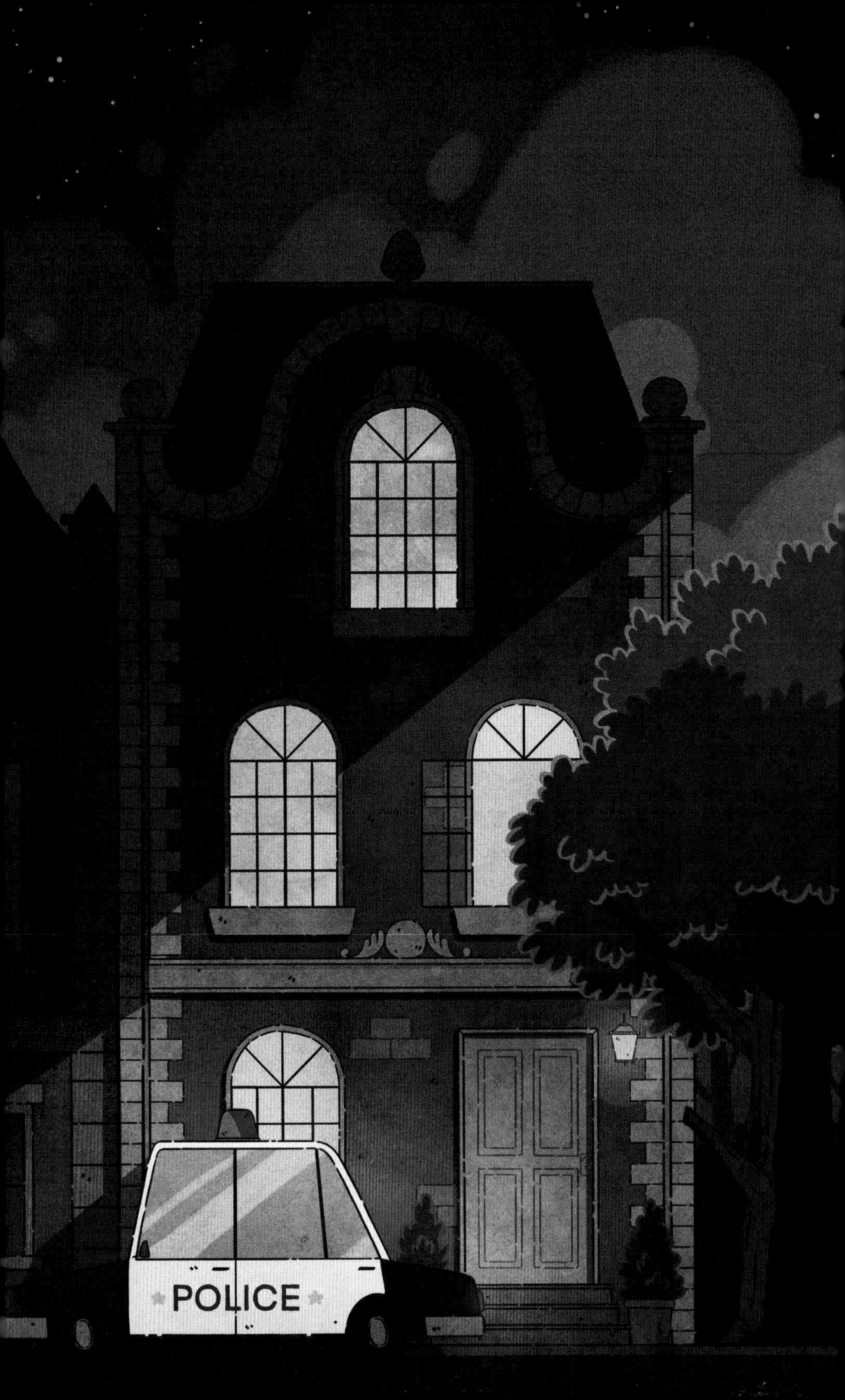
POLICE

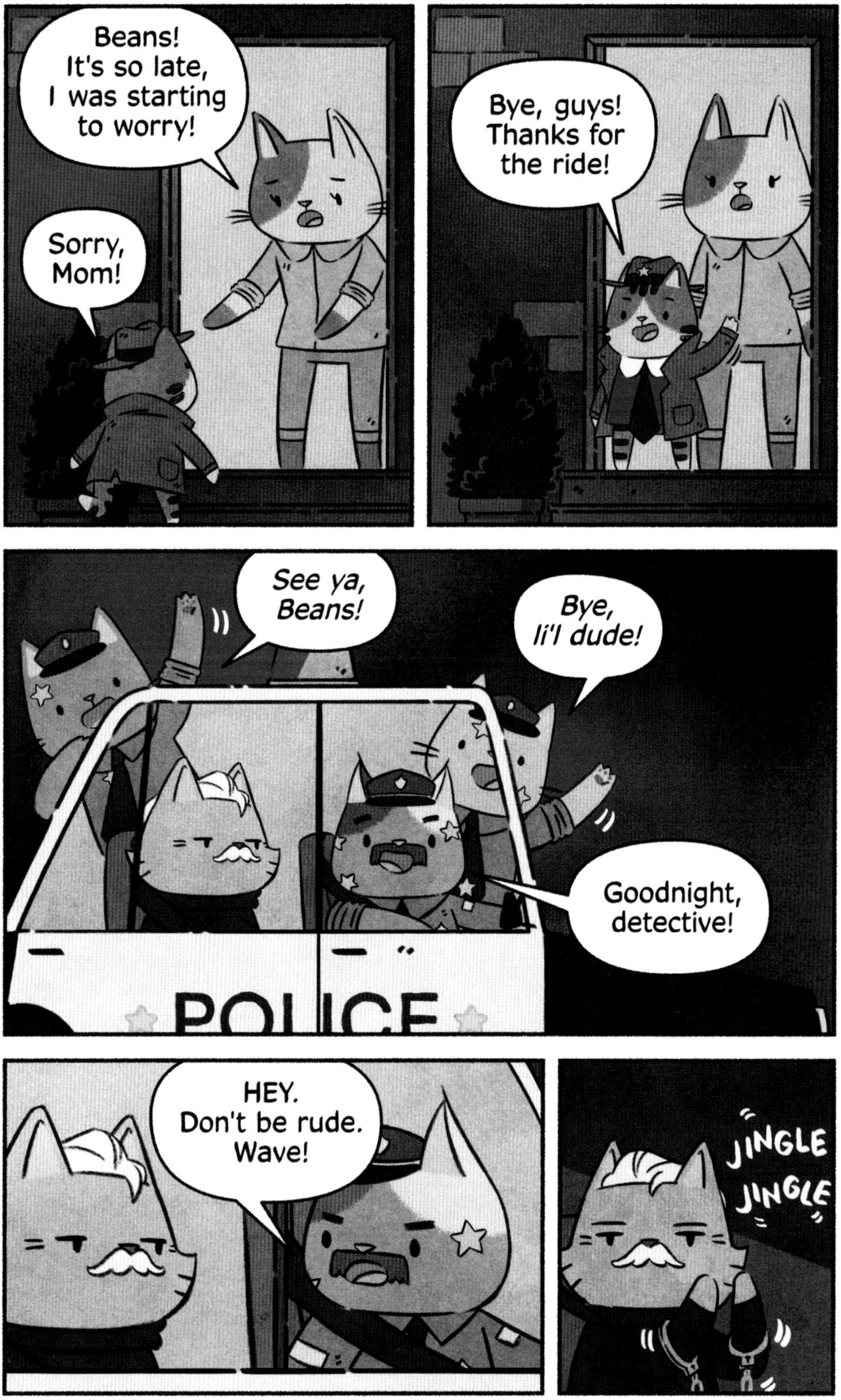
Beans! It's so late, I was starting to worry!
Sorry, Mom!
Bye, guys! Thanks for the ride!
See ya, Beans!
Bye, li'l dude!
Goodnight, detective!
POLICE
HEY. Don't be rude. Wave!
JINGLE JINGLE

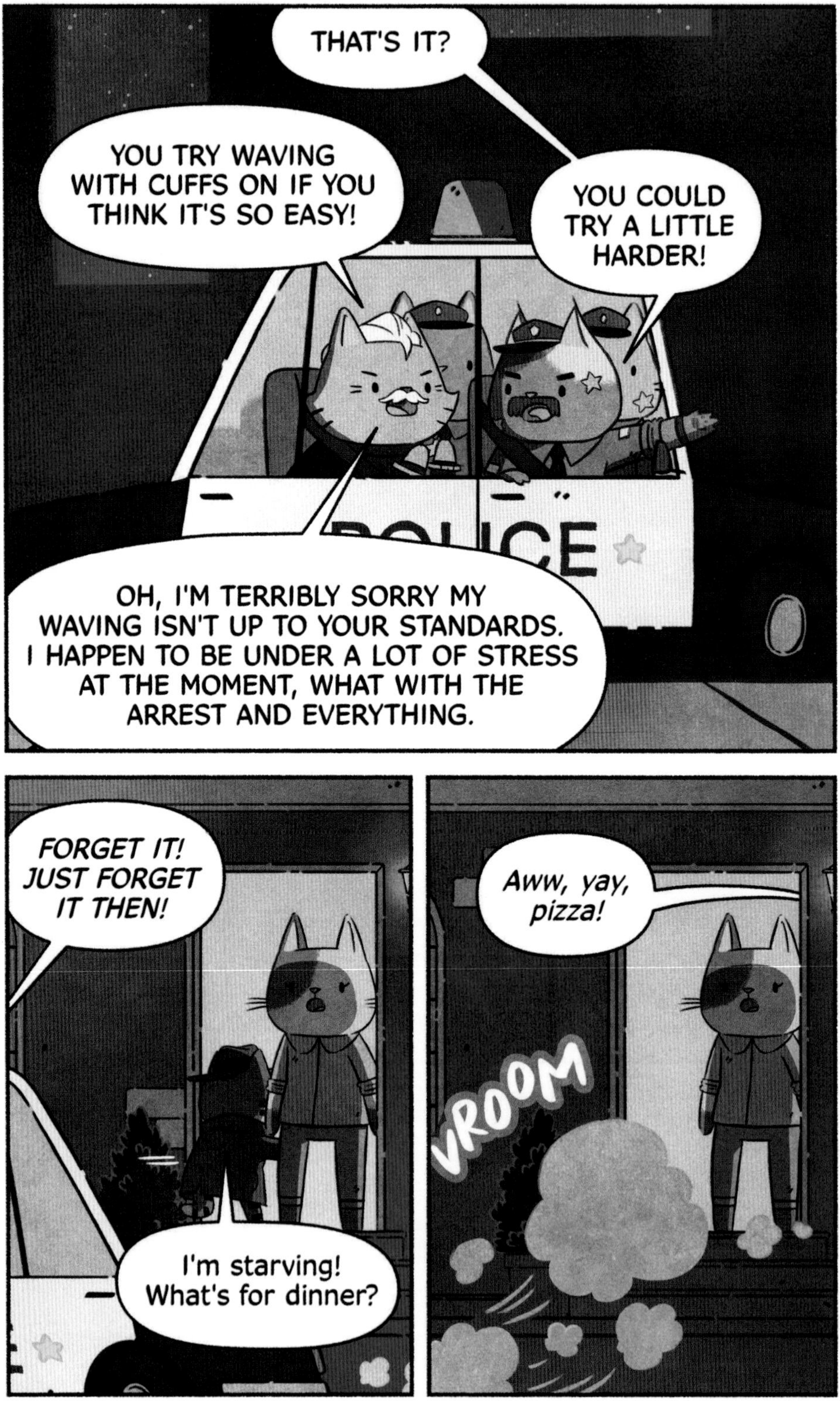
THAT'S IT?
YOU TRY WAVING WITH CUFFS ON IF YOU THINK IT'S SO EASY!
YOU COULD TRY A LITTLE HARDER!
POLICE
OH, I'M TERRIBLY SORRY MY WAVING ISN'T UP TO YOUR STANDARDS. I HAPPEN TO BE UNDER A LOT OF STRESS AT THE MOMENT, WHAT WITH THE ARREST AND EVERYTHING.
FORGET IT! JUST FORGET IT THEN!
I'm starving! What's for dinner?
Aww, yay, pizza!
VROOM

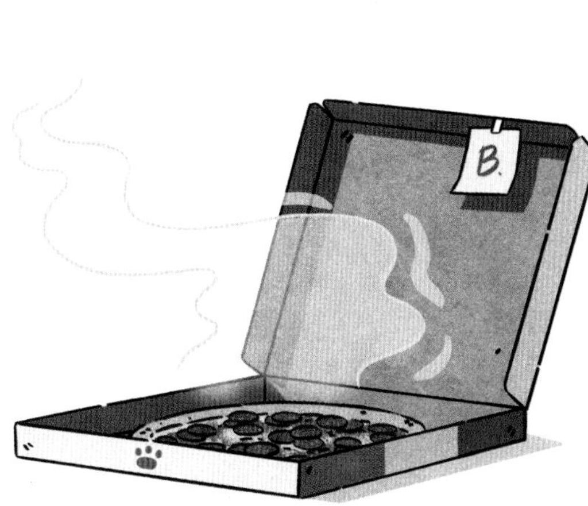
B.

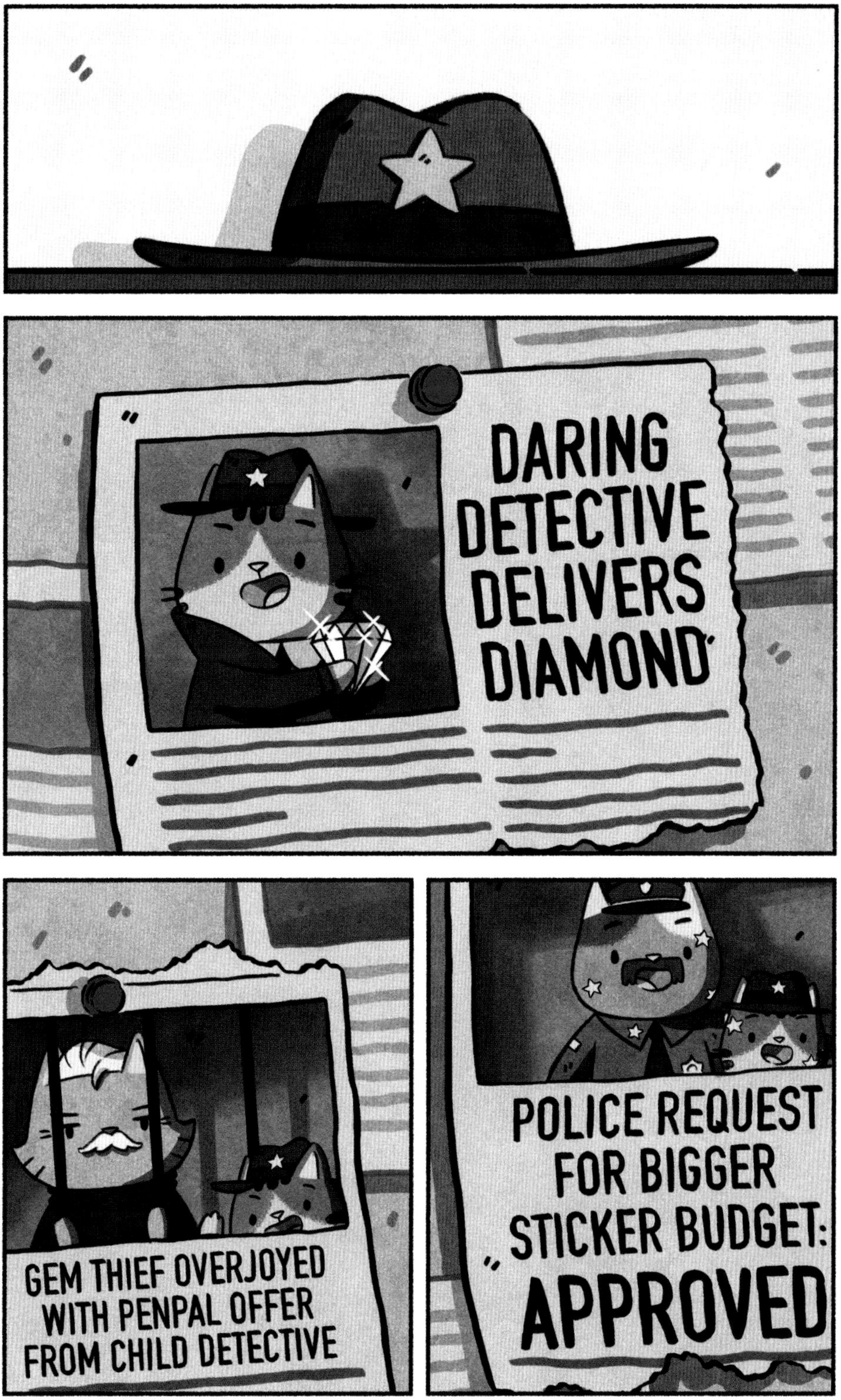
DARING DETECTIVE DELIVERS DIAMOND
GEM THIEF OVERJOYED WITH PENPAL OFFER FROM CHILD DETECTIVE
POLICE REQUEST FOR BIGGER STICKER BUDGET:
APPROVED

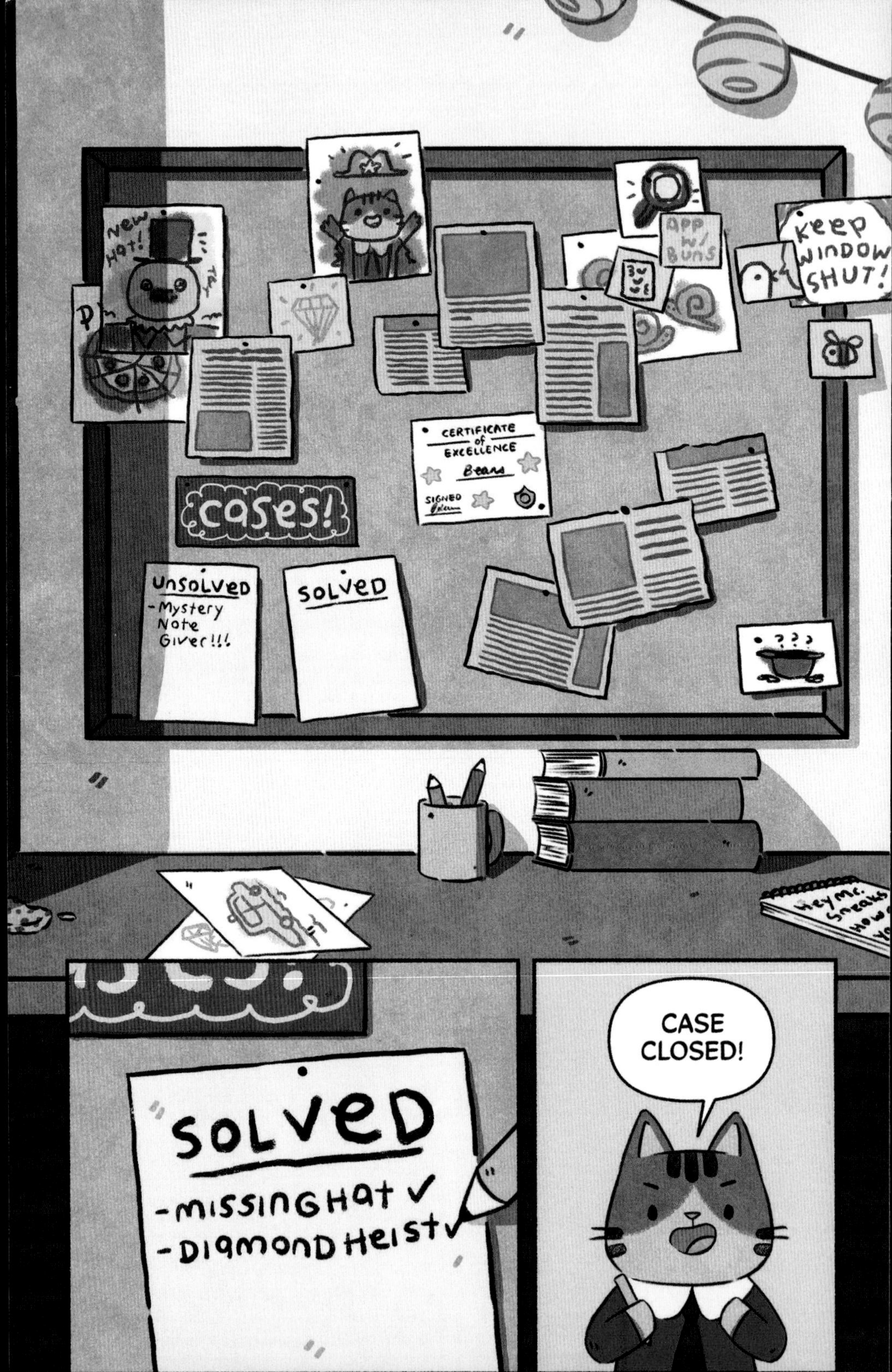
New Hat!
Keep WINDOW SHUT!
APP w/ BUNS
cases!
CERTIFICATE of EXCELLENCE
SIGNED
UNSOLVED
-Mystery Note Giver!!!
SOLVED
SOLVED
-MISSING HAT ✓
-DIAMOND HEIST ✓
CASE CLOSED!

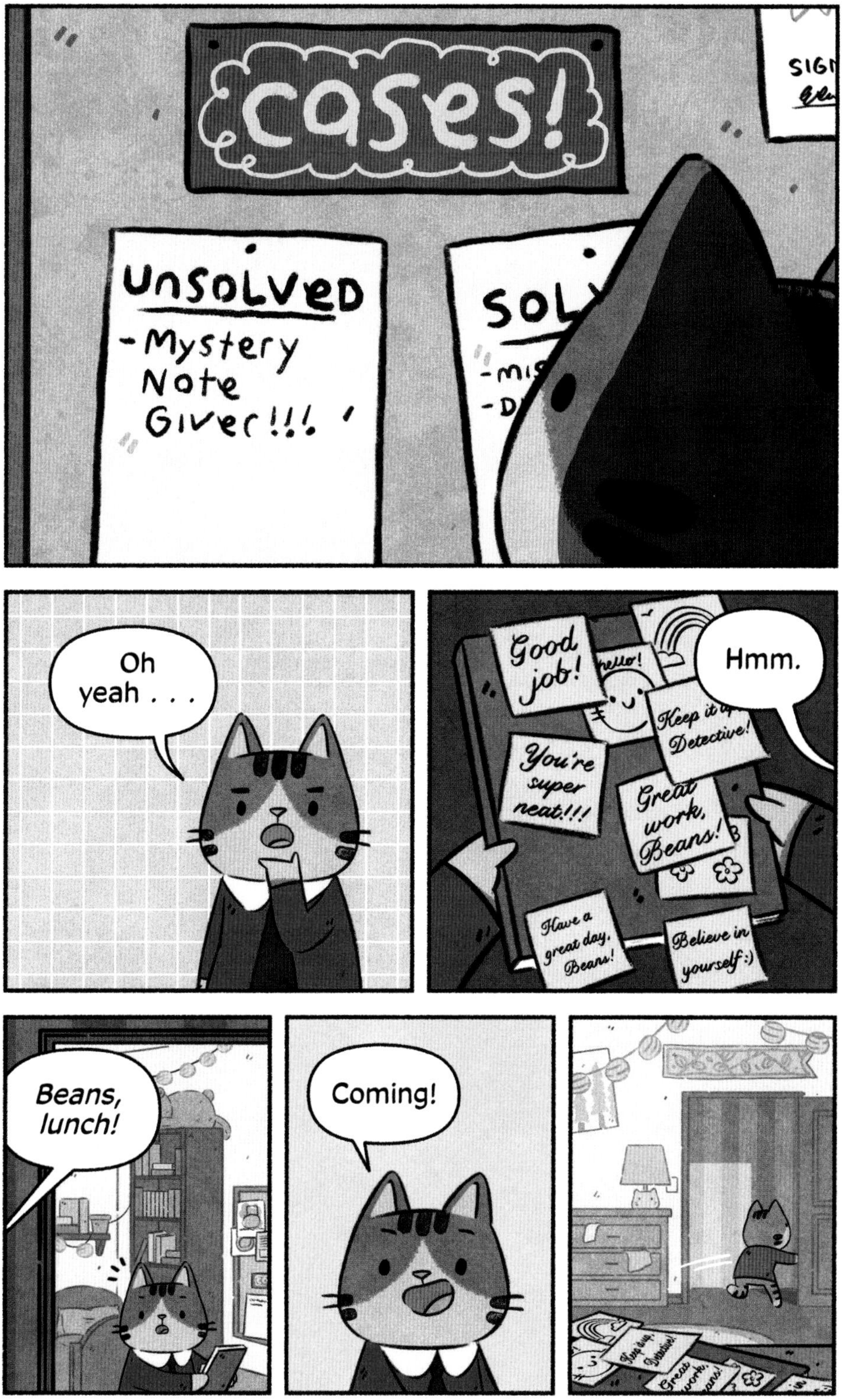
cases!
UNSOLVED
-Mystery Note Giver!!!
Oh yeah . . .
Good job!
hello!
Keep it up Detective!
You're super neat!!!
Great work, Beans!
Have a great day, Beans!
Believe in yourself :)
Hmm.
Beans, lunch!
Coming!

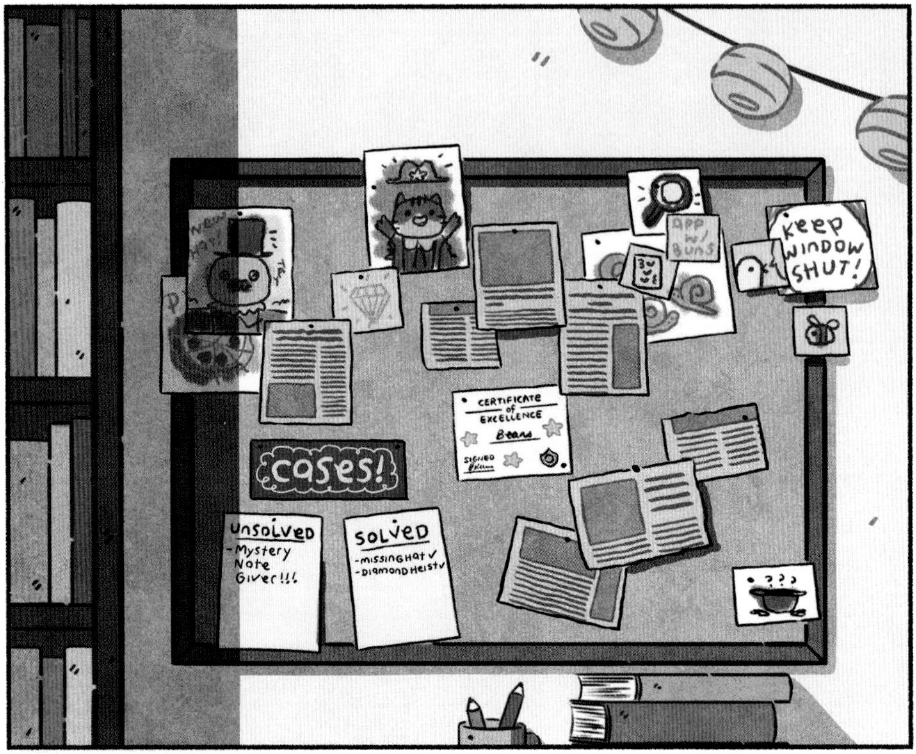
Keep WINDOW SHUT!
APP w/ BUNS
CERTIFICATE of EXCELLENCE
Bears
SIGNED
cases!
Unsolved
-Mystery Note Giver!!!
Solved
-missingHat ✓
-Diamond Heist ✓

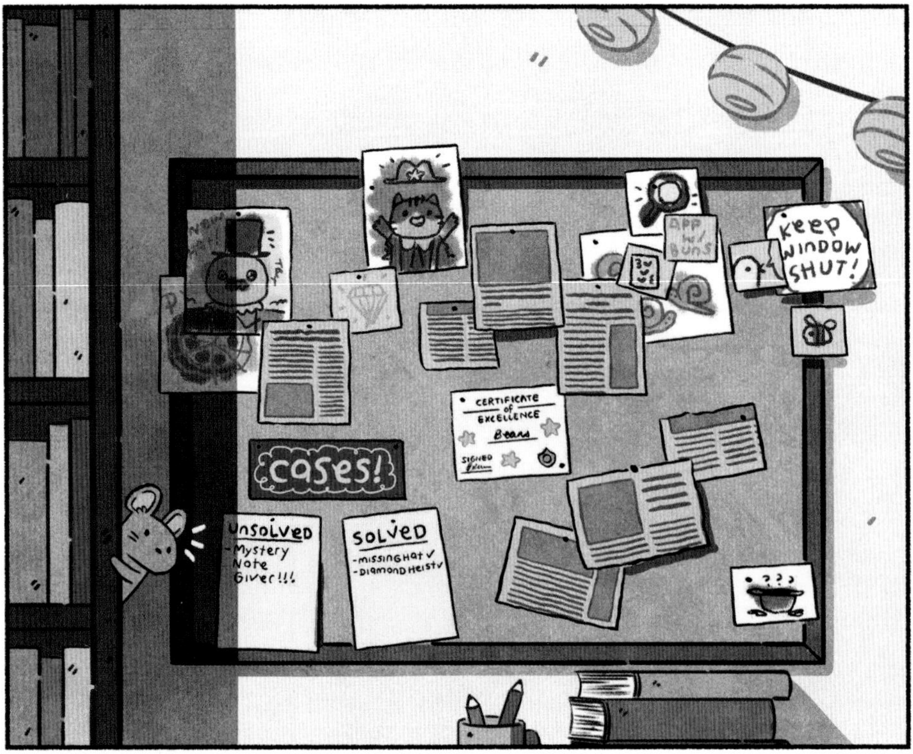
Keep WINDOW SHUT!
APP w/ BUNS
CERTIFICATE of EXCELLENCE
Bears
SIGNED
cases!
Unsolved
-Mystery Note Giver!!!
Solved
-missingHat ✓
-Diamond Heist ✓

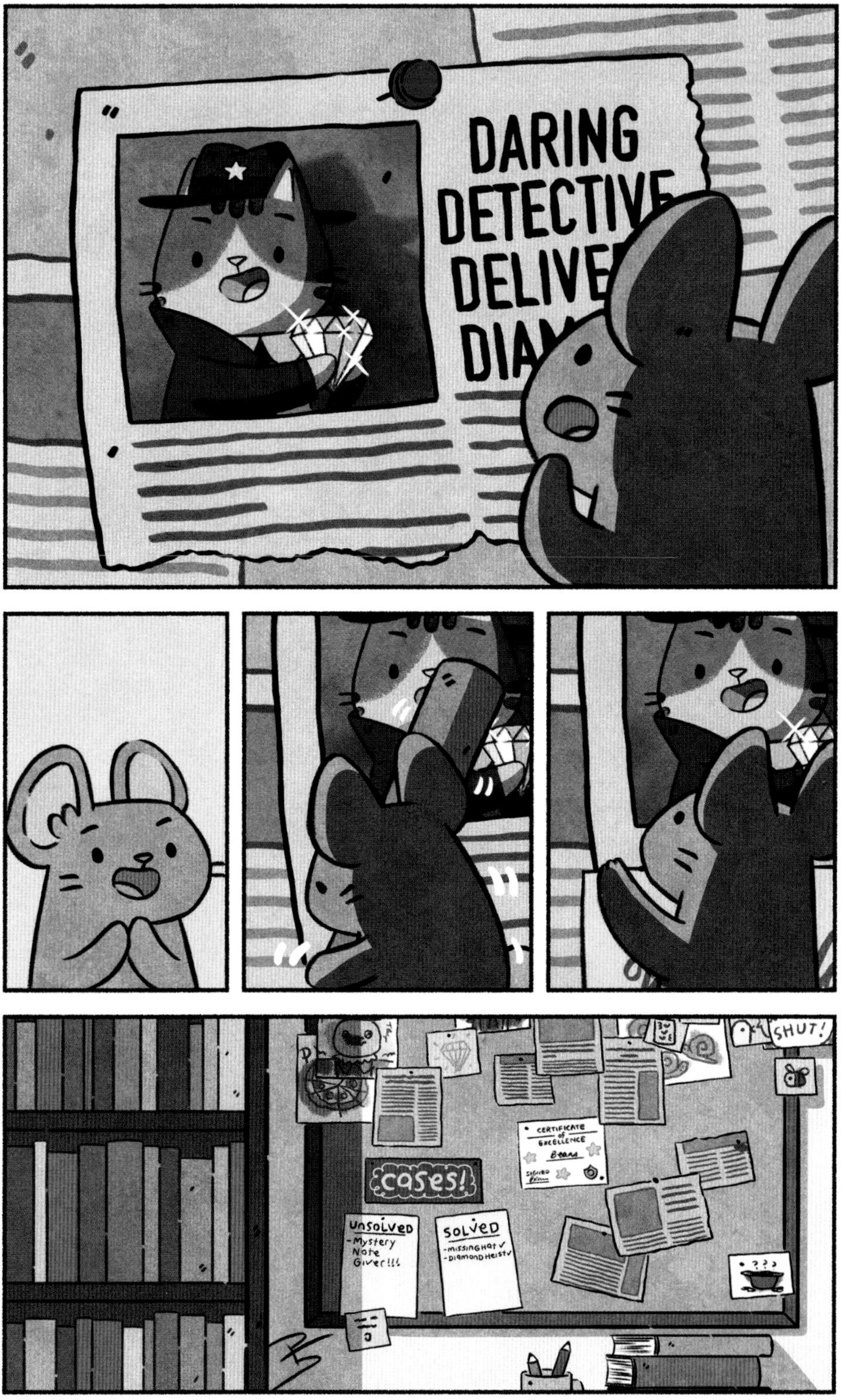
DARING
DETECTIV
DELIVE
DIA
SHUT!
CERTIFICATE of EXCELLENCE
Beans
SIGNED
cases!
Unsolved
-Mystery Note Giver!!!
Solved
-missing hat ✓
-Diamond Heist ✓

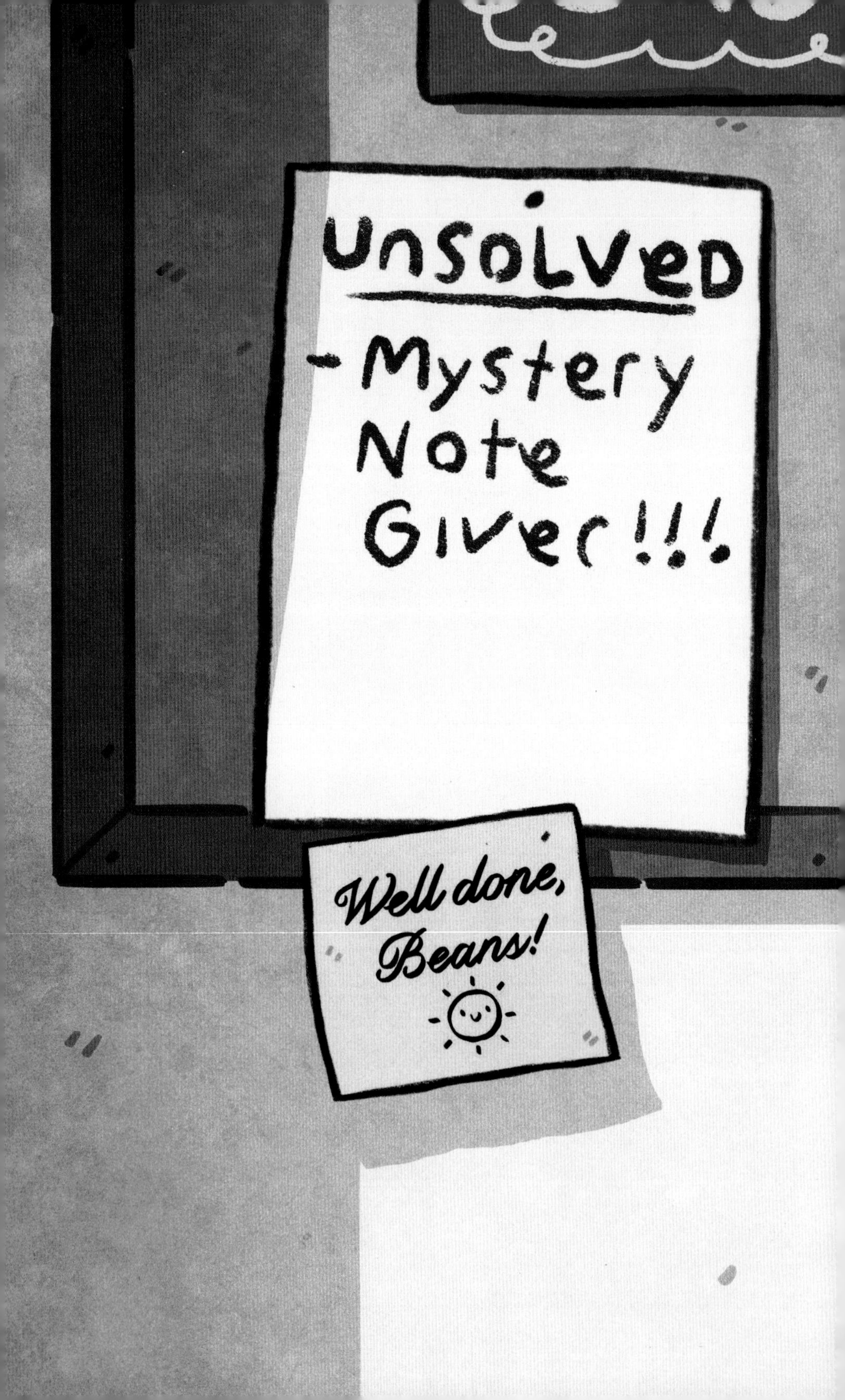
UNSOLVED
-Mystery Note Giver!!!
Well done, Beans!